FORBIDDEN FABLES

SAVVY ROSE

CHAPTER 5
FENRIR
WALES, 1678

"HUT! ONE. TWO. HALT...AND THREE... CHARGE!" My body jerks, instinctively knowing the urgency to pursue, to fight...to kill.

The need inside of me to prick blood from skin, to drain it from their bodies in spurts—victory.

I charge, and the heady smell of my brothers' blood and sweat pushes me on—a war cry spilling from my mouth.

I wake up in a cold sweat, clutching the ax at my side —the hatchet that never left my sight. The feel of the wooden handle causes me to exhale in relief.

My cock stretches up the length of my torso, thick and red.

I reach down and grip the head, furious.

Laying back on the piles of fur pelts, I close my eyes again. Sybil's moans fill my ears, but I shove the noise away, trying to summon myself back to sleep.

It is futile.

I watch as my hand nearly covers the shaft, working it slowly up and down. I challenge myself not to think of the woman who rejected me. The only love I've ever known was hers. I knew no love from a mother or father, as they abandoned me in the woods as a pup, until Sybil's father found me and took me in as his own. I knew nothing of the ways of shifters—my mother died before I could walk, and I have no memory of my father.

Groaning, I continue my strokes, longing for the feel of a maiden's tight, warm mouth. My wolf comes alive, unexpectedly.

I have not brought myself to climax since I came to these woods. For if I did not have a mate to spread my seed to, what was the point?

My hand quickens, feeling the wetness from my excitement slick the head.

"Up against the wall." I breathe into her ear, and she obeys.

I am at her entrance now, but I wait to sink inside her,

allowing her lust to build. I feel between her thighs, and she is ready, the sweet dew waiting for my cock to plunge inside.

I guide the head, pushing inside her, slowly, as she lets out a sharp gasp.

Holding her hands above her head, palms flat against the wall, I thrust up and into her. Sheathed in her tight warmth, I slow, feeling my balls tighten.

Letting the fantasy consume me, I pump harder until my balls pull up tight to my body and I'm rolled onto my side, fucking into the bed. Warmth erupts over my hands and furs, sweat running down my brow. Blood pounds in my ears as I roll onto my back, staring into the blackness.

I am empty and alone, my wolf and soul ravenous for a love to call their own.

I nod off, fighting the urge to make a kill just to mask the pain, but I let myself fall into a dreamless sleep.

～

The sunlight creeps in through the doorway, taunting me with its victory of rising before I.

I stand and stretch...feeling my age. Yet my wolf refuses to accept such a fate. He knows no such number.

He stirs tonight, and he has not stirred since Sybil. However, the way he paces in my mind tonight is not the same. It is deeper, stronger. This morning, he rumbles low in my belly for his true mate, and it seems that it could not be her.

I was never taught about mate selection; the men and women of my clan knew nothing of what I was. Most stayed away from me, out of sheer terror and whispers about what happened on the battlefields.

Confused by this curiosity, I pull my long hair back and grab my leather strap, securing it behind my head in a loose braid.

I missed the battles, and I missed my brothers. It was easy to withstand living in the elements alone without a clan. I could feed myself and hunt. I needed no one.

Hunting down the men that did evil deeds in these woods curbed my hunger for war. Not entirely, but the screams made it less lonely.

I pulled on my trousers and tunic, layering it with my chain-mail and fur. My days started early, tending to the fire and hunting for food. I keep my storages full, and I don't enjoy staying still for long. My wolf likes to run, and

I know these lands better than anyone. It was mine, and I knew its plants and trees and the ground knew my padded paws.

Two lonely years.

The cold stings my face as I step outside my hut. The structure is not much, but it gives me a warm, dry place to sleep at night.

Stacks of wood lay to the side of the rickety structure, and pelts of animals hang from the lines linked from tree to tree. I was becoming skilled in tree climbing, and the exhilaration when I reached the top was comparable to shifting.

Sliding the hatchet into the loop at my waist, I hoist a rope around the tree and pull myself until my boots scrape the bark. I brace my body and shoulders against my weight and whip the rope up higher onto the trunk. With each footfall, I creep higher until I can see the tops of the trees.

I can see for miles.

The woods are quiet this morning, but too early to tell if it will stay that way.

The men in the black coats have been scarce these days.

~

There did not seem to be any neighboring clans. The closest sign of life was a single, but large, house to the east. It hid the abandoned structure I found against the thick shrubbery that had grown around it. There was only one large room, a sleeping room to the back, but an oversized fireplace still stood at its center—a lucky find.

After weeks of hunting and preparing my home, a man in a black coat and brimmed hat knocked on my front door.

"Good morning, Brother." He removes his hat and places it in front of him.

I stand in the doorframe, bare chested and standing almost a foot taller than the man. Without greeting him, I continue eating the dried meat in my hand and wait for him to continue.

He clears his throat after landing his eyes on the landscape of tattoos that cover my chest. "My brethren and I were just wondering...um. Do you come here as a friend or foe?"

His head is bald, and the lines around his eyes suggest his age. Perhaps he is the leader of a nearby town. Regardless, his words make me laugh. "That depends."

The man's eyes grow wide, and he looks past my shoulder inside, a fresh kill hanging next to the fire.

I can smell his fear, and I see sweat form at his temple. He almost seems familiar to me somehow, though I have never seen this man...it is the way he smells. "Come here, small man." I crouch just a little, so our eyes are level, and I wave him in closer to me. He leans in, hesitantly clutching his hat. I roughly grab his collar into my fist and pull his face to mine. "Perhaps if you leave me be, I am a friend. If not, I will rip apart you and your entire family in the night. Would that make me foe?"

He swallows, staring at my mouth, where I can already feel my canines lengthening. My fists double, my claws pricking into his neck. He nods his head slowly as his feet leave the ground.

With a thud, I drop him back to his feet and he struggles to regain his balance, slamming the door in his face.

The offerings began the next day.

~

I discovered the pyre deep in the woods once I smelled rotting flesh. My wolf was insistent on knowing the trespassers on our hunting grounds.

In the early morning dusk, fog had settled over the grass, the days growing warmer. Sniffing the air in my wolf's form, the odor of sulfur stings my nose—the unmistakable smell of cooked beef and burned hair.

I examine the pile, wood neatly stacked against an iron pole protruding from the ground and rock circle.

The circle of stones lead me to believe this had been some sort of ritual, perhaps an initiation.

It still wasn't exactly clear what the men wanted from me. I only assumed the spot belonged to them, the only others I had ever seen in these woods. I would neither help nor hinder them, but if I picked up the faintest scent of my true mate, I would make them understand just why I was named after Fenrir the Wolf God.

CHAPTER 6
LUX

She let it happen.

It was her fault, and nothing would change my mind about it.

The carriage ride bumps my body about, my hat falling off my head. All of it only stirs my irritation as I glare toward Gran, a woman completely oblivious to anything but herself. Her hair was tucked into a tight bun, and she always wore the same color dress day after day. I wasn't sure if she owned ten of the same color, or just washed the same one every night.

How could someone wear the same thing day after day?

Mum told me I was curious, detailed, and sometimes cunning. But I liked that word: cunning. It made me feel like a fox in my bedclothes.

I guess I wouldn't know what the chatter of a normal ten-year-old girl had inside her head. Gran told me I was too curious.

Well, so what? Curiosity was why you ask questions and asking questions gained your knowledge.

What was the problem?

Gran needed a man to tell her what to think, and who would want that? My father and his brethren only talked about God and money, those who possibly deceived the church. Praying, praying, praying.

I could think of far better things I could do with my time besides praying. What good was waiting around for a miracle? I wouldn't wait for anyone. I knew how to help myself.

Even mum said I was helping myself to freshly baked bread before I could even walk.

I had a bible next to my bed, untouched. I had no interest in praising someone I couldn't see.

I knew for certain that would never be me—I planned to stay as far away from a church now. What better excuse than locked away in the woods?

I would rather spend my days reading or making fires.

Playing with fire was captivating, but I was forbidden.

I hold back my tears as we round the cliff side with woods all around it. I won't let her see me cry. She doesn't deserve my tears.

I wanted her blood.

Her absence instead of my mother's.

The intellectual part of my brain was a pesky thing. It asked so many questions all the time, something my mother didn't seem bothered by.

It bothered Gran, though.

I wanted to know why they called my mother a 'witch'. I had only heard fables of green hags who flew in the air and killed children. My mother loved me and never made me feel like she would hurt me.

She was brave, but more than that...she was charming.

She had a way of turning every situation on its head, spinning it happily in another direction when disapproval reared its—or should I say, Gran's—head.

Maybe that's why Gran didn't stop them from taking her—always to snuff out my mother's flame...telling her to hush.

"Cleanliness is next to Godliness. Your mother is not

one to idolize, Lux. She is lazy and promiscuous. When you scrub these floors, you scrub hard and get all the cracks. And then you shall be even closer to God."

I never seemed to get the floors clean enough for her. I also didn't know what that word meant.

Promiscuous…I kind of liked the way it rolled off my tongue.

It took hours to get to the holiday cabin. I hoped the amenities here were just as good as those at the manor. Only here, it would just be Gran and I.

My insides coil, and I feel the pressure building in my neck as I worry about what would follow in the coming days.

Would she feel sorry for me and for my loss? Would she punish me even further now that my mother was out of the way? Did she care that I no longer had my mother?

Deep down, something told me that this would not benefit me, and I felt sick.

I collected what I could of mother's hidden items. The items that were most likely responsible for her death. Though I wasn't scared, the worst that could happen already had and if I died the same, I would be with my mum again.

The cabin was dusty and old. We had not come here on holiday since I was a small child.

It was mostly how I remember it, but I was eager to set up my space—I did not want to see my gran's face for a while.

Gran says I'm lucky to be alive. But what does she know?

Did that mean she was the reason I was saved? Or did she have bigger plans for me I wasn't aware of just yet?

It scared me to find out, but I also wanted it all out in the open, once and for all.

Walking up the dark stairway, cobwebs hanging from the posts, I make my way to a small corner room with a bed under the window.

The moon hangs perfectly in view from my bed. This room would be mine.

CHAPTER 7
FENRIR

The screams of women woke me in my sleep the second summer at my new camp.

I thought it had been my own dreams, screams of children from the villages my clan used to raid. A child's scream was a haunting thing, and one very hard to shake. Especially when you wanted a family of your own.

At first, I was mildly bothered. I tossed and turned until sleep took me again. Tonight, however...the noise wakes me, and I decide to hunt beneath the full moon. Freyja will shed light on the mischief of these woods, and perhaps I will fight once again.

I step outside, and I am met with a light fog. The days had abruptly turned warmer, the nights slightly colder. I raise my nose to the air and inhale deeply.

Blood and oil.

A chilling scream rips through the air. It is female, and it is no child. I break out into a run, adrenaline pumping through my body and my wolf demanding to be freed. I hold him back as long as I can until he is bursting through the small cracks of my skin. Hair sprouts, legs lengthen...my snout, now fully formed and snapping at the air as I make my way into the thick of the dark. My paws dig into the earth, edging me on further, the chilled winter air filling my lungs. I shake out my fur and sniff again, but this time I can smell something foreign. The pungent smell of alcohol rushes my nose, and I halt. I sneeze, roving my eyes over the trees, trying to identify where.

Ice fills my veins and stills my blood. I pick up a faint scent of daisies and realize I am looking for someone that I do not even know yet. I keep my eyes through a clearing in the trees and spot the circle of rocks. There is something sinister about the air, but I cannot take my eyes off what is happening just feet from me.

Just past a hemlock grove, two men and a woman struggle. The men wear black coats and brimmed hats, just like the man who came to visit me that day.

One holds a cloth over her face from behind, while she fights against his arm. The other holds up a wooden cross and a bottle of anointment. Her eyes grow wide with fear, and she bites the man's hands until he shouts. Screaming expletives, her hair is wild around her and the veins in her skin protrude from the struggle. The man holding the cross stuffs a white cloth in her mouth and binds and ties it around the back of her head. A smell similar to alcohol is stronger now, and her body goes limp, as I hide behind the brush, watching. The taller man says a prayer of some kind over her lifeless body. I am unsure if she is dead or not, but I decide not to find out.

I slink into the shadows, as to better hear them. "There are men who pay wealth to the ministers to save their souls. We cannot let another witch go. She dies tonight!"

I laugh at the word 'witch'. This is a word for children, a character from a nighttime story. She looks nothing like a witch. She is young and beautiful.

Perhaps these women need saving. I have plenty of warmth in my cabin for a soft maiden.

I needed to keep watch, as far away as I could, and wait for her to smell...the scent of my mate. This woman was nothing but a stranger to me, so for now I will let them live...and do what they need to.

CHAPTER 8
LUX

The long days of washing linens and dishes wore on me. It appears my only purpose here was to take care of the house, along with making sure we had a fire.

I barely had any social interactions, aside from my tutor Benjamin and his father, a trader who could get us any materials we needed.

My punishments were a daily affair—whether because the laundry wasn't hung properly or the more severe punishment that came with any insolence. I suffered whippings from her cane, seated at the altar with my back bared to her.

Insolence, however, I was forced into a freezing cold bath until I begged to be released, my gran holding me down with her cane when I relented.

My mother would have let none of this continue. She

would never have brought me here; she would have continued to protect me from Gran. I didn't care that Gran hurt me...I cared she wanted to.

The hate she harbored for me reflected from her eyes, and I swear it was not me she saw, but my mother, with red hair exactly like mine.

One afternoon, after her tea and biscuits, Gran told me of the way my parents came together. As if it brought her satisfaction to reveal my mother's wickedness.

"Your father met your mother at a brothel. Do you know what that is, Lux?" Gran always had crumbs littering her lap, and today was no different.

I shake my head no, silently.

"Let us just say it is not a proper place to meet a wife. But your father fell in love and was determined to make an honest woman out of her. Well...you can see what good came of that." She leans over to grab her knitting bag as I seethe.

I did not know yet what a brothel was. And when I finally found out from my tutor, it made quite a lot clear about my mother and father...they were both sinners.

A man with a black brimmed hat came to visit us that same rainy afternoon, about two moon phases since we arrived. "Hello little one, I am of your father's flock, only checking to make sure you are safe. Is all well within these walls?"

I look at the man with the unfamiliar face, his eyes nearly black, and I fix my expression into a frown.

"Does she not talk? Is she mute?" he asks after my gran, while she drapes her arm around my shoulder, smiling at the stranger.

"She is clever, full of questions. She is not mute." Her hand squeezes my shoulder roughly, pushing me toward the man.

He bends down to my eye level, grinning through yellow teeth. "Such a beautiful young lady. Smile more, it becomes you."

I don't like the way he says young lady, almost as if the word is comical. I wind back my knee, landing it square between his legs.

The man doubles over, grabbing himself and groaning in pain. "Little wench!"

My grandmother violently grabs my ear, pulling me into the large downstairs bath. There is already dirty and cold water sitting in the tub from the bath this morning, and she shoves my head over the side, dunking me under the water. I hold my breath for as long as I can, fighting my head back against her hand. She doesn't release me, but shoves my head deeper down, until I choke.

When I come to, I am on the floor of the bathroom, my wet hair tangled around my face. I sit up, alone and wet...and sob. It was night now, and time for me to discover what genuine pain felt like, at my own hands.

CHAPTER 9
FENRIR

Today was the day, the day I would trek to visit Emon atop the mountains they call 'the black mountains.'

My dreams quickly became more like torture. The realization that my true mate was merely miles from me, and the pain of being unable to attain her, was like a hot knife—searing and uncomfortable. Her sweet nothings had turned into shouts, and my dreams turned into nightmares, causing me to avoid sleep at all costs.

My body was weary, and a cough that would not go away no matter all the hot water I drank. I needed Emon's herbs and foretelling.

The hike was at least a day's trip, not very far from where my old clan still dwelled.

My boots held up well, and the bag I packed was full of dried meat and ale. Only stopping once to make a small fire to heat my hands.

My beard kept my face warm, and the fur hat Sybil made me worked well enough.

Keeping warm was not the most challenging portion of my trip; finding the cave that Emon hides in was.

The opening to the cave is small, barely enough room for me to squeeze my body through. And it was possible the last time I had been was when I was just that of a teen.

A small stack of rocks marks the entrance, and to the naked eye would only look as if it was part of the rocky crest.

I knew because of the crows that had gathered.

He must have been out to hunt recently.

Setting down my pack, I clear away the brush and snow, revealing the entrance on the side of the hill.

I just hope he remembers me.

~

"Friend, come in, come in. I've been expecting you."

I squint my eyes into the darkness, as I hear him speak before he's even been spotted. A small fire is set up at the rear of the small room, candles littering the floor and the surrounding rocks.

Emon shuffles to a wooden chair beside the altar.

As if my muscle memory knew exactly what to do, I walk to him, sitting at his feet.

"Emon. Brother. I see that you are well and still thriving." I bow my head, allowing him to take the ash from the fire, swiping it across my eyes.

He laughs, and his voice is rasped with age and living in these harsh elements. "I am still serving my purpose. Close your eyes."

My eyes shut at his command, and as if a match had been struck, her face appears to me and Emon gasps.

Red, snow, and screams fill my ears, images of crows and a cross with a body draped from it.

"Ahhh...yes." The old man is completely bald, with ears that stick out. Ash covers his face, branding the creases of his wrinkles with black. "Having trouble sleeping, I gather? She visits you, because she needs you."

"I do not remember having any such dreams before. Why now?" I lean back from his hands, both reaching out for me and suspended in midair.

Dropping his hands to his lap, he cocks his head to the side, observing me. "It is simply time."

I can remember being confused by Emon's vagueness whenever Frode would bring me here as a boy. It seems he was still vague.

"She is not mine for the taking. I do not know who she is." Hanging my head, puzzled by the realization that our fates were tied and I had never even spoken to her.

Emon waves me back toward him, and I obey, his hands resting on the sides of my head again.

"It will not be easy, but she is yours." He closes his eyes and begins to hum, the vibration sending my dreams into overdrive, spilling inside of my thoughts until he releases me. "If you do not wish for your bond to be broken, it needs to be sealed by a blood oath."

When our contact is broken, the dreams disappear like the fog. Slowly dissipating into the void.

Confused at this, I falter. "Blood oath? I have no desire to harm this woman."

He smiles, broken and cracked teeth lining his dry lips. "No harm is needed. Just her blood."

CHAPTER 10

LUX

WALES 1688

Ten years, ten long years have passed since I have lived in this too-quiet house in the woods.

"Are you bloody crazy, Lux? Just like your mum..." Benjamin spoke the words under his breath. Let him. I didn't care what thoughts came out of a stupid boy's mouth. My mother always taught me a man thinks with what's between their legs.

'The shorter it hangs, the more dubious the man.'

I giggle to myself as I watch my feet skip the broken sticks and jagged roots covered in snow.

Ben looks at me a few times, waiting for the explanation of my giddiness. I wouldn't give him one. Let him wonder.

"Just because you read lots of books and go to some fancy, private school, doesn't mean you're smarter than I am." I continue my careful foot placements on each root space of the trees. The Ash trees were covered in green moss, and I let my fingers graze over the wet dew. I close my eyes and inhale, peace flooding my senses. Wrapping my arms around the trunk, I smile, pressing my cheek to the rough edges. I could feel Benjamin's eyes watching me.

"Hug the tree, Benjamin. Come on, it feels nice!" I remain where I stood, waiting for him to join me. I hear a dramatic sigh, and suddenly he's there beside me, doing just that.

Pleased with myself, I step back from the tree, grinning. He looks rather childish standing that way, his cotton jacket sticking to the bark. I giggle again, biting my fingernails and taking in his submissive form.

"Satisfied?" He backs away from the tree, arms outstretched.

Benjamin was my only friend, the only person my age that I could ever remember knowing, but he was my tutor.

Did that make him my friend?

He stayed at Gran's cabin frequently, since the trip from England was more than a day's ride. My gran paid to have his tutoring discreetly. Perhaps it did not matter to Benjamin who I was at all.

I lower the red hood of my cape, freeing my locks. I

have been told to keep my red hair hidden away, especially while I was outside. Snow was rare here, but the contrast of red will give me away to God's mercy. This was all according to my gran, however. I'd like to see these cowardice men try to take me.

I untie the cape and let it fall to the ground, holding eye contact with Benjamin. He licks his lips and stares, taking in my sheer night-robe.

I know why he gives in to my silly requests, and as I feel my nipples harden against the fabric, Benjamin's eyes widen. His boots crunch on the snow as he approaches me, and I lift the hem of my dress gently over my head. Throwing the garment aside, I hiss as the cold hits my naked body, goosebumps exploding across my flesh.

My breath is a cloud around my lips as I survey the thick of the woods.

Wouldn't it be dreadful if I was caught out here? Maybe by Gran, or one of my father's men. But what would be even more exciting?

I stand before him, daring him to deny me what I want, and what I know he surely wants himself. God fearing or not, men had needs and desires. Something women had far more control over than they. Most just didn't even know it.

Ben meets my eyes and stalks to me, calling my bluff.

"And why do you enjoy teasing me like this? You are going to get yourself into trouble…"

"Trouble? Me?" I giggle as he scoops me by my waist, crashing his lips to mine. We tumble together on top of my cloak and it kicks the air from my lungs in a small whimper as we hit the ground.

Benjamin fumbles with his jacket and breeches, his erection pushing up against my thigh. He grunts and grinds, trying to find the slick spot between my legs.

Padded footfalls stop Benjamin dead, and he looks into my eyes. Fear and realization cross his face as he whispers, "The Wolf of the Woods. Don't move."

Excitement fills me again, and I feel my pulse quicken in anticipation.

Did I have a death wish? Perhaps. Did I want something exciting to happen in front of Ben just to prove him right?

I did as I was told, trying to tilt my head backward so I could see behind us, hiding a smile creeping up my face. Two holographic eyes caught the moonlight, a low growl escaping the bushes. My body goes rigid, and my blood pounds inside my ears.

I clutch the amethyst stone hanging from my neck, reciting an incantation silently to myself.

"Run!" Benjamin screams, tripping over my body as he goes, leaving me behind and laying in the snow. I wrap the cloak around my naked body and jump up to sprint behind him. My hair trails behind me like a royal flag, but I cannot stop to hinder it. Surely this wolf will catch me and rip out my throat. My heart pounds, and the woods look endless.

Finally, I see the clearing ahead, the cabin not far now, smoke billowing from the chimney. I have heard nothing following us for a while.

Benjamin is already inside. Obviously fine with sacrificing me to the beast.

I turn to look behind me, right before running up the stairs to the porch. It is silent, and nothing lurks in our wake...

Once inside, I close the door behind me and lean against it. My breath still coming in heaves, sweat beading my brow...

I smile.

FENRIR

The fox-haired girl and her small guard walk through the trees together, and her sweet scent flows to my senses. It is her, the one my wolf has been searching for.

She seems distracted and I worry she is lost. The guard looks like a boy rather than a man, and I can't help but feel concerned for her safety. Perhaps she is trained with a sword, or to fight. It was common for women to fight alongside the men in battle where I came from—perhaps she is a shield maiden.

I sniffed at the air, and in my wolf's form I could smell for miles. My stealth was unmatched, and I could easily remain unseen. If he attacked her, I would be on him in a moment.

The girl from my dreams, my true mate—my tail wags furiously, and I try to keep it from rustling the branches behind me.

It is her. She has finally come, and here she is teasing me so. A low growl rumbles through my chest, but I keep myself from leaping on the boy and taking what is mine.

I let my tongue dangle as I taste the surrounding air. She smells of sex and rosemary. I lick my chops.

As they approach nearer now, I can almost hear what she says, and her words come fast, like a song melody. She backs against the trunk of a tree and laughs, her eyes mischievous as she looks at the boy.

Her laugh reveals her presence before her body does —along with that blazing mane.

Perhaps I would laugh often as well—if she was mine.

Without warning, she tosses back her flowing red cape and lifts her dress.

I pant, my muscles stiffening. I watch her as she stands naked, looking at the boy with need.

Displaying her vulnerable body in the open?

This maiden intrigued me beyond the dreams that have come to me. In her proper form, she is a goddess, and beauty plucked straight from the stars above.

Her head tilts to the side, and I can see her teasing smile driving me wild. How I craved to wipe that sly smile from her face and turn it into yelps and whimpers.

The tips of her breasts like pink rosebuds and hips that curve sharply outward and dip down to a plump patch of red curls.

When the lad rushes toward her, I move closer in a few steps and brace myself for an attack.

Her head rolls back, and her overturned gaze is on me. For a moment, I think she sees me, as our eyes almost meet through the thick brush. A shiver runs down my spine as the sun hits her eyes, and they glow like golden honey.

The boy is scared and runs. I watch as she scrambles to her feet behind him, gathering her cape and shoes. She looks over her shoulder behind her, a mix of fear and amusement. I sniff the air that trails behind her, a sweet perfume of pheromones that tickles my wolf's belly.

You can run, but you cannot hide.

CHAPTER 12
LUX

As I walk to the back sitting room, I can hear their low conversation in the dim light. It's late, and the fire is nearly out now. I tip toe to stand next to the doorway, still breathless and full of excitement. Sweat trickles down the small of my back, inciting a reaction between my legs. My nipples push against my dress, eager for release. Perhaps I can talk Ben into sneaking upstairs with me.

Was it man or beast that stalked us in these woods tonight? Either thought was better than living out another day caring for a woman who enjoyed punishing me.

"I trust you, Benjamin. I have no doubts that you will make the perfect predecessor to my son." It was my gran's firm voice, speaking the praises of my selfish father.

I swear, if a man took a shit on the floor around here, they would reward him. All hail the man's digestive track!

I roll my eyes at the thought of Benjamin taking over for my father. He didn't want to stay in England. He constantly boasted of his uncle's ship and how his family would sail to America.

"Yes, Ms. Bryce. You can trust me." I can hear in his voice a waiver of nerves. I have known him for nearly ten years now, and he was terrified of my gran.

I found that quite amusing—a man afraid of a female.

"She will make a proper wife...someday. But you need to use your skills and teach her about our savior. He washes away our sins, and she badly needs direction to repent of the very thing her mother died for. Sinful pleasures of the flesh." Her voice sounds morose at the mention of my mother. However, I know it's for show.

Sinful pleasures, huh? I'm sure Benjamin wasn't thinking about that last night while he pounded into me from behind.

I peer around the frame, and they are in an embrace, Gran's head on his chest. I move into the doorway, visible to both now. Benjamin turns to leave and walks by me as if I am invisible.

I stand almost two feet taller than the feeble old woman in front of me. Her back is hunched and she cannot walk without her cane anymore. I am left to take care of her, something I've always taken seriously. Until now.

So, she planned to marry me off to Benjamin? Well, what if she isn't around to see to it?

She turns her head up to me and grins. "Don't you worry, Granddaughter. I will make sure you are well kept after I am gone." She hobbles by me, and when I offer my hand on her arm to help, she swats it away, smacking my forearm. I pull back, coils of fire pricking under my skin.

Why do I even bother with this woman? I could easily take her life, no one knowing the wiser. She was old, and I knew just the herbs that would take care of my problem.

"Don't touch me with your tainted fingers," she hisses and looks me over as if I am the Devil himself, standing in her sitting room.

I watch as she struggles to the back bedroom, contemplating what would happen if she had a nasty fall...

What a pity it would be to have this house all to myself...at least I would still have Ben around for a good fucking.

CHAPTER 13
FENRIR

"I need you, Fenrir...come."

I am in complete darkness, and cannot see in front of me, but I know I am outside, and I know I am in my wolf's form. The pads of my paws slowly tread against the hard, cold ground. I have no direction, only the pull of her sweet voice.

My wolf wants her, needs her. It is a hunger inside me that cannot be satiated until I have had her taste in my mouth. I want to devour her sex, bite her—mark her.

"Fenrir! Please!" Her shouts are coming more urgently now, and I can tell she is scared. The primal need to protect the one I love is strong, and I cannot tell if the woman I need to save is Sybil or the fox-haired girl.

The darkness lifts, and the sun rises faster than normal. I am in my human form now, and the fox-haired girl is laying in a field of daisies. She is laughing, and it makes me want to laugh as well. I go to her, but I look down and realize I am not clothed.

Neither is she.

I kneel to her, and she looks at me and smiles. "Hello, my love." Her eyes of copper...eyes that I lose myself inside of each time she visits me in my dreams.

She stands, and I reach for her, feeling her absence like a cold gust of wind.

Suddenly, we are inside now, and she lifts her arms above her, dancing in front of the fire, tossing her head and hair around as if she is unaware of my presence. This place is unfamiliar, the fancy mantel lined with glass jars and candles.

Her eyes are closed, and she hums a tune that can only be described as a lullaby. I sit, watching her become lost inside whatever God she is channeling. She is a wild woman...my wild woman.

I lay back on a soft cushion, lacing my fingers behind my head, smiling over curves and dimpled thighs. She knows I am watching but pretends not to as she lights another candle.

"I fear if I touch you now, you will explode with pleasure instantly." Leaning down over me, hands on her knees, her breasts are inches from my face. I lick my lips, so parched for her sweet nectar.

Now she kneels over me, her hand trailing down my abdomen. It feels like an eternity before I feel her wrap her hand around my throbbing cock. I lift my hips up to meet her strokes, but it isn't enough, and I feel myself building at an achingly slow pace.

I reach out to stroke her cheek, but suddenly she is screaming—her face melting into the sunken hollows of her skull.

When I wake, I am drenched in sweat. I sit up and reach for my hatchet, but it's gone. I stand from the furs and charge out the door.

I can no longer take the dreams of my ripe, nude goddess. I wished to see her red hair spilling over my lap, to lay her down and nuzzle the apex between her thighs until she sighs.

Each tortured dream is worse than the last. Now, in the dreams, she is touching and teasing me, and when I reach for her, she is gone again. What I would give to feel her skin pressed to mine.

I hadn't seen her in these woods since, and I hunted more than normal, just on the off chance that I would get to see her rosebud lips in the flesh.

When I hunted this time, I would hunt for her.

. . .

~

It was hours before my nose led me to the house beyond the crested hill; the sun rising now. The tall trees disappeared, and a clearing held a gigantic structure with a chimney full of smoke.

This was a place unlike the clan from where I came, even the structure where I now live is abundant.

This was her home, where she lay her head each night while I fever dream of her soft skin.

The fires in the woods stopped once I dreamed of her...the fox-haired girl. My search, bringing me here without the nerve to do a thing about it.

I kneel behind a wide tree stump, knowing what I was doing was dangerous, never coming this close to any human since leaving my clan, accepted as a pup. I tipped the scales in heavy favor once my King witnessed the blood I shed in my Wolf's form. He called me a secret weapon, and rumors of what I was spread for miles amongst the others.

Fenrir, the great Wolf God.

I am a fool for coming here. I am a fool for believing I could take what was mine, my mate. In pure self-ishness....

She didn't know what I was. She was a soft maiden with barely enough experience to understand what love was. Specifically, what love was to a beast such as I.

Cold air strikes my bare chest and I let out a growl, the emptiness the dream left in my mind inescapable... burning me from the inside out. I have to leave.

I break into a run, away, as far away as I can get before I lose every ounce of self-control, and seize her.

~

When I make it back to my camp, dusk has settled over the copse of land nestled between the trees.

I sniff the air, the scent of a male hanging near my front door, heavy pepper and sweat.

Walking toward the back, snow crunching under my boots, I stop in front of the neat stacks of wood.

My hatchet is lodged in a log on the top row, a black brimmed hat hanging from it.

I bare my teeth, my wolf growling, hackles raised. If this was a threat, I would surely rip them all to shreds without hesitation.

Fist clenched, I pull the hatchet from the wood, pivoting my head in both directions, looking for any signs of movement. The morning is still, and the smell of sulphur and ashes has finally left the air for good. It has been a full moon's phase since I last had seen the men in the black coats. I had no reason to strike at them, for now. I did not mind turning a blind eye to the sacrifices to one's God, but if the fox-haired girl came to these woods in peril, my wolf will leave no survivors.

CHAPTER 14

LUX

Safe and alone, upstairs in my bedroom, I close the door behind me and plop down on my bed. I sit for a moment, re-living the chase through the woods...the fear, the urgency. The excitement.

My skin still tingles, and I think about watching Benjamin getting ripped to pieces by the beast. Would it be bloody...with his insides spilling from his body? Would he scream like a woman?

The fantasy makes my nipples peak and harden under my dress, and I lay back on the bed and close my eyes.

The wolf is at our door, scratching and menacing. The door, unable to hold him back any longer, bursts open and he is inside, hungry. This wolf isn't a normal wolf, no. He is three times the size and has shoulders wide like a man's. The cold creeps inside and his breath comes in thick bursts of fog. He sees Gran first, but charges Benjamin.

My fingers drift down over my breasts, my thumb stopping to rub tiny circles around the tight pebble. My breath hitches at the sensation, the tingles zig zagging down to my belly. I spread my legs and tilt my hips up, straining to fill the ache that builds deep inside my core. My hand dips down over the small curve of my belly, and I lift the hem of my dress.

Only, it is not my hand. It is the wolf's tongue.

I cup my cunt, hot and slick. Sliding my middle finger between the crease, I plunge two greedy fingers inside. I cry out but bite my lip so I will not repeat the mistake again.

He is massive, his weight pressing down over me, covering me. I pump my fingers in and out, bending my legs for a deeper angle. My head pushes into the pillow, hair sticking to my forehead.

I pull out my fingers, slick with my arousal, and find the sensitive bud that built with need and throbbed when I touched myself. As my fingertip finds the tender spot, I cry out again. Slow, small circles making me buck my hips and cup my breast.

It is the wolf's tongue now, lapping at my cunt, until I feel the pressure building, cresting. I pick up my pace, mimicking the strokes of a tongue, and I can feel the wave coming, my body trembling.

He is no longer a wolf now. He is a man. His blue eyes

look up at me while his tongue drags long strokes through my swollen cunt. Like the spark of a match, I feel heat coil through my abdomen as I jerk my hips up to his mouth. My toes curl and my body fights against the waves pulsing through me. I am needy and hungry, and even as I buck against his mouth, he chases my wet sex with his tongue, never losing contact.

I orgasm, lights bursting behind my eyes and another shout of pleasure leaving my lips.

I roll to the side, fingers drenched, and body languid.

Whatever magic this was, I never wanted it to stop.

~

I toss and turn repeatedly. Flinging limbs and hair, angry sighs, and grunts filling the room.

When I couldn't sleep at night, my mother used to coax me back to sleep with a candle.

Watch the flame as it dances, let it dazzle you and concentrate on your breathing. In and out.

Relax your body, Luxy, and envision yourself walking toward your true path. Yes, that's it...stare into the fire and let your mind wander. Soon, your eyes will close, and you will be fast asleep.

I push myself up from the bed, the memory of her voice too real, and I grab my hip satchel from the windowsill. I gather a tapered candle from the box under my bed—Benjamin snuck them to me if I continued to fuck him. At least he was good for something.

I run down the stairs, flinging my cape about my shoulders, and quietly open the front door.

The air outside is frigid. Pulling the hood over my head and stepping off the steps, I shiver. Taking a deep breath in, I hold it for a moment, allowing the sounds of the night to fill my ears.

A slight wind rushes by me, rustling the dead leaves at my feet, carrying me deeper into the trees. There is a hill behind the house, a hill I was never allowed to climb on my own...until now.

The stream flows just beyond it, where every memory I kept of my mother took place.

Dare I cross this line, this late, knowing the wolf may just be beyond? Was it he who nearly caught us today?

Climbing the hill, I clutch the candle and the flint, ready to light it once I reached the stream, saying a silent prayer to the moon.

As I make it to the top, the woods seem to stretch out endlessly. I stare too long, and the trees move on their own, taking on the form of bodies with arms and legs reaching...

I blink a few times, striking the flint and cursing under my breath as my hands shake.

The flame catches, and the candle's wick is engulfed by the red and orange glow. I stare as it dances, waiting until a drip of wax skitters down the side, almost landing on my hand. I concentrate on the flame, and it grows larger, greedily licking the wick until it overflows with hot wax and spills onto my knuckles.

I hiss, a memory of the first time I felt same pain that turned into pleasure between my thighs.

I am sprawled, naked and flushed, replete with orgasm. There is dried wax spilled over each nipple, white splashes decorating the pink nubs.

It streaks the insides of my thighs with red, the remnants of the wax long washed away after my thrashing. It wasn't long before the bite of the wax didn't hurt enough for me to climax and I needed more. After I lit the candle, I warmed the edges of the metal flint box until it glowed, burnishing the insides of my thighs until I screamed. That was when things with Gran took a dreadful turn...

The sound of footsteps takes me out of the flame's trance, and I snap my head toward the sound to my right.

In the distance, two slanted eyes glow a greenish yellow. A small puff of fog plumes around its mouth, and I see fangs in the moonlight's glint.

The trees before me cement my feet in place, and my body refuses to move.

I want to see it...I want to see just how big he is.

The candle blows out as I bound forward, right toward it. "Come out, wolf! I see you! I am not afraid!"

I am in pure darkness now; the candle is no longer in my hands anymore. My stomach turns, and I stop myself, wondering what my mother would think if she knew of the careless choices I was making in the middle of the night. Hanging my head, I turn back toward the house. The house that I surely will die inside of.

I must have been dreaming, the desperate need to experience anything besides the old woman.

CHAPTER 15

FENRIR

Ever since the day I witnessed the nakedness of the fox-haired girl, I've dreamed of her every night.

I run in my wolf's form more than ever before. Was I avoiding her by not sleeping? Running only fed my wolf's desire to find her, to seize her as only a savage would.

Omens and signs can come to a man in many forms. But dreams, dreams are sacred and a holy belief to our Shamans. The ones sought after of foretelling and what the future held.

My insides twist each time I see her face, and the need to reach for her rips me in half. I want to cradle her in my arms, kiss her brow.

Drag her back to my furs.

But I do not know her. I only know of her.

In each dream, I am so close to touching her. And each time it takes her from me—an illusion to tease my senses.

Every night, I roam the woods searching for her scent. I couldn't understand why I had seen none of the men in the black coats, but they left a single hat behind.

The offerings faded, and I was no longer treated to fresh baked bread and wine. No matter. I did not care about the offerings. I cared only about finding this woman and making her mine.

I stayed close to the home that I believed was hers, watching for any signs of the men in the black coats. I wouldn't allow them to have her.

This must be what it felt like to be a parent and have children of your own—constant fear and worry about always being able to keep them safe at any cost. I would give my life in place of hers. The urge from deep within my core to mate with her and carry on my lineage—fill her with my seed until she was round and ripe with healthy babes. Powerful, half-pup babes.

I would raise a son into the Viking way, but show him how to use his wolf.

A fierce hunter named Garm—Sybil's father; the only father I had ever known—rescued me, abandoned me, and left me unwanted in the deep woods.

Did I have a chance at happiness once again? Or was I

bargaining with Odin for something that would never be mine?

I light the candles that line the fireplace mantel, silently asking for Odin to deliver her to my feet.

CHAPTER 16

LUX

"It's that bloody book, isn't it? That book you told me you found under your mother's floorboards?" Benjamin rushes to my bed and reaches under the mattress.

I grab his arm and tug, but he easily throws me off.

"You know nothing about that book! So why be angry about it? It's just a book!" I screech, half-panicked that Gran would hear us and discover the book herself. I would be locked in my room forever.

"The School of Venus: The Lady's Delight." He holds out the yellow, tattered pages, the cover almost unrecognizable.

"Yeah, Venus. You know it? It's the planet of love." I stop trying to grab it from him, crossing my arms and acting bored.

As he opens it, I brace myself, holding back my delight.

"Fuck's sake! This book is straight from the pits of Hell!" He throws the book on the wood floor beside the fire, as if it has bitten him.

Gingerly, I pick it up and place it back under my bed. I sit, unfazed by his reaction...I already knew I was going to Hell. Better make the best of it.

"Hell? Hell? For what? Coupling before marriage? Sounds like something silly to suffer for in eternity, if you ask me." I look him straight in his face. His nose is slightly bent.

He looks at me with disgust and says, "You will never find a husband if you keep your mind in these dark places, Lux. And then you will end up burning just like her." He leaves the room, taking my horn book with him.

I guess the day's lessons are done. Good, then. I'm glad he's leaving.

Even though he is the only one I can have a chat with besides Gran.

Before he leaves, he turns to me and opens the wood tablet. "And lead us not into temptation and deliver us from evil."

The Lord's prayer.

With that, he leaves, and I heave myself at the door, slamming it loudly behind him. I feel hot tears stinging behind my eyes, but I swallow them back and walk to my only window.

"Luxy, don't you ever forget that you can be just as intelligent as any man, no matter what's between your legs. You remember; we are powerful women. Do you know why that is?" I would nod expectantly at my mum, eating up the words as she spoke. "We are powerful women because we use our minds—as well as our spirit. Our spirituality comes from deep within." She presses her hand to my heart, and I instantly flourish at the thought of being powerful, as if it ran through my veins.

"Evil? What is evil? Desire? Lust? Freedom?" I pull out the tinder box from my bedside drawer and light the single white candle perched upon a pewter candelabra. The flame lights the windowpane and flickers ever so slightly.

Walking to my dresser, I pull out my nightgown and four cinnamon sticks fall from the rolled-up garment. I hadn't worn this since the day I was ten, the day I discovered my mother's room was empty. I smell it, my mother's scent rolling through my senses and invoking a memory of her willowy face.

I prayed to the moon, to the stars, and to the sky. I prayed for rescue, maybe even tragedy.

I pull the candle out from its holder, marveling at the flame and the wax dripping down the sides. I hear the front door slam, followed by my gran's sharp yell. "Lux! Come down here at once!"

I cringe, pouring the candle wax into my palm with a hiss.

Any punishment she gave me was well worth every orgasm that had ever ripped through my body.

~

"I know you are summoning the devil. Using herbs and candles for your own gain. You cannot fool me, girl. I have arranged for a minister—not your father—to bless the house and exorcise the demons from you." Gran coughs and wheezes, struggling to get out the sentence. She is completely bedridden now, which means I have the pleasure of emptying her bed pan and giving her sponge baths daily.

At least now she can no longer assault me with her cane, or force me to kneel for hours, praying for forgiveness at her replicated church altar.

"Do you mean the same herbs and plants that help your pain, Gran?" I roll my eyes and pull the handmade quilt up to her neck. I thought how easy it would be to take a pillow and end my misery...hers, too. "Is there anything you need? I'm going for a walk." I already had the red cape draped around my shoulders; my basket ready for whatever treasures I find.

Luckily, she's too far gone to realize what season it is. There were no flowers or herbs to gather this time of year.

I added a few more logs to the fire at the foot of her bed. The flames licking up the sides of the wood, growing. I stare, letting the orange and red dance mesmerize me.

Standing, I am looking back at the sleeping, ancient woman. I did not choose this life. I wanted to see boats, maybe America, and get my hands on more books. Gran said that books were bad for a woman's mind—textbooks were the only acceptable literature.

I allow myself to ponder what life would have been like if my father wasn't a minister.

My eyes travel to the small window of Gran's room. It is dusk now. The wind howls outside, and I feel the night beckoning.

CHAPTER 17
LUX

"My father is coming early today, and he is bringing a minister to assess your...condition." Ben clears his throat at the last of his sentence, careful not to look me directly in my eyes.

I want to smack him across his plain, childlike face for even thinking such a thing of me...There was nothing wrong with me. Nothing a minister could help me with anyway...

"Well, isn't that lovely, a visit from a holy minister? How lucky am I?" I elbow him in the ribs as he jerks away from me.

"You shouldn't joke about it, Lux. What a pity it would be if curiosity really killed the cat..." He glances at the woods, then back at me.

Entirely over waiting for him to finish, I stand with a sharp sigh and grab the ax from his hands. "Let me have it, if you're just going to stand there all day looking at it." I raise the ax over my head, bringing it down as hard as I can onto the center of the wood. It breaks in half on contact, the two halves falling to the ground.

"Give me that back! What are you thinking!? This is dangerous for a woman." Ben snatches the ax from me, nearly hitting himself in the face with it.

Rolling my eyes, I sit on a stump in defeat, wrapping my cloak around me, wishing Ben would hurry and finish splitting the wood so I can start the fire. "Do they talk about me back home? Does Jamie ever ask for me? Do they even care that I am gone?"

Jamie was my best friend growing up, and we regularly teased the adults and their 'invisible rules' until we were clutching our bellies with tears in our eyes.

Ben swings the ax, the wood falling to the ground, uncut. "You are full of questions, Lux. That is reason enough to summon a minister."

I wonder if the minister would be handsome...gentle. His holy water and blessings will be wasted on me. This would be the third time they had exorcised me since coming here.

Maybe it helps Gran sleep at night.

****

"Have you seen him? The Wolf? I have heard he burns the women's bodies and then eats them. Bones and all!" Jamie's voice is hushed, but then she screeches, as if her own question has scared her.

I wanted to scare her, to tell her tall tales that she could take back with her, to tell the others. I might as well make her trip out here worth it.

"I have seen him...he is monstrously large. I barely got away with my life this last time," I lied, the rush of excitement flooding over me in a wave of heat.

Jamie's eyes grow big, and she follows me through the dining room, to the stairs.

"Lux, stop. Come, come." I have one foot on the first step, and I look toward the booming voice. The voice belongs to minister Finley and his wandering hands. I'd lost count how many times he'd accidentally brushed one of my breasts.

He certainly was not handsome, with a shiny bald head and saggy jowls.

Walking close to me, he is tall, with small, feminine arms. He places a hand on my back, guiding me into the sitting room where Gran is propped up in her chair.

Front row tickets to the freak show.

Father Finley reaches for his crucifix beneath his collar, holding it up in front of my face. It is almost as if he knows to expect nothing but giggles from me now. He barely finishes the rites anymore, and it makes me wonder if Gran stopped paying him to come.

Placing one hand behind my neck, and the other pressing the cross to my forehead, he mutters quiet prayers for absolution and purity. As each prayer falls from his lips, he closes his eyes tighter and pulls me closer to him, my breasts pressing into his sternum. Sweat beads on his forehead as he recites the last prayer, the demand for the demon to leave my body.

Father Finley's body feels like fire against mine, and his head falls back, his body shaking as he presses his leg between mine.

I decide I will give Jamie a petty show for the road. They would tell stories about me and my demons back in England. Perhaps if I returned, I would be celebrated.

I let my head fall back, fluttering my eyes and bouncing on my toes. I let out a long groan, and Father Finley's eyes snap open as he watches me thrash my body. My noises cut his words short, and I feel him harden against my leg as I grind on his.

This asshole is enjoying every second of this, and I doubt it has anything to do with his holy purpose.

I open one eye to get a peek at Jamie, and her eyes are wide with horror. She notices me looking at her and I wink as she giggles behind her hands.

I close my eyes again, but I still my body and stand on my own, backing away from the minister.

He adjusts himself, clearing his throat and straightening his collar. "You are healed, my child."

I smile at him from under my lashes, and he looks slightly irritated.

Perhaps he knows that I'm into him.

"Lux, kneel at the altar. Four hours at minimum." I look at my gran, every drop of blood in my being wanting to—needing to—tell her no.

Only I don't, and as I walk to the altar where I will be for the rest of the evening, I silently ask the moon goddesses to save me from this Hell on earth.

CHAPTER 18
LUX

Stepping outside, I quietly pull the door closed behind me. I draw my hood over my long hair, a few small strands whipping around my face. It was the middle of the night. Gran was sleeping peacefully in her chair. My knees ached from sitting at the altar for so long, and as I breathe in the fresh air, I am reborn by the night.

The dirt of the small yard crunches under my laced boots, and I stare out into the endless rows of trees that seem to form a black hole through the middle. The moon is waxing, and I can feel the magic around me stirring. Excitement runs circles over my skin, and I eagerly press forward.

Follow your true path...

The satchel at my hip contains a small hunting knife my mother gave me after my father found it under her pillow. I believe that was when the trouble began.

I've brought a candle and my tinder box just in case, but use the light of the moon and my lantern to find my way.

As I enter the wood, the branches break beneath my feet, but I don't feel scared...I feel powerful.

Benjamin was certain there was a splendid beast inside of these woods. His uncle told him that if the beast didn't receive his offerings, he would sacrifice a woman. They rumored his dwelling was somewhere a few miles from the long stream.

Did I believe these rumors? Not particularly. I believed little to anything about what a man had to say.

Did I want him to be right? If that was the case, perhaps I had a death wish.

I make it to the long stream that runs along parallel to Gran's, but the path up over the hill ends where the stream winds.

I pull out my fluorite crystals and cleanse them in the cool water. It would soon be time to lay them under the full moon at my window.

I hop on rock after rock, to the deeper part of the water, slipping slightly when I land on the biggest one. Bending down, I sink my hand and the crystals into the icy water.

Taking a deep breath, I slowly release it, holding it a little longer and wishing for a different life than this. Happy memories of my mother and me coming to this stream on holiday...her kisses in my hair and flowers in hers.

I hear an owl somewhere in the distance, and as I turn on the slippery rock to peak, my heeled boot slides.

I fall so fast that I don't have time to recover. I fall, hitting the back of my head against the large rock I once stood upon. Pulled into the blackness, the icy water pulls me under and swallows me whole.

~

I turn my head, choking and spitting out the water as I struggle to regain my normal breathing. When I finally pry open my eyes, I am looking into a sea of stars and jagged branches lifted toward the sky.

My body is stiff, wet. Pin pricks cover my skin and I

lick the dry split on my bottom lip. Blinding pain at the back of my head, reminding me of the impact.

I'm slightly aware of the red cloak flung about my shoulders, heavy and saturated from the stream.

Cinnamon sticks...the bloody stream. I would surely freeze to death out here now.

Pain splinters my head and the cold snow against my face burns. I exhale slowly, trying to regain my resolve...to move...to just get up.

I dig my fingers into the packed snow beneath me, the shards of cool ice stabbing my cuticles.

A deep, chilling howl fills the sky, and my eyes grow wide.

The sound is so close, I can feel it reverberate down into my eardrums, causing me to shiver.

"He only comes out to feed during the witching hour of night. Beware full moons, lost daughters, you must stay inside and lock your doors tight."

Benjamin's voice echoes inside my mind, bringing me back to when he first told me the tale...

"Oh!...Why? Is he large? Is he...Oh! Monstrous??" One last thrust deep inside me, and he grunts with his release.

"He's a beast, Lux. What do you think??" Benjamin pulls himself from inside of me and looks down, horrified.

"Do you think he is responsible for the lost daughters?" I knew next to nothing about the rumors, only the ones from Ben himself.

I stand. "What? What is it? What's the matter?"

"Blood! Is it your menses? For fuck's sake, unclean blood that poisons everything it touches!" He flails around the room, looking for the pitcher of water and rags to clean his hands with.

I suppress a giggle.

"Oh, you think this is amusing? You...with your wandering womb. You know a woman's menstruation blood is tainted...vile." Benjamin buckles his breeches and stands to grab his books.

I know exactly how a female's reproductive organs worked. Perhaps he didn't.

My face is flush, but I choose to ignore his ignorance. I look at him with a sneer. "Do you think he's hairy? With sharp teeth, too?"

"Christ almighty, Lux. Yeah, I think probably. You and

your incessant questions...Here's an idea. Maybe you should go find out for yourself." With his dick tucked back inside his pants and his books stacked neatly in his hands, he turns to leave.

I did not care what Benjamin, or the brethren, thought of my menses. It wasn't any of their business. I wanted to know more about the enormous beast of these woods.

The solitary conditions of my life push down hard on my lungs. All desire of wanting to get back to a warm fire leaves me.

I lay still and allow the black behind my eyes to pull me under, back to a dreamless sleep of swimming in the stream. Only my body is numb from the cold, and it rolls through me like an icy finger.

I hear another howl, closer now.

Time passes. A few minutes, perhaps.

Now, I hear an animal's snorts and puffs so close that I think I can feel its warmth on my neck. I can no longer muster the energy to even care.

If I died out here deep in the dark woods, would Gran even notice?

No, she would die most likely, and who would then notice my absence?

I vaguely remember giving her an excuse for my sneaking out. I always blamed it on her medicine. Even though I already had the flowers and herbs I needed.

Which ironically was the recipe my mother had taught me—and just the things that the brethren accused women of for witchcraft.

Something fluffs my hair, and it almost sounds like heavy panting. The snorts come louder as I feel something cold and wet press against my forehead. I sink back into the warm darkness and pretend my mother is wetting my brow.

CHAPTER 19

FENRIR

"What happens, Fen? You can tell me." Her voice purrs in my ear, but I do not respond.

She is teasing me, trailing her fingers up and down my chest and stomach. I eye her fingers, my cock tight against my belly, throbbing.

"I take my wolf's form." My hands are linked beneath my head, and she is draped across me.

"I want to see." She climbs on top of me, positioning me at her entrance. I close my eyes and groan as she slips me inside of her.

"Fuck," I say with a groan. She is so warm and wet... for me.

I grab her hips as she circles me, the head of my cock hitting her deepest pleasure spot. It only takes a small moan that leaves her lips for me to lose all control.

I flip her onto her back, hooking her long leg over my shoulder. With her ass raised, I slam into her over and over. Our skin smacking together and I feel my balls tighten. I fuck into her with one final, hard thrust up and I'm spilling inside of her.

I feel my body quake, every hair standing on end. The change is coming swiftly behind my release and my body stretches to twice its size until I am standing over her in my full wolf form. Her eyes are wide and her small, naked body arches. A smile blossoms on her face and she bites her lip, looking pleased. It was the most beautiful smile I had ever seen.

I let out a chilling howl and turn from her.

I run to the door and don't stop until I've reached the woods.

I wake up drenched in sweat, my cock rigid and angry.

This woman was made for me, her very ingredients a calming salve to the aching of my lonely soul.

She was mine. She just did not know it yet.

~

I can't fall back to sleep. I need to fuck or fight, and the first one was impossible.

I would hunt, then.

The moon is almost full now, and my wolf is restless. If I sleep, the dreams come.

Why did these dreams keep coming to me? Was this a sign from Odin? Should I be heeding a warning, or was she the reason my wolf had been sent into a sexual frenzy?

I break into a run as I let myself be consumed with thoughts of her. I wanted to know what she smelled like, what she tasted like. What her face looked like completely breaking in pleasure for me.

I shift mid-run into my wolf's form, shaking out my fur and feeling a small amount of relief.

I perk my ears, an unfamiliar sound in the distance. Carefully, I sneak toward the sound and lower my head.

The small stream is nearby, and I can hear the water splashing as if someone treads through it.

It is bitterly cold. It could only be an animal who's lost its way.

A small scream and a loud splash cause me to run toward the commotion.

As the stream comes into view, I see a red flash of cloth.

I freeze.

Do my eyes deceive me? Did my dreams bring her to life?

I run to her, pulling her lifeless body from the swirling water.

As if she has sprouted from my dreams, the fox-haired girl lays unmoving under the ash tree that I've dragged her to.

I sniff at her wet clothes and look side to side, wondering where the red cloak is.

The men in the black coats. A trap, perhaps?

My wolf whines, the smallest bit of red catching my eye. I sprint to the small stream that cuts across the land, grabbing the cloth with my mouth and dragging it to her. I cover her as best I can, but my legs will not move.

I watch her for a moment. Her back rises and falls

slowly. I sniff at her brow and a nostalgic feeling takes over me.

I cannot leave her here to die. I have no choice but to take her back to my fire, and I can only do so in my human form.

CHAPTER 20
LUX

Deep down, I luxuriate in the warmth. My body thawing from the stiffness in my arms and legs.

Perhaps I am dreaming again, only imagining the heat and comfort.

I look down over my body and I am only wearing my sheer white sleeping gown, nothing else.

My cape is gone, and I seem to be inside of a cabin that looks like it was built by a cave dweller.

I shiver and realize I am laying on the floor on top of a fur pelt.

I go searching for a mythical creature and end up captured by some...savage.

It is what you wanted, Lux. Who are you trying to fool?

The stone fire is roaring, and I feel for my satchel, but it is gone, along with my cape.

I mock myself with my own dirty thoughts. Just like Gran always says.

Your mind, always in the gutter!

I hear heavy footsteps coming from the adjoining room, and I cringe, keeping one eye open. The tallest man I have ever seen stood before me. His hair was tied back and shaved at the sides, a wild look on his tan face. A long, tangled beard the same blonde color as his hair hung nearly to his chest.

He's carrying a hatchet and has murder written all over his stone face.

Does he want me to know he plans to kill me? Why would he bring me inside to warm? Why not just let me die out there?

Then my heart is in my throat.

He wants more than your life, Lux. He desires what's in between your legs.

After I take a large gulp and tame my nerves, I can't help but wonder if his beard would tickle the inside of my thighs. He is one of the most beautiful men I've ever laid my eyes on.

"Where are my petticoats? And cloak?" I move slightly closer to the fire as a shiver runs through me.

He leans up against the doorway that connects the two rooms. "Wet," is all he says.

His accent differs from mine. His 't' is much softer, almost like a Scottish burr. I have learned about all the surrounding countries in my studies with Benjamin, and he never resisted a moment to brag on his father's ship that would 'discover new land' eventually. And Benjamin would be famous; just what he needed—a bigger head.

"Do you plan to kill me?" I wanted to hear more of his deep voice and smooth accent.

"Are you not afraid to die?" He laughs, but it is an amused laugh. My cheeks redden.

"My mother wasn't, so neither am I. I am brave like her." I stick my nose in the air, feigning a bravery that I wasn't sure I had just yet. After all, I did just venture out into the night alone. Even men were afraid of these woods when night fell. They feared the dark, but I did not.

He chuckles. "Fortune favors the brave. I think tonight is my lucky night."

His eyes are an icy blue. It reminds me of the bitter cold frost that covers my windows at night. He is shirtless, tattoos sprawling across his chest and an unkempt beard that nearly reaches his equally furry chest. His abdomen was tight with muscles, and I let my eyes travel down to the dark trail that leads to two toned lines disappearing into his trousers.

I flush and realize I am thinking sinful things about a stranger.

Your mother was guilty of the sinful pleasures of the flesh! I forbid you to be like her. I see it, Lux. You cannot lie to me.

My ear rings as I remember Gran's constant pestering. My only memories left, being of her and her discipline and religious ridicule. The hate I had made for myself over the years didn't even match the hate Gran had for our entire situation. She was proud of my father and ashamed of my mother. Surely, that meant she was ashamed of me as well.

If only Gran could see me now.

The thought brings a smile to my face as I look down over my womanly body. The fire's flames lick my pale complexion and dances over my curves. I am warm, all over my skin and deep inside my belly.

"What do you plan to do with me, then? Skin me like a deer? Strip me naked and hang me up like a kill?" I decide I will take my normal approach with this one, sure of myself. A man can smell weakness for miles, and by the look of this bloke, he could sniff out a rat in a brothel.

He walks to the shelves in the room's corner near the fire, near me. His footsteps are heavy, and I hear the floorboards squeak beneath his weight. He turns to me and says, "There are far worse things in these woods than me, I assure you. I have no such plans for you."

CHAPTER 21

FENRIR

Fenrir, the warrior, the killer...tries to resist the raw hunger to rip that fancy little dress from her and ravage her soft body. Beneath those petticoats that dried near the fire, or whatever she had called them.

I could smell her arousal and hear her heart beating as swiftly as a bird. "Why are you wandering alone in these woods?" I grip the hatchet in my hand and look down at her.

Her chest rises and falls delicately, her lips bright red against her snowy skin.

I want to bite it, ravage it until she bleeds.

"I...I was looking for poppies. For my gran." She cocks her head up and to the side, trying to look at me, but fails miserably.

I let a chuckle roll from my chest and stand at my full human height. She looks terrified and my Wolf is amused.

"Liar. Poppies only grow in the warm months. What were you really doing out there?" I furrow my brow at her little white lie.

Her eyes turn down, but then back to me, and I can see a flicker of anger flash behind them. "Escaping."

I turn my thoughts to the men in the black coats. Was she running from them?

"Escaping what, exactly?" I lean down to where her curvy body is laying on the floor of furs and think back to the number of times I've heard the screams of women in these woods.

"My life." She doesn't look at me when she says it, and I wonder what could be so terrible about her life. It looks as if she has riches, things I never knew existed.

I let out a long breath as I sharpen my hatchet while we sit in silence, with the fire crackling now and then.

"These woods are dangerous." I continue sharpening the blade with long strokes of the steel bar.

"Why? Because of you?" she says, sharp and full of condescension.

I stop, looking over her face. She seems to be unafraid of me, but I can hear her heart thumping hard. "Tell me about these poppies that you're lying about. What do you plan to do with them?" I am intrigued by her wily mouth and quick wit.

"Lance the seeds and grind the gum with the other herbs I have. Not that it's any of your business." She tugs at her restraints, eyeing me.

"So, you are a healer?" Intrigued, I stop sharpening and pull up a wooden stool beside her and grab an apple from one of the many baskets that lined the floor. "The men here—Is that why they take the women?" Her face is that of a nymph, round and supple. Her hair is just as red, if not more so, as the dreams she visited me in. I chew the apple slowly, the sweetness covering my tongue as I watch her nervously hug her knees.

"What do you know about women? You live in the woods...a filthy savage of a man," she spits, but her face flinches in shock as if she has surprised herself with her sharp words.

With two long strides, I am on her, pushing my face close to hers as I growl loudly. I wrap my hand around her neck, my thumb and forefinger nearly touching. Her head is against the beam in the middle of the room, and she watches my lips as I grind out the words, "I am no man, little lamb."

I squeeze slightly. Her face strained, eyes bulging. Her cheeks turn bright pink as she wraps her small hand around mine, relenting.

It pains my heart seeing her face that way, so I let go.

Releasing her, I stand and turn as she violently wiggles her body around until her hair is covering her face and she is panting.

I have no sympathy for this one. It appears she has done this all on her own; come into my woods looking for a plant that only blooms in the summer.

A healer. She would make for the perfect mother and wife.

I shut my eyes and walk to the shelf beside the fire, full of stores and gifts from the men in the black coats.

Are the men stealing these women of their magic?

No matter the answer, I couldn't understand why these women wander alone in the woods at night, but perhaps these men are stealing them from their own beds. Our clan went to great lengths to protect our women, but it seems these men had no intention of protecting them...Rather, they sacrificed them.

And for what?

Was their God a greedy one? Demanding a sacrifice of only the most powerful of humans?

Odin only asked us for our bravery, strength, and honor—a sacrifice of a powerful shaman or woman would only cast a man to death.

"If you are not a man, then what are you? Are you the one they call the Wolf of the Woods? Did you not get your offerings this day? Is this why you have taken me?" Her plump lips distract me as she speaks, never stopping for a breath.

She is asking too many questions.

"I am not the one collecting women, if that is what you are asking." I sit back down beside her, an effort to prove that I had no intentions to hurt her. I must figure out what to do with her, although all I can think about is keeping her.

The sting of Sybil's words—the way she looked at Erik that night—still burned my heart. The memory solidifies my reasons for being alone...I did not need a woman...

My wolf stirs, and I realize he is pleased with her and will not relent until I've had her. The dreams surely brought to me by him, or perhaps Odin. The realization that these dreams I have had of her—I never had them before Sybil...Perhaps dreams are the call for my true mate.

I just hope Emon was right.

"What is your name?" I stood again, her eyes

following at my back as I fill my cup with ale—a part of the Viking way, infused in my blood.

At first, she didn't respond, but after a moment's thought, she whispered, "Lux."

It shocked me, the way her name fell so easily from her lips. It was as if...I already knew it. The letters of her name looped behind my eyes and the wolf inside of me invoked a vivid vision.

Red hair, laughter, and sunshine. Running fast through a green field of daisies as flashes of her bright smile hit the sunlight. The sight of her fills my belly with warmth and consumes my heart with rapture.

Lux, Lux, Lux.

As if a lost key was returned to me—unlocking everything I had ever shoved down, deep inside me. The overwhelming need to protect her, to help her...to claim her as my own. I shook out my head at the thought, and decide it is best for her to stay here with me until I can figure out who she belongs to. She would fight me, but it was for her own good.

"I think it is best you stay here with me until morning." I leave the room, my word final, and set down a pot at her feet, along with a pitcher of water.

"Are you mad?! You expect me to stay here on the floor, bound with no food?" Her face scrunches into a sour expression, but still looks as angelic as Freyja herself. Her top lip curves into a sharp bow, her closed mouth mimicking the shape of a heart—her eyes swell with tears.

I did not plan to bring her here, but the inherent need to protect her was too overwhelming. The familiarity of her, like a long-lost lover, returned home.

I needed to be alone and pray to Odin for answers.

Was she a gift? Had I finally lost my mind from the seclusion and loneliness, and imagined her? Was I dreaming now? The throb deep in my balls told me different. I needed to find out more about her. I needed to know who she was. Where did that fire inside of her come from? Perhaps she was not just a healer, but a sorceress.

One thing I knew for certain: I didn't want to let her go.

She stands, her figure glowing in the firelight beneath the white shift. Her hands in fists at her sides, she says, "I am leaving now. You are the scariest thing in these woods! Just look at this place!"

She walks to the shelf, moving baskets and bottles, clearly searching for something. "I have your things, if that's what you're after." I cross my arms and puff out my chest.

"Fine! Then I'll leave without them!" She walks to the door, half naked with no warm clothes, and I take two long strides to stand in front of it.

"I didn't want to do this, but if I must do so to keep you safe...I'll have to tie you up."

CHAPTER 22
LUX

The following morning, after a tortured night of not being able to find a comfortable way to sleep, I am bound and badly need to use the loo. I barely touched the water he gave me, and my neck throbs from the way I was sleeping.

Though she was a wretched woman, Gran still made sure we had the finer things available to us, even in these woods. Deliveries came once a week, rain or shine. Expensive soaps, linens, and tea. Granted, it was not for me, but for her. I missed the rich taste of the hot, brown drink she called coffee.

I am still wearing last night's dressing gown, and dirt cakes my ankles and feet. My mouth parts, dry beside the now almost extinguished fire. The room is dark besides the morning light that barely shines in through the small windows.

I must get out of here. If Gran is alone too long, she will rot in that bed.

The thought makes the corner of my lip turn up, but I break my morbid scheme when he appears.

"I need to use the loo. Now." I don't even give him the chance to speak. He says he has no plans to harm me, but I do not believe it...I do not know this man. I will have to find a way out of this...

He slides the chamber pot beside me with his foot and meets my eyes. "Oh no! I am not going...in that! In front of you!" I am near hysterical now. I badly want to stretch my body and have a bath.

"I will not watch." He kneels beside me and loosens the ropes enough for me to stand. He smells of wood smoke and leather, and I absentmindedly bite my lip. Standing, he turns his wide back to me, walks to the front door, and leaves me inside alone.

I stand as best as I can, and bend my body over the pot, lifting my dress, with ropes around my wrists.

Bloody bastard. I would get out of here, and it didn't matter how I did it, I would.

I hear the door open, and back away from him up against the beam I'm still loosely tied to, standing awkwardly next to the pot, holding out the dress from my body.

Silently, he walks over to the stove, a pot of water sitting on the stand in the middle of the hearth. Gloving his huge hand, he picks up the pot and sets it down on the stone mantel. Pulling out a cloth and what looks like a carved piece of soap—glorious soap—he wets them both in the water.

I take the warm cloth, resisting the urge to press it against my face and inhale the clean scent.

He walks to the stool and sits, grabbing his mug of ale from the previous night off the floor.

He is filthy. He wants to watch me.

I am so full of rage and exhaustion that I no longer care to fight the urges I'm having. Determined, I meet his gaze.

I lift the hem of my dress with my right hand, exposing myself, but never taking my eyes off him. I wipe the cloth from thighs to cleft, dropping it back to the floor when I'm finished.

If she is dead by now, Gran is surely rolling in her grave after that!

He stands, and I can see the outline of his half-hard cock.

It is enormous and my mouth slacks as he strides forward, lightning fast, his teeth bared in fury. Fisting my hair in his hand, he violently yanks my head back. My breath catches and my adrenaline kicks up in my throat —I can feel his hot breath on my neck, and my body tingles all over.

Down to the tips of my toes.

In a husky whisper, he says, "Are you teasing me, Lux?"

CHAPTER 23
FENRIR

The heartbeat in her throat slams against my hand.

She is not scared. She is excited. I know what fear smells like; sharp and pungent. But excitement, that smell, was almost as sweet as wine and just as intoxicating.

"Why pretend? I can smell your arousal. It clings to you like a perfume." I sneer, daring her to deny it.

Her eyes go to my lips, then back to my eyes, and she is so close that I can smell the flowery scent of her hair. I resist leaning in to inhale more.

"Teasing you? Nary full of ourselves for someone alone in the middle of the wood—with a captive woman." She holds my eyes, and I see a flicker of something behind them—mischief and curiosity, like that of a fox.

"What would you do if I touched your soft skin? Would you come undone at the seams? Whimper for me to fill you up inside?" I bring my mouth down, inches from her ruddy lips, and I cannot help my snigger. "And what are you going to do about it, my captive little fox?"

She licks her lips and leans forward slightly, nipping at my beard.

My wolf is jumping and whining, tail wagging. He is pleased with this mate, but he must remain dormant inside of me...for now. A growl rumbles deep in my chest, as I fight back the urge to take her mouth to mine, claiming it just as I would claim the sweet fitte between her legs.

I must admit, seeing her tied in my ropes is enticing. The way she fights against them ignites something inside of me. I'm not sure how she thinks she can manage her way out of those ropes. My knots are expertly tied.

"Do you like that? Perhaps you would come apart at the seams first?" Her amusement at herself is obvious, and I smile. I have been told by many maidens before that my smile makes their legs weak. Looking down briefly at the wooden floor, I remove my fist from her hair and take two steps back. "I do not intend to hurt you, but I want to know what you are running from."

Was I the type of man to look the other way? The last time I received a visit from the man, I was asked to turn a blind eye, so the rumors would be extinguished. I knew not what a rumor was, but by her inflection, I understood it as gossip.

"Aww, you do not wish to play with me, wolf?" she asks as she sticks out a pouty bottom lip.

The girl must be a powerful woman, with the way she speaks to a man. Roaming through forests in the middle of the night.

I hold my smile, and it seems to make the corners of her mouth rise to meet mine.

"Play with you? And just what do you mean by that?" She is toying with me, but I am finding enjoyment in all aspects of our banter. My cock stirs in anticipation of which words she will lash at me with next.

~

Lux

This was the most fun I've had since I was a child. A fun game of...who is the predator and who is the prey?

I felt powerful...It is as if he cannot take his eyes away from me.

Standing there in front of him, I'm certain that my white night gown is transparent in the light. I almost cross my legs, the excitement throbbing between my thighs.

While his eyes are still fixated on my body, I survey the room for something sharp. Pots, knives, and skins hang from the walls in the far corner of the room, near the window. Dried blood is caked on the floor near some hooks that hang from the ceiling. A large tin tub is pushed against the far wall, and it looks as though it had never been cleaned once.

I wouldn't be able to reach any of the weapons without him noticing. Blasted one-room dump.

The only way I was getting out of here was if he untied me himself. Besides, I wanted to have a little fun with this man-beast before I escaped—and if he killed me, I would become a Lost Daughter legend and be spoken of by everyone.

The number of times I have talked myself out of a dangerous situation was endless. If I didn't, I would receive a caning. This was going to be simple; since he wanted me.

"Untie me, then undress me, and I will show you what I mean." My cheeks are flushed with anticipation. I want him to ravish me, leave me breathless. The thought of it has me clenching my cunt and biting my lip. I wanted it to be rough, wild.

His expression is blank, but his icy blue eyes dance with flames.

I see contemplation pass over them as he stalks toward me. "You must be hungry. What is it you enjoy eating? I have stores aplenty, as you can see." He motions to the tall shelving beside the hearth.

Changing the subject? Interesting way for a man to gain self-control.

I am hungry, but I doubt he has anything I would put in my mouth. I did not know where that food had been. Perhaps I wasn't hungry enough to care. All I could think about was his lips claiming mine, and how good it would feel to have him fill and stretch me, a pleasure I could never provide for myself. No matter how many fingers I used, I could never reach that ache deep within me, and I imagined how big it could be...

"Come on then, big fellow. Come ravish me just the way you know you can." I push my breasts out a little, the pink circles pressing against the sheer fabric.

He runs his hand over his hair, but keeps his eyes fixed on the floor. I watch his forearm flex, and the tattoos that adorn it come to life. I think for a moment that I see a trickle of sweat at his temple, and it's confirmed when he slowly walks closer to me, his eyes never leaving mine. My throat is tight, and I struggle to swallow. He leans down to my ear and whispers, "When I take you, it will not be gentle. I have waited too long for that."

I am confused by his words, but he speaks to them as if he knows me. "Tell me who you are. Why are you living in the middle of the woods? Alone and with no kin?"

His face is close, and I can see the weathered skin around his eyes. "As you said, not that it is your business...I was outcast by my clan. I am simply destined to be alone. Written in the stars the day my parents left me to survive on my own."

His tongue snakes out of his mouth, teasing small flicks against the corner of my mine. I feel his beard tickle my face, his breath on my ear making my eyes flutter shut. I shiver in anticipation, a small groan escaping my lips.

A familiar tingle begins at the base of my spine, and my cunt weeps at his words.

My heart blooms at his admission—and I am only left with an aching need to fulfill his heart with his wildest desires.

CHAPTER 24
FENRIR

She is a seductress. It explains my dreams and the inability to control my cock. But then, my wolf mocks me: She is your true mate, your hjarta.

If I took her now, I would change. I couldn't bear to think of the terror that would grow behind her beautiful golden eyes if she saw me in my wolf form. I never wanted to see that look of terror on her face—only pleasure.

My wolf wanted to claim her body, and I would have to stop him.

I toy with the idea of giving her the pleasure she so desires, but it would all be for her. My wolf jumps and spins at the idea.

I can keep her here tied up forever. She cannot outsmart me. The image of her surrendering her deepest pleasures to me day after day; assaulting her body with climax after climax.

I lift my hand to her face, nearly covering it from small chin to cheek. Brushing my thumb over her bottom lip, her body goes rigid.

I let my hand travel down over the plump mound that fit perfectly into my hand, her nipples tightening at the contact. I let my gaze slip down and brush my thumb over the nub softly as she whimpers.

"Have you never received pleasure from something other than your own hands?" I tease.

At this, she blushes and her are eyes glaze with need.

How badly I want to give her everything.

I let my hand travel lower still until my hand cups her warmth. She sighs, letting her head fall back against the beam.

"You don't need to be untied for this," I growl into her ear, but she is too lost in the moment to reply.

Her thin dressing gown is moist from my pressure, and I push my fingers into her center. Her hips buck as I find the swollen bud that brings women to their knees. I circle it, and her head falls back with a cry.

I make small circles with the pads of my fingers,

pressing the nub, growing harder. My cock is steel against my belly, and the head rubs against the top of my breeches as if to reach for her warm cunt.

The need for release is almost unbearable now. I grind my teeth together to control my need for her.

I bunch up her gown, revealing her slick lips, and I slide into her wet folds with two fingers. I easily find the bud again, expertly swirling around it until she is panting into my neck and her legs have parted.

Sliding down her slit and feeling the warmth of her entrance, I am greedy for her, and I push one finger inside, hitting her in the spot that I know will drive her mad. "You take it so good for me, sweet little lamb. Do you want more?" She looks at me with lust-filled eyes and red is now covering her from chest to cheeks. She nods and whimpers. My wolf growls deep in my chest, and I feel it vibrating to my core.

"I need you to say it, little lamb." I plunge my fingers inside again and again, as deeply as I can, without lifting her off the ground. Her knees buckle and she screams so sweetly that I imagine what my cock would feel like buried inside her tight cunt while she did that. I pump my fingers, finding the rough patch of pleasure within her. I groan, unable to hide what she has done to my body —without even touching me.

In that moment, I knew...I would never rest again until I could bury my cock between her legs.

CHAPTER 25

LUX

My body is lifeless against his, save for my center bouncing on his hand.

His massive hands.

I use what little leverage I have and grind into his hand, pushing him deeper inside to the spot where I needed it the most. Riding his digits, I hear him groan as I almost climax right there—but I don't want it to end. I don't want it to be finished until he has filled me with his cock.

He removes his fingers from my needy core and toys with my sensitive bud again. No one had ever touched me there, and as he circles it, jolts of pleasure shoot through me.

I want him to take it in his mouth and use his tongue to make the circles, not his fingers.

I am a tight ball of shooting stars, and as he moves over the ball of nerves, a warmth fills the bottom of my belly and I let go.

"I want to hear you. Let me hear you as you reach your highest peak...just like that..." His deep voice sends shivers through my body, and I cry out. "Let it out, sweet lamb."

I come apart, and I feel his hands steady me as I tremble and soar into an orgasm that rips me in half. I bite at his neck as wave after wave crashes over me and I whimper.

"Look at you, little lamb. Writhing under my touch. So perfect." His breath is on my ear again, and I realize he is holding me up as my arms strain against the ropes behind my back.

I open my eyes, and his face is softer...almost remiss.

He backs away, but as I regain my balance, he turns, walking around to the back of me. Grasping the rope, he unties it and drops it to the floor.

I stand for a moment, stunned. However, a small sliver of disappointment crawls over the back of my neck. I rub my wrists, burned from my wiggling.

I want a bath. I want properly prepared food, but I also wanted to see him again. "That's it? You show off your sexual prowess and then just let me go? What was the point? I guess you're not as savage as I thought."

"I'm not letting you go until I know why you were face down in a stream last night." He moves to the shelf again, taking down a basket that looks like it is full of bread loaves. He sets the basket down next to me. Fancy fruit spreads and glass jars of olives and pickles adorn the bottom, and two loaves of bread sit on top, untouched.

I poke at the softness, greedily ripping it in half and taking a mouthful. "What does everyone run from? An enemy."

He laughs at this, or maybe he is laughing at my cheeks filled with bread. "I do not run from my enemies. I kill them."

I roll my eyes at this, trying to elude his question. I wasn't running from anyone...I was running toward anything else. "Well, I don't have that option in this situation."

He chews on a piece of dried meat, his jaw muscles flexing, all the while never taking his eyes from me.

Maybe escaping would be harder than I thought.

"And why not? You escaped whoever it was." He looks at me with a cocked head and raised eyebrow.

I roll the word around on my tongue. 'Escaped.'

Did I? And to where? A run-down cabin in the woods?

Not much of a difference, save for the dashing man standing in front of me. What was I even going back for?

I want to admit it all to him. Lay out my soul on a platter. Spill the details of my pathetic existence onto his feet. But every instinct my mother hammered into my psyche, said to keep quiet.

Perhaps I won't be quiet simply because I've been told to all my life. What harm would it do? I don't know this man, and if I made it back home, I doubted I would ever see him again.

My desire for him has clouded all reasonable thoughts, and I remember his words right before he filled my body with pure sin: I've waited too long...

Then he knew me? Had he been watching me? The realization causing my adrenaline to return, and as if he could read my thoughts, we lock eyes. My eyes dart to the front door, and he follows my gaze, bracing his muscles.

Now, it must be now before I decide to stay with this madman forever.

I move, shoving open the door, not missing a beat. It isn't until I am nearly upon the stream that I see him from the corner of my eye.

~

Fenrir

The way the fire glows against her skin, casting hallows in her neck and down her chest, makes my heart ache. Her whimpers and whines echo in my mind like sweet torture. I want her to give herself to me, but not by force. Part of me wants to set her free, just to see if she would come back to find me. Perhaps this way I could get her to trust me.

What enemy does she speak of? Did she escape the men in the black coats? If so, then why was she trying to get back so badly?

Her eyes flick toward the door, and I know what she plans before she even flees.

I give her a head start...there was simply no way she could outrun me.

Her red hair trails behind her in the wind, and she looks over her shoulder ever so slightly. Her cheeks are reddened, and her bare feet stumble over the rocks and branches. I sprint after her, my abs tightening and my thighs working. Cold air pierces my lungs, and my wolf threatens to break free if I allow this high to take hold. I slow just a little, and Lux trips, but deftly counters it. I smile to myself, wondering where the thrill of this chase is tickling her. Up her thighs? Down her back? I revel in the victory of what I will do with her when I catch her. Perhaps I will punish her and see if she enjoys that thrill as well.

Would she fight me? Would she scream and resist what I know she desires so? Or would she open herself to me, the way she did for that puny boy?

I would seize her mouth this time and make her feel exactly what was like to be mine— hjarta.

CHAPTER 26

LUX

There is no way I will outrun him, but I have to try. I am running so fast that each tree I pass looks as if it is reaching for me...trying to catch me. The branches slice through the frosty air and my hair trails behind me, a loose strand betraying my vision every now and again.

The small branches of the trees whip my face and sting my neck, but I don't stop; and I don't look back.

Blood trickles down my neck, and I can feel the tears biting at the corners of my eyes. My feet are on fire, and I can feel the dirt sticking to my heels.

Just keeping running straight, the clearing must be close by.

My heart pounds against my ribs, and I can hear his footsteps gaining. I lose my footing on a cluster of rocks and I go down, hard.

My palms hit first, and it knocks the breath from my lungs.

He is behind me, kneeling behind me. Grabbing a fistful of my hair, he forces my head back to meet his eyes.

"I can bloody well take care of myself! I got away from you, did I not?" I wrestle myself onto my back. All the while, his firm body is pressing down on me.

"I told you, it isn't safe out here. Stubborn one, aren't you?" He grinds out, assaulting my ear with his warm breath. Chills run through me, as I arch my neck back, and I can see the white of his teeth.

I want his bite marks...to fill me with pleasure until I bleed. I dig my fingernails into the snow again, pricking me with needle sharp bites. The heat between my legs is a dull ache, and I want to roll over and grind my hips against his.

"Lux! Lux! Can you hear me?!"

Shouts break the tense moment between us. I know it's Benjamin, and he is shouting from only a few feet in front of us. My heart races, and I see Fenrir's head jerks toward the sound. My blood stills, and I can hear every functioning organ in my body. Blood pumping, heart pounding.

Fenrir's low growl rumbles behind me, and my muscles tighten.

I just want Benjamin to go. I want him to leave us to this game of chase that I'm enjoying every thrilling minute of.

Benjamin's form appears from the fog as if from a dream, and his shocked expression lets me know he has seen us.

I can feel Fenrir's anger pulsing into my back, and suddenly I realize I don't just want Benjamin to go away, I want him to RUN. This game was not worth the life of my only friend.

For the few moments frozen in time, while all three of our eyes lock, I feel Fenrir lean down into the crook of my neck, steam from his hot mouth mingling with the frozen air. His soft, wet tongue glides up my neck and over my chin. All the while, Benjamin stares in disbelief.

I mouth the words, *run*.

CHAPTER 27
FENRIR

I hold eyes with the boy I had seen Lux with before, while I lick the blood that's dripped down her neck, the marks on the branches left in her escape. It is salty...wet and warm.

My wolf pushes against my thoughts in a frenzy to claim what was ours. I have tasted her blood and brought her pleasures that were nothing but a gift. Gifts I wanted to give to my mate.

I hear her hushed word to her friend, glad that she is urging him to leave us. After all, she possibly just saved his life. "That's a good girl. He is not your master."

She groans as I lick her neck clean, taking one last, long lick up to her earlobe. I bring it into my mouth and suck hard, nibbling at it until I am satisfied. I release her hair and flip her to her back, her hair splaying across her face. Tears prick her eyes as I gently wipe away the hair from her eyes. The tears only make the gold of her eyes glimmer, and the way she is looking at me, I can think of nothing more than to kiss her.

"Tell me. What is so terrible about your life that you would run straight into the dark woods?"

She wipes her eye with the back of her hand, and I notice my hair has fallen free and mixes with hers...and I wonder what our children would look like.

Choking, she says, "It's my gran...she is not what everyone thinks. She wished I was dead, just like my mother."

Running my thumb over her lip, I allow myself to stare deeply into her eyes. Sinking into the smoky depths of her irises. She blinks the tears away, and our eyes lock, the world spinning as I fall. A life in the future with her flashes before me...oceans, kisses, and laughter.

Her lips are on mine, mauling my mouth with hers. Her kisses are hungry...desperate, and as sweet as nectar.

I want to protect her from any finger that causes her pain, physical or otherwise. She will only suffer at my hands now, the pleasure dripping from her lips as she asks me for it.

Lux's escape was answer enough for me. I knew that if I felt safe to her, this was something bigger than us both. What madness would drive away such a complex creature like her?

Our tongues meet, but I break the kiss. Kissing down her jaw, I nibble at her neck and inhale the heady scent. "And what shall we do about that?"

Her eyes rove over my face, as if she is trying to find a reason for what she's about to say. Running her fingertips through my hair, she breathes and whispers, "Take me."

I stand, scooping her up and into my arms. She lays her head against my chest as I carry her back to my den.

Joy fills me, and my wolf howls inside my brain, itching to reveal himself.

CHAPTER 28
LUX

Those words could never leave my mouth before today.

Take me...

The way the words carried from my mouth, as if the admission had given me life. I felt more alive beneath his heavy body than I ever had before. When he looked into my eyes, I could no longer deny the fire ebbing inside me, as if my soul finally recognized his.

He carries me back to the hut, my feet cut and my body freezing, as he lays me on the bed in the back room.

His bed.

Effortlessly, I fall into a deep sleep, filled with images of blood and moons.

. . .

~

Waking up in a place I don't recognize has me recoiling. But then I remember the powerful man that carried me here.

Standing from the bed of furs, I smell myself, making a disgusted face. I desperately need a bath, and I am missing the stacks of books by my bed, along with the treasures that belonged to my mother. Walking to the doorway, my heart races at the prospect of seeing him again. I do not yet know his name, but somehow, I covet his protection. Even more so, I wanted his pleasure to erupt within me, giving it all to me.

The front room is dark, and only two small windows cast a ray of light into the corner, where I see movement.

He stands at his full height in a tub...completely nude.

My jaw nearly drops at the sight. His body glistens from the sheen of the water. Ripples of muscles work under firm skin, and his broad shoulders curve down to a sculpted chest. I watch him as he grabs a finely made towel from the tub's edge, wiping it over his face and beard. He looks over to my stare, fixed on him. "You are fast, like a fox. Perhaps a rabbit…but you are certainly cunning, convincing me to untie you like that." He stands in the deep tub, droplets plopping into the water from the impressive head of his cock.

I breathe in slowly, my cunt squeezing at the thought of his massive hands covering my neck again. Or maybe I could try taking him into my mouth as Katy did to Roger in my book.

Tattoos of runes and pictures of mythical beasts covered his chest and arms…a serpent eating its own tail. I marvel at his abdominal muscles, which flex under my stare. He's proud of his body, and I struggle to keep myself from reaching out to touch this godlike man.

Perhaps this was why Gran worshipped God so, with all faith. I will worship God as well if he looks like this man.

My eyes fixate on the length of his cock, swinging slightly back and forth between his thighs, as if to taunt me. I clench the walls of my insides and bite my lip. "Yes, cunning. I am…" I try hard not to trip over the words, and I can't keep myself from looking down. I squeeze my eyes shut and the only image that comes to mind is him above me, working my body into a coil of pleasure and release.

I snap my eyes back open, and he grins. "Do you like what you see, sweet lamb?"

He does nothing to hide his nakedness, and it inflames me. I do not want him to know that he has made my body feel things I never have before.

Possibly, even the presence of God.

He steps out of the tub easily with his long legs. The smell of mint soap and musk draws me in, my feet carrying me to him absentmindedly.

I walk a little to the left side, the opposite of the side he stands on. "Are you afraid of me? Even after all I've done for you, sweet lamb? I may be big and bad, but can I be your big bad wolf?" He walks to me, placing both hands on either side of the tub, leaning down into me... his eyes are close to mine, sky blue with tiny flecks of yellow. My eyes dart down to his lips momentarily, and I shudder at the fullness of them. I want to bite it, badly.

His eyes shine as he looks me over, his hair wild and wet around his shoulders. "I think maybe I'm just confused." I bite my lip, looking down over my rumpled attire.

Feeling his thickness press against my belly, he runs the back of his fingers down my cheek, and I fight back a smile.

"Get in," he growls, and he places his hand on my lower back, the warmth lighting me up. I look up at him, his eyes daring me to defy him.

Me? Defiant?

"Am I your prisoner again? Is that why you think you can control me?" I squint my eyes at him.

He smiles, and my hackles raise...wondering if maybe he would strike me.

Pressing his hard body into mine, he leans forward until he is arching my back and I nearly fall into the tub. Wrapping his arm around my waist, he lifts me to the tub edge. "I can make you do whatever I want you to...I'm the big bad wolf, remember?" He breathes into my neck.

My pulse quickens under his mouth, and I realize he knows how excited I am.

Surely, he can smell me, and I can already feel myself getting warm and slippery between my thighs.

"Or else...?" I am panting again, wanting nothing more than to give in, to let him possess me.

"There is no 'or else'. Don't tell me you don't want this. I can already smell your sweet flower soaking for me." He brings his hand to my throat and slowly wraps his fingers around my neck, gripping it tightly. He pulls my mouth to his and blesses me with a kiss so fierce our teeth clack together, and I surrender.

He pulls back, sinking a thick finger into my mouth and as I suck, he closes his eyes and groans. Claiming my mouth again, we lash tongues, and I pull his lip into mine, biting it until it bleeds. He hisses, pulling back...but he grins and licks at the blood.

"Fiery little fox...I think you like pain."

He pushes me back and into the water, his hand still around my throat. The steam envelopes me, and I close my mouth, so I won't choke. Releasing me, I come to the top, gasping for air as he climbs in the tub beside me, a grin on his face.

Was it strange that I did not fear this man? That he makes me feel safer than I ever have before?

I laugh as I wipe my face and brush the hair from my wet eyes. My nightgown floats around me, and he helps me lift it over my head, dropping the soaking garment to the floor beside the tub.

I decide to allow my body to relax and enjoy the smell of the minty soap, along with the roaming eyes of this muscled, naked man.

He sets both elbows on the side of the tub, then takes one thick arm into the water, cupping a handful of bubble. "I have used none of these useless gifts until you came."

One side of his mouth lifts into a smirk, and he looks younger, possibly even slightly charming.

Plunging beneath the water, I submerge my smelling hair and hide the smile that I can't keep from spreading across my face. I breech the surface, taking in a deep breath as I do, wiping the water from my face. I blink a few times. "What is so special about me?"

He does not respond, just continues to stare.

I think back to the way he made my body come undone earlier, and the strange faces I must have been making.

"Perhaps you are my genuine gift. A gift from the Gods." The way he looks at me makes my belly all fluttery. No one had ever looked at me that way.

Benjamin only gave me looks of disgust and lectures after our boring coupling.

"There is only one God. That is what my gran says, anyway." I play with the few bubbles that have formed on the surface of the water.

He ticks with his tongue and retorts, "There are many gods."

I look at him again, his face as serious as stone, as if I had just insulted him.

I think on it for a moment, remembering the nights my mother would sing of the maiden, the mother, and the crone. Three moon goddesses that protected me and always watched over me. But I was never to tell Gran the secret of the moon, or its phases.

"You mean like the moon goddesses?" I am curious now to know more about these gods. I did not care for the God that was my gran's. Perhaps she simply chose the wrong one.

"Yes, Freyja is one. Odin is her husband." He is hovering over me now, his eyes hungry to see more of me. I oblige him, sitting up straight and exposing my bare breasts. He reaches out and cups one, cocking his head to the side. His eyes meet mine, and I am lost to him again. Pinching my nipple, then rolling it between his forefinger and thumb until he has me whimpering.

Breathless, I finally say, "Tell me of this God, Odin."

CHAPTER 29
FENRIR

The last time I felt the supple skin of a woman's breast was many years passed. I held my tongue between my teeth to keep it from lolling from my parted mouth.

She wants to know of my gods, and I would sing their praises to her all night long if she wished.

"Odin is the God we take our Oaths to. We fight in battle for him and are rewarded with the splendors of Valhalla." I move my hand to cup her other breast, and she arches her back.

"Val..hulla?" she asks me, watching my lips as I speak.

Her question makes me smile, and I correct her. "Val-halla."

"Like Heaven, you mean?" Her eyebrows shoot up, and I cannot understand what this word Heaven is.

"There is no way to tell. I know nothing of your God." I sink my hand below the water, finding her soft thighs. Stroking down the length, I find her warm center.

Her breath hitches as I slip a finger inside, her entrance greedily accepting it. Then, I push two inside, sheathing myself to the knuckle.

Lux's head falls back, and she cries out, "He is a cruel God..." She whines as I pump into her, "punishing us for our sins and..." She's losing her breath and all I want is to watch her come apart for me again, while she rides my cock.

My eyes are closed, and I fight my swollen erection, resisting the urge to explode at the sight of her bare chest rising and falling. Feeling her tightening around my fingers, it drives me mad. My cock is rock hard, the veins angry and protruding, the tip slick with need.

"Stop." Her wet hand is on my arm, and she looks at me with such ferocity that I do as she tells me.

"Let me please you, but continue to tell me of your gods while I do. Stand up and let me show you how unafraid of you I am." She kneels in the tub, facing me. I grasp the sides and slowly stand, my cock now towering above her.

She blinks a few times but reaches out for it—her feminine fingertips barely able to wrap completely around the shaft. She stares in wonder, taking in each stroke she gives me. I bring myself closer, and she straightens up, her eyes perfectly level now. Placing my hands on my hips, I close my eyes and let her enjoy her curiosity, but it isn't long before she is taking me into her mouth.

Gods.

Looking down over her, I purr. "I have dreamed of this very moment, of you with your tongue wrapped around my cock." Groaning, I tell her, "Never once did I think it would feel this glorious."

I hold it in, but the tight warmth of her mouth nearly takes me to my knees right there. I allow myself to watch her mouth work over me. At first, she is slow and tender, but once my shaft is covered with her spit, she begins a steady rhythm. She grips the base with her fist, sucking me wetly until she reaches the head again. She laps at the underside of my crown and my balls pull up to my body. The pulses come faster now, and with each stroke of my cock against the back of her throat, I feel myself slipping on the edge.

I want to seize her head and pound into her mouth until she is swallowing my seed. When I look down, my fists are already in her hair, gripping. I thrust forward, feeling the tightening of her throat around the head, sending shock waves of electricity down my spine. She looks up from under her lashes, her pupils nearly eclipsing her iris, water pooling under her lids as she gags.

Immediately she regains her focus, but she is moving her head faster now and I push on her head again. I watch myself torture her throat, tears streaming down the sides of her face.

She dips her head down, all the way to the base slowly, and I brush her hair away from her neck, marveling at the column of her throat, moving up at down at my pleasure.

I let my head fall back, allowing her to milk my cock at her own pace. The softness of her tongue, her lips, and her throat...

"Look at you, taking all of that for me. Such a good girl..." I fist her hair while she looks up at me, and I groan. She moans around my cock, and it is then I notice the splashing water between her legs.

~

Lux

I am choking, I can hardly breath and I am enjoying every bloody minute of it. I free one of my hands from his swollen cock and let him fuck my mouth while I desperately find the swollen bud between my legs with my hand. His groans edge me on, and I want nothing more than to feel him fill my mouth with his warmth.

What would it taste of?

My fingers mimic the motions of my mouth as I find the most sensitive part of me.

My head is spinning. I feel dizzy with each violent thrust he pushes inside my mouth. Each moan that drips from his lips was like a reward, and I pump my fist harder down his shaft for more. My tongue wraps around the head, and I look up at him, and I can feel tears running down my face.

With both his fists still in my hair, he looks down at me with a soft face of pride. "If any of this is too much for you...you only need to say mercy. But this...ah...I think you like this."

I did like it, maybe a little too much. He was giving me a choice; he was making this all...my choice. It was never my choice with Benjamin, and it certainly was never my choice with my gran. Her purpose was to protect me, and all she did was convince me of my dubious presence.

My mother's things. I have to go back.

Withdrawing my mouth from his stone body, his phallus angry and swollen, he watches my face carefully.

Kneeling again, he takes my face into his rough hands, studying my eyes with his.

"Mercy," I say, and he drops his head in disappointment, but nods.

"I will return you safely in the afternoon tomorrow, but I want one more night with you." He strokes my cheek, glancing at my lips.

"No...that word...mercy." I place both my hands on top of his and move to his lips. They are soft yet coarse and it fills me with excitement. Parting my mouth slightly, I allow his tongue to sweep inside, sending a shiver through me. I open my mouth more and allow our tongues to dance together in a sensual rhythm. I have never been kissed this way before, and I never wanted this feeling to end.

I am dizzy and once I open my eyes, our lips are still locked, but I am in his arms again. He lifts me from the tub, and with his arms linked under my legs, he lays me on the furs beside the fire, near the neatly tied ropes on the beam.

"Mercy is what we ask of our God...to forgive our sins and show us mercy. Why do you ask me for my mercy? You are not God." I sit up, and cross my arms over my bare breasts, suddenly feeling very aware of my nakedness, and hearing another one of Gran's words coming from his mouth.

He stands beside the beam I once was tied to, and fiddles with the ropes still attached to it.

His face is set, un-knotting and knotting the ends of the rope. "I only want you to understand that you are safe, little lamb. I may not be a God, but I am named after one."

Did I want to remain here with a man I did not know, living in sparse conditions within a two-room shack?

I wanted my mother back. I wanted to be in England again where I had all the riches thanks to my father...

But at what cost? My father was wealthy and well-known, still living amongst his brethren. A place that I was not privy to, a woman not worthy of that knowledge.

I was a witch—and bringing me here to these woods saved my life. I must learn to accept this about myself...I am a sinner, my fate is already sealed.

I deserved to be in this dark hell, a feeble plaything under the hands of a savage.

"What is your name?" Bringing my hands back to my sides, I brace myself for his answer.

Never have I wanted to hear a name as much as I wanted to hear his.

"Fenrir." He reaches for me, and I take his hand, pulling me up and into his arms. "After Fenrir, the great Wolf God." Taking my hand, he places it over a black sigil in the shape of swirls and circles on his neck.

I trace the lines over his skin, and he slides his hands down my back to the swell of my behind.

"This here? Fen-reer." I roll it from my tongue slowly, and he lifts me in one motion, both my legs wrapping around his hard waist. He kisses me again, only rougher this time, nibbling at my lips, and dragging the bottom one through his teeth. I feel the sting of his bite, gasping, blood warming the spot. Sucking on my lip, Fenrir watches my face as I close my eyes.

My entire body is on fire, and I fear if he takes me now, I will shake the tiny cabin down to its foundation with my screams. The tips of my breasts prick against the hair on his chest as we devour each other with kisses and hands.

The high continues as I feel my back slam into the beam. He sets me down on my feet and I whimper in protest.

"Let us play...little fox. Do you trust me?" He takes my hands into his, raising them over my head.

My eyes grow wide, and my body stretches, forcing my chest up and out. Holding both my hands together with just one hand, he leans down to swallow me whole, and I am lost.

CHAPTER 30
FENRIR

I bring her tight nipple into my mouth, suckling like a ravenous babe. If I only have one night left with her, I will take my time and enjoy every inch of her.

I remove my mouth from hers, and I see her eyes are still closed. My wolf is howling now, and he has been taking any thoughts I've had of returning her and growling in response. He does not accept this, but I am in control now. He is only inside of me.

The wolf inside of me shakes with anger and a growl builds deep within my chest. He doesn't like the idea of letting her go, but I am in control now. I need to enjoy her for tonight. We will work out the rest later, but for now I want her needy and shaking on my cock.

Her hands are high above her head, and with her body pulled tightly on her tiptoes, I almost drop to my knees. But I will worship her cunt soon, showing her just what it feels like to be devoured. No, right now she wants the thrill of a chase...and she will have that.

"I trust you will wring pleasure from my body...Is that not the highest trust a woman can give to a man?" she says coyly. She is playing with me, and a tingle of satisfaction sends fire up my spine. Pressing my body into hers, I grab the dangling rope that is secured at the top of the beam, tying her wrists. I coil it around her arms, just below her elbows, where I secure it tightly.

Grabbing another rope, I lash her breasts around to her back.

With each loop I bring around her, I jerk it tightly before I begin the next. Her breath hitches at each tug, but soon she is stifling them, and her body squirms, so I slow my pace...

Once I reach her hips, I bring the rope around to the back and make a tight knot.

I take a step back, marveling at my work. She is bound tightly to the beam by her arms pointed at the sky, looking like the vulnerable prey that she is. Submissive and willing...just for my touch. She is bound down to her curved hips, her flesh bulging against my ties.

I want to mark her, leave my imprint so that she may never forget this night.

Stepping up to her again, I can already see her fair

skin reddening under the rope's bite, her breasts straining against the cords.

I palm one of them, bouncing it free it from its constraints. I tease her nipple, pinching it gently until she cries out. "Mmm, I think you like the pain more than the pleasure."

She nods her head. "I do...Hurt me more."

The wolf that lives inside my mind licks his chops, his bloodlust palpable. I smile wide, allowing my sharp canines to show.

She has not blinked once. Her eyes are wide and famished for what will happen next. "Yes, you are right...the highest honor one can give. Trusting me to fulfil your body the way it is begging to be." I kiss her supple cheek, and trail kisses and sharp bites down her neck until I am kneeling.

"I can smell you...adrenaline mixed with fear." I continue wrapping loops and jerking it tightly as I grate the words, "It's driving me mad."

~

Lux

I cannot move an inch, and the rope that binds me is biting my skin red. Prickles flood my body, and every piece of me is pulsing like a heartbeat...throbbing.

My legs are quaking now, and I'm glad for the ties that hold me.

Fenrir brings his hand down between my legs, brushing the folds. "Does fear arouse you? So slick and ready for me already."

His words send a wave of need through my body, and my eyes flutter. I swallow, my body feeling heavy.

"M-M-" I stumble on the word.

"Mercy, sweet lamb?" He sinks his fingers inside me and I shudder.

"Mmm...more." I gasp, and he's moving in and out of me painfully slow. I try to meet his hand, wanting it deeper, but I am bound here too firmly for that.

"Ahh...more. I cannot wait to give that to you." Removing his fingers, he grasps his cock, my wetness still covering them. He glides it over the veined shaft and rounded head, lightly twitching.

Grabbing my left leg, he hoists it up over his arm. Reaching for the other, he does the same until both legs are draped over his biceps.

He pushes in closer to me, and my legs are nearly folded up to my chest. I gasp and my eyes connect to his.

Bending slightly, he watches as he guides his cock to my exposed entrance. With one rough thrust, he fills me to the hilt. I cry out, squeezing my hands as I adjust to his size. Disbelief that I can accommodate him has me panting. He doesn't move; he stays still for a moment, and I revel at how filled I am. My cunt throbs, and I keep myself from jerking my hips. Little prickles of pressure shoot through me to my core.

"Gods, you are perfect." He moves, slowly at first, but soon his eyes turn on me, feral. He is struggling to hold back his need...

Each thrust sends jolts of pleasure through my belly, and I roll my hips the best I can, bound this way. He pushes into me, a satisfied growl passing from his lips once he is completely sheathed.

The throb that runs through my body has pooled at my center, and I am squirming and ready to explode around him. His pleasure is almost tangible, as I feel his body growing; hair pricking my thighs.

He slows, then stops...I buck my hips in an effort to squeeze more pleasure from him.

His size has doubled, and I marvel at his height, pulling me tighter against him. Claws replace fingertips and his hands double. Grabbing the beam above me, his face lengthens and changes as he lifts himself onto the pole.

I am gasping, relenting to his solid frame, as he stretches me to ecstasy. No longer am I in control of my limbs. I am reduced to nothing but nerves and shock waves as he rocks into my body. My eyes roll back, and I feel the hair of his chest biting at my cheeks.

Suddenly, he stops, and I can feel him withdrawing himself, reducing in size.

He backs up a step, breathing heavily...his shoulders are hunched, and he hangs his head.

Why is he stopping? Did I do something wrong? I open my mouth to protest, and he looks at me. "I cannot...and even if I explained, you wouldn't believe me."

It is then I notice the sharp teeth behind his lips, and the claws that adorn his fingertips.

CHAPTER 31

FENRIR

Just as I tumble toward my release, losing myself in her softness, I feel my body shiver and my wolf threaten to break free. He wants to taste her blood, claim her body in every sense of the word. Spill inside over and over until she is full of my seed.

With every drop of self-control I have, I use it to pull away from her before the change. Her face contorted as I break the sexual ward we had created together. Her face screwed up into confusion.

Kneeling before her, I lift her plump thigh over my shoulder and bury my face in her sweet center. Crying out, she grinds into my face with ferocity, and I open my mouth wide, sucking her lips until I find her entrance with my long tongue. A loud whine leaves her, and as I sink my tongue inside her, she cries out again. I plunge it deeply, wiggling its length along her walls. Her juices soak the coarse hair of my beard, droplets pooling below my lower lip.

I replace my tongue with two fingers and bring it back to the bundle of nerves tucked inside her folds. I wiggle it gently, plundering to find, and when I do, I nibble and bite, mixing pain with pleasure. She cries out and I smile, sucking and licking at it until she isn't crying out my name.

"Fennn....Ah fuck..." She rides out the climax on my fingers, jerking and twitching until she is limp.

Kissing the insides of her thighs, I notice red streaks of blood, and worry that I have hurt her with my razor-sharp teeth.

Gently setting her down, her legs shake, and she looks up at me in horror. I take her face into my palm. "Did I hurt you, lamb? You are bleeding."

"Your...f-f-face is covered in blood," she stammers.

"I did not hurt you?" I reach between her legs again, and she is still soaked, but there is also blood.

She is quiet, embarrassed perhaps, her face reddening. She said I was not her first, so it couldn't be that.

I bring the sticky, red-stained fingers to my mouth and lick at them while she stares. I suck off the blood, never leaving her eyes. Grinning, I wrap my bloodied hand around her neck and squeeze, capturing her mouth[SL1] . She whines, but her tongue swirls inside, coiling with mine.

I pull back, a wolfish grin spreading across my face. Our fate is sealed as we share this private blood oath. The warm taste filled with salt and iron, cultivated from the very heart beating within her.

A love fully quenched by the sticky, sweet mixture between her thighs.

I untie her, gently but quickly, kissing each spot that I uncover. Her head lulls, and I can tell I have wrought her of all her energy for today. I would take her to my bed and feed her sweet grapes and soft cheeses, kissing every spot I bruised.

Once I am finished untying her, I swoop her up into my arms and carry her to the back bedroom.

Picking her head up off of my shoulder, sleepily she says, "I like the fire. Let's sleep there...please?" I kiss the top of her head and turn back to the furs on the floor. I set her down, and she sits up, rubbing her eyes. "Is it night-time now?"

"I would say so. About the time to eat some food and drink some wine." I remove the pot of water from the hearth, pouring it into a wooden bowl. I pluck another handmade soap from the tall shelf of items, placing it into the bowl. Kneeling, still naked and covered in her blood, I gently wipe the cloth over her mouth, neck, and chest, ending the wiping at her inner thighs as she lazily spreads her legs for me.

Bringing the bowl to the butcher's table, I set it down and finish the process by washing my hands and face in the flowery scented water.

I walk back to her sprawled body, tucking her under the blankets.

"Hungry?" I ask her, but she lays her head on top of her hands, resting atop her folded red cloak, eyes closed.

With a sleep-filled voice, she says, "Why is pleasure a sin, when it feels like every part of my body soars? I just don't understand..."

I lean into her lavender scent, her hair brushing my lips. "You can find pleasure in things without calling them evil. Perhaps your gran never felt such happiness."

LUX

My body is replete; satiated until I can no longer stand.

Was it the Wolf or the woods that I loved so much? Maybe a bit of both. But is this my wolf, or is he only a man who I have created in my darkest fantasies?

"Food?" Fenrir's voice is close to my ear, and when I look up, he is holding a poorly made plate with an array of fruits and cheeses.

And here I thought he didn't have manners or taste…

My belly growls loudly. I move to sit up and I see he has been busy while I've slept. He is wearing trousers—no shirt, though—and his face brings back tremors to my legs as I recall the shattering orgasm he gave me with his mouth earlier.

I am mostly shocked at what just happened between

us, although there was something different about this man. He didn't look like the men I had seen in my childhood.

I bring myself to sit upward, feeling a rush of dizziness come over me. "Yes. Food, please."

He feeds me the cheese and I close my eyes, thinking of all the food I'd missed from England.

"Tell me why you hate her." He chewed loudly, his jaw working.

I gave it a moment of thought, not sure where to start. I figured I would just lay it all out. What could it hurt?

"She let them take my mum—didn't even try to stop them...and neither did my father." I pinch the skin on my inner thighs, brushing my fingertips over the scars that adorned them. With each caning I took from her, I would retreat to my room and make myself hurt worse. Candle wax was my preferred method, and nights when it was bad, it was the actual flame.

"I am sorry for your loss...a mother can never be replaced." He brushes a strand of hair behind my shoulder, scooting in closer to me and pulling me into his arms. His enormous frame easily wraps around mine.

He kisses my bare shoulder, and I lean back into him, finding humor in our odd situation. I could never bring him back with me. My gran would not be pleased.

Could I really stay here, in this place? The thought wasn't terrible...I could get used to being in his arms.

"I just don't understand why he let them take her. He didn't even fight for her...or at least, not that I recall." I snuggled against him more, and the heat from his body makes me feel sleepy.

"A man is supposed to protect his family at all costs. I would allow no one, man or monster, to take you...to hurt you." He kisses my neck, nuzzling his face and nose into it.

Family?

I close my eyes, remembering how I thought I could fight off those men by myself when I was all of ten years old. I had convinced myself that the only reason I didn't fight them was because of Gran.

"What is a sinner, exactly? Someone who pushes against God's will? This should be explained at length, and yet, I am expected to accept this God that I cannot see." I am looking up at him now, craning my neck to see his thick beard.

"Your God sounds daft to me. A woman is the vessel that brings life into this world." At this, I sit up and turn to face him completely.

"You do not think I am wicked? After the things that I just let you do to me?" My tears are brimming now, speaking about the God my mother refused to accept, and paying with her life because of it.

"Aye, little lamb, I can assure you there is nothing wicked about you, save for the nectar between those lush thighs." He smiles, stroking my hair.

I try to hide my smile, but I push him with my shoulder instead, and he gives me a low growl. At this, I giggle, tingles running down my back.

"Gran beat me when I didn't pray. She beat me when things weren't clean enough. My mother collected crystals, herbs, and candles—and when Gran found out I had kept them...she locked me in my room without food for days." I fight back tears as Fenrir pulls me close to him.

Leaning into my ear, he whispers, "An eye for an eye... a life for a life, perhaps?"

I watch as the shadows dance over his face, his brows and cheeks looking more prominent, even sinister. My belly flipped and flopped, and I could not think of anything more than kissing him again. I tug and bite at his beard, and he rumbles deep in his chest each time.

"First, I want to tell her exactly how I feel." I pull on his beard, bringing his face close to mine. "Then I want to skin her alive."

CHAPTER 33
FENRIR

The more time I spend with this woman, the more surprises I uncover. A temptress, a healer, and a killer...

The moon was high in the sky this night, and it would be full by tomorrow.

I needed to shift, and I needed to run soon. For now, I am content lying next to her body that fits so perfectly tucked next into mine.

We drift by the fire, speaking of dreams and desires.

It isn't until the early hours of the morning that I wake with a shiver and realize the fire has burned out.

I step outside and walk to the neatly stacked pile of chopped wood, stacking large and small pieces in my arms, and still bare chested.

Fog has rolled in—the nights getting slightly warmer during the spring equinox—and in the distance I see two black figures.

Each one wore a black hat and coat, carrying a lantern filled with fire. The men rarely came to the woods since Lux had arrived.

"Fenrir," one man calls, sternly.

He cannot feign bravery with me. I can smell his fear clinging to him just like that hideous coat.

Setting down the wood in my hands, I feel for the hatchet looped around my waist, but it is not there.

So much for a bit of intimidation.

I step in closer as they approach me. "Sirs."

One is almost as tall as I am, the other is much shorter. I could kill them both easily, even in my human form. I was itching to shift, and my wolf howls in the recesses of my mind.

A visit from these men in the wee hours of the morning only meant trouble.

"We know you have her. Thomas has told us as much." The taller man steps in a little too close to me, his bravery fighting his fear with equal measure. He doesn't appear to have any weapons, only the fire blazing inside the glass of the lantern.

"I do not have anyone. I do not know who it is that you speak of." Bored, I pick at my teeth with my nails.

The shorter man steps up to me now. "We have no reason not to believe Thomas, for God has delivered this message himself."

I chuckle at this. Gods do not address a mortal man, they would not waste their time on such things. "I assume Thomas is your leader, the one who first came to pay me a visit."

The taller one clears his throat. "It would be in your best interest to hand over the girl. It is God's will—to rid the world of evil. Our work here is not done. We need to continue, beginning with the girl."

I do not appreciate his demand, and I do not owe his God anything. "Leave, now. Or you will meet your God this morning, at my hands." I bend down to retrieve the wood and turn to leave, giving them a chance to rethink their request.

"Fenrir, she is Thomas' daughter...a Lost Daughter. She belongs to God now." The shorter man steps up to me, and I do not smell fear, only anger.

She belongs to God now.

The man who visited me that day long ago, the one who politely asked me to keep to myself...was Lux's father. The realization sparks me with rage, remembering that she told me they took her mother and she could not understand the reason. It was him, then. Burning his own wife alive for his false God and his even falser promises.

And I would never let him, or these foolish men, near my little lamb. Let them try to take her.

I turn to the smaller man. "Well, Thomas is wrong, and so is your God."

I take a step toward the cabin, but I feel the small man's hand grip my arm.

My wolf rears, and the rage burns behind my eyes until I am incinerated by it. The wood drops to the ground, clacking together as my body stretches and cracks. Fur sprouts over my body and I double in size, as do my snout and fangs. The relief of accepting my primal instinct in its physical form.

The small man is struck with a look of pure horror, holding his lantern out in front of him as if it could protect him.

Foolish man.

The tall man reaches into his pocket as I shake out my form and bare the sharp canines, already wet with saliva. My head snaps back and I howl, enough to send the men running for their lives.

But this is not over.

The pads of my paws beat down the cold ground until I am nipping at the short man's heels. I could easily grab his leg and be done with it, but I wanted to be sure I was far enough away that Lux wouldn't hear his pleas.

The tall man drops his lantern, easily escaping me in the darkness—not the short man, though. I grasp his foot and toss him into the air, shaking him like a rag doll. My size nearly triples his, and I easily lift his flailing body into the air. He screams and begs for mercy, but I rip out his throat to end his racket.

Satisfied with a kill, my wolf is content, but I am covered in the man's blood.

I shift back into my human form, bones cracking and my legs shaking.

I fall to my knees, shaking out my hair as I try to stand. I am completely nude and vulnerable to the elements, and need to get home. Doubtful that Lux slept through the screaming, I brace myself for her questions.

I enter the cabin, realizing I am most likely covered in more than just blood. She is awake, and her eyes squint into the dim sunrise, nothing less than enchanting.

"You are filthy." Her voice is thick with sleep, and she rubs her eye. "And why are you naked?"

CHAPTER 34
LUX

I feel the absence of Fen's warm body, but sleep keeps taking me under until I hear a loud howl.

My body aches, but I desperately need water, so I force myself to sit up.

Fenrir quietly opens the front door, his body splashed with what looks like mud and deep red blood.

Then I remember the voices of men outside, scream-ing...followed by the howl.

Realization floods over me and I look over his tall, marked body that drips with strength and instincts.

The Wolf of the Woods.

"You...You are..." I stutter over the words, but my heart is beating out of my chest at the prospect of my fantasy becoming a reality.

He approaches slowly but doesn't speak, his face almost morose.

Sinking to his knees in front of me, he covers my hands with his. "Yes, little lamb, I am the monster that lives in these woods."

I squint my eyes, confused by his words. I already know that he is a killer, a savage...born and raised that way.

It is all he's ever known.

"Tell me what happened." I squeeze his meaty hands, tucking the loose hair that brushes his shoulder behind his ear.

He takes his hands from mine and stands, disappearing into the back room.

When he returns, he is wearing a fresh pair of breeches, but still no shirt...perhaps he enjoys reminding me of his wild ways.

"Could you hear the men?" he asks, studying my face.

"Vaguely, I remember voices. What men?" The only men that lived near Gran were the people of a neighboring town, but the rumor of the Wolf kept them well enough away.

"These men...they know your father. I think they are

his brothers." He pulls the stool near me and sits, bracing his arms on his knees, leaning forward.

"His brethren?" I ask, excited at the idea of my father finally returning home.

Fenrir nods, understanding the difference after our conversations the night before.

"Did you kill them?" My voice raises, unsure if I even want the answer.

He doesn't move. He continues to stare at the floor, but nods again.

"And my father? Him as well?" I am standing now, wondering if I am angry or just overwhelmed by everything that has happened in the past two days.

"He was not with them, but they came here for you, and I could not let them have you." His hands are clasped together tightly, and for the first time since I have been here, I see fear in his eyes.

I did not know the men that my father associated with. I was not allowed to partake in any rituals or meetings that involved the world of men and worshipping their God. It mattered not to me if they were dead or alive. My stomach squeezes at the thought of Fenrir defending me, standing his ground...just as I wished my father had done for my mother.

"So...then my father didn't come back for me." I fight

back tears, swallowing them down. I should count my blessings on the number of times my life has been spared.

Fenrir's voice is a low timbre, and he stands from the stool, taking my hands into his again. "Your father sacrificed your mother to his God, and now he wants to sacrifice you as well."

I back up, looking down and un-linking our hands.

No, my father saved my life by hiding me away. This can't be true.

"I don't believe you. He saved me." My chest heaves again, and I feel a line of sweat drip between my breasts.

"I am a monster. I never should have kept you here." He turns to the shelf of stores and grabs my leather satchel, filling it with water, skins, and food. He plucks my red cloak from the nail it hangs on beside the fire, handing it to me.

I take the cloak, dumbfounded. "Wait, I am not done discussing this with you. Where is my father?"

Fenrir is standing with the door open now, the sunshine beaming through the trees. "He is not here, little lamb. He is the one responsible for all of this."

~

Fenrir

My heart is breaking, watching her golden eyes gloss over with sadness at the betrayal by her father. I couldn't let them take her. I would spend the rest of my days keeping watch over her from afar and wouldn't let any man make it near her. No matter if I needed to sleep outside her door each night, I would.

I stand, holding open the door for her with a few things packed so she could take the lead alone.

I can't keep her here. I need her to see these things for herself, even if it meant letting her go.

Only she wouldn't move. She just continued working that beautiful mouth of hers.

I cannot read the emotions on her face. She is too lost in thought.

"Come, Lux, I will bring back to your gran's." Even the words stretch my heart, and my wolf whimpers.

"I don't believe you and I also don't need your escort. I came here on my own and I can leave that way too." She snatches the bag and cloak from me, throwing the cloak around her shoulders.

"If I remember correctly, you fell face first into a river

and I found you." I followed her out the door, surveying the land for any uninvited guests.

She whirls on me, furious, and I cannot tell if it's because of her father, or because of what I had done.

"Yes, you saved me. But now, you are throwing me back..." She sniffles, but keeps her strong composure. "Maybe I don't want to go back. Did you ever think of that, you big...big...beast?!"

I want to laugh at her adorable outburst. She may think she is fighting me, but she is only making me fall for her even more.

"I simply want no more blood on my hands, and if you stay here, there will be much more." I spread my hands, showing her the evidence left behind.

"If I go back now, my gran will not protect me. She despises me, and I reckon she would have rather I burned right beside my mother." She is shouting now, her cheeks flush with the cold, her breath misting the air.

I step in close to her, her lips so plump and red that I can't help but cup her face. "I only want to keep you safe, and perhaps if I return you home, you will be, but I will be there to make sure."

Tears wet her cheeks, and she pulls her head away, backing away from me.

I hang my head again, wanting nothing more than to return her to my furs, where I know she will be safe.

I had to let her see for herself.

CHAPTER 35
LUX

"And what should we do about it, sweet lamb?" He reaches for my hand and looks into my eyes as if I am the most divine sight he has ever laid eyes on.

I could never go back now, and the thought of it makes my stomach turn. I had been gone two days and tonight was the full moon. Surely, if I returned home, I would walk straight to my death.

I choke back the thought that perhaps he no longer wanted me as his problem, and he was done playing his deviant games with me.

The games that I enjoyed so much.

I walk to him, and I kneel before him. "If you keep me, I promise to worship you more than any man God has ever made. I will give you offerings of my body...and my soul."

He sinks to his knees as well, removing my hood and grabbing my chin tightly. "You owe me no offerings, and I would be a lucky man to have you grace my furs every night."

I run my fingers through the coarse hair of his beard, tugging lightly, and he smiles. He is seemingly the least terrifying man, in my eyes. He was strength and savior, but also a cold-blooded killer.

I wanted him to be my killer.

But even after all this, part of me still cannot accept the fate handed to me by my family. I needed to go back to her, to where the last few items remained of my mother's. If I needed to have acceptance, the time was now to face it.

The words come stern and certain from me, a vengeance that had been brewing for years. "I want them all dead."

***

Fenrir

This woman drives me wild. My wolf is pleased, and ready for another fight to defend her honor. When she kneels at my feet, I am lost to her...I want nothing but her, and I will do anything for her.

"You cannot say such things to me, or I will take you right here. The way you are stroking my beard makes me want to throw you over my shoulder and take you back to our bed." I lean in and kiss her roughly, her head forced back and her mouth welcoming me wide.

Leaning back, she wraps her arms around my neck, and I bring my arm around her waist, pulling her onto my lap.

Snow begins to fall around us, and I need to feel her. I am desperate to press our skin together. I want to watch her shatter beneath me over and over for the rest of our lives.

Her words send me into a frenzy, and my wolf howls in response.

Bending over, I lay her on her back and un-lace her cloak, spreading it around her. Her face is soft, but dry of tears, and she bites her lip while I untie my breeches.

Reaching under her shift, I slide my hands down her thighs and under her knees, hooking my hands beneath them. I push her legs up and apart, exposing her pink flesh, readying my tongue.

She gasps as I lash her folds, flattening it wide. I have not splayed her this way to only taste her. I want to lick her from seam to seam.

I prop her up higher, so her ass is splayed under my

lips, and I flick my tongue over the tight hole. Her hips buck, but I hold her in place, sinking my fingertips into her skin. I plunder the hole with my thick tongue. Leaning back, I drip spit over both holes.

"Ohhh...Fen," she says with a whimper, and I pick up my pace. Darting my tongue in and out, tracing a line to her sensitive nub. She shudders as I use long strokes up her center, meeting her eyes with mine each time I reach the top. I can feel her climax climbing, and her pleasure forces my cock tight to my belly.

I am ravenous for her, and I bite the insides of her thighs, leaving a trail of red marks.

I pull back, savoring the way the snowflakes fall on her skin, melting on impact. "This body should be praised every day. Does your God praise you, sweet lamb?"

"He does nothing for me," she says breathlessly.

"If your God can see us now, what would he say?" I free my cock now, readying for her to see everything that I am.

"Sinful..." Her hands are reaching for my hips, pulling me deeper, stirring her to the direction she needs.

I bring the tapered tip to her sex. "Ah, but it feels so good, does it not? And how can something so sinful feel so sweet?" I groan, piercing her, the walls of her cunt embracing the shaft.

Her back arches, and she cries out, pulling my hair, driving me into a frenzy.

My face is smeared with her blood, and she strokes my lips as I stroke inside of her.

She spirals, every string of self-control broken. I let her ride me, legs wrapped around my waist, her fingers still in my mouth.

I watch her until she is replete and panting, my eyes fixed on hers while my mouth works through her orgasm.

I trail kisses over her thighs where my bite marks are, and its then I notice the burns.

CHAPTER 36

LUX

Never have I brought myself to climax the way Fenrir had. My climaxes left me feeling drained, dirty, and wrong.

My body was not supposed to bring me such pleasures. It was sinful.

But his mouth brought a euphoria that could only be explained as holy.

Of all things that stood out to me from my tutoring, from my long Sunday mornings in church, it was the word holy.

Described as devotion to one service or God, entitled to reverence and respect. This man deserved my devotion.

As I pull down my dress and adjust my cloak around

my shoulders, Fen is still kneeling in front of me, breeches untied. "Who did this to you? These marks on your thighs?" He looks concerned, but his brow is furrowed, angry.

I realize he is speaking of my burn marks, the only way I could handle the abuse of my gran.

"I...I did it." I stand, straightening my dress and cloak.

He stands along with me, towering over me now.

I walk away, toward my gran's, not wanting to broach self-mutilation yet.

He follows closely, but says, "I don't believe you."

~

We make the clearing to Gran's house by dusk, and every light on the house is on.

I find this unsettling; I am the only one who lit the lamps and took care of the fire. Smoke was billowing from the chimney, and I notice Benjamin's father's carriage outside the barn.

"There is someone here. You should stay here and let me figure it out myself." I am unsure what it is I will say exactly, but I have enough confidence in Fenrir to know that I will be safe.

He grabs the back of my cape as we hide behind the large ash tree together, "I am here...and I am watching."

I can tell he doesn't want to let me do this on my own, but I must. If not to end this once and for all, but at the very least, I can salvage my mother's apothecary.

I trot down the small hill to the large cabin, and once I am on the porch, the door opens abruptly.

"Lux?" It's Benjamin, and he brings me into a hug, as if he did not know where I had been.

He knew...He saw.

Benjamin's father—a tall man, dressed all in black—appeared behind him. "Lux...Are you well?"

I can sense his unease; he is looking around the woods behind me.

"I am fine. Can I come in, please? It is cold out here." I push past them both and I see my gran, propped up by pillows in her wingback chair in the sitting room.

I remove my cloak and walk to my gran's side, resting my hand on her arm. "Are you well Gran? I lost my way, but I was able to find shelter in a cave…I'm here now, though."

She shoves my hand off her arm with whatever strength she could muster. "Don't touch me," she says with a rasp.

I step away and look back at the two men standing in front of the door.

My blood runs cold, and their eyes are fixed on me.

The hair on my arms stands on end, and it's then I see the hunting knife in his hand.

Bolting to the stairs, I make a run for it.

I hear Benjamin's clunky footfalls at my heels, but I know I am faster. I almost fall at the top of the stairs, slipping on the wood floors.

I make it to my parent's old bedroom, but he catches my arms before I can slam the door in his snide face.

He falls on top of me on the bed, my face nearly hitting the headboard. I feel his hands capture mine over my head, and I feel his hot breath in my ear. "Went and got yourself a monster, huh? A one-way ticket to Hell. Let's see that dirty pussy one last time before they burn you alive."

I try to shove him off with my shoulder, but he is bigger than me. With my face pushed against my mother's pillows, I hear Ben unbuckle his trousers, and his clammy hand is pulling up my dress, over my rear.

Tears sting my face as I feel him. With no priming, he forces himself inside me, slices stinging my insides like knifes. The pain is unbearable, my screams muffled by the pillow. I struggle and fight, but he outweighs me and I cannot budge. I know my beast is waiting for me. All I must do is call to him—if I could only free my face from this pillow. Taking a deep breath in, I gather all the strength I can manage and push. Ben loses his grip on my head and I'm able to free my mouth.

"Stop! Stop it, Ben! Please!" I beg him to remember the times he was my friend, the times we laughed about sex and the human body. He didn't stop.

"Mercy! Mercy!" I scream as loud as I can, while Ben shoves my face back down. I imagine Fenrir, my wild beast, ripping him limb from limb.

"There is no use asking for mercy now, whore. You will be dead by this time tomorrow...and I will get paid a nice amount to get me started in America—just for your body. I guess men aren't so stupid after all?" He chokes as he pumps into me.

The room spins as I regret not trusting my intuition and staying away. I should have listened to my intuition.

Was it that far off, or was this just part of the game? Fighting for my survival, even if it was from my family.

FENRIR

As soon as she leaves my side, warning bells ring, and my wolf picks up the scent of two men.

I try my hardest to stay hidden, to allow her to do what she believes needs to be done...to be said.

Staying low to the ground, I prowl toward the side of the house, a large window giving me a full view of Lux standing in the living room.

It's when she runs up the stairs that I decide I can no longer just sit by and watch.

I resist the urge to shift, but rip off my shirt instead, just in case.

The front door is ajar, and as I walk into the large room, I'm awed by the interior.

Never had I seen such things, paintings, and cloth

chairs...it was as if Lux's family had all the riches in the world. Why she would hate it confuses me.

That was until I saw the old woman sitting in the darkness, her face half slacken, unmoving. I stalk to her chair, her eyes following me, but I realize she cannot move on her own.

She smells of mint and a sickness I cannot identify, perhaps her rotting insides.

"You must be Gran. So nice to make your acquaintance." I circle her, her eyes struggling to keep up. Many things pass my thoughts—like slicing her throat in one simple movement and putting the old woman out of her misery before she even knew what happened. I decide I will let my little lamb have the last word.

That's when I hear Lux screaming..."Mercy!"

I am flying up the stairway, polished and perfect floors beneath my boots. I make it to the end of the hallway, and a tall man stands in front of the bedroom door she is behind.

"It's too late. She is ours now. Her destiny is in God's hands." He holds a small knife, but I am unfazed.

I lower my head, a growl rumbling in my chest as he lunges. We roll, but I am easily twice his weight in muscle alone. When we stop, I am on top of him. His face is pale, and his knife is in my hand now.

Pulling back, I let one slash fly across his neck, the blood spluttering from the wound in bubbles and spurts. His face goes slack, but I hear Lux. "Stop! Please! MERCY!"

Her cries send a slice of rage through me I can no longer control. I open the door and my body is already stretching and changing into the beast that I carefully tried to hide from her.

I am on top of the boy, whose body is assaulting my sweet lamb.

He will die for what he has done to my mate.

I drag him from the bed, his screams of terror reverberating off the walls as Lux looks on in horror.

I thrash his limp body around, dropping him to the floor in a heap. I bare my teeth, already covered in his father's blood.

"No! Please! I don't want to die! I'm sorry...please forgive me!" He is shaking beneath me, begging for his life. My wolf is feral, but more concerned with my soft lamb, who is scared silent on the bed.

I turn back on the boy, and I know it is time to seal his fate.

He cannot take what is mine without punishment or death.

"I cannot offer you forgiveness."

I rear my head and clamp my jaws around his neck, blood spilling out and over my teeth. His head hangs at an absurd angle, blood gurgling from the gash, as he struggles to find his breath.

His body sags, his eyes empty, and the floor of the room begins to pool with deep, dark blood.

Lux pulls herself up on the bed, swinging her legs to the edge and gently placing them on the floor.

I whimper, laying down at her feet and in the blood of her friend.

Unmoving, I wait as she settles her graceful arches into the blood of the floor. I lay my chin at her feet, ears flattened back, waiting for her to run from me.

But then, I watch as she kneels in front of me...her white dress sticky with thick red. She strokes my head. "Good boy...That's a good boy. You have saved me again."

The stroke of her hands guides me back into my human form, and I change under her fingertips as I lap the blood from them.

I bring her into my arms, and she wraps her body around mine as I lift her off the blood-stained floor.

"It is you...you are The Wolf of the Woods. Your coat does not match your hair. It is black as night, but...incredible." She kisses my fingers, taking the middle one into her mouth.

"My coat is as black as a winter's night, as am I. Is my soul too dark for you, lamb?" I trail kisses down her neck, her pulse throbbing under my lips.

"I love your darkness, just as you seem to enjoy mine." She strokes my beard and I lose my balance on the slippery fluid.

Landing in the blood, Lux laughs...and I join her.

Ripping the dress over her head, she climbs on top of me, never breaking our deep kisses.

Flat on my back, I link my hands behind my head and allow her to take control.

I am rock hard for her, whirling at the thought of her loving me as a man and a beast.

Good boy.

She guides me to her center, impaling herself on me with a loud gasp.

The tips of her hair nearly touch her waist. They drip with blood, painting her body in red stripes as she writhes on top of me, swirling in wide circles.

I grip her hips, pounding up into her, meeting every swirl she uses me for pleasure.

"Watching you kill him, ripping him to shreds, I was wild with lust. Seeing you lose all control like that. I like the blood, Fen...the blood spilled at your hands." She cries out my name with a long moan, and I am on the brink.

I pump into her as if it is the last climax I will ever chase, feeling her tightness pulse around me until I am spilling inside of her in utter agony, pulse after pulse of warmth wringing me dry.

She falls on top of me, the slick wetness of sweat mixing with the sticky blood that surrounds us. "I love you, Fen. I love you in a way that is a masterpiece."

"And you are mine, sweet lamb. My masterpiece."

Maybe I am wicked, after all. I am on a high... and I have never felt this happy ever before.

The last happy memory I have of my mother was the day before she was taken away.

"Luxy, let's make a picnic and take it down to the stream. I can show you how to cleanse crystals and show you where all the rare herbs grow." Her hair was long and auburn, and she had a beauty mark just above her lip.

The sun shone high in the sky, casting shadows from the trees on our faces. We unpack the food, all prepared by her. The sun warms our cheeks, she laughs, and I dance. The temperature climbs high in the summer and we decide to go for a swim in the stream.

As we strip our clothes and climb into the cool ravine, she tells me stories of our ancestors passed.

It was the day she passed her wisdom to me, handing me a weapon in my mind that I knew nothing about.

"You are the filthy one now." Fenrir's baritone voice breaks the memory, and I remember I am not submerged in spring water, but the blood of my enemy.

I crawl under the bed, retrieving the box that I hid there long ago, holding it to my chest.

I walk out of the bedroom, naked and covered in blood, down the stairway. I don't stop until I am standing in front of my gran, clutching the box in my arms.

"I am leaving here now; with every piece of knowledge my mother ever gave me. Including this." I hold it out, almost placing it in her unmoving lap. I wanted to say all the things that I thought about when I was young, but I was a smart woman now, and didn't need to waste the time. I was free to be whoever the bloody hell I wanted to be.

"I should have...let him..." She wheezes on the words, but her inflection still reeks with contempt.

"Let who? My father?" I crouch down closer to her, eager to hear what she had to say after the bloodshed today.

"This is...my punishment...for allowing you...to live." She coughs, closing her eyes briefly.

"Allowing me to live? Do you think the way we have lived here...? Is this living?" I laugh, disbelief in my voice.

"All to settle a debt. Your father was...a fool. You are pure...evil," she sputters again, only this time, I don't want to hear any more of it. I had finally had enough of being told I was tainted, not worthy—it was enough.

I hold the box high above my head, my gran's half-paralyzed face looking at me, blank.

I bring it down on her head, as hard as I can manage, hearing the dull thud of her skull smashing against it. I swing it down repeatedly until her head is a pulp of gushing blood and skin.

I back away, the wooden box covered in her blood, pieces of her hair and scalp sticking to it. I feel Fenrir's arms come around me, and I fall to the floor, sobbing.

~

Fenrir

I place kisses on her shoulders; her back. I stroke her hair and whisper into her ear. She is wrought, and I am in awe of her strength amidst this betrayal.

"I am here. You are safe." I stroke her hair, and her golden eyes finally find mine.

"I want to go home." She curls her body into mine, and the only thought I have is getting her body clean and her weary body into our bed.

She is mine...and my little lamb is too fierce for that title anymore.

A wolf in a red cape.

LUX

I am covered in blood, and my hair is a sticky mess. I can barely get my fingers through it. "I want to cut my hair."

Fen stops sharpening the hatchet he always carries, looking up at me with shining eyes. "You can do whatever you please, little lamb. It will not change the way I feel about you."

I finish filling the bath with hot water and toss in a couple of the soap bars that were newly delivered to Fen's doorstep today.

I ease my body into the steamy water, dunking my head underneath, running my fingers through the strands.

I come up for air, and Fen is standing beside the tub, watching me. "Your beauty comes from deep inside. It has nothing to do with the length of your hair, or the curve of your bottom."

I smile, but I pull myself from the tub, dripping water all over the wood floor.

He hands me a cloth that barely covers my hips, and I dry myself off as he watches intently. Even his stare brings excitement to the bottom of my belly, and I bite my lip as he comes closer.

Wrapping his arm around my lower back, he pulls me to him and kisses my neck until I am breathless.

"I want to fill you with my children. Watch your belly swell with pups." He runs his fingers over my belly, jiggling it as he swipes down, his fingers disappearing between my thighs.

I watch his hand as he strokes me, igniting the flame that burns for him almost instantly.

My cheeks are flush with heat from my bath, and lust for my lover. I saunter to the corner that holds his knives and blades, grabbing the smallest one, and gather my hair in a low bundle near my neck and saw at the strands. I grip the ends, being sure to keep a firm grasp so it would not fall. Pulling the last strand through the knife, I hold out the bundle proudly.

"Should we keep it? An ode to what once was, and no longer is?" Fen tries to take the swinging hair from my hand, but I pull back, knowing exactly where I wanted it to go.

I walk to the fire, tossing it inside. "Too wild, Gran? How's this for wild?"

The smell is putrid but fades quickly as the flames engulf the hair. I feel lighter, and I toss my head about, my hair swishing around my shoulders.

Fen swoops me into his arms, easily lifting me, and I kiss him as he walks us to our bedroom at the back. Laying me on the bed, he says, "I have something I want to try...roll over."

The thrill of his command runs through me, and I obey. I hear him light the flint, and I peek around my shoulder at his towering frame and still feel the thrill running up and down my spine.

He lights a white tapered candle, watching the flame as it heats the wax, pooling at the top. "Is this what you like, little lamb?"

Kneeling behind me, he adjusts himself between my thighs, my rear propped up. I am entirely exposed, my sex open and vulnerable under his eyes.

He spreads my cheeks with one hand, dripping hot wax down the sensitive crack, and I hiss. Pleasure jolts through my bottom, and I grind myself onto the bed.

The wetness of my sex is open to him, vulnerably so. I

look back at him, his eyes lit with mischief. I lay my head down and watch his hands as they roam over my body, letting his touches soothe me.

Both rough and gentle, the skin from his calloused fingertips lights my skin on fire, creating a mixture of warmth and happiness.

"So, you do enjoy the pain, then?" His smile creates a wave of wrinkles at the corner of his eyes as I nod my head, smiling in return. I see a flicker of something behind his eyes, a flash of something wild, feral.

Rising to his knees, he gives my ass a paddle, the strike sounding like that of a whip. I gasp, the force of it shoving my head into the furs beneath me. He reels back and does it again, only this time, I cry out.

"Ohh, you do like that, don't you?" His words are low and husky, as if he can feel my pleasure. "Do you like it when I nibble at you as well?"

He bends down, bringing his face close to my cheeks, sliding his tongue into the crease and nipping at my flesh.

He leans back again and spreads my cheeks, spitting on the hole as I gasp. I am already slick for him, this man who saved my very life.

He wastes no time, plunging two fingers inside of me. "That's it. Fuck my fingers, sweet lamb. Take what you want." He gives my ass a few more smacks while he pumps his fingers, curving inside of me until the pressure makes me feel like I might wet myself.

I let the sting of his smacks swirl together with the pleasure, as he strokes inside of me.

THE PRESSURE behind my hips builds until I am reaching under myself to find that place that sets fireworks off behind my eyes. I easily find it, stroking myself to the same rhythm as his pumps.

I hear a low growl from behind me as he unsheathes his fingers. Craning my neck, I see Fenrir's cock exposed and sticking straight up into the air, hard and ferocious.

FOR ME.

GENTLY PLACING each hand on my hips, he guides himself to my drenched hole as I lift my ass to accommodate him.

HE SLAMS inside of me to the hilt. I cry out, and I feel him slump over my back, his arm wrapping around my waist. The weight of his body feels delicious covering mine.

PANTING A FEW TIMES, he whispers, "I have dreamed of you for years. Your smell, your smile, your taste. I want to fill your insides with my seed until you overflow with babes."

. . .

His words send shooting stars down my limbs, and I arch my back in approval, squeezing my cunt around him until he groans.

Reaching between my legs, he finds my sweet spot and kneads it gently with his fingertips.

I am panting now as I quietly say, "Fill me."

My words push him deeper inside of me as he violently pumps his hips into me. I bite the blanket under my head, feeling him bite my shoulder as the pressure builds between us.

Pulling back from me, he sits on his heels, holding his cock in his hand. I look back at him, my ass still high in the air.

He stares at me like that for a moment, stroking himself. "I am going to watch my seed spill into your womb...you stay just like that."

I watch him as he pumps his fist up and down the veined shaft, droplets of liquid beading on the head. I lick my lips, my body quivering with the need for climax. "Touch yourself, lamb. Show me how you make yourself feel good."

· · ·

THIS DEED SENT shivers of thrill through my body, and I did as he asked.

STROKING MY FOLDS, I find the place again, watching his eyes on my sex. We stroke together, in harmony, as we feed each other's visual senses. I slip over the edge when his mouth opens and his hooded eyes watch my face as I squirm and ride out my climax, falling onto the bed.

I FEEL him grab for my hips. "You keep that in the air, just like that." He grunts, still pumping.

MY BODY IS ON FIRE, and Fenrir releases a roar as I feel his hot seed spill over my ass. "Oh, yes. That's so fucking perfect."

HIS EYES ARE FIXED on the spot, smiling.

"THAT WAS INCREDIBLE." I sigh, keeping my ass under his hands.

"You are incredible, sweet lamb."

BONUS SCENES

BRECON BEACONS FORREST, WALES 1700

"I'm beginning to love this belly you have grown full with child. I think I may need to have you forever, this plump and swollen." I watch as Fen strokes my exposed skin with his thick fingers, and I cover his hand with mine, holding it on the spot where I can feel her tiny toes poking just under my ribs.

"Shall we name this one after another God as well? Frigg, perhaps?" I giggle, fully knowing his amusement with my jests.

It appears our luck changes every few years or so. My father did not relent his ownership of me, insisting I needed to be 'taken care of,' explaining that if I bore any children, I would be further damning us all to hell on earth.

Fenrir did not kill my father purely out of love for me...he could have, but he did not.

It wasn't until my father brought a slew of men I had never seen before while I was first pregnant with Freyja. Their demands became threats, and their noise ignited

Fenrir's change—if not to protect me, but the wild need to keep his unborn child alive.

Ten men lay dead, my father begging for his life, his bloody and mangled hand tucked to his chest as he crawled away from Fen.

He may not have been able to bear the burden of killing my father, allowing him to escape in fear. But in my eyes, my father was already dead.

TWELVE YEARS LATER

"Mum, when is the baby going to be here?" Freyja asked, her voice high and sweet, forever the curious one.

I wonder who she gets that from?

Fen would have laughed if he heard her question; I think he has asked me this question more times than even she has.

"Well...very soon. I have grown her in my belly for nine full moons, so I have a feeling it will be on the next." I wink down at her, sitting crossed-legged beside me on the fur rug.

"The next full moon is in Capricorn, the goat, am I correct?" she states, continuing to clean the dirt off the carrots and potatoes in her lap.

"That's right, Freyja. You've been paying attention to the stars in the sky, hm?" I struggle to get up from the rocking chair Fen built for me and tousle her long, black locks.

How I would even begin to explain to a ten-year-old child what exactly she was capable of still stumped me. I was only beginning to understand the capacity at which my own mind can operate—the powers I have come into knowing Fenrir and what he is.

It still wasn't clear just what abilities Freyja would have just yet—her ears were pointed, and her canines resembled small fangs. She tells me she has nightmares filled with men that look nothing like we do, watching her...wanting her.

Just as any mother before me has done, I tell her she is only imagining the men and must remember her mind is a powerful part of her, and she must learn to control it. Each time the dreams wracked her, in the middle of the night with tears in her eyes, she would nod and return to her slumber.

"Come, come little helper. It's time to wash your hands and get ready for bed." I say, collecting the remainder of the vegetables and placing the full basket next to the sink.

Freyja steps up and washes her hands, drying them on the towels that hang on hooks beside the pots and pans.

The house is unrecognizable compared to how Fenrir lived before I came. I had never watched a man so excitedly build cabinetry or tables in all my life. I stand and stare at the sitting room that now inhabits the space where I was once tied to the beam at the center...twelve years ago.

We had used that beam for many other nights of pleasure following that day.

"I'm going to decorate this house in the richest cloths and most divine jewels I can find. I can't wait." Freyja is tucked into her bed, an empty bassinet beside her, looking up at me with wide, green eyes.

I sit on the edge of the bed, the weight of me sinking into the mattress, "I'm not sure how much longer we will stay, your father and I have befriended a man near the coast. A man who ca—"

"I'm not leaving here. I don't ever want to leave these woods." she says plainly, picking at a piece of lint on the blanket. I narrow my eyes at her stubborn nature, but I knew this conversation wouldn't be easy.

"Freyja, you cannot stay here alone. Perhaps if you were older, but you are coming if we decide to leave. We are family...blood. We stay together."

I stand, blowing out the candle next to her bed, the words final. She would have to learn to obey us the hard way. I was easy on her up until this point, but once she realizes what she is, will she want to be with me? I would have Fenrir walk with her tomorrow and change her mind. He was a more patient teacher than I was.

∼

Freyja

Walking beside my father in his wolf's form feels normal to me, and I follow him along the footpath that has been trodden from our daily walks.

The stream is the best place to find flowers, and I know a thicket of roses is behind the large Ash tree.

Pay attention to the whispers of the trees, and the songs of the streams...nature will never steer you wrong...

The voice was getting stronger the older I became.

What felt before like whispers carried through the wind have now become something of a caress across my face, a guiding hand like a mother's.

Tell them.

What exactly could I say about this mysterious voice I've had for as long as I could remember? For all I knew, it was just my imagination, although it felt like it belonged there as if the voice was familiar.

What little my mother had shared with me about our past, I knew men hunted down the women who spoke of voices in their heads—my grandmother, for instance.

I was smarter than that, and I listened to the voice quietly telling me of the powers I possessed. I needn't worry mother or father over such things; I was strong enough to carry this secret on my own.

There is a large house just beyond the crested hill mother told me she once lived in. It was where she first saw my father in his wolf's form.

I had become a little obsessive with the house; it held the history of my mother and father's relationship—the spot where they committed their first murder.

I am unafraid of the beast that walks beside me, his back almost level with my ten-year-old head. His paws are larger than my own feet, and when his tongue lolls out of his mouth, his sharp teeth shine with strings of saliva.

Perhaps I should be afraid, but I am not. No harm would ever come my way with a beast by my side.

I reach out and ruffle his black fur as we walk side by

side. He nuzzles my long black hair, almost the exact color of his fur, and I giggle.

As we reach the clearing before the house, he stops, whimpering.

"Oh please, father. I just want to see it one more time!" I say, taking off in a run to the top of the hill.

The house is large, three stories with windows in fancy shapes, taller than me. I look back at my father, hidden in the shadows but watching me closely. Each step I take away from him, I feel wary...yet empowered.

"Are you looking for wood as well?" I hear her before I see her. Turning to the left, I notice a little girl with curly blonde hair.

She was beautiful, with a perfect row of pearly whites and dimples to match. She wore a necklace with a deep red stone, nothing like the rocks mother and I have ever found in the steam. The stone is clutched by the foot of a bird, and her dress is beautiful. I blush as I look down over my own tattered dress of mud brown.

"I told Reeve I would take care of the wood today, and silly me, I came out here with a dress and my best shoes on." Her voice is light but careful, and she laughs at herself as she points to her shoes while I stare.

I look down at my hands, a small rosebud rests inside, and I cannot recall stopping at the thicket to pick any roses.

I step up to her, compelled to share it with her. "When this rose blooms, she will return."

That was the day I gave that little voice a name, and my gifts began to multiply.

THE WICKED WITCH OF THE WOODS

Charity, a quiet and proper girl, believes everyone is acting ridiculous over the recent killing of a young boy in the Welsh woods. Things happen. Certainly, it wasn't a punishment for their sins.

Charity's new stepfather wants to marry her off and continue his role as town leader, intent on bringing back the practice of witch burning. On an errand for his father, Charity stubbornly follows Charles into the woods, hoping to stop him.

The pair soon become lost, delirious with hunger, and stumble upon a house so magical it looks good enough to eat.

Freyja is like no one Charity has ever seen, but Charles knows exactly what she is...The witch he's been assigned to find. Freyja's fearlessness sparks something inside Charity—a longing suppressed for years—and Charles lust for Charity follows soon after.

But Freyja has one rule: no one passes through her woods without payment.

PROLOGUE

BRECON BEACONS FORREST, WALES 1735

"*I am The Dark Mother. Do not forget that you are a child of Lilith.*"

She speaks to me again. She means no harm but likes to remind me of this from time to time.

My fangs tingle, my mouth slowly opening around his pulsing neck, "Yessss, just like that. You are doing so well," I rasp, closing my mouth around his warm, sun-kissed skin. My blood lust is strong tonight, The Mother Moon Goddess shining bright and full above us.

His brown eyes stare up at me wide, never leaving my face. Black curls stick to his sweaty forehead as I work my hips back and forth over his rigid cock, the only part of his body he has control over while I'm here.

He called for me, and wanted me to ease his pain. I did not come here uninvited.

Most often, my victims find me.

A man who is lonely, perhaps a man whose wife does not satisfy his carnal needs the way I can.

Or a lonely widower, who hasn't felt the heat of a woman in many years.

Most men have such an inherent desire to fuck, they will use it to heal wounds. They often think it is the only salve to soothe their sins.

I can take all the pain away with the flick of my tongue on their paralyzed lips.

I have the power to end wars, appeasing the appetites of the male ego. Only tonight, this man will not live. I needed to feel the warmth of a soul inside me again; it has been too long.

Biting down on his strained chords, I feel the warmth of blood breech my mouth, gushing and gurgling forth as I suck.

I feel him explode inside of me, his cocks pulsing in tune with the artery that sprays inside my mouth as he climaxes.

My body feels light, then full, and then...

I lean back, eyes closed, blood dripping from the corners of my mouth and down my neck. I smile wide, looking down over my willing sacrifice.

I didn't *need* to kill; I *enjoyed* it.

The man below me stares at the ceiling, motionless. The life force has gone from him; his blood is still warm from the final beats of his heart. The heartbeats that pushed his seed deep inside of me.

Wiping my mouth with the back of my hand, I stand naked and towering over the corpse with satisfaction.

The Mother's whispers became louder with each kill, and the vengeance she demanded for all her lost daughters is done through me.

It is my job to find and take care of them all. These were my woods, and I needed to protect them for generations to come.

Spilled blood on the Welsh lands, magic flowing through me as a reward.

I survey the large room, finding a window that overlooks a dry desert, the sun rising along the horizon.

I look down over my bloodied hands and turn my palms upwards, closing my eyes and imagining my home.

Well done, daughter. Your magic awaits you.

This is my purpose.

CHAPTER 1
CHARITY
1730 BETHLEHEM, WALES

My belly grumbles loudly, and I stare down at the wooden plate that barely contains enough food to call it a meal.

Placing my hands in my lap, I push away from the table, muttering the words *excuse me* as I stand.

"Where do you think you're going, girl? Sit and eat with your family." Thomas shovels a heap of potatoes into his mouth, his share more than all our plates combined.

"I'm not hungry." I lie, walking quietly away from the table to the cot at the back of the house.

I can feel his eyes on my back, but I try my best to ignore him, praying to God he will leave me alone for once.

My prayer is unanswered as his one good hand slams down hard on the table, sending the wooden forks flying and causing me to stop in my tracks.

"Sit. Down." He bellows, standing now, but I do not move.

I must say, for a man of his older age, he still has a lot

of fight in him. He has to be at least sixty, and when he married my mother everyone whispered their *whys*.

The promises he made to the three of us a year ago never came to fruition. A hefty reward is coming his way from London; he just wasn't quite sure when.

"Do you think Troy and his family will tolerate your insolence when you marry? You need to show more respect for men, little girl." He speaks while his mouth is still full of food, and my stomach turns as I make a face of disgust.

Little girl?

I have had my blood for five years now and am soon to be married off to a man. I am *far* from a little girl.

I sit on the cot, now facing him, and I feel rage boil inside me, but know better than to speak out of turn. I nod, looking at the floor.

His son, Charles, who did not look anything like his geezer of a father, stands, "Please, Sir. Leave the girl alone. We have been here but a year—let her get used to the idea of having a new family. Sit down before you give yourself a coronary."

I smile at him beneath my lashes. Charles gives me a shy smile, and something inside of me stirs. Something I have tried for years to turn off...my friend tells me it's called desire.

Although, him and Thomas are a part of our family now, it feels wrong somehow—a puzzle piece that just doesn't fit into the picture.

Marriage is the only way a traveler, or I should say stranger, will ever be accepted into a small village like ours. I knew Thomas is just using my mother for her vulnerability, something that came with a widow of her age.

I tried to question Charles about their arrival, where they came from, and why they chose our small farm town.

I know I will never choose a place like this voluntarily.

No questions were ever answered, and now, Thomas is vying for the role as town leader and pastor...and the uncertainty of their identity only left me wondering— why?

CHAPTER 2
FREYJA
BRECON BEACON FOREST, WALES

When I wake, I am once again in my bed, covered in silk and furs from continents far away.

The sacrifice rewarded.

The latest rewards of my travels spill over from the bed onto the floor beside me, and I remember the man whose soul I claimed the night before.

I stretch my naked body in the sunlight from the circular window above me, dried blood still covering my left breast and hands.

I will make a trip to the hot springs this afternoon after my chores and a hot meal.

The birds must get their bread soon; the loyal pets I have gathered over the years depended on me now.

Lilitu slept in the corner of my room, a cacoon of furs surrounding her. Her black-tipped ears perk up as I move off the bed. Foxes have impeccable hearing, and she has warned me of the squirrels inside the roof long before they made it into my food stores.

I stride into the living space, full of tables, mirrors,

pillows, and altars. I light the white and black tapers, hand-dipped candles I have conjured from across the oceans, far away from here.

The weather is still warm, but a chill has crept in during the early hours of the morning, a sure sign of autumn.

The Sun God will soon turn into the Lord of Shadows, and it will soon be time to prepare for the winter.

I enjoy the solitude and seclusion of my cabin. The only connection left to my family after they sailed for the Americas.

I doubted they will return, and I refused to leave.

My mother cried for hours, begging me to go. I shook my long black hair 'no.' She knew I will not be swayed, stubborn as I was.

My grandfather, Garm, returned when I was a child, joyful at seeing his kin prosper. But it was only because of his protection my mother agreed to let me stay.

Garm is a werewolf shifter like my father, and although he wasn't related to me by blood, he is part of my father's clan...something just as sacred. The things my mother and father were afraid to show me—Garm did. The fangs I always ignored were put to use, and Garm will tell me of the legends of Lilith, The Dark Mother of Witches.

It is she who speaks to me; I am a creature not like any other. I do not need blood to survive, but I thrive on the kill.

At times, men will pass through my woods, entering my realm without realizing what they were walking into. Once they were inside my wards, they will never leave.

When I am feeling kind, I will release them just to watch them run away in fear. The word 'witch' is rarely uttered anymore, but it is a label I wear with pride. I know all about the men in the black coats, and when my mother told me what they have done, I swore I will never rest until I have claimed them all.

I am no ordinary witch, no, I am a Volva Witch—Viking blood running thru my veins—and when I captured them, their eyes will grow wide with terror, even the men of large stature, armed with ropes and pyres.

Running did them no good...they can not leave my wards without payment—their pathetic lives.

Each time, I will stalk through the trees after them, ash from the fire decorating my eyes and fingertips, the bow made by my father in my right hand...and I will hunt them.

"We have work to do today, Lilitu. Will you join me, little furry one?" I busy myself with the jars of herbs and dried meat I left on the table to dry. The garden will need harvesting and re-planting before the ground froze, and today seems like the perfect day for it.

I pulled on my gardening shoes, my pet fox at my feet.

It took years to cultivate the large expanse of a garden in my backyard. My grandfather did most of the heavy lifting—tilling and carrying buckets of water in from the stream.

I planted seeds and whispered spells into the ground while my animals fertilized the rows.

A large hot spring is tucked behind the raised beds and tall thatches of flowers and grass. It is the place where I manifested my lovers and washed before my rituals under the new and full moons.

I clutch a large jar to my chest, filled with salt, rosemary, lemon, and peppercorn. I take my time walking in circles around my land, to the edge of the woods and back, chanting my protection spells.

Lilitu follows me the entire time, and I smile to myself as she sniffs the mixture I throw and sneezes.

I welcome any and all strangers here, but whatever their purpose, they can never escape.

"Don't! Give it back, Frigg!" my preteen voice is strained, and I can see my sister's small hands cupping the doll I made.

"But she's pretty, she has blonde curly hair…"

I snatch the doll from her hands, tucking it inside my dress and walking away from my annoying kid sister. "It is a poppit, Frigg, it's enchanted…with my magic…don't touch it!"

I leave her standing in the middle of the rose bushes, sobbing. A tiny part of me feels sorry for yelling at her, but I also know her fingers will wipe away the magic I have placed on the doll.

I can't let her know that The Dark Mother needs this doll for her curse. I have to do this for her, even though I'm not quite sure why yet.

CHARITY

"Is it true, then? About the girl that disappeared into the woods all those years back?" my voice is high, and the anticipation of his answer sends a shiver through my body. Nothing exciting ever happens in this repressive little town called Bethlehem, currently up in arms, chattering and gathering in meetings to speak of the evil that lived near the black mountains.

"A woman, my age, escapes the clutches of an evil witch in these very woods, but never lives to talk about it? How do we even know if it's true?" I shake out the sheet I try to fold in the whipping wind; it smells like it might rain soon.

The story of the girl resurfaced recently after the bloodied body of a boy is found in a nearby stream. His body is dismembered and torn to shreds; his face nearly unrecognizable. It wasn't until our neighbor, Kathryn, knocked on our door late that night in tears that word got out.

"And why do you care about myths and legends all the sudden?" Charles' smirk bothers me, and not just because he is a dashingly handsome blonde with blue eyes.

"Oh, Charles... you're so *dreadfully* boring." I smirk back at him, but he only smiles as he continues to help me fold the linens.

Charles is my brother, but only by marriage, and since we are similar in age, I enjoy his company...and his stories.

"*Pssh,* I've *seen* the way you look at Tris Morgan's ample cleavage. You have an odd obsession with beautiful women, fictional and the like," Charles says, quickly turning his back to the large wooden table fixed tightly to the side of a tub of suds, stacks of towels and blankets beside him.

"Charles, shouldn't you be doing something other than the work of women?" Clarise quips. Clarise is my older sister and appointed caregiver while my stepfather is at the church, and my mother did what she did best: gossiped and ate too much bread at the neighbor's house.

I never understood what my mother saw in the old man I am now forced to call father. He is grey with age, and his hand mangled with scars.

My mother is attractive, in my opinion.

The only reason I can find for my mother's poor choice is his sharp tongue and bold attitude—two things that were sure to gain him recognition in this town as Pastor.

"I am just leaving," Charles sighed, his impressive height warranting the attention of the young, blushing girls who walked by. I admire his broad shoulders as he jogs down the stone pathway to the church nestled between the hills.

Clarise, my mother, and I kept quietly to our home when my father died of a black sickness that swept through the town like a tidal wave. It is not long after that Thomas and Charles arrived.

They came as a package deal, just as my sister and I did. But soon Charles became my friend, and it is better for me since I didn't care for making friends with females my age anyways.

Tris is my only friend, and it is obvious to others I preferred *her* company.

Oh well, their loss.

"Not attending church today, I see," Clarise states, with her perfectly placed bonnet and braids that mirrored mine.

The men here are boring, lazy, and have mouths that never cease to run from them. Mostly, the men of my stepfather's brethren. We never had a *clergy* before, but ever since he came, many things have changed.

It is no secret that men are the ones in control. Huddling in groups and speaking low amongst themselves in the corners of the village. It didn't bother me so much that they were men, but the fact that there weren't any women allowed.

"Actually, I think I will attend church service today. I'm not finished speaking with Charles just yet." I wipe the wetness of my hands from the tub of suds on my apron, turning to face my sister, who looked so much like our father.

"Cher, I think you will be better off just staying behind as you have been. You know your mouth has a bad habit of not staying shut. Do you remember last ti—"

"Yes, Clarise! I remember what happened last time,

do you think me daft, *sister*?" I stand before her and our small cottage, hand on my hips and ready for a fight.

Only Clarise never stood up to me once.

When her face turns to shock, I grin at her playfully and wink.

She knew I willn't listen regardless; it didn't matter what she said.

As I walk down the cobblestone pathway and down the hill to our church, my stomach begins to twist into knots, and my skin flushes into a clammy sweat.

It is summer still but nearing fall, and the evening's chill begun the week before.

It's early morning now, and I pull my shawl closer around my shoulders and neck against the whispering winds.

As I approach the church, I notice the men standing outside the doors and beneath the stone steeple, wearing their long black jackets and tall hats, looking like a murder of crows.

My stepfather stands next to an older man whom I do not recognize, but his overgrown eyebrows are scrunched up into a pointed expression at my sudden appearance beside them. Even at nineteen, I stood taller than most of them.

"Thomas, I'm so sorry for missing your *captivating* sermon, but I need to speak with Charles."

Adjusting his hat, his wrinkled face looks to the ground and steps out of the group, taking me by my elbow. "I will prefer it if you didn't announce your absence of my sermon in front of my brethren in particular, Charity. I have told you before to think better of these bold choices you continue to make."

"*Father*, I *want* to be involved as much as possible...I

only want to help." What I really want to ask is, *what is it you say to your flock that has them following you so unquestionably? What do you talk about at all hours of the day and night with no women around to hear?*

I take his hand into mine and smile as he looks at me with speculation.

"Cher... women cannot speak directly to God as a man can." Gently, he tucks my unruly brown hair behind my ear, and I shudder.

"Charles, escort your sister to the market, she needs to fetch more carrots and beans with the last of our coin." Patting me on my back, he pushes me towards Charles, eager to be rid of my curiosities.

Charles leans into my ear, sending little tickles and tingles down the side of my neck as he says, "If you come with me without a fight, I promise to tell you all about the men in the black coats and the succubus girl."

Charles is already walking ahead of me but looks over his shoulder to make sure I am following him.

"A succubus!? What in God's name is that?" I whisper back as we leave the church behind us. Away from the men, Charles and I can speak freely, as we usually did. He didn't seem to mind my questions, and I didn't like the way he acted when he is around those men.

The recent attacks blanketed our village with questions ever since, although the men liked to pretend they have it under control. According to them, they already knew exactly why this happened.

Charles and I walk side by side in silence.

"Listen, I'll tell you what I know, but you cannot tell my...father, or anyone else these secrets or our covert communications will end." He looks back over his shoulder, grinning back at me like a prince straight out of a fairytale—a man you can trust with all your secrets.

Well, a prince in peasant's clothing.

If only the other boys in this town were as charming and funny as Charles. Perhaps, I will stop fantasizing about Tris and the delicious curve of her mouth.

"Tell me!" I shout, punching his arm hard and stifling back a laugh.

"Ow! You hit bloody hard!" He rubs his arm, mocking me but grinning at the same time.

I can already smell carts of food and the chickens that hang from the stout butcher's cart. The one that always found a way to brush his hand over one of my breasts during a sale. "Come on then, tell me." I stop walking, folding my arms over my chest.

Charles pulls me into a shadowed alley between two tall houses made of brick. "The story of the Wolf is very real... one of the older men of our flock remembers the Wolf-man storming a house on the other side of the forest. He *saw* them...both the succubus woman and the Wolf with his own eyes."

My eyes grow wide, and, although it takes a lot for me to believe these wild claims, I am interested... *a demon?*

"Who is this man? Is he worth his word? Are you sure he is not lying for popularity?" I ask, always trying to get the full story from every angle. The way gossip travels, there has to be a way to filter out the rubbish.

"You cannot lead on that I've told you; do you understand? My father will never forgive me. The Wolf and his devil woman companion were after my father, and that is why we have to flee to London. I can't tell you much more than that...he told me it is better for my safety if I didn't know more about it."

I didn't believe him for a second. It seems strange to me that he willn't know why, especially if Thomas is his father. Let him lie; it is nothing new to me…I will rather hear more about the legend than his boring father, anyhow.

He leans in closer to me, eyeing the narrow road at my back. "It is said, he is as large as two men, and she is like that of fire, dressed in a red cape with blazing hair on her head to match."

I cross my arms tighter to my chest now, my mind trying to paint a vivid picture of a wolf-man and a fire-woman.

I giggle.

"Oh, it's funny, is it? Cause I find it downright terrifying. What if he is responsible for the boy's death? Perhaps he has finally found us." Charles grips his warm hand onto my forearm, pulling me close to him. I look down at it, his thick digits clean, his nails as polished as a girl's. My insides squeeze as I look up into his glossy-blue eyes. Just for a moment, I think I see a flash of something mischievous behind them.

"Now, we share a secret, Charity. A secret that no one can know, or they will blame my father for this. Promise me you will tell no one." His lips are so close to mine I can feel the heat of his breath. Absentmindedly, I tilt my head up slightly, licking my lips.

"There is something else that you cannot share with anyone."

I nod…eager for more scandal.

"Thomas believes there is a witch here, and it is part of the reason we have come."

"I knew it! I knew all along there is more to your… *arrival*. Why will he think that?"

Charles releases a deep breath and says, "Well...he is married to one once. He plans to bring back the burnings, and he will not stop until God gives him a sign."

My chest tightens, and I remember the stories I was told as a child about witches—women with strange markings, healers, and husband's who dropped dead without warning. It makes me think of my father's death and my mother's teas that helped ease his pains.

will she have burned if we lived in those times?

I am silent, pondering what this can mean for the women of our town.

A heavy beat of silence passes between us, and he leans down to place his soft lips on mine. I close my eyes, letting the warmth of his mouth melt into mine. It is over far too soon, and I am left standing before him with my eyes still closed and lips still puckered. "Sealed with a kiss. Now, promise." He says, and I snap open my eyes, my body still humming from our contact.

"I promise."

I turn from him quickly, making my way toward the smelly meat merchant while butterflies fill my belly.

CHAPTER 4
FREYJA

"What do you mean he wasn't *the* boy?" I gather my cloak around my neck, passing my eyes over Garm's towering form.

His hair is held back in a leather strap, fashioned by me, and the loose hairs around his face are grey and frayed. His weathered skin looks exceedingly creased today, and he smells like he hasn't had a bath in days.

"Aye, woman. What part of that don't you understand?" He stretches his large hand to me, tugging on the long strands of my hair.

His accent is a thick burr, and sometimes I struggle to understand what he says unless I listen closely. It took some time to adjust from my parent's patient, calm demeanors to Garm's savage ways.

He always slept outside, no matter the weather, and he ate his food the way beasts devour a kill, smacking and tearing his sharp teeth through the flesh without care.

I prefer *most* things to be done neatly...meticulously.

"Did you let the boy go, then?" I cross the room to the

fireplace, hot water boiling for the salve I am making for his cuts.

He laughs a loud and rumbling tone that sends a shiver through my core. "Let him go? And what's the fun in that, *sunnedatter*? You should have seen his face," he mumbles as I apply the soaked bandages to his skin and place a steaming mug beside him on the table.

"Perhaps, at the very least, it will send a message. We know where they are now." I move to the largest altar in the room, the one that serves the purpose of rituals and spells. Flowers and grass litter the baskets of offerings. Wine and bread to the side for Brigid and Lilith. I light the bundle of herbs beside the mirror, carrying it over to Garm and brushing his body with the heavy curls of smoke.

He coughs, waving his muscular arms around, "Fuck off with that, will ye?"

I gasp at his outburst, setting the burning herbs back down on the altar. He is always so crass, especially when it comes to my magic.

"I can always just find him in his dreams, it willn't be so hard. I have been meditating and—"

"No. You will not. It is too dangerous. If there was one thing I swore to yer Dad, that was to keep you safe no matter what."

He stands, his aged body showing signs of weakening; it willn't be long before I will need to watch out for *him*. Age taking its inevitable hold, even if he is half man, half wolf.

"You are tired, *Afi*. Rest, I will tend the fire today." I pull a thick sweater on over my dress, preparing for the morning's chores.

"Aye, I will rest now, but not too long. I have a debt to

settle, and my soul cannot rest until I find the man who took my love from me."

I nod and walk to the door, stepping outside and into the sunshine.

~

Night fell quickly after I kept myself busy in the gardens and splitting wood for the week.

Fog pours over the sides of the hot spring and over my naked body, the slanted rocks and branches molding around me like a throne.

Closing my eyes, my body begins to feel weightless, and my spirit lifts away from my body. I am no longer a languid human lying naked in a pool of water. I am floating above myself, looking down.

When I leave my body this way, I am vulnerable. When I enter the dreams of anyone...even more so, it is why Garm insists I do not find the man through his dreams.

The trail ends in London; his tracks do no' exist there. I cannot risk being seen in my wolf form, so I retreated.

It wasn't until Garm followed the renewed indistinguishable and pungent sulfur smell that lasted for days. He tracked the man by the ashes of women left in his wake. It wasn't a hard trail to follow for a wolf shifter.

I hoped he will return to me with blood on his hands and a head I can add to my skull collection.

The man settled in with a family, so luring him into the woods will take some creativity and time.

Garm will have to wait to exact his revenge for just a little longer...

I did not mind Garm's company or protection, but I didn't need it. I revered myself as a creature of the night, more than capable of protecting myself with fangs and claws of my own.

Learning to wield my powers of seduction came early to me, and when I reached the time of my blood, I claimed two lives.

It is time for me to find him now.

The moon hangs in the sky like an old friend as I rise closer to its glow. My nude body shimmers as I look down over my curved belly and hips. I bend my legs and raise my arms above my head, thanking the Goddess for her gifts.

I ascend from my steamy bath, higher and higher, until the tips of the trees are far below my toes. The thick green and black become a swirl of shadows until I am high enough to see the border of the land around it.

I hover, drawing closer to the small town until I see his mangled hand—the hand my father tried to take from him and failed.

Come sit with me, Freyja, little moon child. I want to tell you the story of how your grandmother and I were created. will you like to hear it?

I nodded, fascinated by my father's size and yellow, blue eyes.

There was once a Goddess so powerful, men feared her. She was cast out by her creator after she refused to submit to her husband. She believed she was his equal, and because of that, she was damned to Hell. Only, she did not stay for long there, Lilith's powers only grew, and she returned to these very woods to start a family anew.

As a child, I feared little. Perhaps I am accustomed to creatures because of my father and then Garm. But Garm's return is fueled by his love for my grandmother, Annabelle. And while he said he will protect me, he also needed me.

We agreed to take down the men in black coats together.

I concentrate on my physical body, peacefully soaking beneath the warm water until I am returned to my form. I open my eyes; the dark woods quiet, except for the crickets and the owls.

Running my fingers down my body, goosebumps cover my skin beneath my dexterous fingertips, the warmth of the water soothing my aching muscles. My nipples tightened under my touch, the silky skin below my breasts soft, and I tease tiny circles down my abdomen until I'm arching my back.

My thoughts fall back to my latest conquest: a prince with dark eyes and hair, Hookah's, and jeweled tunics. We spent some of the night smoking a green herb that made me feel light-headed and warm between my legs. He has perfect, straight teeth and a large nose, mimicking his cock—impressively thick and long. I trail my fingers to the apex of my thighs, cupping myself until my insides throb. Sinking one finger inside, I imagine not the cock of a prince, but the tongue of the blonde maiden that lives in the tall house beyond the stream. It seems I preferred a fantasy with a woman tonight.

I tease my inner lips, stroking and pulling on them until the bud at the top of my cleft swells. I tease myself, picturing her pink tongue dancing over it and pulling it into her mouth. My breathing is heavy now, and I lift my hips out of the water so I can watch my hand work over my cunt.

Cunt, fuck that felt good to think. A word that sounds so deliciously dirty I had to whisper it out loud, *"cunt."*

My chest blooms with red, and the water splashes as I fuck my hand. My mouth hangs open, and my tongue is bereft of contact, lapping at the air and wishing it is her wet mound.

I do not know why I am drawn to her. Thoughts of her invade my mind often as if she sleeps all the time. I do know she is beautiful, with ringlets of white and soft thighs.

I rub the erect ball of nerves as I jerk my hips, figuratively fucking her face until the coils of pleasure build into a tight ball at my center, and I gasp. Crying out, I come, bursts of light behind my eyes, and my body collapses back into the water with a splash.

I lay still, allowing the currents of bliss to wash over me, smiling to myself like a fool. A loud snap of a tree branch breaks my little piece of paradise, and I sit up, reaching for my bow.

"Who's there? Show yourself." I stand naked and tall, unashamed and unafraid of meeting an enemy in the nude. I have fought many times on my own, man and beast. It is the reason for the thick scar above my lip.

I squint, trying to make out eyes or a silhouette through the trees, but I only see a flash of black, and they are gone.

The men of the town on the other side of these woods were getting braver, something they will pay for with their lives.

There is no one who can defeat this wolf and witch duo. Not a mortal with only two eyes.

CHAPTER 5
CHARITY

I kneel beside my bed after my mother plaited my hair and pray.

Dear Lord,

Please protect my family from whatever is menacing our town. Though I know you are not fool enough to think it is that of a witch. Please feed this animal that has such an insatiable hunger as so he will not take any more children.

I must ask for forgiveness, again, for what I am going to do tonight. I cannot suppress this ache inside of me; I need to see her.

In your name, Amen.

I climb into my bed, belly full of butterflies at the thought of seeing Tris' long lashes and pink lips. I only need to wait until Thomas is snoring, and then I will slip out into the night.

I smile to myself as I close my lids, imagining the cold air brushing against my face, my cheeks flush with excitement. Only two more hours until freedom.

~

"Please, Tris, let me taste you just this once. I can't stand it anymore; I need to know how you taste." I tremble, eyeing the shadows that rove over her face as I lift her dress and run my hand up her thigh.

I knew it is wrong; I knew I shouldn't be thinking of her this way, touching her like this. God will never forgive me for lusting after another girl.

"Not here! My brother will be in soon to milk the goats! Oh!" her voice wavers as I find the apex of her thighs with my fingertips and stroke gently over her dewy lips. I push her against a bale of hay, our bodies pressing together tightly. With my left hand, I hoist her leg around my waist, hooking my arm underneath it and capturing her mouth with mine, unsure where this hunger inside of me came from.

Her lips work over mine as she accepts my tongue into her warm mouth, tangling with mine. Her nipples pebble against mine, and my body flourishes with sparks and tingles. My brain spins in a fury of bliss and fire, causing the world around us to fall away.

In this moment, I don't care about God.

Breathing heavily, she says, "I have a book for you, here, quickly. Don't let anyone see it."

I wrap my fingers around the spine of the book she shoves toward me, and I fling it onto the ground, kissing her deeply once more—not ready for it to be over yet.

Our kiss is broken when a hand around my arm jerks me backward, causing me to tumble to the ground, right onto my plump ass, tits bared to the wind.

My breath wooshes from my lungs in shock, and I look up into the glaring brown eyes of Tris' older brother, Troy.

"Don't you have some stray animal to save, *rat*," he spits onto the ground beside me, nearly hitting the patched, cotton dress spread around me. Quickly getting to my feet, I dust off the hay and dirt, standing eye to eye with him, his sister staring in shock from behind him with her dress still pulled up around her waist.

"Don't *you* have any other females you need to harass besides me?" I wipe my wet fingers, tucking myself back inside my dress and stepping up to him until we are nearly nose to nose.

Why should I be afraid of him? Because he has a cock between his legs, and I do not?

"I will never waste my time on you, *rat*." Again, he spits on the ground, but this time he hits my faded, worn boots. The boots that used to be my sisters.

I hear Tris whisper behind him, "She *made me*. I didn't like it, Troy. You must believe me!"

I glare at the pair as Tris follows Troy out of the stable and into their backyard, glaring at me momentarily.

It isn't until I'm storming out of the barn that I realize my breathing is labored and my fists are clenched.

I will not cry. I will not cry.

The times I have kissed and fondled Tris were too many to count, but all in secret. She can lie to her family all she wanted, but I knew what she sounded like when she came. If she didn't like it, she willn't have been begging for me to finish her off before church was over last Sunday.

Thomas planned to wed me off to Troy, likely because the Morgan's were the wealthiest family in this town.

When I was young, my big brown eyes and unkempt hair—rarely having clean water will do that do a girl—proffered the nickname *rat* from Troy and his asshole friends. The next generation of men in line to join the brethren, the ones in charge of the church and this town.

I feel the tears sting my face, and I sniff them back with a swallow until my face is composed again. I walk back inside the barn, picking up the small green book from the floor, and tuck it safely under my arm.

Silently, I trudge down the dirt path to our house, my belly full of anxious flutters as I approach the door. I reach for the handle but hover over it as if I considered turning around and going...

Where?

The door opens before I can even make sense of my thoughts, and my sister Clarise stands in front of me with a concerned look on her face. "And to think, that was just a thing of the past—an awful history! This! This is bullshit!"

She shoves past me, hurrying down the pathway that weaves between the other small cottages where we live. Surely, she is off to her *secret* boyfriend's house. Only, it wasn't a secret, my mother is aware.

I pass through the door, eager to check on the two stray cats I rescued when I was thirteen. If I didn't feed them, no one else will. I named them Thyme and Rosemary.

"She is fornicating before marriage, Sophia. It is a sin

against God. I shouldn't need to explain this to you! This will bring more bad luck, and that includes lack of coin. She must be stopped!" Thomas stands beside the main table with his hands braced on top of it.

"Stopped? *How?*" My mother's voice is soft and gentle; it is just her way. Even in an argument, she is genial.

Thomas raises his fixed stare from his hands to my mother, standing opposite the table. "There's a witch among our people, and they must be found. How about we start with Clarise, eh?"

I swallow, a knot in my stomach dropping like a stone.

"What's the matter? Has something happened?" I held my hands behind my back, waiting to be dismissed. It is uncommon for women to be involved with any politics or decisions, but I pried anyways.

"Another boy has gone missing. I knew when I came to this town I was needed. There is a rotten crop among our harvest, and we must get rid of it before it poisons this whole town." His eyes are fixed on me, and my cats appear out of nowhere, winding between my ankles and rubbing against my legs. My cheeks redden, thinking back to my own discretions back at Tris' barn.

"I will be speaking in the square tomorrow to announce the curfew. We must take drastic measures if we do not want to lose another innocent life." Thomas turns toward the stove, giving himself another heaping helping of greens and sitting back down at the table.

"Curfew? What is a curfew?" I bite my lip and churn my hands behind my back.

His eyes do not leave his plate, but he stops chewing and thinks for a moment. "You will not be allowed out of this house after dark unless you have an errand and a chaperone."

The throb that lingers between my thighs turns into an ache as I stand in the middle of the room, crossing my legs.

Nearly every night, I snuck out of the house to meet up with Tris, usually carrying bread and cheese with me. Tris and I will trade gossip of the men and women, followed by deep kisses and dry humping until we exhausted ourselves on top of one another.

If there is a curfew put into place, how will I ever see Tris? I can not just ignore this gnawing inside my chest—this urge to be near her, to touch her. An urge that felt like a shadow mocking me from the dark corners of the room, and if I took my eyes off it for a moment, it will consume me.

Perhaps this is my punishment from God...never feeling her lips on mine ever again.

CHAPTER 6
FREYJA

This cabin, these woods, are my home. The wind whispers through the trees as the creatures of the land flock to me. It is a rare day to pass that I did not make a new furry or feathered friend.

I rip thick pieces of buttery bread from the loaves, spreading them throughout the forest floor. My dress drags along behind me, the heavy material sweeping the dirt at my bare feet.

It will not be long before the ground is frozen at the frigid blusters of winter. I already gathered the necessary stores I will need: wood, food, and herbs.

It is time to retreat and rest.

I've always have the ability to travel to lost souls in need of comfort, and in return, I will observe their treasures, recreating them with my magic when I made it back to my home. A talent that made it so I am never without.

As I walk along the borders of my land, the ravens begin to gather, carefully at first, but once an unkindness gathered, they all joined.

"Ah, my pets. I see you come hungry. Are there no dead animals for you to feast upon today?" I say, speaking to the two larger ones who often visited my backyard. I throw them both two large hunks, and they caw sharply in response at the same time. "Good boys. You have certainly outlived your feathered friends, my pets."

I continue my walk along the footpath that has formed from years of walking inside these woods with my father. Even after he left, I maintained the tradition on every new moon, casting my wards anew and manifesting the gifts to come.

I circle back to the cabin, where Garm surely waits for his breakfast. For a foraging-savage beast, he regularly relied on me for his meals and my mulled wine. He is all I have since mother and father sailed to the Americas, taking my younger sister with them.

And you have me as well; I am always with you, my child...

I smile at her voice, impeding my thoughts in times of need.

It is the voice that never left me, the woman who showed me what it is to wield the powers I have, teaching me exactly the way a mother should.

She will never leave me.

"Freyja! Freyja! Gods be damned...where is tha' girl." Garm stands outside, at the back of the cabin, shouting my name with a cross look on his hairy face.

"Hush, hush...I am here, I am perfectly well." I hold the basket tucked under my arm out for him to take filled with the herbs and two rabbits from my traps.

I pat him on his muscled arm, walking past him and into my fenced garden. Shutting the gate behind me, I inhale the sweet scent of lavender and roses. I kneel beside a small patch of tomato seedlings, running my hands over the top and chanting a spell. The seedlings sprout almost instantly, and I smile.

I walk to the one thing my father left behind, a chill crossing over me as I ease myself into the braided hammock. My father is a master at knotting and strung this hammock for my mother when she was pregnant with me. It was the only way she can sleep at night.

I close my eyes, envisioning my life with them before they left. My sister, my best friend, and the one person who shared the woman's voice within us. We vowed never to tell, but it was not long before my father sensed something was going on when late one night, he found me naked and writhing in bed.

"Fee! Wake up! Wake up!" my father screamed at me, my body lifeless in his hold. It was only when he smacked me across my face that I returned to my body, gasping for air. My eyes were wide and scared, and my father, relieved that I was alive. "What happened, father? Who was that man? It was as though I was no longer here...I was somewhere else entirely." He held me close and whispered into my ear, "Don't ever leave your body again, there will always be a chance that you will not return."

My eyes open, the memory making me wince. I sit up, letting my emerald green eyes scan over the years of hard work...my garden.

I still leave my body, and I'm not sorry.

I had become a powerful woman with magical powers because of those travels, and I will do it all again, given the choice. I craved the blood sometimes, the soul sacrifice that only seemed to add to my magical gifts.

I have my watchdog now, and he will never allow my vulnerable, sleeping form to come to any harm.

"What now, of the boy? Whoever Thomas has with

him is hidden well. There are many small towns around the outskirts of these woods."

Garm bellows as he enters the garden gate, now standing in front of me with his arms crossed over his barrel chest.

I stare down at my blackened fingertips, a stark contrast to the silver and jeweled rings I wore on my fingers. "Do not fret, he will come. The Mother commands it, and so it will be."

CHAPTER 7
CHARITY

"We must keep a clean *cunny* if we want to stay closer to *God*," Clarise mocks Thomas' words behind me as we walk up the hill and toward the community garden. Of course, he will never, ever say *that* word, but Clarise mocks him with it.

I roll my eyes and lift the hem of my dress so I don't trip. The garden looks overgrown and dull, with not many vegetables viable enough for food. The few herbs in the upper right corner have done well, mostly because they are mine. I watered them daily and spoke kind words to them before I took my leave, sharing stories from my days...and nights.

"He didn't *really* say that Clarise. He said, 'Clean mind, closer to God.'"

"Perhaps that's what you heard, but I heard different. I bet that man has the vilest thoughts of all, his guilt projected onto all of us—the *young ones.*"

I giggle. "Clarise!"

She sits beside a small patch of daisies, taking a soft

roll of bread and cheese wrapped in a towel from her dress pocket.

"You didn't," I chide, both hands on my hips looking down over her petite frame.

She cocks an eyebrow. "Oh, I certainly did. Sit."

I do as she tells me, my belly too empty to argue.

"Breaking *all* of the rules...you better ask for forgiveness," I said, raising one eyebrow and breaking a small piece of cheese from the lump.

Clarise lets out a puff of air through her thin lips, shoving a piece of bread far too big to fit into her mouth.

"Afternoon, ladies!" a sweet, lilting voice calls from behind us.

I look over my shoulder, hardly believing my eyes.

Tris sprints up the hill, her skirts ruffled in her hands, her lush thighs peeking out from beneath.

As if she hadn't betrayed me just the night before.

The wind moves her sun-kissed hair gently in the breeze, and she's wearing a new corset under her tightly hugging dress. I can tell just because her tits spill triumphantly over the top in a way I have never seen before.

My sister gives me a long stare, but I turn away, cheerily waving over my friend.

I truly suffer a weakness for her, and I pray to God silently to take it away.

When Tris is seated, I stare at the plump mounds spilling over her low neckline, and I can feel my lips twitch and my mouth begin to water.

What I will give to see one released, so I might capture it in my mouth.

I snap my eyes back to her face, and she is smiling sweetly at Clarise.

Clarise gives a generous sigh and begins to stand.

"Well, I'll leave you to it..." she eyes us both but keeps her eyes locked with mine as she smooths her skirts to stand.

I'm not sure if she knows about us, but I have an inkling she knows my feelings.

"Good morning, Charity."

"Good morning, Tris." I smile, looking around her shoulder to make sure my sister has disappeared down the hill.

I reach for her, eager to feel her mouth on mine, but she pulls away.

"I need to talk with you...and I know this isn't going to be easy to say," she says, her blue eyes shining brightly through her thick lashes.

"Easy? What do you mean? Do you not want to be my friend anymore?" I ask in a panic.

"It's not that...I...I'm engaged to be married, and *this* cannot continue." She scootches back a little on the grass, and I look down at her small hands, a gold band with a pin-pricked gem at the top, sitting on her left ring finger.

My voice catches in my throat, and I blink back tears. I know how foolish my reaction is; these illicit acts only began between us over the last year. But it takes the air from my lungs to think of her absence—no more stolen kisses or gossiping during chores. No more quiet walks through the garden complaining about all life lacked. The thought of not being with her every day made me feel as if I am falling.

Falling with nothing to catch me.

I smooth my skirts with my hands, unable to make eye contact with her. I am afraid I will break under her gaze, and I do not want her to know how much this is breaking me.

"Oh...okay. I understand. It must be the will of our Lord." I smile, taking her ringed hand. "I'm happy for you."

She smiles awkwardly and says, "I did...enjoy our time. I just think...it was sort of like practice for me. Do you know what I mean?"

I cringed slightly at the word *practice*.

If there is a sharp dagger between my breasts, she just turned it slowly, and now the ache begins to burn.

"Me too." It is all I can manage.

Tris stands, a sigh of relief leaving her chest. "I'm so glad you understand, Cher. I'll see you around."

She turns, running down the hill, a freedom in her step I didn't recognize. I hold back tears as the wind picks up.

If it is Tris' fate to be married off, I am sure I willn't be far behind her. I have a feeling Thomas has already secured an arrangement with her father, the Doctor.

If I am to be married to her brother, seeing her every day without being able to touch her is surely a punishment at the hands of God.

CHAPTER 8
CHARLES

"I cannot keep lying this way, even if it is God's will." I sit with steepled hands atop the meeting table inside Thomas' chambers.

"It is *not* just God's will. You are one of the chosen, are you not grateful?" Thomas says, tossing back a second chalice of wine.

"With all due respect, it will give me great pleasure to lead the church, but not at the price of a woman's life." I glare down at my hands, willing them to stay still and not shake.

"*They* are not women. They are demons inhabiting a woman's already extinguished soul. You are doing Him a service!" he yells, slamming down the cup on the small altar. "What you need to be thinking about, Charles, is the larger picture. The life in London, aligned with one of the most powerful men of our flock. willn't you find *pleasure* in that?"

I don't say a thing, only continue to stare at my hands while I give him a small nod.

Charity's round face and brown eyes come into view, her enchanting laugh and even more enthralling lips. I have an inherent desire to protect her since the very moment we met. Something perhaps unexplainable yet necessary. I will never let anything happen to her, even if it meant sacrificing myself in her place. I didn't need to be a respected man of the church; I can start a family and live a humble life somewhere else, somewhere far away from Thomas.

"Now, we will announce the lockdown at once, and tell everyone that they need to stay inside before dusk falls. We cannot go calling for witches to be burned if the town is not in anything less than a panic." He rests his fingertips on his lips, pacing around the small room until he stands in front of me. "Do you know of any… promiscuous, perhaps, curious girls?"

Charity immediately comes to mind, but I refuse to give him any inclination of my knowledge.

His breath is sour, and his face is far too close to mine for my liking. "Promiscuous? Sexually insatiable you mean?" I ask.

He nods, leaning his head back and raising his eyebrows.

Abruptly, I get up from the table, pacing just as he did earlier. My first thought darts back to Charity, all those nights I came to bed late, and I can hear her soft whimpers and moans. I shake my head no, but I don't meet his eyes.

He grabs me by my collar and shoves me against the back wall, my head slamming into it. "What did you expect to happen when you agreed to be ordinated? Did you think you will only need to sit on your knees and pray?" He seethes into my face, spit trickling down his beard.

Certainly not burning women. Here I thought Domenico is trying to help me.

Call me ambitious, but I wanted to use this opportunity to finance my way into a school for the Arts in France. Hailing from London, the only job that paid well is this one—appointed to me by the man who took me in. According to Domenico, it is an atonement for growing up in a brothel.

I'm shocked that Thomas' old, weathered body can lift a tall bloke like myself. I hold back the deep urge to push him off me and throw him to the ground.

"I didn't think it will involve punishment for sexual promiscuity, *father*." My voice comes out low and unrecognizable.

Setting me down, he turns, rubbing his mangled right hand with his left.

"Find one. And let me know who she is. Soon. I have debts to pay...a town to *save*." He grabs his jacket and leaves, the heavy wooden side door of the church slamming shut.

All I can think about is warning Charity not to sneak out anymore and do whatever vile things she is doing in the dark of the night.

I have seen her sneaking out, and everyone knew nothing righteous happens beyond midnight.

Did I think there were witches hidden among the women of this village?

No.

will I pin the murder of a boy on an innocent person? I can never.

So what is the real reason Thomas wanted these women persecuted and possibly *burned?*

I have a feeling it is far more personal than holy, and the only one who can shed light on this matter is Domenico.

CHAPTER 9

CHARITY

Reading lips has become something of a survival instinct for me, years of putting my nose where it didn't belong. Call it self-preservation, or maybe it is simply a survival skill.

My mother will scold me, and my father will encourage me. He had always wanted to stay one step ahead of the church and the gossip...always wary of following un-seen forces led by blind faith.

Charles and Thomas have been meeting privately at the church since the attacks, and what puzzles me is what business Charles has in the brethren's decisions since he is so young.

This is the second night in a row they met late at night, long after the sun has set.

Only the older members were allowed inside the Pastor's chambers, and since the death of the latest Pastor, the town has been anxiously awaiting a sign for a new leader of the church and the town.

It can't be Charles; he is far too immature to be

named a leader of the church, yet Thomas is too old. Isn't he?

Surely if they appointed either of them, they were all daft. I already have my doubts, and this decision will only solidify them.

And what will I do if that is the case? Leave? No woman makes it far without the companionship and voice of a man.

I creep up to the side of the church, careful not to kick up any gravel. I lean my ear against the heavy door, jerking back slightly as I find it slightly ajar. I poke my head into the open slot, listening and watching Thomas' lips move quickly.

"...cannot find out who we are. We must continue to lead and be righteous Champion's to God. You will tell the people that God has chosen me to be this town's new pastor as told to you by God Himself."

I pull back a little, hidden more by the shadow of the small roof, gasping in disbelief at Thomas' bold lie.

I stare intently now at Charles' face, waiting for his response.

"...I will not lie. There must be another way. Perhaps we can encourage someone else to say it by way of repayment or an owed debt."

"Now you're using your noggin, boy. Find out who is sneaking around at night, there is bound to be some pent-up teen with a tiger in his pants. Once you know, I will take care of the rest."

A carriage drives by, and the words that came next are lost to me at the distraction. I lean in a little further, eager to know what Charles' response is, but instead, I trip over my untied shoes and fall into the door and inside the room.

I stay like that for a full minute, not wanting to see the shock on their faces.

"Get her out! A woman's blood will erase every holy aspect of these chambers!" Thomas yells, and Charles is already helping me to my feet before he can finish yelling. Wiping the dirt from my palms, I back up and out the door, Charles firmly gripping my elbow.

"You're hurting me!" I shout as I jerk my arm from his grasp. He shuts the door gently behind us, and I watch as he brings his finger up to his mouth to shush me.

He walks up the dirt road toward our small home, waving me to him. His tight breeches hug his muscular thighs and I chastise myself for enjoying the view of his rear.

Perhaps I am full of the devil, these sexual thoughts occurring to me more and more since I started touching myself...touching Tris. I am a needy ball of pent-up sexual desire, just waiting to be explored.

I stand in place, scowling at him, but follow anyways since this is the most excitement I've had in days.

Stomping up behind him, I hiss, "What lies do you have to tell me, Charles? Or are you the good one and Thomas is the bad one?"

He strides towards me in two quick steps, and my breath catches, unsure of what he will do. Shoving his large hands into his pockets he growls,

"You need to ignore these...urges you have. I know more than you think and see more than you know," he looks around and behind us as if someone will be interested in this illicit conversation, "because I have them too, sometimes. But Thomas is hell bent on finding evil in this town...and he's using sex as a reason."

"Burn women as witches because of *sex?*" I let out a loud laugh, half out of terror and half out of disbelief.

He stops, a serious look crossing his face. "It's not funny. It's quite possible innocent women may lose their lives because of his outlandish beliefs. I'm not even sure the Deacon knows about Thomas' intentions..."

"The *Deacon?* So, there *is* more to this story."

"Honestly, I probably know as much as you do. I am trying to figure out if the old man is crazy or if he seeks vengeance. His passion over the subject makes me believe the latter."

I squint my eyes, the sun setting behind the forest. I wonder when Thomas will announce his wild claims and at what cost will come of it.

"Tell me, what *urges* do you have, *brother?*" I step closer to him, my heart thudding against my chest, and I swear it beats so loudly that he must be able to hear it too.

With his hands still deep inside his pockets, he takes my hand, his lips once again close to mine, only this time, the velvet in his voice sends chills down my spine. "Bringing pleasure to oneself is a sin, and so is sneaking around after dark to lay with another, unmarried. But this...," he moves my hand to the hard outline of his cock beneath his breeches, "this is what you do to me...and it is something I must ignore."

My cheeks burn, and my nipples tighten. He turns from me, but not before dragging his blue eyes down over my lips. My hand slips from the spot, and my palm tingles with the need to stroke it just a little.

"You're saying we need to stop, then?" I ask, level. Desperately wanting to explore more of him...if only he will stop following the rules all the time.

He stops, turning back to me again. "Well, it seems we both have some things to work on."

I want to stomp my feet, tell him no, but the well-mannered girl I am always forced to be carries my feet dutifully to the house beyond us.

~

Everyone is gathered around the front of the modest church the next morning, awaiting the announcement of who will take on the new role of Pastor and town leader.

I wear the best dress I can find, a tattered blue floor-length piece that is cinched at the waist. Though I didn't have nearly the amount of money it cost for a corset, I have hand-crafted my own from some stretched fabric and twigs, giving me that curvaceous form I have only read about in literature. My pinched waist hid my plump thighs beneath the bell of my dress.

Although I will much rather be laying in front of the warm fire with my nose in a book, I am required to be present, as is everyone else who lives here. Not only did the pastor lead the town but reported directly back to London once every few months.

Becoming the pastor is a coveted role for many, but only those of the male faction.

My family never bothered with politics; my mother nothing but a homemaker, and my father brought home pennies running errands for the wealthier side.

After father became ill, Thomas arrived with a remedy for the sickness. Word has traveled quickly of the black death sweeping the countryside, and Thomas arrived as if sent from Heaven on a sturdy steed. The only catch is the heavy coin attached to the medicine, something my family can not afford.

Thomas took pity on our family and sat with my mother as my father's body faded away from fever. The comfort he brought to my mother remains still, but now his things were there, and my mother only looked back at me in defeat when I will meet her eyes with questions.

While we are taught as children to respect our elders and never speak out of turn, I will often bite my tongue until it stings. holding back the desire to tell this stranger to get out of our house—a home that has not yet grieved the loss of a husband and father.

"Fucking twat. I hope he chokes on a piece of bread someday with no one around to save him." Clarise steps up beside me, looking as beautiful as a just-blossomed flower. She smells like vanilla and is one of those girls who squeals over anything with more than four legs.

"I doubt we will be so lucky, we already lost one father, what are the chances we will lose another?" I say, adjusting my hood against the wet fog that has settled.

"We can kill him. I doubt anyone will miss him besides Charles. And I'm sure you can distract him..." she teases, elbowing me and wagging her eyebrows.

I laugh but shush her as Dr. Morgan steps up to the pulpit.

"Good morning, friends and family. I understand that everyone is very upset at the recent events over the last week. One boy who lost his life at the hands of a wild animal and another missing already. A memorial will be held for the boy tonight at the church, all are welcomed."

"Do you think he will name Thomas as Pastor? Or, perhaps, Albert? He has been vying for the position for yea—" she whispers before I shush her again, only louder this time.

Dr. Morgan continues with a prayer and a warning of the dangers of being outside alone late at night. A point I felt is obvious, he continued, "I will like to formally announce the new placement of pastor and leader: Thomas Bryce."

Everyone remained silent, most likely in shock at a renaming right in the middle of a tragedy like this. One we have never once experienced since I am alive.

I look around me at dirty faces and ripped clothes. It sickens me to think of the two families whose children were taken from them. The loss of my father was a pain I will never be able to express in words and nothing I will wish on my worst enemy. There were times I didn't want to move from my bed, days when mother wouldn't.

Thomas hobbles to the pulpit, looking old, wise, and as modest as ever. He was the perfect image of humility.

He makes a dramatic movement of the cross in the air above him and places his hands together in prayer. "Our God is a loving God, but at times can be a punishing God. While this death pains our hearts, we understand that God has a purpose. Perhaps these sacrifices necessary for us to continue to live and thrive."

A lump forms in my throat as I hear a woman wail.

Is he justifying these deaths through God? As if that will be of some comfort to a mother bereft her child?

"Protecting this town and its people is the only way we will ensure the safety of our wives and children.

Which is why I—we, have decided to place everyone in lockdown until further notice." Thomas sighs dramatically, the people moaning and arguing at the announcement.

He holds up a single leaf, bright orange and yellow. It is hard to make out from where I stand, but as he shows the crowd, he rotates with a solemn look on his face.

"Blood. Upon a single leaf found at the edge of the forest. You can see the discoloration. The work of a witch."

Gasps ripple through the throng of people, and I watch their faces of shock.

He speaks, following his outlandish statement, "Let us pray."

Everyone recites the Lord's Prayer in unison, and I turn away, suddenly overcome by nausea and sticky sweat.

A lockdown? What did that mean? We were never to leave our homes? The town?

All because of a turning leaf?

The ground pitches beneath me, and I stumble, my sister catching my elbow before I fall.

"What is it? Cher?" she asks, but her voice sounds far away and muffled. I close my eyes, suddenly feeling very sleepy. I will just rest for a while, then I will feel better.

Surely when I wake, I will remember this all as just a bad dream.

CHAPTER 10

FREYJA

She spoke to me mostly at night, The Dark Mother. The stealer of souls.

It is a huge responsibility listening to a Goddess. One must have a keen sense of reality—an inward acceptance of all one can be. I have reckoned with my demons and made friends with my nightmares. I welcomed all the blessings she bestowed upon me.

The Dark Mother gave me unconditional love.

A man has wandered into your wards, ready for your taking. He is one of them.

The end of my name is left in a whisper like the wind, forcing my eyes open. I sit up on the raised dais covered in furs and silk pillows of red and purple. Tucking my hair back over my naked shoulder, I light two red candles and two black. Picking up the gold candelabra, I walk with my robe draped around me—the finest woven silk from India, in colors only available to the wealthiest of patrons. A luxury I afforded through my magic.

I walk down the short hallway, lined with more woven carpets from Asaahn. I allow him to live because his gifts are abundant and worthy of my approval. I lick at my fangs, the sharp points grazing my tongue, sending a sting of pleasure down my spine. With my robe open, and the tips of my pink nipples exposed, I step outside into the night. My bare feet meet the cold ground and dirt, making me smile. I take a deep breath in, smelling his sweat already. I can feel him inside my wards, a small tickle at the back of my neck. My pupils double in size as I adjust to the dark night. Parting my mouth, I salivate at the smell of his fear. I drop the robe to the ground, the crescent moon washing over my glittering skin. I hold out the candles in front of me, lighting his way straight to where I stand. As he comes into view, the candlelight highlights his dark eyes and long beard first. Toe to toe, I smile, showing him the sharp fangs inside. He stares, unmoving, just focusing on my mouth and my breasts. His black coat and hat are covered with moisture from his long walk; it is a wonder the poor thing didn't drown.

He walks to me as though compelled, enraptured by my wards and pheromones.

"Come to me, sweet, lost soul." I say, opening my arms to embrace him.

"*Dem...on...bitch,*" he slurs into my neck but licks it all the same. "*Tastes...so sweet.*"

"Shh...hush. You are free now." I steady him by placing my hands on his shoulders, gently pushing him down onto his knees. He kneels before me, his head upturned, awaiting my next command.

He closes his eyes, a languid fluidity in his motions. Tears wet his cheeks as he licks his lips again, a hunger behind eyes that rival possession. His desire for me runs deeper than my spells, the forbidden fruit to a man of

Christ. Men denied the fleshy juice between a woman's thighs because of a purity unseen.

Pureness is a thing for fairytales and children.

"Lick." I command, spreading my legs apart for his mouth. With my hand curled into his wavy hair, his hat falls to the ground as I shove his face to my cunt, his slippery tongue eagerly wiggling up and down my slit. I gasp at the contact of his mouth to the little hill between my nether lips. Looking down over his wet face, I roll my hips over his nose, rubbing the sweet spot that throbs with need. I bare my teeth, fangs tingling and body humming.

I shove him onto the ground, my naked body on display above him. His eyes roam over my heavy breasts, nipples peaked. His cock is hard against his thigh as I crouch down over him, pushing my face into his neck, grinding myself into him. "Are you ready to die for this sweet cunt?" I whisper into his ear.

His face remains unmoving, his eyes wide with wonder. I lean back, my knees on either side of him, and look down over my torso to my pubis mound, cleanly shaven. Running my right hand down over my breast, I cup it but continue running my other hand down to my cunt. Spreading my lips slightly, I watch his face as he stares at it in awe, mouth agape.

The last thing he sees is the majestic contours of the female organ that births the very breath of life.

I circle the tiny hill with my middle finger, and he begins to drool. Bloodlust throbs inside my veins, and I can already taste the metal running over my tongue. I rear my head back and strike the main jugular artery that pulsates beneath his skin. My aim is perfect, for I feel the blood squirt into my mouth as I suck, swallowing over and over. I reach behind me and grab his stiff cock from his trousers, impaling myself until he cries out. He is larger in size than most of the men I have encountered over the years. I begin to suck again as I ride his cock until the pressure cannot build any longer, and I explode above him. I buck and scream over his corpse as blood decorates my face and neck.

I sigh, still seated atop him, replete.

I will leave his body here and tell Garm. He will get rid of him for me before morning.

Right now, I need a bath.

CHAPTER II

CHARITY

I wake to my mother and sister's worried faces. My mother holds a warm cloth against my brow, and as I peel my eyes open slowly, she smiles.

"Oh, Cher. We were so worried! Are you alright, love?" My mother's soft voice comforts my aching head, and her smell of freshly washed linens make me smile in return.

"I'm alright mum, I didn't eat breakfast this morning. I'm sure that was all it was." I feel warm and flush but sit up slowly, taking the tray my mother put together of stale bread and the last of our canned peppers. I knew it is the last because it is my favorite.

"Here is some tea. The neighbor brought some over." Clarise sets a chipped mug down on the tray like a royal with her pinky in the air. She has always wanted to visit the palaces in London but is humble enough to understand that is a far reach.

"Thank you both. I think I'll rest some more. I have plenty of books to read."

The last word I remember before I fall asleep is *lockdown*. I'm not sure why this word triggered me so physi-

273

cally. It felt like a solidification of my already less-than-desirable circumstances. I will never be able to openly care for Tris in a way more than friendship. It is a sin. Something people are damned to hell for, and I did not want to go to hell for all eternity.

Eternal damnation all because of a pulse beating between my thighs for both a man and woman.

A short burst of satisfaction for such a sinful crime. Father Patrick's voice slithered inside my ear as his hand slipped between my thighs.

That short burst of satisfaction is everything to me, and the one time I chose to confess out loud I am chastised...corrected.

The stars that lit behind my eyes with her fingers in my mouth. They exploded over and over until I rolled my hips against her thigh, panting like a wild animal and sweating just the same. Those moments were my most cherished ones, and I wasn't ready to give them up.

The thought of coming into Tris' sweet mouth has me squirming under the covers after my mother and sister leave.

After Charles' warnings, it made it all the more difficult not to think about the pleasure I am able to give myself with just a flick of the wrist.

The forbidden is thrilling; it created an illusion that the idea is more exciting than the act itself. I pull my hand between my legs, dragging my thin undergarments up with it until I reach the warmth between my thighs, pulling aside my panties, my lips ready and wet with fantasies of Tris, as my slit meets my fingertips with eager need. I sink one finger slowly inside, my breath hitching at its firm entrance. One more finger follows the other as I roll my hips up to meet it. I whimper, needing to be filled by more than just two fingers, but not brave enough yet to try. Pulling out both, I skitter over my sensitive nub, my hips jerking at the contact. I try rubbing it gently, but I feel as if I will wet myself if I continue stroking. Instead, I flick it, sending jolts of pleasure through my body before I reach for the wooden doll beneath my pillow. The paint faded from all the times the foreign object entered me, bringing me to orgasm over and over again. I slide the doll down the length of my body, finding the tender spot that I wanted to be filled.

"Jesus, Mary and Joseph! What are you doing!?" Thomas' graveled voice rips through my cloudy fantasy. I pull the covers up over my half-naked body, the book that laid across my chest falling to the floor at his feet.

Clutching the blankets to my chest, I watch in horror as he roars, tossing the book into the fire at the foot of the bed. I gasp, and he turns to me, looking down over my body in silence. His face is that of shock, which must have matched mine.

With a hard, abrupt motion, he strikes me with the back of his hand. My head is tossed to the side as I whimper, grabbing my stinging cheek.

His eyes are dark, sweat trickling down the side of his forehead, a slimy rivulet of hate.

Wiping his forehead with the back of his arm, he's out of breath from the exertion and says, "Now you must repent. Ten hail Mary's and fifty our fathers." He turns, slamming the door behind him and leaving me in a pile on my bed sobbing—a mess of confusion and shame.

****

After a lukewarm bath, my body still feels as though I have been injected with poison, slowly seeping its way through my blood and curdling my soul. I vomited directly after his outburst, feigning something rotten I must have eaten when my mother asked my what is really going on.

I can never tell her.

How can I take away my mother's false sense of security so selfishly? She is happy, and I have not seen him raise a hand to her. I want her to be happy, regardless of my misery.

I still think he is rotten...a rotten root of a man hiding behind God's protection.

I flip to the page in my favorite book where Miranda accuses her love interest of rape, and he is thrown into prison forever.

Although I am no galloping nun...so perhaps no one will even believe me.

I only need confirmation of my marriage to Troy from Thomas, no doubt, because his father is one of the most wealthy and powerful men in our town. It will not only gain Mr. Morgan as an additional ally but will unload Thomas' responsibility of me anymore.

It's the middle of the night now, and Clarise is snoring on the bed beside mine, the candle on the bedstand flickering dimly as the warm wax pools around the wick. Sitting up, I grab the candle by the handle and crouch on the floor beside my bed. Looking over my shoulder, I arch my neck to see my sleeping sister's body. Satisfied with the small amount of privacy I have for a moment, I grab the hand mirror from under my bed and bring it to my face.

My cheeks are streaked with red from crying. Swollen patches under my eyes match my puffy, red lips. I have always been a little bit plain, with fair skin and brown hair. My sister is blessed with the blonde hair of our father to match her fair skin, creating a luminous sunshine that beams from within her when she smiles.

I feel jealousy creep up my cheeks, but I swallow it down—I loved my sister and didn't want to leave her sarcasm and jests behind.

I will have to marry a man I don't love very soon, move away from the only comfort I've ever known, and deny my true feelings for a girl I've cared for since I was a child.

I begin to sob again, understanding the weight of my next choice.

What am I going to do? Sit here and sob? I prayed to God every single night and saw no help, no pity. It must be because I am a sinner, and I do not deserve to be happy. Only how can that be true? I help mother with chores without argument. I care for the garden every day, even when others refuse. I sat by my father's bedside night after night when he was sick and dying.

Am I doomed to hell all because of a few small indis-cretions?

It cann't be; I willn't accept it. If God isn't going to help me, then I will help myself. I need to come up with something.

Thomas may have shown up here with a plan, but I can devise a plan of my own.

I will find out what is really going on from Charles, he

will know, and he will tell me. I've seen the way his breathing quickens when he looks at me. The way his pupils grow larger when his eyes meet mine. Perhaps Charles and I can run away together. Find a nearby town to take pity on us. I laugh to myself as I entertain the forbidden idea of Charles and I starting over somewhere new...together.

I wonder if Charles really thought a witch is behind it all; he is the one who told me about the succubus woman and the wolf.

If it is *really* a witch, will he want her killed? Burn her alive?

I shiver at the thought of a human burning alive, my brain is unable to comprehend the pain of fire consuming a body from toe to hair.

Tomorrow, I will get Charles alone and get him to talk.

Perhaps the pest isn't a witch at all, but a man. Thomas can try and get rid of me, but not if I get rid of him first.

CHAPTER 12

CHARLES

This sham of a family is quickly eating away at me and my spirit. If it weren't for the debt—the debt I owe to Domenico for saving me—I will have left by now. I have to focus on my mission, and I willn't be able to do that if I continue obsessing about Charity and the soft curls that wisp around her face so perfectly. She is as fragile as an open wound; it felt as though I may destroy her with just one touch.

Part of me wanted to take her beneath my body and show her what it is *truly* like to be touched by someone. I want to destroy her in the most beautiful way, break her open and explore her from within.

Did she feel the same way about me? Did she wonder what it will feel like to have her body pressed against mine?

It wasn't long before a letter from Domenico came following Thomas' announcement. Thomas' suspicions of witches are his own. Domenico is looking for someone in particular. Someone who I knew little about, only that I will know it when I saw her.

You must journey into the woods without Thomas and draw her out. Bring her to the tall house beyond the river, and I will be there...waiting.

"How will I know?"

"You will just know."

I laugh to myself, thinking back on our conversation before Thomas and I set out to Bethlehem.

My futile response is an attempt to call off the search, but in the end, I only ended up agreeing.

Weak.

After all, Domenico is the very reason I am alive.

There are no signs of witches in this town, and I believe that Thomas will only make us look suspicious to the people here. I have met women who read and others who have been allowed into the church at an older age. This does not align with our task at hand. I encourage you to pull Thomas from this place and insert him elsewhere. I will remain, continuing our endeavor to find the one you seek, even if it means I must enter into the woods.

"And you may need to do just that."

When I finish penning what I believe to be a straightforward, albeit vague, letter of communication to the Deacon,I sit back in my chair, studying my hands—long, dexterous fingers with veins that begin to fit the hands of a grown man. I was soft when I was a boy, one who is meant for love, romance, and poetry. My mother will chase me away with paints and paintbrushes to the House Madam. I will swish deep paint strokes of red and blue to the soft moans of pleasures that belonged to my mother and her lovers. A symphony of sighs and moans as I painted, creating an art piece that left a bulge in my pants.

The night she was killed, I was auctioned off like

cattle to a man with sad eyes and gaunt cheeks. Domenico—the Deacon—stepped in, insisting I was being called to God. I was to leave with him and enter an honest and clean life of worship.

I never knew my real father anyhow, and since my mother was a French courtesan, it was likely I will have grown up following the same path as her. No longer a virgin by the young age of twelve, I developed my height and thickness somewhat quickly. A curvaceous, older woman milked my cock at the request of my mother, so I can *'just get it over with already.'*

I begged her not to make me, but she insisted, sighting it as a distraction that will keep me from my everyday tasks.

She wasn't kind or patient, and that was the day I realized how selfish she really was.

I didn't realize just how much of a distraction sex will end up being—I hadn't stopped fucking until the night my mother was murdered.

There was no sympathy for the son of a whore.

I am thankful for Domenico and everything he has taught me. He

saved me from a life of sin and sex; therefore, this is the path I will continue to walk on.

Painting and erections be damned.

This is my true path. The righteous path that will lead me to my destiny; it is the reason Domenico was there that night; God told him so.

The thought of the many courtesans I bedded has my cock growing hard against my leg, and I close my eyes, fighting back against the urges.

My mind wanders back to a fair-skinned dame, tits swinging into my face as she rode me, groaning my name and begging me noy to stop. I grimace, forcing my hand to stay where it is, clutching my left knee. My leg begins to shake, but I redirect my thoughts to Domenico and his holy work.

The moment doesn't pass, and I decide it's probably time to lie down.

The door to Charity's room slowly opens with Charity standing in the shadows as I observe from the dimly lit table just down the small hallway. Grabbing a pack and her cloak, she quietly opens the front door and disappears outside.

What in the bloody hell is she doing? I warned her to stop this...stubborn as she is.

I quietly scoot back my chair, standing up and following her out before the door even closes.

"Get back inside, Charity." The sternness in my voice surprises me, but I stand firm in my rigid posture.

"Go away, Charles. You're annoying me." She huffs, tucking the satchel under her arm and beneath the cloak, continuing down the steps.

The crickets chirp happily, and the smell of wet grass and moss fill my nose. Breathing in a gulp of air, I follow behind her, quietly closing the door.

The moon only lights the ground in spots, and I find myself struggling to keep an eye on her as she expertly darts from house to house in the shadows. I stop for a moment, watching her. One can see for miles from atop the hill with a little light. I observed her nightly patterns while I silently watched from the shadows. She liked to pretend that she is compliant, well-mannered even, but just as I am afraid of—she is quite the opposite. She is cunning.

I settle against the outer wall of our tiny house,

knowing damn well I will never give her to Thomas without a fight.

I watch as she stops at the Morgan's house, disappearing into the attached barn.

You sly little minx. Visiting Troy's little sister...I knew I saw them watching each other a little too carefully at the church gathering a week ago.

I didn't need to stick around to see what she is up to; I already knew. But something kept me standing where I am, a need to protect her.

I scan the rows of pale white and stout cabins with chimney smoke puffing from the tops. Did I believe there are truly witches roaming these lands? Perhaps not, but it didn't hurt to keep a watchful eye for whatever it is— witch or beast.

I keep a sharp blade in my boot, just in case. I've been in scrapples before, but not with the likes of a creature with sharp fangs and nails.

The thought sends a shiver down my spine.

I will wait until she is finished, then I will see her home.

It seems like a beast will be the worst thing to find her out here, vulnerable and hardheaded, but now I think that's not true.

Thomas will be.

CHAPTER 13
CHARITY

I know Charles is following me; I am well aware of my surroundings. *Let him.*

Perhaps I can show him what true bollocks look like.

I knock softly on the barn door and wait, but Tris doesn't come.

I tell myself this will be the last time, and I will tell her that as well. One more night of pleasure, and maybe this time, she will touch me. My body yearns to know what it feels like to have her fingertips trace the hallows of my body. My cunt throbs and I squeeze my legs together, the anticipation of her touch overwhelming my body.

This is silly—pathetic even. She told you she didn't want this anymore. Go home, and be the boring girl they all want you to be. It will be so much easier.

There is a small chance she will even answer, and I know there's also a chance her father or brother might catch me.

I didn't care; I have to try at least once more.

Do I tell her I love her? That I desire her so much, I don't think I can be without her?

The questions flash through my mind, but I've already made my decision, and there is no turning back now.

My stomach drops, and I swallow, looking at the surrounding woods, menacing and black. I watch closely for any signs of movement, but I know my eyes are playing tricks on me when I think I see a shadow crouching low beside a large willow tree just at the forest's edge.

A small shiver crawls down my back, but I shake it off. I am no longer a small child who can be scared by fables and fairytales.

Just as I turn towards the dirt path leading away from Tris' house, a man's shouts assault my ears, "Witch! Witch! I have seen a terrifying, blood thirsty demon woman!"

I tighten my grip around the hood of my cloak and watch as the man falls at my feet, sweat staining his ripped shirt. He grabs at the bottom of my dress, nearly pulling me to the ground with him.

Charles charges us both, slipping from the shadows of the house next door, and I jump back as the man sinks down beside me to his knees.

"Get yourself together, Callum! Tell me what it is that you saw."

Charles shouts at him, helping him to his feet.

The man is gasping for air, and I absentmindedly step back, eyes wide.

"She was naked...and deep within the wood, I only went in to find John...to help him...I...I heard his screams. He went too far, and it started to get dark..."

Charles turns to me and nods towards the house. I know he is silently telling me to get home, he doesn't want me to hear what the man is about to tell him.

I take the path, looking back over my shoulder as I do, walking as slowly as possible.

A naked woman? In the woods? The man was daft!

I don't believe it for a second, especially since there hasn't been a report of witches in decades, and I know there is no woman in this town brave enough to venture into these woods after the attacks.

Charles leads the man by his arm back up the dirt path to our house. I look behind me, towards the large barn that belongs to Tris' family. No one is there.

This is my sign to give up, to let go of whatever it is between us. A small part of the past now.

We are met at the door by Thomas, who has clearly heard the man's screams.

He narrows his eyes at me, and I cast mine to the ground, not wanting to make eye contact with him...ever again. I hurry inside and past him, hoping the commotion and Charles will be enough to distract him from my curfew breaking.

Thomas steps outside and closes the door behind him, more interested in what is happening with hysterical Callum.

I quietly take off the new cloak I borrowed from my sister—a gift from her lover.

The front door is bracketed by two small windows, and I pull back

the rough curtain, watching the three silhouettes in conversation, the man from the wood's voice panicked and high.

I press my ear to the window, but I can only hear the

terror in the man's voice and Thomas' low, muffled words.

Suddenly, all three men are marching inside our house, and I run to my room. Cracking the door slightly, peering into the living area, and listening.

Thomas enters first, followed by the man who is clearly out of his wits, his black coat trailing the floor as he walks to the large table in the middle of the room and sits.

Charles enters last, and he walks toward my door. I leap onto my bed and feign sleep, Clarise already snoring in the bed beside me.

I see his shadow blocking the light that creeps in, but he doesn't shut the door.

Once the light in the small crack returns, I hop off my bed again, my nightgown billowing around me as I land on the floor and run back to my listening spot.

I push my ear to the crack, so I can hear everything.

"I swear it, I swear on our almighty God—I saw her... covered in blood that dripped down her neck. It was too late for him, so I just ran...I ran as fast as I can and didn't look back. She was a demon...I can smell the sulfur in the air."

There is a brief silence, then Charles' soft voice, *"Are you sure? Absolutely sure?"*

I move my ear, replacing it with one eye, and I watch as the man clutches his hat to his chest, nodding slowly.

Thomas rubs his forehead, one elbow resting on the table, and he looks at Charles.

"It is time to bring back the witch hunts—clearly. God has sent Callum straight to my doorstep, we need to act...now."

Charles looks at the floor and back to my door; he knows I'm listening. *"I will go...tomorrow at first light. I will find her, and I will bring her back..."*

Thomas watches Charles' face, almost puzzled but runs his hand through his beard and nods. *"Alone? You should take someone with you."*

"No. I will do this on my own. I am not afraid of a woman; I have God's protection."

Thomas nods, *"Yes, It is Gods will, and so it will be done."*

CHAPTER 14
CHARLES

"I'm coming with you, if anything, to prove how foolish your father really is. A *demon woman?* Do you know how crazy that sounds? Maybe a wolf or a mountain cat, but not a *possessed* woman. It's ridiculous!" Charity says, following me through the quiet house after Thomas is already in bed. I hear a disdain in her voice I never have before.

Did I think the man is telling the truth? Perhaps.

Is it more likely that I will pass through the woods, give up, and turn back?

Whatever the case, if I found a mad woman—naked or not—I will need to bring her to Domenico first.

He will be waiting.

"Why were you sneaking around at the Morgan's house? I thought I told you to stay inside?" I grab her arm roughly, something I have done a lot lately. Feeling a need to control her, not wanting her to run from me.

She looks down over my hold, incredulous. "Let me go, I don't want to hear what you have to say. You're just as crazy as they are."

I follow behind her to her bedroom. "Please, just sleep on this, and we will talk more in the morning."

"Fine, I'll sleep on it, but I'm coming with you." She stands inside her room, looking like a disheveled angel in her white nightgown, and I must keep myself from reaching out and stroking her cheek.

"Cher—"

She shuts the door in my face, and I'm left standing there, alone.

I walk to the cot at the back of the house, and I find myself staring up at the exposed beams, thinking about my mother and the life I lived with Domenico before I came here.

The Church was his home back in London, and it was amongst one of the most modern architectural structures in the city.

His chambers alone took up a good portion of the second floor, and my room was just off his, with murals of angels and clouds decorating the ceilings. The furnishings were velvet and silk, and deep red tapestries with gold edges draped across the windows. I wish for a moment I can show Charity just how beautiful the world is on the outside of this small town. I imagine the amber around her eyes shrinking, the blacks of her pupils expanding at the sights. I close my eyes, letting that look of shock that will surely cross her face fill me. I have seen things she may never get to witness in her lifetime, and it pained me to think of the sheltered life she will live once I left here.

What is the harm in her joining me? Did I think I will stumble into the woods and find a woman possessed?

Not likely.

But did I also know there were creatures lurking outside, waiting to eat us alive?

Certainly.

I scrub my face, feeling the weight of her words. She wasn't wrong; everything the man said tonight sounded insane, but I have to remember my purpose here:

Look for the signs, follow them, and rid this world of the daughters of Lilith. It is my mission in life.

Domenico was adamant that these women were still in existence, showing me photos in books of the woman known as Lilith. He has seen her himself when he was a lad, a woman so monstrous and terrifying he went crying for his mother.

If their existence was real, and I was able to bring even one back, the payment for such a woman will have me set for life, never wanting for a thing. Then I can decide if I wanted to stay and serve God forever. It was not something I had taken lightly before, but after meeting Charity, my choices simply weren't as clear anymore.

I shut my eyes, praying to God for guidance, not only for strength to face the possibility of facing Lilith's kin— but for resisting Charity's innocent, soft body.

CHAPTER 15
CHARITY

I stop, looking inside the cave of tall trees. Nothing but darkness, bark, and pine-covered roots. My blood runs cold.

"Stop. Charity, you are being senseless." Charles stands firmly in place, blocking me from the entrance into the tree line. Surely waiting for me to realize my foolishness at the idea I can accompany him on his mission, let alone stop him. Turning back in fear.

Only I didn't.

"Blasted women's movements." He curses under his breath, hands on his hips.

When I packed my things to leave, I recited the Lord's prayer repeatedly. I knew that if my faith were strong enough, God will protect me. God will always make sure his faithful children were protected. Although, I am beginning to have doubts after Thomas' crude actions the night before.

I also have doubts after seeing the mangled body of the child they found, even though my mother insisted I not be a part of the burial that rainy morning. She said there is no benefit in seeing the body of an innocent child gone too soon...she told me it will haunt me forever.

Surely those missing children simply forgot where their home was, stumbled upon a den of wolves, and paid the price.

Going with Charles will put an end to this nonsense, and the threat of the witch hunts beginning again.

I packed the few things I thought I will need: what food I can, a flint, a blanket, and a flask of water. It willn't take me long to prove there is nothing to fear, and we will be back before nightfall.

I want to return the book Tris gave me and tell her of our plan.

She is still my friend; engagement be damned.

I fantasize about Tris begging me not to go, perhaps declaring her love for me when I return...my heroic bravery sending her running into my arms.

I smile to myself.

"I will like to visit Tris' before we leave," I say, wishful thinking refusing to let her go fully. She didn't want me. If anything, I should tell her I don't want to be her friend anymore. I willn't be anyone's *practice*, I am worth more than that.

"You're *not* coming." He grits out, his own pack strapped beneath his arm.

"Listen, you know it's dangerous for only one person to go out there. What if something did happen? You will need me to find my way back to get help. Besides, I know these woods better than you..."

He rolls his eyes, but I can see the realization cross his face that I'm right—he's only been here a year, and I have grown up playing inside these woods before all this tragedy.

"Fine, but we go in, and we come out. If there is no sign of a witch..." he falters, as if he's searching his mind for what those signs will be, "we come right back."

"Deal." I say, smiling.

He almost gives a smile back to me, but instead, walks up the dirt path towards the Morgan's.

I sprint to catch up to him, pleased with my convincing speech.

Gently opening the door, I ease myself into the stuffy barn. The crunch of hay under my feet makes my heart leap, a reminder of our nights alone together.

It reeks of scat and oats, and I try to hold back a gag. Looking behind me, Charles waits by the door...my own little lookout scout.

I sit on a hay bale and wait, knowing her chores are always done early morning.

I flip through the pages of *The Fair Jilt* and caress them as if they are a living, breathing thing. I hate to return it, I want to keep it, but I have to let go.

The morning is chilly, steam clouding around my mouth as I shiver.

She isn't coming.

In defeat, I leave the small tome on the bale of hay I sat atop. I kiss my fingertips and place them on the book.

My heart squeezes, and a sob forms in my throat.

Who am I kidding? She will never love me back.

I am a fool.

Goodbye, my friend.

"Don't you see? Thomas is in a hurry to marry me off to Troy and out of the house. One less mouth to feed. I will know that better than a pure and perfect *pastor* in training. You belong to the church, and to God...." I say, stopping just at the tree line of the forest's shadowy entrance.

I am angry—angry that I am forced to accept a new father, one that is nothing like my *real* father. Angry because I will never truly be happy with whomever it is I am to marry, because I don't want a man to touch my body the way I touched Tris'.

Charles steps up to me, meeting me at my height. So close that I can feel his breath on my nose. "That's not true, Cher. I am not yet ordained... I still have free will. I'm sorry that you don't..."

In the single year we have known each other, he never once spoke a harsh word to me, and I feel a little guilty for giving him such a hard time.

He avoided me mostly.

Only recently, we have begun to trust one another with jokes and secrets, and I began to look forward to seeing him each day.

If he ever left, I will miss him...

Is that why I *really* want to follow him?

He takes my hand inside his, warm and gentle. "I want you to come."

For a moment, tingles rush through my body, and my breath hitches at those simple words.

I look over his full lips, wondering what it might feel like to kiss him again. Only longer this time.

The wind suddenly picks up around us, forcing my hood off my head.

What a horrible, perverted thought, Charity.

He is the only boy I have ever had these thoughts about...

I turn from him, hoping he can't read my face. I want him to think I am unafraid and brave, but I'm not sure why.

I didn't doubt I can survive one night in the woods. I have a bit of dried meat and fruit...a knife. I can do it...I have to. However, I am not so sure I can do it alone.

It is time I did something constructive about this hysteria that is sweeping the town. In all honesty, I am growing weary of praying to God for help that never comes.

A small voice in the back of my mind silently makes a prayer that Charles will be braver than me.

The only weapon I have is a small hunting knife my father used to use to kill squirrels and racoons that made their way into our food stores...when we have any.

Charles may not be a hunter, but as I said, at least two minds were better than one. If we really did come face to face with a terrifying wolf, then what will we do?

"Wait! Charity, wait!" he shouts at my back.

For such a pretty boy, he sure did know how to shout. The memory of the night with Thomas in the dining room sends a shiver down my spine.

The leaves crunch under my frayed boots, and I lift my dress to gain some distance between us. I don't want to look at his perfect face right now, and for a moment, I wish he never came here with his decrepit pest of a father.

Thomas will lead our town into more worship of God

and less focus of the real problem of poverty and lack of trade. He will be sending us right back through time and further away from real changes.

It didn't help that night after night I cann't help but think about how Charles' soft lips will feel kissing between my thighs. I only ever entertained thoughts of Tris', and these sinful thoughts I had of him—the only boy ever—sent my body into multiple shuttering orgasms.

"Charity! Stop!" Charles calls, but I continue walking until I'm breathing heavily, my muscles burning with exertion. I'm not sure if I'm flushed because of the exercise or the filthy thoughts of him that continues to run through my mind.

When he finally catches up to me, I stop, bending at my knees, and gasp for breath. I'm thirsty, and hungry and don't have any real reason to be angry with him—other than these new, scary feelings.

It feels more like running away now.

My mother and sister must be aware of my absence, the sun rising higher in the sky, and my chores left unfinished.

"Maybe we should just sit here for a couple hours—then return. They will believe...that we came out here unscathed... and lift the lockdown." I struggle to get out the words, a sudden panic washing over me at the realization these woods aren't so familiar after all...

"Oh hell!" Raising his arms in an emphatic gesture to the sky. "She wants to turn back! Little girl has gotten scared! Do you really think it will be that easy?" He laughs in my direction, looking handsome against the backdrop of orange leaves and blue sky.

I glare back at him, wanting to continue on despite

him. He may have shown me kindness and been fun to banter with, but this...this is just rude—I am *not* a little girl.

I stride to him with purpose, shoving him hard once I reach him. He steps back, blonde brows furrowed. His tall, warm body feels solid under my itching palms, where they rest on his chest.

A few branches crack in the distance, echoing through the empty forest.

Getting in my face, leaning down only slightly, he whispers, "will you like me to fuck you right here, Charity? Take you down to the ground and lift your dress, pillage you until you scream out God's name? I know lust when I see it, and I have a feeling that will shut you up for a while."

My mouth drops open, his breath so close to my lips that if I tilted my head up just a little, our lips will brush.

Never hearing a curse leave his lips before, I bite my lip at the shock of it as though I have been smacked in the face. Perhaps that's what I want, the sting of his skin burning mine. Perhaps then I will have something tangible to cling to.

Maybe I did want that, and then I will finally be rid of this throb between my legs and the ever-foreshadowing virginity that seems to be used as a bargaining piece in marriages.

I take a step back, looking at my feet and the forest floor littered with leaves. Fall is here, and how foolish it is of me to think we can do this without incident.

"I.... I'm sorry Cher. I shouldn't have said that. I didn't mean it...I'm just scared. There really can be something out here, you must know that on some level. Somewhere inside that stubborn brain of yours."

He lifts his hand to my elbow, but I turn and continue walking into the woods, the tall trees creating the illusion of a never-ending landscape of green, orange, and brown.

"And how do I know you and Thomas aren't just making this entire thing up? Perhaps it is you who killed the boy. Panic is a powerful tool to use to control the masses." I say into the wind as he tries to keep up with me, walking beside me with a look of concern on his face.

My chest tightens, and just when I think I can't stand his presence anymore, he rushes in front of me, stopping me in my tracks.

Bending slightl, and as gently as a feather, his lips touch mine, lingering for a moment. His tongue wets my lower lip and I whimper, waiting to feel the pressure of his lips on mine, but it never comes.

His teasing has my insides wound tightly into a ball, and just one firm touch will have me undone. I squeeze my eyes shut, frustrated with the yearning that has begun for him. It no longer beats only inside my core but in my chest as well.

My face burns with the cold air shocking my cheeks with the absence of Charles in front of me. I open my eyes, watching his muscled back walk away again.

Where is he going? I want to turn back!

I guess maybe I am acting a bit confusing, the back and forth between wanting to prove something and wanting to run back to my bed and cower under the covers.

"Where are you going? What will we do?" I shout, half in a panic.

"WE are building a fire and making food. Hunger is the only reason I can think of for your—*erratic* behavior!" he shouts back to me, rolling up his sleeves.

I hold back the tears that threaten to breach my lids, and I fist my hands in anger at my own stupidity. This is the worst idea I've had since asking the previous pastor for a library. I was laughed at and quickly dismissed, given the excuse that women didn't need to read.

I am not one to think out the long-term of my decisions. It is something my mother always lectured me about. I rarely listened; I am too busy living a fictional life to avoid my very real one.

This will be fine; I sniff back my tears, deciding it will be far more practical to remain determined in my decision.

We can sleep tonight and wake for the morning refreshed and go back to the town, proving we were unharmed.

If we made it through the night.

CHAPTER 16

FREYJA

I wake up at dawn, her whispers caressing my neck, weaving lullabies inside my ears. There is unrest in these woods, the insects and creatures too silent. No owl softly hooting, nor the rustle of water on the rocks in the streams.

I close my eyes once more, my spirit lifting from my body in a weightless ascension. Keeping my eyes shut tight, they roll from side to side, eagerly awaiting the vision of who I will feed from next.

The weightlessness around me suddenly turns cold as ice, a shadow entering my mind before the girl.

She is blonde, with tightly curled hair and a smile that feels familiar.

I hover over her body, which is tucked into a pure white linen duvet. She looks innocent...that of a bright white light.

I slowly sink closer, smelling her lemon-scented hair and licking my lips. She did not smell of loneliness, sorrow, or desire...so how did I get here?

It is her—she is the one.

The one? The one of the prophecies?

I did not hear The Mother speak again, not until I turned to the window to see where exactly I was. This place looks familiar, as if I have been here before.

Turning to the window, I press my iridescent hand up to the glass, taking in the woods—my woods—sprawling out before me in the black of night.

It is the house where my mother lived.

Bryce Manor.

Turning back to the bed, I watch her as she sleeps, her beauty almost too perfect to be real. I reach out to touch her, and she is as cold as snow. Not once have I ever encountered the cold when I astral project. Warmth, sensuality, and fire all fuel my powers, and under my spell, I can seduce anyone—man or woman. Only something tells me my glamours will not work on this one.

Put whispers in her ear...so she will know.

I do as The Mother tells me, tenderly weaving the prophecy of Lilith's return into her mind, envisioning it whispering through her ears like a lullaby on repeat.

Her blue eyes shoot open suddenly as she grabs my throat with her steel-like grip.

I choke, instinctively smacking at her hand and closing my eyes, envisioning my sleeping body back where it lay in the furs inside my cabin.

I awaken suddenly, returned to my body, choking and gasping for air. I look down and my throat and chest are covered in small red bumps.

There is no other creature who has the power to slay me—the only other magical creature to exist in these woods is my grandfather.

She is not human.

Her voice never brought me fear, but this time, I feel a chill of uncertainty pass through me.

I quickly remind myself of the powers I hold within… there is no need to fear; I am powerful.

I light the candles on my altar to Lilith, refilling the chalice of red wine, and pray.

I pray for her to make me understand what role this girl plays and to tell me who she is…. what she was. I pray for revenge on the man responsible for my grandmother's death.

Closing my eyes, I admonish my gifts….

So mote it be.

CHARITY

The following morning, I wake up huddling against Charles' chest with his arms wrapped tightly around me. I squint up at him with one eye, and thankfully he is still sleeping. I shut my eyes again and allow myself to enjoy this one moment of privacy we have together, me inside his warm embrace. He smells of soap and pine.

I am rarely left alone with a boy, and I inhale his peppery musk, smiling to myself.

"Do you always wake up so cheerful?" His voice is thick with sleep, making me squeeze my eyes shut again in embarrassment.

I gaze up at him fondly from under the wool blanket, biting my lip. His gaze lingers for a moment, and I feel his hand squeeze my hip. I scoot my body closer to his, and in response, he moves his hand down to cup my bottom.

I allow myself to be drawn into this moment, unhindered by anyone's scrutiny. Moving his mouth down over mine, he blesses me with the pressure I wanted from his lips yesterday. It is a small kiss, ending with him pulling back from me and sitting up abruptly.

I shiver, wrapping the blanket around my shoulders, the cold air reminding me we are in the middle of the woods with the potential of a bloodthirsty beast at our backs.

I'm a downright fool, and I have followed Charles here at my own volition—blinded, stupid puppy love.

"I'm afraid I'm not even sure which direction we should be heading in at this point. Hunting and trapping were never my strong qualities." He scoots over to the pile of ashes from the fire last night, poking at the embers until they burn red again. Adding some small twigs and spruce needles, the fire ignites when he blows on one small ember at the center.

I am still shivering, and my stomach grumbles loudly. It had begun late last night, but I am too afraid to reach for my pack, wanting to save the small amount of food I carried.

Reaching for the satchel, I look inside to find it's empty.

"Fuck sakes. Did you eat the food I brought?" My chest burns, and my stomach aches, and at this point, I am far beyond what hunger felt like on a normal day.

"Sorry...I got hungry in the night. At least we have a fire..." He grins, his cheeks still pink from our encounter.

Selfish boy.

I throw down the satchel, raking my hands through my hair and standing. I pace back and forth near the fire.

We will have to hunt, and we need to kill something if we want to eat. I have my knife...I can kill a rabbit.

But can I catch one? I barely remembered my father teaching me how to set a trap, even the simple ones only involving string and a sharp stick—did I even bring any string?

My stomach grumbles again loudly, and I feel the panic seeping into my bones. I want to cry, to yell...to stomp my feet.

But I am a woman now, no longer a child. I need to calm myself, I didn't need Charles seeing me break so soon.

Warming my hands against the fire, I toss back the last of the water. If he ate the last of the food, then I am going to drink the last of the water. That will teach him.

Now neither of you has any water to drink.

"Let's keep walking. There must be a house or another town on the other side of this massive spider web of a forest." I stand, placing the water skin back inside the satchel, and roll up the wool blanket.

Charles looks over at me with his soft blue eyes and nods.

It seems as though he will do whatever it is I said, and as much as I didn't want to admit it, I liked that.

~

My feet throb, my calves burn, and it feels as though we've been walking for the entire next day...because we have.

I watch as the sun begins to make its disappearance

behind the trees, far earlier than it will have if we were simply at home, by a pleasantly warm fireplace.

Charles has a large walking stick now, his clothes covered in dirt and ash, giving him a wilder look than before. It made the side of my mouth twitch in amusement.

After staring for a while, he begins to resemble a bowl of sweet cream with a swirl of chocolate. I dare say he looks downright edible.

I follow slowly behind him, chastising myself for thinking these thoughts of him. Bloody hell, he is my stepbrother!

"What in the—"

"What, what is it?!" I sprint up beside him, clutching my skirts, terrified we will be looking at the demolished body of the missing boy.

"Bread... it's bits of bread..." Charles leans down and picks up a larger piece, sniffing it. "It's fresh..." He bites the hunk and closes his eyes as he chews. My eyes grow wide, and I search the ground for more, feeling ravenous.

As if someone has magically sprinkled the earth with food., just for us, I grab a hunk as well, biting into it— closing my eyes and licking my lips at the buttery crust, the dough melting in my mouth.

I groan. "These taste as good as candy! My God..." I grab up the largest bits I can find, shoving them into the satchel at my hip.

"I shall give Assahn's chef the compliments. Who knew humans will enjoy bread just as much as birds do."

The woman who stands before us is something straight out of one of my books. She is adorned with jewelry and cloaks of different colors, her black hair hanging past her waist, tied back in loose braids.

The robe she wears is embroidered with intricate patterns of roses and snakes; I have to blink a few times before I can even gather an intelligible response.

Ravens gather around her bare feet, feeding on the food she has obviously thrown about for them—not us. The largest raven I have ever seen perches upon her shoulder, its beady eyes watching us from the side.

Charles' face freezes in shock at the sight of her. Women from our town are not allowed to wear fancy jewelry or makeup...or even bright colors. This woman is like a beacon of everything a female is not supposed to be. I am sure Charles is shitting his pants at the sight of the ravens, a well-known bad omen from God himself.

"I...I... we're lost." I blurt out, unsure of how to speak to someone that looked like her.

"Lost? Poor darlings...come inside and get warm...I will take care of you." Her statement is simple, and full of confidence. She turns to look behind her as we follow, unobjecting.

I gawk at the trees and gardens, the different color flowers lining the house and the backyard like a bouquet of brightly lacquered lollipops. Everything looks as though it's sparkling, and I can't help but feel a childish wonder wash over me.

There is so much to take in, and I keep myself from exclaiming at the lush surroundings.

I elbow Charles as we follow her up the wooden stairs to the inside of her cabin, and he narrows his eyes down at me.

Perhaps he didn't view this place with the same wonderment as I did, but men were funny like that.

"But...how?" I gasp as we enter, and the house seems to triple in size.

Both Charles and I stand in awe, taking in the high ceilings and rows of bookshelves. Some are lined with dusty tomes, others lined with glass jars and boxes.

"Ah, you like? Something told me you might. This humble house of mine." Her voice is velvety smooth, with edges of sweetness to it like a rough caress. Her hair is a glossy black, with blunt bangs that hang above her emerald green eyes glittering beneath thick, black lashes. The shape of them is nothing like I've seen, sort of... enchanting.

Two dark lines ran above her cheekbones, and a crescent moon bridges her nose with what looks like ash. My eyes dart to Charles again, wondering if he is thinking about the woman Callum is wailing over.

Impossible...she is too...beautiful.

"What she means is... there have been attacks on our town. One boy is dead, one has gone missing. She's just scared. Have you noticed anything amiss?" He says, true to form from a leader-in-the-making.

She softly titters to a small fox that sidles up to her feet and sits. She gently shakes her head no, looking down over the small, red creature with bared teeth. "What awful news...shh...shh...Lilitu. They are only visitors."

I walk over to one of the many bookshelves that line the back wall, two plush chairs catty-cornered beside it.

We don't own sitting chairs—stiff table chairs are the only option.

Grabbing a book with a purple cover and silver edges, I open it and sit, surprised by my instant comfortability— the place looked like a library straight out of one of my dreams.

I almost forgotten that we're in the middle of the woods with a stranger and empty bellies.

"What are your names, sweet ones?"

"Charity." I blurt without even thinking. Charles walks to my side and grabs my hand, squeezing it, but I smile stupidly at our hero.

She looks at Charles, and he hesitates. "Charles."

"Charles and Charity," she purrs. "Such beautiful names. I am known as Freyja. Stay here tonight, it will be cold soon. I will take care of you."

Her words are so simple, yet they are an order.

Charles squeezes my hand harder, but the stupid grin plastered on my face only widens. "Thank you so much, Freyja."

CHAPTER 18

CHARLES

This is more than just strange. This is downright *black magic.*

I have not seen such abundance since London. The animals and gardens that surround this land, seemingly appearing out of nowhere, are not *normal.* Not to mention it held the most exotic flowers and fruits I have ever seen—bright yellow petals with six-foot tall stems and wide brown centers. Red roses thatched around the border of each line of vegetable patches. Birds chirped, and dragonflies flew from flower to flower. It is as if we are in a different forest and not the one we have been lost inside of these past two days.

As she leads us inside, the house seems enormous. This woman is not just any woman, she is very different, and a wary feeling in the bottom of my stomach grows heavy like a stone.

Her height and inflection are intimidating, her robes otherworldly and not common. It is hard for me to look away once her stare catches my gaze. Her green eyes shimmer and her heavy black lashes touch her cheeks gently when she smiles.

The smell of garlic and leeks fill my nose, and my stomach growls loudly.

Charity is surrounded by open books beside a roaring fire, a chocolate bar sitting beside her while she happily chews. I watch her eyes grow big as she reads, her face betraying her thoughts. The corner of my mouth lifts into a grin to see her happiness at this sudden change of circumstances. We are no longer lost in the woods, angry with each other. We are in another world entirely.

Freyja is in the kitchen, lined with glass bottles of deep reds and blues. Plants hang from twine above the sink. Countertops flecked with gold line the walls, a modern feature that not many houses can afford.

"Do you like venison?" Freyja calls, her voice sending an involuntary chill down my spine. The smell of whatever it is she is cooking is clouding my thoughts and causes my mouth to fill with saliva.

It has to have been a month since we have eaten real red meat. I nod and try to hide my elation at feeling the salty juices in my mouth again.

She fills two wooden bowls to the rim, tucking a long baguette under her arm and walks toward us.

Charity looks up at the dark-haired stranger and smiles. "Thank you, thank you *so* much."

Freyja looks down over Charity, pleased. She sets down the bowl beside me while Charity eagerly swallows down the steaming broth.

Tearing the bread in half, she hands a piece to me and one to Charity. Two spoons follow, and I can no longer wait, shoveling the sustenance into my mouth, dipping the bread in the bowl, and savoring the juices as they drip over my tongue.

Freyja sits beside me on the floor, furs spread beneath us.

I slowly chew the meat, tasting the familiar sweetness of carrots. I close my eyes and hum, and when I open them again, she is watching me...grinning.

I look over to Charity, whose eyelids look heavy, her empty bowl beside her.

"There is a loft just up that ladder beside the shelves, right above the fireplace. It should be large enough for the both of you. Plenty of blankets as well."

I look towards where she is pointing, and I see the small alcove above the wooden steps, candles flickering against the narrow ceiling inside. My eyes feel heavy after my belly is full.

Before I can say thank you, Charity takes off her boots and climbs the stairs.

I nod at Freyja, who collects the bowls behind me as I follow directly behind Charity.

I can't say I mind getting some much-needed rest, and this woman seems harmless enough. I did not know of any tales of a witch as kind as she, and I knew an animal will never trust someone evil. It is an added comfort she is clothed and not dripping with blood.

Even still, we need to get back home, even if it meant lying and reporting nothing back at all. Clearly, this woman meant no harm and can never kill a child.

I climb into the alcove, filled with feather-down duvets and silk pillows. Charity is nestled beneath one, and I hear her yawn as she blows out the candle beside her.

I lie down as well, careful not to touch her. I lirflat on

my back and place both hands behind my head. I stare at the black above me and listen for her rhythmic breathing, indicating sleep.

"What do you think, Charles?" she whispers, surprising me.

"Think of what? That woman?"

She yawns again and turns toward me. "All of it. How lucky we are to have found a place to sleep. A place with food."

I don't respond, hoping sleep will take her so that I can think in silence.

"Yes, we are lucky."

"She's beautiful, isn't she?" she asks lazily, her eyes closed.

I watch her eyes gently roll back and forth under her lids, her mouth slightly slack with sleep. Her hair is free of braids, laying loosely against her cheek in a way I have never seen before. I brush it back with the backs of my finger, twirling one tendril, wondering if she knows how beautiful she is.

"She is." I whisper.

My dreams are vivid but very real. I am never a dreamer, but when they came, I felt as though I am living them in real-time. I toss and turn as I see Freyja kneeling beside me, stroking back my hair and whispering to me. I feel the urge to reach out and touch her, but my arms feel heavy, and my cock has grown hard against my thigh.

Just relax...you're doing so well...

I grind myself into the soft bed cushions, needing a release so badly. It has been months since I have touched myself—years since I felt the touch of a woman. I will be lying if I said I didn't think about it daily. But my calling required abstinence and what better time to start.

Just let it happen...it will be ok...you can have it this one time...

I flip to my back, and I watch as her naked body climbs atop me. Her waist nips in below her heavy breasts, and her wide hips flare out dramatically. My fingers twitch, and all I want to do is grip her hips and grind her down on me as hard as I can.

Yes, that's it...good boy...

My head pushes back against the pillows, and when I look to my left, I watch Charity's body moving up and down beneath the covers.

She is doing it again, and it made my nipples hard, a shock of pleasure bolting through me. I groan, feeling something clamp around my cock, and it feels *so real*, even though I know I must be dreaming.

Freyja is there again, only now, she throws back her head and undulates her hips over me in wide circles. I feel my balls tighten and a deep pressure at the base of my spine as I prepare for my climax. One small whimper from Charity's writhing body beside me, and I'm sent over the edge, climaxing so hard I see stars. I clench my eyes tightly as I spill inside my slacks, my labored breathing bringing me out of my dream state. I open my eyes, and sure enough, there's a wet spot on the front of my only pair of pants, and I am alone in the darkness, Charity snoring loudly beside me.

~

When we wake up the next morning, I am curled around Charity, my cock rigid against her thigh. I moan through my sleep and pull her closer to me, grinding myself into her.

Charity stretches, and I jerk back, sitting up abruptly.

I grab my shirt and pull it on over my head.

"We should go back...soon." I say, short.

Charity turns to me, her cheeks flush with sleep and hair tousled into a perfect mess.

"Already? I like it here." She pulls her dress on over her undergarments, turning away from me, even though I have already seen the pert, tan circles underneath her shift.

My cock is still half-hard.

I smell coffee beans, and when Charity and I lock eyes, I know she smells it too.

Her mouth drops open, and she scurries down the steps.

The first time she ever tasted the bitter brown juice, it is because of me. A thank you gift brought from London for my new family.

She watched me intently as I added a small amount of milk and sugar with wide eyes. An alchemist, creating a hot drink she sipped with both hands wrapped around the cup, eyes closed and inhaling the sweet scent it made.

The pleasantries never seem to stop in this magical house, and I wonder how much more Freyja has up her sleeves.

CHAPTER 19
FREYJA

Charity happily sips at the cup I've poured her of coffee. I watch as her eyes close, and she savors the warm flavors.

Something about this one's curiosity has caught my eye. She is brave, too, not something I am used to seeing from females.

Her eyes hold a promise, an optimism that only youth bring, bereft of any painful experiences just yet.

Her height matches mine, and her wide, full mouth is mesmerizing to watch.

"The entire town is scared. Perhaps you have seen something out of the ordinary...out here?" the boy asks again, clearly not sure what to make of me. His eyes move about the large sitting room, taking in every item here. I have no weapons, only my spells and my fangs. I did not need anything else.

He is unsure of me, of why I live alone amongst the trees and the animals. It amuses me and equally entices me.

I know exactly what he desires after my visit to his dreams last night.

Charity barely speaks unless she's looked to the boy first. Not uncommon from my observations of many humans.

They do not look to be related, her of darker hair and eyes and his a much lighter. Though, I sense something of a connection or a bond between them. They are both sexually charged this morning, either recently engaging in something or perhaps thinking of it repeatedly. I can smell it, so thick, sweet and sour—a tincture of lust that leaves sparks on the tip of my tongue.

He has made his way to the wooden easel that showed up here a little before he arrived. He runs his fingertips over the bottom of it, looking back at me. "This is...beautiful."

I grin at his passiveness, the way he softly says it. "It is. I think I may have canvas and paint to go with it." I crook an eyebrow, setting down my mug.

He watches me as I walk to my largest altar, lighting the red and white candles, refilling Lilith's wine cup. I break apart more pieces of fresh bread, and I can feel his eyes never leave my backside.

Is this the boy Garm has been seeking? He looks nothing like the men in the black coats. He looks as soft as a blanket, one to curl up beside, not one to cower from.

I should know better than to doubt The Dark Mother. She has delivered him here to me, just as I've asked.

I study them both, youthful yet mature. I feel no threat from either, but I have seen the way he looks at me. I have seen the way both of their eyes have lingered over my shape...my unconventional dress.

The thought of having them both, something I have

never had before, sends prickles of pleasure down my arms and back. The life that vibrates within my fangs tingle and I lick the tips and hiss as it pricks me, a reminder to myself of what I am.

"So, tell me...why were you two alone, in the woods yesterday?"

Charity looks at Charles for the umpteenth time, and Charles clears his throat.

"Errands. We lost track of time and lost our way."

"How careless. It can be quite dangerous here," I say and sip from my mug.

Charity speaks up, "Thank you, so much for your kindness. How can we thank you?"

I grin, knowing full well they will never be able to leave on their own accord. They will only be able to pass my wards if I *allow* them to.

"We should really get back today; our parents will be worried."

They both look to me for an answer as if they need the confirmation. I revel in holding them hostage for a few beats of silence.

"Walk with me first."

~

"Take off your shoes...allow your feet to touch the

growing grass and feel the joy from the Earth beneath them."

They both do as I say, unquestioning, taking slow steps around the garden, murmuring to one another. I smell Charles' fear and Charity's curiosity; hers more pungent and overpowering than his.

Charity hurries to my side, quickly falling into step with mine. I glance at her and smile, her eyes twinkling with questions.

"These gardens are magnificent. Do you tend them by yourself?" she titters; her voice slightly higher pitch than normal.

I nod as we continue to walk the path that weaves its way around the garden and into the woods.

We pass the hot springs, surrounded by tall grass and cascading rocks, and I hear one of them softly whisper, 'amazing.' Though, I cannot tell which has said it.

Lilitu yips as she sprints ahead of us, and the ravens begin to gather at the clearing just before the shadowy trees appear at the forest's edge.

Charity smiles down at the fox, and Lilitu bares her teeth as she reaches out her hand to the fox.

I bar my arm across her chest, stopping her from crouching down to the little feral animal.

"She is not friendly; her job is to protect me. Unless you want to lose some fingers, I will step back," I command, looking down over her tall form from the corner of my eye.

She clutches her chest, and I sense an uptick in her heartbeat, but I cannot tell if it is fear...or excitement.

"I'm s...sorry...I just...like to think of myself as an animal lover." She glances down at my outstretched hand covering her abdomen, and her cheeks flush. She swallows and grazes her fingertips over mine. I feel a small pang of guilt at my harsh tone, but I have saved her the pain of a nasty bite with my reprimand.

"Just because you love an animal, does not mean they will love you back. You must earn their trust, which can take years."

I turn my body towards hers, and I can feel Charles' broad shoulders close behind me, surveying the interaction between her and me. I take Charity's hand in mine and reach behind and find Charles' hand as well, warm and large, surprisingly soft for a man.

"Come, I will show you just how much my pets trust me."

CHAPTER 20

CHARITY

The ravens crow and caw as they flock to Freyja, and it is as if I can't believe what my eyes are seeing. I blink a few more times as they perch on her shoulders, pecking at her glossy black hair. Her delicate collarbone is slightly exposed beneath her green dress, and my eyes linger on her fair skin in such close proximity to the birds' sharp beaks.

She gently motions me toward her, and I take a shaky step next to her, marveling at the size of their long, feathered wings.

"Hold out your arm and stay still. Try not to hold onto any fear, just take breaths and clear your mind."

I obey and do as she says.

Slowly, one of them walks down her arm, hopping to mine. She gently reaches out her other hand and hands me a piece of bread, and as I take it, the bird tilts its head, looking at me sideways from one eye. I gasp at his closeness, the startling black against black making me waver. His eye sucking me in like an endless, pitch-black sky.

I look to Freyja, and she nods while I slowly raise my

hand to his beak. He pecks it, and I take in a deep breath, feeling a rush of adrenaline course through my chest. I look back to Charles, and he has a feeble grin on his face as if he is trying to fake confidence for me.

I try and stifle a nervous laugh, but I can't, and I blow out a huff of air with a big smile, startling the bird.

With a sharp caw, his massive wings take flight, the stray strands of my hair from the tight braids ruffling around my face. I squeal, closing my eyes. Only he doesn't fly away, he lands at my feet, pecking the crumbs that have fallen from my offer to him.

"Good job, he likes you," Freyja says in her deep, sultry voice. I cannot deny that she is unconventionally beautiful and mysterious, and she makes my belly do little flip-flops when she looks at me. A small part of me is thrilled that I have pleased her, and that she thinks *I* have done a good job. I let her hold my gaze, and I find myself getting lost inside the myriad of greens and blues that swirl around her pupils.

If I gaze into her eyes long enough, I may even forget about Bethlehem altogether. I liked the thought of that.

"Um...this is really...interesting...but we should pack up some provisions and get back home, it's a long hike." Charles breaks the heavy connection between us, and I hold myself back from telling him to sod off.

Instead, I glare at him, and he turns from us, heading back toward the cabin.

"Does he know the way back? I will feel very badly if I sent the two of you back into these woods unprotected. Perhaps we can wait until my *Afi* returns, and he can escort you?" Freyja shrugs off the birds, walking towards me and taking my hand again. I feel dizzy for a moment as her spicy scent hits my nose and finishes off with the sweet taste of vanilla on my tongue. She tilts her head, and I smile at her, letting my eyes fall to her deep red lips for just a moment.

"*Afi?* Who is that?"

Lord, Jesus, Charity—she has your head spinning in circles. Get your head screwed back on so you can make responsible decisions.

"My grandfather. He knows these woods better than anyone."

I look over at the cabin in the distance; Charles waits in front of the door for us. He stares in our direction; his hands buried deep in his pockets.

Why will Charles simply want to return when he clearly is set on a mission to find a possessed woman I knew didn't even exist? will he just bring me home, get rid of me, and then return on his mission? Freyja cann't be the one he is looking for; she is of sound mind and a friend to animals...she is harmless.

Doubt pulls at the corners of my mind, and I'm not sure if it is doubt about Charles' intentions or if it is this strange and exciting woman who has materialized into the middle of our path.

Didn't God say there is a lesson in everything?

I want to refuse to leave, to tell Charles that I have a choice of my own and I am not ready to return. The thought of sleeping on the ground after sleeping in a warm cocoon of blankets last night sounded like pure misery.

We will just wait until Freyja's *Afi* came back.

I stride with purpose to Charles, head held high and shoulders pushed back. "I am not prepared to leave yet. I think we should wait."

Freyja makes a noise of agreement, and my heart

beats faster.

Charles sighs, scrubbing his hand over his tired face. He has deep, dark circles below his eyes, and for a moment, I'm concerned there is something he isn't telling me.

"Why, Cher? What's the difference? A few more meals and a night's rest? It will not make any difference. I will wager someone is already on the lookout for us."

"Neither of us is in charge here, we are a team. I do not have to take your orders. I want to stay another night, and Freyja has said that her grandfather will escort us when he returns." I am shouting in a whisper, and just as I finish my small rant, Freyja appears beside us.

"Is all well, little doves?" she asks sweetly, and I nearly melt when her hand gently caresses my lower back.

"Yes, we want to stay another night, and we will wait until your *Afi* comes back to help see us home. will that be alright?" My face is close to hers, and I lick my lips. Her eyes follow my tongue's motion, and she smiles.

"Of course."

I think Charles' head may explode as he rolls his eyes and storms off in silence.

Freyja chuckles, crossing her arms over her pert breasts. I squeeze my thighs together as I imagine what she will look like without any clothes on. I have never seen a woman bare...and I desperately want that first time to be with her.

I bite my lip.

"Men can be childish...do not let him worry you." She steps up close to me, and I can feel her breath on my lips. "I will gather some wine and food, and we can have a soak in the hot springs. That *always* soothes my soul."

CHAPTER 21

CHARLES

Freyja is *the* witch; I am sure of it. I can feel it deep inside my bones.

When Domenico said I will know, I should have just believed him.

I *know*.

Her uncanny ability to draw us in is effortless. This must be what it felt like to be under a spell...although I can feel its effects, I am fighting against it, and Charity has entirely surrendered.

Charity will never believe me. For now, I will need to keep this to myself until I can figure out how to wake her up.

Just how I am going to get Freyja to the tall house beyond the river bend, I did not know.

It is plain to see Charity's instant infatuation.

I must act as though I am none the wiser, or she may just kill me when I least expect it.

I pace back and forth inside the massive cabin, looking like a shack from the outside but a manor on the inside. How else can that possibly be explained? How can Charity not tell?

The only explanation for its size and riches is magic—most likely black magic. Every meal we ate, every book Charity read is just a tool to keep us here.

And who is this grandfather? Another witch? A wizard or demon, perhaps?

Worry bubbles inside my belly, and the longer we are here, the harder it will be to leave.

I rub my temples, trying not to think of all the possibilities. Charity is *naive,* full of curiosity and desperation for a change...I know if I instill fear in her, she will listen to me.

But how? How am I to make her fear a creature so alluring...charming...*illusive?*

My own mind is weaving a web of lies around her, and if I am not careful....

Freyja and Charity enter the cabin just as I stop my pacing and take a seat in one of the over-stuffed chairs.

"How about some food? I have some freshly picked lettuce and greens, carrots and chives." Freyja asks, moving through the kitchen with ease. I watch the curve of her hips, remembering the movements from my dreams, my mouth feels dry.

"I'm not hungry." I choke out, my eyes traveling back to the easel again.

"That sounds perfect, *Freyja.*" Charity drips, kneeling in a chair next to the table where Freyja works. They lock eyes and smile at one another, and I watch as Charity's chest rises and falls quickly. She might as bloody well have hearts for eyes, the way she is falling all over this *stranger* she just met yesterday.

I feel jealousy burn my throat, and I tell myself to stay calm.

This is bad. She is already fully under Freyja's spell.

A part of me can't even blame her...

Freyja reaches high into a cupboard, stretching her body over the counter, and Charity's eyes travel to Freyja's plump behind, cherishing it until Freyja turns around with a dark bottle in her hand. Charity isn't even trying to hide her desire, and Freyja is lapping it up.

As the pair chats and chews their food, my stomach turns at the thought of spending another night here—perhaps battered by another sexual dream. The orgasm last night has drained me, and I don't think I will be able to stand another phantom fucking without wanting to take the *real* thing I wanted... Charity.

I watch Freyja, and her eyes catch mine; a knowing smile plays on her lips.

The sun is setting, another reason why we should have already been on our way back. Fall is here, and the days are quickly growing shorter and colder.

"Can we go to the springs behind the garden?" Charity asks, oozing with eagerness, as she brings their empty bowls to the small sink behind Freyja.

"Indeed...I think that is a fantastic idea," she drawls, eyeing Charity in a way that can only be described as hunger.

Charity giggles, grabbing the corked bottle of wine, Freyja leading the way. I don't think I have ever seen Charity have a drink, even on holiday when each house is gifted with a wine sacrament.

"Cher...do you really think that's a good idea? You've never had wine before...it might..."

"Relax her? Calm her?" Freyja interjects, and Charity raises one eyebrow at me.

"Perhaps, but it can also make you sleepy...silly."

I won't allow anything bad to happen to Charity...If she wants to explore this...whatever Freyja is...I will let her do so with me by her side.

I'm just not sure how strong my own resolve will be.

CHAPTER 22
CHARITY

I am ashamed of how badly I want to sink inside the warm springs ahead of us. Not only have I not had more than a lukewarm bath in the past year, but I want to take in Freyja's bare, curvy body more than anything. The excitement runs through me, down to the tips of my toes.

The feeling of elation and fear is a heady, addictive feeling, and this is one of those times.

The insides of my thighs tense, and my knees wobble slightly. I have never felt the touch of another between my legs, and the need has turned into an obsession.

After Tris rejected me, I haven't brought myself to orgasm again until last night when I cann't help but think about Freyja's dainty collarbone.

I know it is a sin, to covet another woman's body, and to touch myself under the covers. The only duty a woman has is to bear children and show fealty to a man.

The thought sickened me.

I want more than that; I want to be coveted, desired... *loved.*

"Your clothes are torn and caked with dirt at the bottoms. Don't be shy—I will wash them for you...come, come." Freyja sets down the basket of bread and cheese she held, outstretching her hands to the both of us.

Charles looks horrified, his eyes wide, and he looks toward me. I take a long swig from the open bottle of wine, keeping my eyes on him as I swallow. Setting down the dark glass on one of the flatter rocks, I pull my dress over my head, suddenly feeling a liberation I have never felt before in my life.

The cool air licks the tips of my pebbled nipples, and Freyja's eyes are only on the garment she's taken from me as she drapes them over her shoulder.

The water is clear, and steam rises from the center, mixing with the cool air around it. I shiver and dip a toe inside, my eyes rolling back as I sink my foot in deeper.

Freyja's arm is outstretched to Charles, but he only removes his slacks and thick wool shirt, leaving his clean, white undershirt and underpants on.

I blush as I take in the clear imprint of his flaccid penis through the cotton. I bite my lip, curious about its size, shape, and texture.

Sinner.

Charles looks me over as well, frozen still, and goose-flesh blooms over my skin, understanding the power of his gaze on my naked body. I feel the slickness of my arousal between my legs, and I shift slightly to ease myself down into the water so no one will see.

I feel a little dizzy but happier than ever.

Their eyes on me make me feel reckless, and the wine has made my hands and feet feel heavy. I have the undeniable urge to giggle.

I have spent a handful of nights thinking about

Charles' hands and what they will feel like on my thighs. Brushing small strokes up and down until I open myself to him. I halt my devious thoughts yet again because he is my step-brother—another sinful thought, another desire that needs to be pushed down into oblivion.

God sees all.

Charles stands on the edge of the small pool but doesn't move. A thousand thoughts pass over his face, but I don't want to ruin this moment by worrying about his duties. I find a long, flat rock beneath the water that acts like a seat and let my body be embraced by the wet warmth. Closing my eyes, I let out a relaxed sigh.

Freyja sets the clothes down beside the mound of rocks below her.

"May I join you?" she asks me, smiling down at me.

I nod, trying to keep my excitement hidden.

As she ascends the rocks, standing high above me like a grand statue, she unbuttons three baubles and lets her robes fall to the ground.

I nearly gasp at the sight of her but push my mouth under the water instead.

Her breasts are heavy and round, not quite as high as my pert smaller ones. Her nipples are dark and small, resting on her curved ribcage that cascades down to her firm belly and flared hips. A small patch of dark hair covers the dip between her legs, and as she steps into the water, I see a shimmer of wetness on the top of her inner thigh.

I flush, a pulse beginning to thrum behind my cunny.

Darting my eyes back to the water, I spread my hands over my thighs and squeeze, urging myself away from these fantasies. If she wants anyone, it will most likely be Charles anyhow.

She cann't want me.

Charles sits down at the edge, plunging only his feet and calves under the water. He, too, looks down at his feet and everywhere else but our nakedness.

Freyja reaches under a small pile of rocks, pulling out a misshapen block of dark white. I assume it's a bar of soap, and as she wets the bar, the smell of flowers touches my nostrils. I inhale greedily, closing my eyes, remembering the sweet smell of lavender from home... from Tris.

"Let me," she coos, motioning for me to turn so that she can wash my back.

I do as I'm told, feeling her heat behind me, her touch gentle and cautious. I shiver as she roams over my shoulders and down the small of my back beneath the water. Carefully, I look over my shoulder under my lashes at Charles, whose eyes are fixed on the scene. His cheeks flush; I'm unsure if it's from the steam or the slapping of water between Freyja and I as she caresses the soap down my arms and purrs.

Circling around to the front of my torso, I take a sharp intake of breath as prickles of pleasure shoot to my nipples. I bite my bottom lip to keep myself quiet.

Her breasts are pressed firmly into my back, and she dips the soap lower between my legs. My inner thighs tingle and she hums into my ear, "The smell is divine, is it not? Jasmine is a natural aphrodisiac; it makes all my senses come alive."

I close my eyes and inhale the flowery scent again, nodding.

"It smells like flowers. It's not a scent I'm familiar with. What is an...aphro-dees...?" I stutter over the word.

"Ah...it is a smell or taste that makes you think of sex."

My eyes snap open at the word *sex,* and I blink a few times, taking a deep breath in.

She says the word so simply like bread, tree, or hello. That word is never spoken in our town.

The pulse behind my cunt increases, an ache beginning to fill my core. I feel her thighs slide behind mine, and my hips jerk at the contact, and she whispers into my ear, "Is this alright?"

I look back to where Charles is seated, but he is gone, and I am too distracted to care.

I gently nod my head yes, my body craving for more than just a few innocent touches any longer.

Is this really happening? Am I dreaming? Maybe I am still in the middle of the woods—delirious and imagining it all.

Her touch feels *very real,* and I keep myself from squirming with need.

Taking the soap and placing it on the edge of the stones, she circles her hand back under the water and around my waist, only this time, she slides her hand down to the apex of my thighs.

I gasp, but I widen my legs for her, the throb deep inside of me mounting. I know I should stop her; Charles is probably angry with me. I feel so free...so uninhibited out here in the woods. I am surrounded by nature and animals and have never felt more alive. I can breathe easier, and *feel* more.

I want this more than I want food, or clothes or...*God.*

I whimper as she tickles my netherlips and slides a finger between them, finding the little hill inside swollen with need. She flicks it gently and my hips buck, but she steadies me with her other hand, gripping my waist.

My breathing is ragged now, and I manage in a small voice, "Please, don't stop...I'm just...scared."

She stops but places a warm kiss on my neck. "Scared? Of what your body so naturally desires? I can see it all over your face as soon as I disrobed."

"I...I am fearful...of what my punishment for this may be..."

"Ah... tell me, *pet,* what does punishment mean to you?" The way her tongue titters over the 't' sounds of the word pet, prolonging the end into a slight command, makes my insides quiver. Heat kisses my cheeks, and I allow myself to lay my head back onto her shoulder.

"God...I fear *him.* His punishment is swift, and necessary. Our faith is the reason we thrive. I feel I need to abide by his rules...or..."

"Or *what?* You will suffer?" she whispers, continuing to kiss up my neck until she reaches my ear. I groan as she takes the lobe into her mouth and sucks.

Her hand still rests on my cunt, and absentmindedly, I push myself against it, urging her on.

I've waited so long for this, and there is no turning back now.

Any punishment cann't be as bad as this torture, the torture of not being able to have what my heart and body yearn for so deeply, for *so long.*

I want her to stroke me until the throb that gnaws at me is gone.

"Please," I say, my chest rising and falling as her kisses trail down my arms.

"Oh, sweet pet, your wish is my command..."

Two deft fingers apply gentle pressure on the bud between my lips, and pleasure shoots straight through my core. I sigh as she makes small circles around it, and I jolt at each stroke, crying out.

"Good girl...you *love* that, don't you? You *need* this."

I turn my head towards hers, and her mouth captures mine. The kiss is deep, hungry. Her tongue slides between my lips, and her fingers play me like a harp. I moan into her mouth, and her other hand slips up my body to toy with my nipple.

For the first time in my life, I am going to peak at the hands of another. My body is primed and ready.

"Just relax...fear not, I have you."

The circles become long strokes, and she enters me with one finger, and I whine. She finds the tight ball of flesh with her thumb and strums it in rhythm with her finger that explores inside of me.

I grind against her hand, pressure ebbing deep inside my hips, and the two spots she expertly rubs at the same time send me tipping over the steady hill of strokes until I'm climaxing around her fingers.

It didn't matter Charles wasn't here to see, I am certain he will hear my cries of euphoria wherever he is.

CHAPTER 23
CHARLES

My cock is rigid, to the point of being too uncomfortable to sit and watch the two women fondle one another any longer. I have to move away from them before I start to reach for it...for them.

I can feel Charity's eagerness all over my skin, just by her pink cheeks and wide eyes, as I watched the pair caress each other beneath the water.

There is no stopping what is happening inside that damned water spring.

My hackles are raised, and I feel on edge...careful to keep an eye on Freyja's movements behind Charity from afar.

I don't go back to the cabin, I hide like a coward behind a thick rosebush a few feet beyond the hot spring.

Am I a coward for not stopping what is transpiring between them? Or am I just a pervert who wants to watch them...not *really* because I want to protect Charity, but so I can watch her.

Memories of the brothel flood my mind again, and I blink my eyes a few times as if to wish them away.

I can't stay here and watch, but something pulls my eyes back to them, an empty ache inside of me. My breath comes in shallow droves as I watch Charity's head fall back onto Freyja's shoulders, eyes shut. My hands find a branch, and I grab onto it to keep myself steady. A sharp prick bites the insides of my fingers, and I hiss, yanking it back, a small dot of blood left in the wake of the rose bush's thorns. I suck the spot while my eyes continue to observe the women's soft bodies thrash gently against one another.

I'm hard, so fucking hard, leaving me angry enough to fist my cock into erupting fury.

How can a demon woman be as beautiful and intoxicating as her? Did I truly want to undertake such a responsibility by will of The Lord? will I be able to keep a vow of chastity and protection under the watchful eye of Deacon Domenico?

Freyja has me questioning it all, but I know Charity is the one who has awakened this need deep inside of me.

I allow myself to stroke my swollen shaft just once. Hell...I wasn't ordained just yet; I have this test to pass first. So why not enjoy this one little wank in the meantime?

I hear footfalls behind me in the woods, and I jerk my hand away from my crotch, throwing a look over my shoulder. There is nothing but emptiness, but my heart thuds heavily in my chest, and I decide to venture inside the cabin to see what damning evidence I can find.

I have to prove to myself that Freyja is what I think she is, and later, prove the same to Charity.

~

As I walk up the creaking, wooden steps to the small cabin, I am stumped as to why this rickety-old shack looks so delightful and modern on the inside. I try so hard to find reasoning besides magic, but I simply cannot.

I run my hands along the perfectly painted, dark walls. Flowers hang from the ceiling around the room, and there isn't a shelf that doesn't have a melted candle or glass jar resting atop it. The bookshelves that line the walls inhabited thousands of books, the sheer number overwhelming me. I walk to the easel, the familiarity of the paint brushes sticking out of a jar filled with water, and my fingers twitch at the thought of picking one up to stroke lines across the blank canvas.

I turn my focus on a dark doorway to the back of the room, forcing myself to resist the temptation that she surely laid out to distract me. Surveying the room, I make sure I am alone.

Whenever this man—Freyja's grandfather—returned, the risk of our demise will be doubled. But how am I going to pull Charity away from this sex-induced glamour? Anything and everything she can ever want is here. Not to mention the fact Thomas is ignorant and insufferable, not even I like the man.

I breech the doorway, my eyes slowly adjusting to the

darkness. The shelves look old and dusty, nothing like the rest of the home. A large tabletop is dressed in black and red linens, candles, and gems I'd never seen before. A mirror sat at the top, along with what looks like a wooden statue of a naked woman wrapped in a python. I shiver, an icy finger of dread running down my spine.

I have no means to kill this woman—the only choice I have is to get her to the tall house and to Domenico. Armed with holy water and crosses, perhaps he will damn her back to hell from which she came; I did not know.

I pick up a box of matches that lay below the statue, lighting one so I can see the shelves a little better. The match hisses to life, and as I hold the flame to the shelves, I gasp.

Hundreds of jars, filled with water and what looks like tongues, fingers, and...male extremities. I drop the match just as the flame is about to lick my fingers, backing up slowly until I'm pressed against a wall.

This is what Charity needs to see—the proof that Freyja is indeed evil, a witch who casts spells and kills men. How will I get her back here without Freyja noticing...without her watchful gaze on us both...I did not know.

My mind does cartwheels over the images of her emerald eyes and curved lips committing such heinous acts. Even I didn't want to believe it is true. Did she have claws? Fangs? Weapons that we can not even fathom?

My hand finds a latch just at my waist, and I pull it. Falling on my bottom, I brace myself with my palms on the floor, looking around at what seems to be Freyja's bedroom.

It is exactly the opposite of what I have witnessed in

the dusty, dark room next door, much more in keeping with the rest of the house. This room is full of treasures and jewels, plush pillows and blankets, and the sweet smell of vanilla. A lamp sits low beside a nest of cushions, a red, sheer scarf draped over the top. It casts an eerie, sensual color over the entire room...a vision that sends nostalgia of the brothel from which I came all through my body. I crawl to the bed, pick up the silk robe she wore this morning, and bring it to my nose. I inhale her musky, sweet scent deeply ravenous for the thrill it pulses through me. My thoughts turn back to the vision of Charity and her together, imagining what Freyja's magic fingers did to her innocent body, what soft sounds spill from Charity's lips with pleasure.

I slide on the bed and onto my back, rubbing the silk fabric down my body. Greedily pulling down my shorts and running the silk over my cock, a sharp intake of breath leave my lungs. I stroke myself up and down, letting it slide over the shaft and beneath my tightened sack. Groaning again, I wrap it around the thickness and turn onto my belly. I grip the bed blankets tightly and rock my hips into the cushion, fucking into the bed the way I wanted to fuck the witch while Charity watches.

Only, I didn't want to stop there, I want to fuck them both, one after the other until they are soaked with my seed. I cry out violently as I spurt into the robe, feeling the most satiated I ever have in years.

CHAPTER 24

FREYJA

I gather Charity into my arms after her fruitful orgasm beneath my fingertips. My own cunt throbs after watching her mewls crest, then subside. But I will be patient; she is making an emotional connection with me...I can smell it on her skin.

"You did *so* well for your first time, pet. I'm so proud of you."

Her eyes open, and she pulls herself away from me, her cheeks pink with orgasm, and smiles sheepishly. "It wasn't the first time."

I kiss her cheek lightly and pull myself out of the water, handing her one of my many robes from Asaahn. She rises, taking it and marveling at it. "Is this silk? I have only ever read about it, but never felt it...it feels...*glorious.*"

I nod, and she wraps it around her tall, lithe frame, closing her eyes at the feel.

Oddly, I feel pleased with her happiness, and I want to please her more. I want to share with her all the spoils of my hard work and travels. I want her to feel the things

I have felt over these years, harvesting and manifesting this life I have now.

It is a strange feeling, and I think about what it is I can show her next.

I take her hand and lead her back to the cabin, still naked since she now wears my robe.

It hasn't always been this way. My family did not leave me with much, and it wasn't clear why they wanted to escape the Welsh lands where my sister and I grew up. I have an inkling it has something to do with my mother's father—the one responsible for burning my grandmother. I don't think my father can accept the fact that he failed to kill the man who left my mother with that wretched old woman.

I know as soon as we enter my home that Charles has been up to something. Things have been touched, moved and the air is thick with sex. His sex.

Charles is handsome in a charming, boyish way. Not the usual type I prefer. The ones I take life away from... take souvenirs from. He smells innocent, pure...but I can't quite tell the *why* of it yet.

"Can I get you anything, sweet boy?" I purr as sweetly as I can. He doesn't take his eyes off me, and his body sits stiffly, almost aggressively, in the chair beside the easel I have procured just for him.

His eyes dart to Charity again, who is watching me...naturally. It is as though he feels the need to keep an eye on her with me. Perhaps he needs her validation—a strange thing for a man to seek from a woman.

"I want to show you something."

Charity's face lights up, and she kneels beside the table where I stand, ever so eager to do as I say.

I can truly see this one here with me each day—a compan-ion, my companion.

My own little pet.

I turn, reaching up on my toes to the tallest bookshelf full of glass jars, and find the one with the loosened top containing my latest find: a large Huntsman spider.

"Ah, here…" I say, holding up the spider, between the two with their eyes wide and fixed on the dancing body of a light tan and dark brown arachnid.

Charles nearly jumps out of his chair, cringing away from my hand. Charity 'oohs and ahs,' her soft brown eyes wide with wonder.

I unscrew the top, and the spider slowly crawls up my hand with a little encouragement from my fingertips.

"Lord, almighty! Get that *thing* away from us! Are you mad?!" Charles exclaims, which causes Charity's face to turn to him, her eyebrows scrunching up in confusion.

"*That thing* is just a spider…are you truly afraid of it, Charles?"

His face is beat red now, and he is half hidden behind the chair. I stifle a chaste laugh. Charity meets my eyes and covers her giggle with her hand.

Soft…just as I thought.

"What terrifies you, *Charles?*" I ask as the spider steadily crawls up my arm and stops at my elbow.

Charity stands, walking slowly to me, reaching for the spider trying to escape me.

Deftly, she sweeps him up into her hands, cradling him. She moves her head from side to side, observing his arched legs. "Beautiful."

Charity walks to the chair where Charles is still cowering behind it, and he falls back on his hands, backing away as she taunts him.

"A *spider*, Charles? You're afraid of a little spider?"

I grin, amused by her bravery and mocking. I wanted to grab her by the neck and push her against the wall while the spider still roamed her body.

Good girl.

"I.... I'm not scared...just...not use to seeing them. I lived in a church...in London. There was no such insect just roaming about..."

Ah...a church...

The spider suddenly drops and makes a beeline for Charles.

It only takes me two steps to close in on it, and I drop to my knees, capturing it with both my hands.

His mouth is hanging open in horror, and I hold his blue eyes for a long beat and smile, opening my hand slowly.

Eyes darting down, he peeks inside my hands, and I violently slam them together, the spider crumpling into a tiny ball. Charles and Charity both gasp in unison, and I drop the ball to the floor.

"Truly amazing how something can *look* intimidating...yet can be destroyed in one, swift motion. Hm?"

Charles swallows and blinks a few times. Charity crosses her arms over her chest and narrows her eyes down at him as if it is his fault and not mine that the spider is no longer alive.

Charles stands, dusting off his breeches, and sits again as if he didn't just cower like a child at the sight of a bug.

"Balls, Charles, you just had to act like a *little girl*. See what happens when you let fear control you? Now it's dead." Charity announces, and my heart swells at her words.

"Indeed, *my pet*. It's all a matter of perspective. Do you know what that means, Charles?" I ask with hands on my hips.

Charles subtly nods his head. "I do. Some may find a spider perfectly normal...and others might be...threatened by it."

I pace slowly in front of the massive bookshelf Charity can't seem to keep her eyes off of. "Indeed. However, I can remember my mother quoting something her mother used to say, '*Normal is an illusion. What is normal to a spider, is chaos to a fly.*'

~

After the three of us eat a large meal of venison stew, I am able to shoo away Charles to bed with most of the encouragement coming from Charity, insisting she wants to speak with me about 'woman things.'

I doubted *that* very much.

Charity lay her head in my lap in front of the fire while I stroke her soft hair. I undo the tight braids she wore, one by one, wondering why she will hide the wild curls that frame her face so well.

What a pity that she has never been shown freedom.

She speaks to me lazily, her lids heavy with sleep. I

feed her hawthorn berries, and her lips become loose with secrets.

"...he just showed up...out of nowhere...with Charles in tow—a young man who looks nothing like him. I'm not even sure they are related. It's all so very suspicious to me." She yawns as she finishes, and she places her warm hand on my thigh, and for the first time in years, I feel calm...complacent. It feels odd...yet familiar.

Like an old but trustworthy friend that's returned.

"And this...Thomas..." I grit out the name, the name my mother can barely speak, and one my father refused to. "You say he is now the town's leader...the town's pastor?"

She nods, and her eyes are fully closed now.

"He is an awful, angry man. He has never been kind to me."

I stop stroking, anger burning at the back of my neck. "Has he ever hurt you?"

She doesn't respond, and I take her silence as confirmation. I picture the same man that killed my grandmother hurting Charity, and I seethe. He will suffer for what he has done to my family.

"Tell me...where exactly is this town you came from?" I ask a bit loudly, and I shift so that she is forced to sit up, her ivory skin flushed with heat from the fire.

I want to do depraved, vile things to her perfect mouth. I want to mark her body with my teeth, dragging them over her perfect skin until it blooms red for me.

I want to make her mine.

CHAPTER 25
CHARITY

This is the third night that we've stayed here with Freyja.

It felt like nothing more than one day to me. Although I did miss my mother and sister, and my cats; I did not miss the suffocating town or the man that infiltrated my home and my life, turning it upside down.

I never want to leave.

It is inevitable someday I will have to leave my family to marry; to continue the tradition of creating my own family and having my own children.

The idea of bearing a child is more terrifying than the notion of marrying a man I didn't love. I didn't want the responsibility of caring for another human life.

It is too much for me to even think about.

What I did want to think about is the feeling of Freyja's hands on me, pulling her fingers into my mouth and kissing her endlessly.

I want to kiss her from head to toe, feel her tongue slide against mine. Taste her, caress her, *inhabit her*.

The fire reflects in her emerald eyes, and she holds my

stare long enough for my nipples to become erect through the sheer nightgown I wear that is hers.

"Come here..." she coos, and I crawl to her on my hands and knees, capturing her mouth with mine.

Her hands are in my hair, tangled and pulling my face closer to hers.

It feels strange not having my braids secured tightly to my head. The feeling is blissful and freeing.

Our mouths are wide, and our teeth clack together a few times before we find a steady rhythm of strokes and sucks.

She pins me down, straddling my hips with hers, and my head swims with dizziness from her heady scent and delicate hands on my breasts.

Pulling the gown over my head, she hurriedly pulls hers as well, and then she is above me, both of our naked bodies wash in the blazing firelight.

"I...I want to feel you..." I stammer, and she raises her hips off mine, guiding my hand to her warmth. My hand shakes as I cup her cunt, feeling her wetness as my fingers sink inside her folds. She closes her eyes, and I gasp, raising my hips up, fucking the air with my own throbbing cunt.

"will you like me to ride you, sweet pet? Feel my wet lips slide over yours?" she whispers, and I all but fall over the edge at her words.

"Oh, please..."

Notching the cleft of my cunt against hers, our legs crisscross over each other's, and she gasps at the contact of our lips. Bending slightly at her waist, she reaches over, grabs my thigh, and pulls me closer to her as she grinds hers against mine.

She is soft and warm and so wet. Her nether lips

spread easily between mine, and my mouth hangs agape as I watch her throw her head back in pleasure, her hips grinding against my core.

She is slow and determined with her movements, savoring the look on my face as we lay there together, cleft to cleft. I begin to undulate my hips up against her, her legs spread wide on either side of mine. Her eyes watching me from above. I hold the contact, but the warmth that spreads through my hips won't allow me to stay still. I wind my hips, gyrating against her wet warmth, the perfect amount of contact against my pulsing nub, but I want more.

She stiffens her legs so I can get better leverage as I hold her thigh, and the slickness between us increases with each slow jerk of her hips.

"Please..." I pant, "don't tease me...ride me."

Letting go of my leg, she reaches between us and inserts two fingers, her thumb gliding over my throbbing bud with ease.

"Oh! That feels so good...yes...there...there!"

And she gives and gives until I can't take anymore.

I watch her finger fuck me, and she is rubbing herself now as well, eyes closed.

When she opens them again, she looks wild; her thick hair mussed up around the crown of her head. If I didn't know any better, I will have thought she *is* a woman possessed. Only, right now, I didn't care. All I can think about is our shared climax.

Freyja falls on her back, legs spread wide. She is angled towards the fire, and I can see every line, every fleshy curve of her cunt..

"Eat." She commands, and her slanted eyes don't leave my face until I crawl between her legs, spreading her lips with my fingers. I make a circle around her erect nub with the tip of my finger, mystified, and my mouth grows wet at the fantasies I've entertained underneath my covers at night.

I use my tongue, first at the crack of her ass, and wiggle my tongue through her fragile creases, my mind swimming within something that can only be called euphoria.

Her smell is intoxicating, like fine wine, and I want to rub her all over my face, let her juices cover me, let her baptize me with her pleasure.

"Slowly, pet...gently..."

I hum against her cunt, making the sounds of satisfaction after a delicious meal. I do as she says and slow my laps and licks, flicking her nub until she cries out. I pull back, wanting to savor this moment forever, and I watch her entrance throb, knowing immediately what she needs.

I line two fingers up to the pulsing center, face up, and push, "Like this?" I whisper.

Her stomach muscles clench in response, and she nods three times before letting her head fall back again.

I am inside of her now, encapsulated by her pleasure, sheathed inside of her wet heat. I pump slowly at first, but the look on her face urges me on, and I start to move faster, watching her face contort as I go deeper.

"You're a dirty girl, fucking my cunt like that..."

Her words send a gush of arousal straight to my core, and I try to think of what I can say to let her know that I *am* a dirty girl...full of hungry, deplorable things that I want to do to her.

"I love your cunt...*Mistress*. I am your pet...use me."

More moans leave her lips as I say the words, and it

makes me want to prove to her that I can give her more, give her whatever it is she wants.

Keeping two fingers buried inside her, I make a v with my pinky and index finger, leaving room for me to suckle the erect, little hill between her lips at the same time. I begin with long strokes of my tongue, but as I watch her jerk under my mouth, I eagerly suck on the tiny nub until she's fisting my hair, moaning my name.

And Lord…the feeling of her calling my name at the height of her pleasure makes me feel confident enough to rule the world.

Withdrawing my fingers, I watch her ride out her climax.

"Suck them clean…your fingers. Now."

I don't, though, I want to fuck myself with the same fingers that were inside of her, and I lay back, spreading my legs before the fire.

Freyja sits up, looking angry, and grabs my hand.

The look of shock on my face doesn't soften her. "I said…*suck them clean.*"

"But, I want to feel your wetness inside me…please…." She watches my face as I beg. "Let me," I whisper.

Using her hand to guide mine, she inserts my fingers into my own cunt..

It stings slightly at first but melts into pleasure as she slowly moves in and out. "You should have listened to me…"

Mimicking my actions earlier, she assaults the throbbing bud between my lips with her tongue, sucking with such ferocity that I am convulsing, the pleasure too much to handle any longer. I have wanted this for too long…needed the release too badly. My entire body shudders as I am hit with waves and waves of orgasms.

It has to be more than one; they don't stop for a full minute.

"I...that was..."

"...not a gentle orgasm, pet. Did it hurt?" Freyja is on top of me, running her hand down my chest.

"No...well, I mean...it was intense..."

"You have pleased me, pet, but also awakened my hunger."

I stare up at her with wide eyes, wondering what she means.

"This won't hurt...too much. Just lay back and let me take care of the punishments. If it is punishments you seek, then *I* will be the one to give them to you."

My eyes are wide, the heartbeat in my chest beating furiously in my ears.

Freyja opens her mouth wide, and I see the small fangs just before she strikes my exposed neck.

There is nothing but blackness that follows.

CHAPTER 26

FREYJA

"The boy is innocent in all of this, you must believe me." I whisper, careful not to disrupt Charity's blissful slumber on my lap.

Feeding from her weakened her body, but I know she's resting peacefully from the slow thrum of her heartbeat against my palm.

Garm's face is screwed up, the shadows of the fire casting sharp lines across his furry eyebrows and overgrown beard. He looks every bit a frightening werewolf in this moment.

"Aye, and her? Is she innocent as well? Another *toy* for you to play with, *Fey.*" He growls, teeth bared.

I pause, reflecting on the few moments I shared with Charity. I have not felt a deep intimacy with anyone... ever. My heart skips a beat each time she smiles at me and tucks a hair behind her ear or leaves a lingering touch. Looking at me as if I am forbidden fruit, waiting to be plucked from the tree of knowledge. I want to give her everything she ever desires and more. I want to keep her with me, sharing treasures and secrets and climaxes forever.

"You must not harm them. I will not allow it."

Garm's large body barely fits in the chair Charles hid behind earlier. With his face in his hands and broad shoulders hunched, he shakes his head like a dog. It startles me, and I jerk back, my hands leaving the tangles of Charity's hair to brace myself from falling back into the fire.

"You won't *allow* it?"

No one garnered respect from me the way my *Afi* did. He is the only man besides my father to frighten me into submission. I didn't know how much longer I can distract him from his love-sworn task, avenging the death of the woman he loved—my grandmother.

"I understand your anger, and your oath to your *true love*. We will have Thomas' head on a platter, I promise you that." As I gently whisper the words, I know my candied tongue cannot coax him the way it has others. I reach out and stroke his muscular thigh, but his teeth are bared, and he glares at me behind years of wrinkled anger.

"I will *not* stalk any longer, biding my time while you *play*," he spits, staring down over Charity's unmoving body. "I want him dead, but more so, I want him to *suffer* the way my Annabelle suffered."

"And we *will*. I promise you that."

Garm looks around the house I have created especially for our two guests, and he huffs, "How long do you plan on keeping up with this *fantasy*? You are incapable of keeping *any* relationship, and I know you leave your body to *feed*. This will never last."

I narrow my eyes at him, a fire rising in my veins that

makes me want to say vile things. But he is just an old man who stalked around these woods for a decade waiting for a woman to bed him until he found Annabelle. A woman just as wild as he was.

I must not forget he raised me and protected me.

"You are just angry...you don't mean that..."

He stands, wrapping a wool blanket around his body and stomping away from the nest of blankets on the floor.

"Perhaps, but even secluding my Annabelle to the woods can't keep her wild ways tamed. I have a feeling it is the same for you."

CHAPTER 27

CHARLES

As I lean over the railing to listen, I can't help but feel my throat tighten at the size of the man that stands in front of Freyja's seated body. He is massive, not the size of a mortal man at all. His shoulders look as wide as my arms when spread.

Just like the tale of the Wolf-man in the stories.

My eyes will not look away as I watch him nearly break the chair I sat in earlier.

Leaves her body to feed?? My God...does she eat children? will she do the same to my Charity?

I rub my eyes as I try to focus on her face, but I can't stop watching her graceful fingers trace lines over Charity's sleeping form. They both look utterly beautiful in the fire's light, and I feel my fingers twitch with need.

A need for what? To take them both at the same time? A tangle of kisses and hair and warmth all wrapped up inside all three of our bodies.

We cann't stay here any longer. Not with that massive troll lurking about. I needed to get Charity as far away from this house as possible.

Nothing good will come from this place.

Bring her to the tall house beyond the river.

Domenico's letter is still inside of my jacket pocket, and as I peek over the edge of the loft again, I see it draped over the arm of the chair the oversized man is seated in.

I swallow hard as he becomes agitated with Freyja, yelling at her abruptly, and standing taller than I can ever imagine.

I swallow again.

A plan...I need to come up with a plan.

After I hear Freyja tell the man she will have Thomas' head on a platter; I can feel my heartbeat pounding inside my neck. Small beads of sweat trickle down the sides of my forehead, and I realize it feels like it's a hundred degrees in here.

I strip off my shirt and pants, trying to close my eyes and make sense of everything I've just seen.

So, the Troll-man wants Thomas dead, and Thomas wants all the witches dead...

Why did Domenico want Freyja brought to him alive? How will I ever get her away from her house and her pets?

It is then that I realize the only way to get Freyja to leave is to promise her what she wants.

Thomas.

I toss and turn for what feels like hours, and soon, the birds begin to chirp outside, the daylight breaking in through the windows.

I know what I need to do, but I doubt Charity will ever forgive me once she realizes it. She will know I am lying to Freyja about Thomas' location; there has to be a way around it.

How am I to face that beast of a man? I nearly wet

myself just listening to him speak, watching the way his movements are like violent strikes.

Pulling on my pants, I climb down the ladder quietly, looking around the large room, and finding Charity and Freyja tangled with each other in front of the fireplace, asleep.

I kneel beside Charity; her cheeks are speckled with tiny brown dots across the flush of sleep on her skin. I reach out, stroking one with the back of my hand. Her fingers are intertwined with Freyja's just under her chin, and I place my hand on top of theirs.

I am not large by any standards, but I am tall and fully grown. Both of their feminine fingers fit perfectly beneath mine, and I cover them with mine.

"Charles?"

Charity's sleepy voice snaps my eyes away from the three-handed masterpiece, and I smile at her.

She looks like disheveled, satisfied like sex, and I can't help but bring my lips to hers. I want it too much.

My resolve shatters there in the morning twilight. I don't know if it's the magic or the cabin or maybe even blatant fear coursing through my body. All I know is I want to feel her lips caress mine for longer than a moment, and I want my fingers in her hair. She smells like flowers and divine feminine—a musk I can't quite name.

She releases a small sigh into my mouth, and I almost come undone at that very moment. My hand is on her jaw, then around her neck, and the pushing and pulling of our mouths are ravenous.

Her tongue glides over mine, and I slip my hand under the covers eagerly.

My body is pressing against hers, and I resist the urge

to grind myself into her hip, remembering we are not alone.

Her hands run down my back, and she opens her legs for me. Two more sets of hands caress the backs of my thighs, followed by a light touch removing my undershorts. Four hands are on me all at once, and the feeling is mesmerizing. My senses can't keep up with who is touching where and when, but my cock is hard, throbbing against Charity's thigh.

I pull back from her and turn to Freyja, whose eyes are a blazing green surrounding the deep pool of black in the center. Her skin glows with uncanny youth, and I stand, stuttering apologies to Charity.

"I...I'm sorry, Cher, I can't."

Charity sits up, one of her hands still entangled with Freyja's. "Why *not?* You *can.* You are not a pastor...or ordained, or anything like that. You are just a... lamb."

"A *lamb?*" I ask, a little shocked.

She looks at Freyja from beneath her lashes, then back to me again, "I just meant...you *follow* them."

I run a hand through my hair and reach for my shirt and jacket that hang from the chair behind me.

"I've had enough, Charity. It's time to go. *Now.*"

The sternness in my voice surprises me once again, and I can feel my heart racing in my chest. Whatever I do, I need to make sure we are leaving together, even if it meant sounding like an angry husband.

This isn't you...you are acting. This isn't what you really want...who you really are.

As if reading my thoughts, Charity narrows her eyes at me. "You know, you sound like a real *twat.* You sound exactly like Thomas. I don't want to go *back* there...back to *them.*"

I know she is stubborn and strong-willed, albeit a little weaker because of her gender. Although was she? Does her being a woman also mean she is bereft of choice and decision? Is she only weak because I am taught that women were weak?

What if the thing men *truly* feared is a woman stronger than them?

I feel like an ass, but I also feel as though Freyja can't be trusted.

I do the only thing I can think of, with Freyja's eyes fixed on me with a murderous glare. I pull Charity up by her arm, bringing her face close to mine in one violent tug. "Do you trust her more than you trust me?"

Her soft face is scrunched up in disgust, and it pains me it is me who has caused it.

I will rather watch her head fall back onto the pillow again in unbridled pleasure, not this face that looks like she never wants to see me again.

She snaps her arm back and steps back away from me.

Shit.

I thought she will cower or she will take my tone as an order instead of defying it. I thought she will cave under pressure and submit to me.

"I'm beginning to think I cannot trust *any* man." she spits out, gathering her dress in her hands and storming off to the small bathroom at the back of the house. The heavy wooden door slams shut, and I am left in the middle of the elaborate and over-the-top library with Freyja.

I turn to the large canvas that sits on the easel to my right, knowing full well my mind has already created a thousand possible masterpieces. The Deacon told me artists are some of the most brilliant men of our time, but artists worship the canvas and do not have time to worship God. All my focus should be on God.

And how much praying have I done since I arrived in Bethlehem? None, not since the day I laid my eyes on Charity.

Thomas is always angry, always on the hunt for righteousness and repentance—two things that went hand in hand. He didn't care about Charity's mother, and never gave a thought to the well-being of her and her sister. He only thought of himself and his God.

How is that *Godly?* Isn't it about showing kindness and understanding to your neighbor? To your kin? Did he really care to punish who is responsible for those children's death, or is he just pushing his *Godly* agenda?

I rub my face with my right hand, my left hanging at my side as I reel.

I denied myself the things I desired *daily;* the things I wanted so badly. All things that will bring me fleeting happiness. My mother never wanted this kind of life for me, she told me she will only ever live in the moment—that life was too short.

I fight back the lump in the back of my throat, the tears that threaten to break. So instead, I pull back my hand and punch the easel with all my strength, sending it flying into the nearest bookcase, and shattering into pieces.

It is then I know exactly what I need to do...for Charity...for myself.

Before I even notice she has moved, Freyja is behind me, stroking my hair and whispering in my ear, "Lost little boy, why do you think you wandered here? It is all meant to be...for you...for her. You are *home."*

An icy finger runs down my back, and I close my eyes as her hot breath hits that sensitive spot inside my ear. I shiver, and let my tongue wet my lips.

And I surrender.

My cock moves, and instead of berating my thoughts with how wrong it will be if I just let her touch me, I say, "Then show me what's meant to be."

CHAPTER 28
FREYJA

I knew it will not be long before I broke him—the lost little boy inside of him, the one who grew up in the house of sex.

I lead him into the back bedroom, the same room he defiled my robe in.

He is fighting me on the inside, and I can see it on his face. I can also smell his arousal, and fighting his desire for Charity for so long is finally wearing on him.

"Lay on the bed," I order, and he obeys.

Peeling off my robe, I let it fall to the floor while his eyes never leave me. I command his stare, and he gives it to me, his eyes wide and his mouth parted.

He is not like my usual conquests—blonde, slightly feminine, but tall in stature, and surely his cock will be the same. I crawl over him, his eyes never leaving mine.

"Pull out that perfect cock. Now."

He does more than I have asked, like the good boy I know that he is. Ripping his shirt off over his head and shimmying out of his breeches, he lays back down on the bed, spread eagle for me, waiting for his next command.

His cock is like metal against his abdomen, and it stretches past his belly button. My fingers tingle and there is an innocent smell that rolls from him, and I know just how much he has held back his desire for me. I have visited him in his dreams before, but this will be nothing like that—this will be carnal...real.

I begin at his thighs, and his balls instantly tighten as I stroke the tip with my fingers. Wetness has gathered there, and my mouth parts at the thought of tasting it.

His groans are soft and guttural, and I take my time licking him from base to head. His eyes stay focused on what my mouth is doing, and I can feel my cunt tighten, eager for what he can give me.

I feel Charity's presence in the doorway, and I know that with my ass in the air, she has a full view of my arousal.

I look at her over my shoulder as she watches the two of us playing with one another.

I wonder if she feels jealousy...or lust.

"Lick." I command, and I turn back to focus my attention on Charles. I hear her fall to her knees and obey, crawling to me until her face meets my cunt.

I gasp as her tongue parts my lips and discovers each fold gently with the tip.

I watch Charles as he peers around my body to see her face buried inside my ass.

I suck his cock with eager, deep motions, making sure the moisture from my mouth coats it until it's dripping down my chin. His eyes slam shut again, and his moans come louder this time.

Charity's tongue finds the tiny nub that sends jolts of pleasure through my body, and I stop sucking, overcome by the penetration that comes next. She moves back down to the nub and plays with it as I groan, Charles's dick popping free from my mouth.

"Such a good girl...you're doing so well. Make me proud..."

CHAPTER 29
CHARITY

I can hardly believe what I'm seeing, and I am shocked by how much the sight of Charles' euphoric facial expressions while Freyja sucks on his manhood makes my cunt clench. When Freyja orders me to her, I am on my knees in an instant, ready to please her while he watches.

The thought is absolutely thrilling.

I find her hole, feeling a tiny flutter between my legs, and the urge to touch myself is overwhelming. I kneel, pressing my hand against my hot mound, and let a single finger slip inside.

Her channel accepts my tongue, and as I feel her, I pump my finger inside myself in rhythm with my tongue and groan.

"Ohh, like that...that's so perfect...just like that, sweet pet." Freyja coos and I steal a glance at Charles as she guides his hand to his swollen cock.

If I keep watching him as his face contorts with pleasure, I will come in waves over my hand, and I don't want that yet. I want to feel my orgasm push free under his hands so, so badly.

"That's right, lost boy, stroke yourself...make yourself feel good. You've waited so long for this...you deserve it."

Freyja's sighs of pleasure have me furiously circling my sensitive bud, and I slam two fingers inside myself as I flick hers with my tongue. Using the pad of my hand, I rub my mound and work myself inside until I'm bucking my hips.

"Ohh...fuck...feels so goo—" Charles grinds out, and I watch his large hand covering his cock while he pumps into it, and I feel a deep pressure inside me, threatening to spin out of control. I pump harder, and a sensation like I may wet mysef came over me, and my face leaves Freyja's cunt.

"Make yourselves climax...together...now."

Just as Freyja commands it, I tip over the edge, and I sit back on my hand as I orgasm, watching Charles' cock spurt milky seed over his belly.

How badly I wish his hand is mine.

I cry out, wetness spilling into my hand as I climax, crying out his name just as I finish.

I collapse next to the bed, and all my thoughts are consumed by the idea of keeping this forever, day in and day out, playing with my two favorite people—food filling my plate and orgasms filling my body.

I want *this* to be my life, no fear, no guilt, just pure satiation.

I want these two to fill my loneliness...together.

I want to have them both, even if it meant staying here forever and leaving my family behind.

FREYJA

Later that night, Garm's agitation is palpable, and I know I have made him wait too long.

"These *games,* end tonight. I have had enough of your *playthings*. They are too young. Too naive. You are treating them like *toys*."

"They are *not* too young. I have begun to enjoy their company, and the girl knows nothing of Thomas except that she hates him."

Night has fallen on my garden, and as we stand amongst the roses, I can see that the last of Mabon's offerings are dwindling, and the feast must be tonight.

Am I ready to let go of the independence I have so carefully crafted around myself over the years? Can I *truly* allow love inside of my heart again for two *mortals*?

Conquests inside of dreams were not real, and even the men I allowed to live were not lovers but hosts.

I want to keep Charity by my side; her looks of wonderment melt the insides of my chest and land heavy inside my belly. She looks at me as though I am a holy treasure, and through her eyes, I see myself as a hero and not a monster.

"Thomas does not deserve to live; he is nothing but a vile human who took my beloved from me for no reason but resentment. Annabelle was miserable inside that house. She has only found true love before her death, although it was brief.

I will kill him, and he will suffer greatly for what he did to her." Garm's voice booms, and I shush him so our guests won't hear his anger.

He stands much taller than six-feet;the werewolf man that he is. His hair and beard are wild tonight, and under the full moon, the black pools of his eyes look menacing. He is trying to keep his change under control, and I can only hope that he returns with Thomas in one piece for our feast this night.

I imagine him ripping the man limb from limb, blood spraying his coat as he roars, and Thomas' screams puncturing the veil of the skies.

My Afi's love for my grandmother was short-lived, for even her captivity can not tame the wildness of her soul... and she paid for that with her life.

Garm will watch my mother and father together with fleeting joy but also pain, seeing what they have together as a ghost of what he had with Annabelle.

Retribution was the only thing that will allow him to live out the rest of his days in peace.

I gather the remaining carrots and potatoes buried inside the dirt for tonight.

Summer is behind us now, and it is time to celebrate Mabon and show gratefulness for its harvests. Passed down for centuries, my mother taught me of 'the witches thanksgiving' since I was a girl. It is not commonly practiced, a tradition that died at the hands of the Christians, just as the witches burned. Tonight, we will bring it to life again, with beloved guests to entertain, and I can't wait for Charity to see the gift I will bestow her.

"Grandfather, please return the man in one piece, I have plans for him. I promise, you will have his blood and his neck when the time is right."

Garm shakes out his head like an animal, closing and opening his eyes as he clenches his hands, waiting to run wildly into the woods.

"Fine," he grits out, and as he breaks into a run, I watch his bones grow and snap as his skin stretches, casting a chilling shadow of a tall wolf against the backdrop of the moonlit sky.

The full moon glows brightly above him, beaming with pride.

**

When I make it back inside, Charles is painting long strokes of red against the canvas he threw across the room just this morning. I pieced it back together with magic, but he wasn't asking questions this time, and that made a small smile draw up one side of my mouth.

He is embracing himself, that I can clearly see. Why he wants to resist the things that make him so happy, I do not understand. Must be because of his father.

Perhaps after tonight, that will all change.

"Please, let me." Charity smiles, and my lower back tingles at her kind demeanor and desire to please me.

Taking the woven basket into her hands, she sets it down beside the pots of boiling water on the hearth.

I reach into my robe pockets, pulling out three silver chains with clear vials hanging from them.

Walking over to Charles, his attention rapt on his artwork, Charity follows behind just as a loyal pet will.

"A gift, one for each of us, filled with water from the hot springs...where we first shared a special moment together."

Charity's eyes are wide, and she clasps her hands together, taking it and immediately pulling it over her head. I do the same, and we lock eyes, hers glimmering with happiness.

Charles looks skeptical, as always, but he takes it from me.

"Perhaps you will appreciate this gift a bit more...if you had a *special* moment in the springs as well..." I laugh, "No one enjoys being *only* an onlooker..." I grin, nodding towards the door.

Charity bites her lip, looking at Charles.

I know how badly she wants this; I only need to gently nudge them in the right direction.

I bend down to the table next to the chair, picking up two sets of new clothes for both of them.

"Here...go to the springs, bathe and adorn your *new* clothes. Prepare yourselves for the feast I'm making for us tonight. *Enjoy one another.*"

Charity eagerly takes the piles and rushes towards the door. A fist squeezes my heart as I see her happiness over-flow...I want to grace her with more gifts each day.

I also desperately want to join them, but I also understood how badly they both want this...they both need this.

It is a heavy burden to bear when you refuse to press the buttons that hide deep inside your mind. They will forever beg to be pressed, until one day, they can no longer be ignored.

"Come on Charles..." Charity holds out her hand to him, and he follows.

CHAPTER 31
CHARLES

Charity takes my hands into hers as we walk, an electric current running up my fingertips intertwined with hers.

The air is chilly, leaves turning brown and red, falling gently to the ground. I put my arm around her shoulder, pulling her to me and thinking about how I have to tell her about Freyja now before I gave into every carnal desire I've carried for her this past year. The back of my neck prickles at the thought, and I can't deny my excitement.

Just this one time.

The rocks surrounding the springs come into view, and Charity walks ahead of me, swishing her hips in a way reminiscent of Freyja. The girl who walks before me now is a woman, holding power within each step—no longer the scared girl who stomped her feet and looked at the floor while Thomas chastised her back.

I want to take her into my arms, sprinkle her freckled face and heavy lashes with kisses; I want to protect her and keep her forever.

If I am honest with myself, I have probably loved her since the day I first met her, falling for her soft brown eyes and naiveté.

I watch as she lets the black and flowered robe fall around her alabaster shoulders, looking at me under doe eyes.

She sets the clothing on the ground beside the rocks and lowers herself into the water. I try to think of how I can gently burst her fantasy bubble she clearly never wants to leave without hurting her too much.

Denying myself the things I love—the things that bring me joy, made me feel a guilt weighing heavy inside my chest.

Is it because of Domenico and the way he has raised me? He never wanted me to be like my mother—living the life she did was a sin. I am supposed to be on a path to redemption and purification...

But what is pure about a life that never gives the seeds of desire planted so deeply inside our hearts the chance to ever fully blossom?

Can I just throw away all I have learned during my time in London? Is Domenico's teachings all a waste of time because of what I am? What is so deeply engrained into my blood? Am I simply a sex-hungry fiend?

My eye travels to her naked skin beneath the crystal-clear waters. Without thinking twice, I remove my breeches, pulling my shirt over my head. I have been naked here more times than I have been in my own company, and the comfort of it makes me feel lighter.

Climbing into the water beside her, my cock bobs, already half rigid with thoughts of Charity's soft, naked body against mine.

Charity glides beside mine, gently rubbing her foot along my calf.

God, please don't do that. I may not be able to hold back another second if you keep touching me...

She rests her head on my shoulder, and lust fills my veins, my cock growing hard against my leg quickly. I close my eyes, taking deep breaths.

"I've never been this happy, you know."

I open my eyes and sigh. I don't want to rip her from this false sense of security. I want her to have everything she's ever wanted.

Can *I* make her happy once we return? Can I even stomach the idea of another man taking her as his wife, caressing her soft skin under the blankets of their marital bed?

I close my eyes against the thought...I don't want to think on it.

"Cher...I have to tell you something..."

She looks up at me, her eyes a lighter brown than I have ever seen before.

Only, before I can say anything—the warnings I know I need to say to save her life before the witch showed us her *true* colors—he places her hand on my thigh, so close to where my cock lays.

I take a sharp intake of breath, and she notices, slanting her head to the side in empathy. "I want you too..."

And with those four words, she slides her hand up a few inches, her pinky stroking the head of my cock lightly.

I nearly fold, swallowing hard, and turning to face her cherry red lips. She pillows them against mine, and I succumb to her; to the need I have been fighting for so long. Her lips slide through mine while her fingers wrap around my shaft, and I come undone.

Grabbing her around her waist, I pull her on top of my lap. While she straddles me, I grip and squeeze her hips, urging her on, and pressing her body into mine.

Her arms are wrapped around my neck, and my grip finds its way to her backside where I palm her lush and plump cheeks. I want nothing more but to feel her warm cunt wrapped around me.

Gripping her hips again, I adjust her so her cleft hovers above my cock.

I look into her eyes with a question without words, and her chest heaves. One small nod from her, and I'm thrusting her down onto me, roughly, unapologetically. An exasperated groan of relief leaves both our lips at the same time.

We stay still like that for a long moment, I am sheathed deeply inside her, and her cunt squeezes me… oh so tightly. Her head is resting on my shoulder, and I hear her whimper, so I ask, "Are you alright? Did I hurt you?"

She shakes her head no and begins slowly rocking her hips against me. I hold her in place, resisting the movement at first. We place our foreheads together, and her breath is on my face, soft feathers of pleasure brushing my nose.

"I've wanted this for a long time…" I whisper, kissing her nose, then her cheeks, but firmly gripping her ass beneath the water.

I turn us so she is resting comfortably on a curved rock beneath the surface, leaning down and kissing her neck. I pull out of her gently but push back inside with one long, slow stroke as she gasps.

"Please," she whimpers out, digging her nails into the rocks, pulling me closer to her, from behind.

"More? Like this?" I whisper into her hair.

I repeat the slow stroke, but two more in succession this time.

"Oh!"

Shivers run down my arms, and my sack pulls so tight to my body that if she clenches just once, I will break into a thousand pieces inside of her.

Flashes of Domenico's sharp features invade me, and I try to focus on the moment, but his words cut through my lusty fog.

A witch resembles a terrible plague, and nothing can be pure again until the root of the problem is destroyed. They all must be destroyed.

"She is a witch, Cher. You must understand, we are not safe here," I blurt, unable to keep the truth from her any longer.

Her eyes are glazed, and she looks at me puzzled, lips parted.

"I don't care...don't stop...*please.*"

I turn her over to face me and take her chin in my hand, "Maybe you don't care, but I do. Her grandfather plans to kill Thomas."

She narrows her eyes at me, squirming for friction as I hold her still. "I don't *care* about Thomas."

She says the words I wish I can say. She is no longer the scared little girl who cowards away from a man. All those times he screamed at her, berated her with his words, I wanted to hit him. I wanted to yell back and tell him to leave her alone.

I never did, though.

I crash my mouth to hers, tangling my hands in her

hair and drawing her closer to me as I allow her to roll her hips over me. Her tight cunt pulses around my cock, and I groan into her mouth, the pleasure rocketing from the base, rushing toward the tip.

Our bodies splash together in the water as I pump into her harder, biting her lips and claiming her body with mine.

I want our bodies to melt together like this with her moans of pleasure playing on a loop inside of my ear over and over as we climax.

Just as the thought ripples through my mind, we both explode. She is biting my ears, and my face is buried inside her neck.

If I ever withheld happiness from myself, and this is how it felt...I will *never* deny myself again.

I will wear the necklace now with the haunting memory of the night I took Charity's virginity and made her a woman.

I will take her exactly as she was...stubborn, strong... and possibly in love with a witch.

CHAPTER 32
FREYJA

When they return, they both wear smiles so broad I almost feel a little jealous.

They are wearing the brightly colored clothes I gave them before with the silver necklaces resting happily against their chests.

A warmth spreads through my body, and I feel a bubble of hope rise inside me.

Two long tables are stretched in front of the fireplace in the library, and the chairs come to life as the shadows from the fire dance on their backs.

Loaves of bread, and baskets of vegetable with herbs litter the top, and I hear Charity gasp as she sees the display of food.

"Amazing! Is this all for us?" she asks, running her fingers over the white tablecloth and silver cutlery. "I've never seen silver like this!"

Lilitu is beside me, looking up at me like she knows something.

"I'm so glad you like it...I have some surprises planned."

I fantasize about the look on Charity's face once she sees Thomas. I think I will let her dictate what she will like me to do to him. I have sedated him with belladonna, and if she will want me to start sawing away at his body parts...yes, that sounds very fitting.

I will have to let Garm have him after we are finished, hopefully still alive enough so the beast may have the pleasure of hearing his screams and pleads for his life.

All sadism and revenge aside, Garm will have his turn, and Charity will have her freedom.

But first, we eat.

**

A black top hat and coat hang on the back of each chair, a placeholder for the souls I have claimed over the years.

The men who thought they will take matters into their own hands—hands claiming to do a Gods bidding; a false God that I have never seen.

When man thinks he is better than a woman and takes lives that are not his to take, a debt is owed. And I, I am the collector of such debts.

They belong to me now, and the women who are burned in an attempt for control and power, are free. All sent back to The Dark Mother of witches, Lilith.

I have thought about tasting Charles, but I must show him I can be trusted first. Trust is something Garm does not seem to understand, and it is what I want to give to him to ensure I can keep them both with me forever.

"Are there others attending?" Charles asks, placing a

hand on one of the hats, crooking one eyebrow, looking downright cheerful.

I fill the three glasses I have set for us with wine and shake my head, the silver beads in my braids clinking together.

Tonight, I have painted my face with lines and sigils of protection from my father's clan. I wear the cloak of my mother's—white and grey wool adorned with the fur of a wolf.

"You look beautiful, Freyja," Charity says, ever so politely, as she sips at her wine.

She is already seated directly in front of the covered mound of our main course. It is nothing but a white sheet, but what lies beneath it is unseen...

"Thank you, sweet pet. I will love if you let me draw these sigils on your face someday soon. I can teach you about my father and his Viking heritage."

"Vikings? Oh, that sounds so *interesting!*" she chirps and takes another long sip of her wine.

I raise my glass to them both, seated in the library I created just for them, and say, "I raise my glass to the both of you...stumbling into my woods so scared, so unsure. Fated. I have watched you two blossom..." I look to Charity, suppressing a smile behind her cup, "from a withdrawn bud, entering spring, into a flower...reaching for the sun in the summer."

Garm enters the library from the back, commanding the room with his tall and bulky form, shadowed eyes cast to the floor in fury. I know he is upset with me...my show...my dramatics. What he does not seem to understand is these two are much more than just pets to me now.

He sits at the end of the table, and both Charles and Charity stare at him uneasy, but from their peripherals, as if they do not want to call attention to themselves.

"This is for you. A symbol of my protection and my promise to take care of you. You came to me in a time of great need and despair, and I saved you."

Charles sits back in his chair roughly, taking a small drink of his wine, eyeing me. Although he shared a moment of vulnerability with me, he still does not trust me.

"Tonight, you and I, *Cher*, take your power back..."

I snatch the sheet from the tabletop, revealing Thomas' oiled, naked body. His mouth is stuffed with an apple, his eyes sewn shut. A decorative wreath of rosemary, thyme, and parsley surrounds him.

Charity gasps and Charles reaches over to grip her hand as his eyes look over Thomas' body.

I stand beside the table with a tincture of peppermint and rosemary in my left hand, and I drip the liquid onto a white cloth. Placing it beneath his nose, he jerks awake, coughing and wheezing, grappling the table with his hands and feet. "Please! Please! I don't want to die!"

I laugh as I watch him squirm above the table, his naked hairy body jiggling and struggling.

Charity suddenly stands, eyes wide and fists clenched, knocking over her chair. Charles rises beside her, watching her face intently.

Thomas sits up violently, knocking plates and glasses to the floor. Garm shoulders are rounded, both hands braced on the table, a low growl forming from deep in his throat. I can see his claws pinching the tablecloth, his knuckles sprouting hair.

I grab Thomas by the back of his head, by his hair. I bring my face close to his. "What do you have to say for yourself, Man of God, who claims to take women's lives simply because they aren't like the others. Let us hear your pleas."

"I...I...He spoke to me! How am I to ignore the word of our Lord!? Please...let me go...p-p-please!" He sobs, and I have to hold back a laugh at his terror.

The terror at the hands of a witch.

"And what if it wasn't God who was speaking to you? What if you simply *despised* a particular woman. I don't believe any of your words, and I don't think your life should be spared after all the lives—*souls*—of innocent women you have stolen." I run my tongue up the side of his face. "Tastes like weakness and *fear*. It's judgement day, *Thomas,* and this *Witch* has taken your fate into her hands. You reap what you sow."

I lunge, his throat stretched wide, and as I sink my fangs easily beneath his sticky skin, I hear Charity say, "Make him suffer, Freyja."

I suck deeply while he screams, blood running down the sides of my mouth in sticky rivulets. I have pleased my Charity.

The table crashes to the floor, and Thomas is ripped from my mouth by the jaws of Garm's hulking wolf form. Thomas' screams vibrate through me, and I fall back, watching Garm shake him back and forth by his neck like a limp ragdoll.

My gift of revenge is snuffed out by the hysterical screams that come from Charity, Charles pulling her into his arms.

I should have known the smell of Thomas' blood will

be too much for Garm to bear, the sight forcing his change with his rage boiling over until he can no longer resist the urge to decimate the man that burned his beloved alive.

CHAPTER 33
CHARLES

After Charity's screams subside, I pull her head into my chest and cover her eyes with my hand, watching in horror as the beast flings skin and blood all over the once-pristine library. Books are splashed with skin, and I watch what can only be an artery or vein fly through the air.

The only thought that can form a rational action is to get Charity out of here as fast as our feet can take us.

I pull on her hand, and as I look back over her tear-soaked face, my heart breaks for her.

I always knew this was a façade. Nothing about this felt real, and although I did feel something akin to thankfulness for Freyja—for taking Charity out of her misery and into a world that existed only inside her mind's bliss-filled eye. What we have witnessed was straight from a blood-soaked nightmare.

Once we are outside, the cold air bites my skin, and I realize we have nothing but the clothes Freyja have given us.

My feet are running faster than my eyes can comprehend, and when we pass the garden and make it to the tree line, Charity is tugging on my arm, digging her heels into the ground and forcing me to a complete stop.

"What are you doing? Come on! I warned you so many times! Did you see that *thing?* It's time to GO!"

The moon's glow make her tears look bigger, her eyes round and innocent. She uses the backs of her hands to wipe them away, and she shouts at me, "I don't *want* to go back to Bethlehem!"

I take two furious strides towards her, placing my hands on both sides of her face, "What is WRONG with you!?"

She begins to sob again and hides her face in her hands.

I feel a sob rise in my throat, half because I know I am callous and half because every alarm bell in my brain is telling me to get far away from here.

"You are *just* like *him.*"

As she bites out the words, something inside of me snaps, and I realize she is talking about Thomas.

And all I can think is...you have no idea how much I am *nothing* like him.

"I'm not, Cher....I...I'm so sorry...I didn't mean to yell at y—"

"But you did! Your sorry's mean nothing! I have never felt afraid of her...I want to stay here with her!"

"Please, just come with me, I will protect you and make sure no one will ever take you away from me." I am trying to cradle her to my chest, but her fists are fighting against it and shoving me away.

"I *want* him to die. I don't care if he's your father—he's *ruined* my life!"

I sigh, but I release her, leading her behind a tree,

watching the door from where we stand. "He's not my father."

I barely know the man that has been ripped to shreds back there. All I want now is to return to London—to Domenico and his wealth. Charity will learn to love it there.

Her eyes grow wide, and she reels back to punch me square in the chest.

"Liars! All of you..."

Something rustles in the trees to our right, and I hear a deep, low growl just as I see a set of yellow eyes glowing in the depths of the trees.

"Call me all the names you want, but if you don't want to die, you'll come with me NOW!"

Charity is already running, and I follow behind her, catching up quickly as trees whip by us. The cold air beats my face, and I try to catch her hand in mine, needing to feel her touch, to prove to myself that she's still safe.

We lock hands as Charity's hair flies behind her, and my lungs burn as we run toward blackness.

I can hear the heavy thuds of something on our heels, but I'm too scared to look. I think for a moment I can hear the beast's snorts and grunts, but I cannot look back because I am too afraid.

I search for the stream I know is up here somewhere, listening for running water, but it never comes.

"I'm scared!" She yells beside me but doesn't release my hands as we hop over roots and rocks.

Just as I begin to lose all hope, a clearing in the distance appears. I smile, and my breath is coming in rapid pants...only a few more feet.

We run faster as a light and a cabin appear. The

moonlight shows through, and I steal a glance at Charity's smile as well.

Just as we breach the clearing, my boot catches on a rock, and I am flung face-first into the dirt, pulling Charity down with me.

And right after my face contacts the cold dirt, I look up and right into the garden that belongs to Freyja.

~

A low growl at my feet raises the hairs all over my body. A smell that can only be described as dog hits my nostrils, and I roll onto my back to meet the creature with my eyes.

It is the largest animal I have ever seen, its size rivaling that of a bear. His fur is a deep grey, with a mouth full of sharp canines and a tongue dripping with blood and flesh. One ear is sliced down the center, and my mouth drops open as he growls so close to my face that I can smell death on his breath.

"Ch...Charles..." Charity sniffs, slowly backing away on her hands and feet.

"*Afi!*"

The wolf juts its head up and towards Freyja's voice, squinting his yellow eyes at her. His tongue lolls out of his mouth and his massive paw grazes my ear as he slinks away from me.

Charity jumps up, flinging her arms around Freyja's

neck, kissing her cheeks over and over, ushering words of thanks inside her ear.

"Witch!" I bellow, and I charge her, knocking her over and Charity out of her arms.

I wrap my hands around her neck, and she only stares up at me, unfazed. She smiles, and for the first time since we have arrived, I see the small fangs that hide behind her full lips.

In a split second, I am on my back, a force of nature that's not tangible, and the last thing I see is her slanted, green eyes and her mouth agape and lunging towards my neck.

CHAPTER 34
FREYJA

I have frightened my pets and perhaps mistook Charity's miseries as something more serious than she intended.

Charles is unconscious, undoubtedly from the shock of witnessing Garm's wolf form. I only bit him a little, just so he will sleep and stop this silly resisting he is always doing.

With one arm slung over Charity's shoulders and the other over mine, we carry him inside the house and onto the furs beside the fire.

"Thank you...for rescuing us...again." Charity says, small and quiet, like a kitten.

I stroke her hair and kiss her forehead. "I will *never* hurt you my pet. I care for you."

My own words startle me, but I allow them to wash over me; to really feel what they mean.

I have never cared for another the way I care for you. I will not let anyone hurt you again.

She nods, and I assess the room, making sure Garm is

safely secure inside the garden's gates with his bone—Thomas.

I go to the kitchen and fill a glass with water; Charles will need it when he came to.

Charity is kneeling beside him, stroking the spot of his neck where I bit him.

I kneel next to her, feeling slightly betrayed she will try to escape.

"Why did you run from me? I thought you hated that man?"

She stares down over Charles' pale face and strokes back the blond hair from his forehead. "That beast! The wolf-man...he was terrifying!"

"Shh, shh. So, you left because of him?"

"Of course!"

I should have known a mortal will be unable to fathom a man turn into beast. He is quite large...

"Do you love him?"

"Who?"

"Charles."

There is a long pause, and she stares at his face a little longer, then looks at me. "I think so."

I grab her by the chin, the hungry animal inside of me rearing its head. I'm jealous, protective, but mostly, I want to hear her say those words to me.

"And *me*?"

Her eyes fall to my lips, and she wets them with that deft tongue of hers. I want to bite it and make her squeal.

"I...I think I love you, too. Is that wrong?"

Her words are like a burst of wind through my bones, and I gasp, taking her mouth into mine. The force of it knocks her back, and I am like a predator on my kill, my hands eagerly exploring her body.

Kissing down her jaw and her neck. I plump her perfect breasts, twirling her rigid nipple through the fabric of the silk robe.

"Stay with me, and never leave me," I say breathlessly.

She moans inside my mouth, and our tongues tangle together, hers tasting like honey and berries from the wine we shared earlier.

She breaks our kiss, her lips swollen and bruised. "Only if Charles stays, too."

I sit back on my heels, my core throbbing to be touched, to be filled. One person has never felt satisfying enough, and the thought of having two sends shivers of pleasure down to my thighs.

When I glance over, Charles' blue eyes are watching us both, and he seems content and undeterred. Pushing himself up on his elbow, he pulls me to him by my hair, and instinctively, I pull back my lips, showing my fangs.

"Bite me again, if you wish. I will happily endure it again, to see Charity's happiness return."

Leaning down, I kiss him gently, licking his bottom lip and grazing the top with my teeth. Charity's face appears beside mine, and she closely watches our mouths move together.

She nips Charles' ear, placing soft kisses down his neck as we share our own intimate kiss. Charles ends the kiss, pulling back, and pushes our heads together. I kiss Charity, but this time, I take her hand and place it on Charles' lap.

"I want to watch, but then I'm going to punish you both for running away from me like that."

Charity's eyes grow wide in that sweet, innocent way

I love so much. She nods, and Charles looks up at her, a need in his eyes so strong, I can feel it too.

I help her shrug out of her robe, and his eyes are fixed on the pink tips of her breasts. He slides down his pants to his ankles, and he's ready, cock already hard. The head is taught, and the tip shines with his excitement. I watch as Charity wraps her hand around it, looking so small in comparison. I lean back on my hands and spread myself wide, reaching between my legs. I know he can see every crevice of my cunt, and I am slick with need. "You want to fuck her, don't you, lost boy?"

His eyes remain on her breasts, and he nods.

Charity stops stroking, looking back at me. She watches my fingers disappear into my folds and bites her lip. "I think...I think I will like to watch you punish him."

I grin. "As you wish."

Charity scoots back, and I lean forward over Charles. "Roll over."

I stand, grabbing a thin, wooden paddle Garm made for me for 'cooking.' He didn't need to know about *all* of my hobbies.

Charles looks at Charity and turns over reluctantly.

"Keep your eyes on her, and if it's too much for you, simply say her name."

He nods in understanding.

His rear is plump, muscular, and perfect for my paddle.

"You must never run away again," *smack*, "Especially when you want to bury yourself inside me so badly," *smack*, "You're a bad..." another smack but harder this time, earning a grunt from him, " ...lost boy. I'm going to get that cock wet tonight."

Charity is whimpering, and her hand is between her

legs now, the wet sound of her messy cunt kissing her fingertips.

"Oh...you're a dirty girl, aren't you? Do you enjoy watching him get punished?" I purr, and she furiously nods her head, her eyes rolling back as I call her a dirty girl. "Are you *my* dirty girl?"

She cries out, plunging two fingers inside of herself.

I leave Charles' bright red cheeks to the air, setting down the paddle and grabbing her wrist. "You don't get to come yet, sweet pet."

She pouts, looking at me from beneath her lashes.

"Don't worry, you will, but not yet. We won't stop until you've both made a filthy mess."

CHAPTER 35
CHARITY

My legs quiver and I can't believe how turned on I am watching Charles' ass get paddled by Freyja.

"Sit up," she commands, kneeling over Charles. His eyes are glassy, and I'm not sure if he's under a spell or drunk with desire for her, for me, or for us all together.

She moves behind me, draping both my legs over Charles', facing him. I look into his eyes, fixed on my cunt. I know how wet I am, and I'm sure he can see. I feel exposed, raw, and I'm eating up every second of it. I feel two small pricks on my neck, and my eyes roll back as warmth fills my chest. I let her suck while she strokes me.

Freyja reaches around to cup me, and I feel her wet heat pressing against my left buttock. I close my eyes as I feel her fingers stroke down my slit, nudging it apart gently. "Open your eyes, pet, and watch how much your brother loves to watch your pussy get stroked."

I've never heard anyone use that word before, but I like it. It sounds a little like 'kitty.'

I keep my eyes on him, and I can tell it's taking great effort for him to keep his hands off himself.

Freyja expertly inserts two fingers into my drenched entrance, but she doesn't go deep; she pushes her fingers against the front of my walls, sending a shock of pleasure through to my core. My mouth falls open, and I cry out as she begins pushing that sensitive spot over and over again in rapid succession until I'm bucking against her hand and grunting. "Oh, you like that? Does that feel right?"

My jaw is pressed to my chest as she continues to put pressure on the spot, and I feel like I may wet myself. "Ugh! Stop! I'm going to w—"

She gives two final pushes and withdraws her fingers, spanking my cunt until a clear stream burst from my nether lips. "Oh! Oh! Fuckkk!" She continues the slaps, and my hips are jerking as the pleasure rolls through my body like a storm, and I watch myself spurt over the blankets.

Charles is sitting up now, his face enthralled with my wet explosion, mouth hanging open.

She inserts two fingers again, pumping out two more spurts of juices, the blanket beneath me drenched in my climax.

Using all of her soaked fingers, she strokes my cunt, the contact over my sensitive nub causing me to lean back on her, letting her take my full weight so I can float inside the euphoria of my sweet release.

"Bad girl for leaving me...but what a good girl for coming like that," she whispers, stroking my body, stoking the residual pleasure from every nerve connected to my womb.

"Lick her clean, naughty boy, then fuck her."

Charles' face is in between my legs in a second, and I pull at his hair as he laps at my thighs, my lips, and my ass.

When he's finished, he's mounting me while I lay between Freyja's legs.

"Wait," I say, and I push Freyja backward, and onto her back, as I scootch upward, so I am laying on top of her, both of our cunnies open for him.

"Oooh, dirty girl...do you think he can take us both?" She coos inside my ear, and she plays with my breasts. The thought of him being inside of us both, one after the other, sends shivers through my body.

"I hope so," I whisper as I watch him draw up closer to us on his knees, between our legs.

He grabs his cock, and I think he will line himself up with me first, only he doesn't. I hear Freyja moan loudly as he drives himself home. His torso is flush with my mound, and as he makes his strokes, his belly hits my erect bud each time. It drives me mad to think of him inside her, but I know he will fill me soon.

Charles groans as he stops himself for a moment, leaning over me and kissing my mouth while he's still inside her.

Suddenly, he withdraws, looking down briefly so he can find my entrance, and buries himself inside me next, his cock already slick with Freyja's arousal. I gasp; he is inside me, but so is she, our fluids creating a cocktail of heady desire.

He finds a steady rhythm of fucking us both, his head bent down, navigating our holes, his hands gripping my thighs.

He slams into me, then withdrawals, slamming into

her and then back to me again. Freyja grinds her hips against my ass, moaning and calling both our names.

Charles pulls out his cock, angry and swollen in his hand, and he pumps himself until he's grunting, his seed spilling over us both.

"Yes! Dirty boy! Make a mess. All over us both."

I climax again as Freyja reaches around to stroke my erect bud once more. I don't hear her release, but her reassurance in my ear is enough to soothe me as we still.

Charles lays on top of us, the three of us falling into a pile on the blankets, hands and mouths covering each other.

Freyja reaches over to the cup of water beside us. "Drink, my pet. You will need to replenish what you just lost."

She reaches into one of the pots beside the fireplace, retrieving a small washcloth and wiping down my belly and thighs.

She returns it to the water, rinsing the cloth again, and hands it to Charles. Looking over the damp blankets, she laughs. "I guess I have some washing to do."

My cheeks are blazing hot, and I sip the water with a smile. Whatever I just did, I want to do it again. I want Freyja to teach me how to make myself do that.

Stroking my face and then reaching over to stroke Charles, Freyja lay beside us, draping her arm over us both.

"You once belonged only to yourselves, and now we belong to each other."

CHAPTER 36

CHARLES

She thinks I have forgotten what she is...and watching her make Charity climax the way only a man can reminds me of her magic.

My body is replete, but the guilt I feel in my soul is searing me. I want to push it out...the guilt and the voice of reason that just won't go away.

I must deliver this deviant of a woman to my Deacon on the full moon...this night.

I rub Charity's thighs, calves, and feet. I kiss and suck at her toes and make a vow to myself to make sure she is always safe with or without Freyja.

I enjoy this one singular moment I have with both of them, and in a perfect, uncomplicated world, I will stay, but I have no choice.

I cannot love more than one, it will be a sin, and I must deliver Freyja to the Deacon.

I pour wine into all our glasses, jesting and laughing with them both. Charity is languid and smiling, and as we drink, it is easy to see they are feeling the effects.

I will just have to keep pouring the wine until Freyja's reasoning leaves her.

"Charles..." Freyja slurs, her voice soft as velvet.

"Hm..."

"Why do you resist the *passions of the flesh* so insistently?"

Freyja stumbles over the word insistently, and I realize she is quite intoxicated.

I snort, taking a large sip of the wine this time, allowing myself to enjoy the bitter grapes that make me feel slightly dizzy. "I don't know if we have enough time for the length of those reasonings..."

"I will like to know as well." Charity states, a small hiccup following.

I stare at the curves of Charity's round cheeks, and she smiles shyly as the orange flames of the fire light her eyes until they glisten.

I have little interest in sharing my lurid past with others, but I want to share it with Charity. I want her to see me...the real me.

"I grew up in a brothel in France. My mother a courtesan, and I a bastard. I have seen some devious things from a very young age."

Charity's attention is fixed on my face, stealing glances at my mouth as I speak.

Freyja leans in closer to me, stroking long pointed fingertips up and down my thigh, urging me to continue. "A brothel? How *scandalous*. Does your counterpart know about this?"

"Thomas? No. He doesn't know very much about me, like most. I guess you can say I've experienced more pleasure than many young men my age. It was a time I both enjoyed and felt ashamed of in a short span of time. Thinking back to it is painful, because I loved my mother deeply—she was all I knew of love. Yet, the man who took me in after she died, he had other things to say of her."

"Tragic..." Freyja soothes, stroking my cheek.

"I'm so sorry Charles..." Charity's sweet voice salves the small ache that lingers inside my heart.

I grapple to change the subject and focus on the task at hand. The job I need to finish. "I have a crazy idea...let's go to the tall house beyond the stream." I pretend to knock back more wine, even though my glass is empty.

Charity jumps up, her breast bouncing in sync with her dimpled thighs. "Yes! I have always wanted to see it! Can we Freyja? I do not fear anything inside these woods with you by my side."

Freyja raises her cup to her mouth with a sober look, and I think for a moment she will dismiss my idea, and my last-ditch effort will fail.

Charity wraps her robe around herself, leaning down to kiss Freyja on top of her head. I raise one eyebrow and flash a charming smile in her direction.

"Anything for my pets."

My mind races while Freyja puts back on the fur robe I'm guessing she made herself. It is still unclear just how powerful she may be, just what she is capable of, but whatever this place is there is no leaving without her help.

"The sun will rise soon, there is no better time than now." I chime, dressing myself again, which feels like the hundredth time in the past three days.

Freyja wavers on her feet, and Charity catches her, laughing.

I scan the outside, the twilight creeping in, but the

full moon is still visible in the sky. Freyja must notice my surveying because she grabs my arm and says, "Do not worry, lost boy...the beast," *hiccup,* "is sated now...he has had his revenge, and I'm sure he is sleeping it off."

Charity grabs my hand, a gleeful look in her eye, and grabs Freyja's hand with the other.

We walk towards the foggy woods, hand in hand in hand...

~

"Wow," Charity drawls, as we all stand in front of the three-story house that once housed the legend of a wolfman and his succubus queen. "Creepy."

Freyja stares as if she is looking at someone familiar, and I look over at her. "Everything alright?"

Leaving us standing in the middle of the dirt path, she walks forward toward the house as if it wasn't of her own free will.

Charity follows closely behind and looks back to wave me on.

My stomach is in knots, and I'm having second thoughts.

will Charity ever forgive me? Can we go back to living an everyday normal life after all we have done in those woods together?

"Wait!" I call behind them, but it's too late.

The front door creaks loudly, and one of the windows has been broken, boarded up with a mangled piece of wood. As I enter, it is dark, cob webs hanging from the covered furniture and lamps. I squint my eyes to see inside, but I can only make out the one uncovered window at the back of the house through a narrow doorway.

"Charles! Make him stop! He has Freyja!"

I enter the doorway, and I recognize Domenico and his gaunt, pointed face. "Deacon?"

There is an iron collar clamped around Freyja's neck, and as she claws at it, I can see smoke filtering through the air around her head. She looks like she's in pain.

"Charles, son, welcome. What a relief that you succeeded in bringing her to me." When he smiles, I see two long fangs and look over his features that seem unrecognizable.

"Wh...what's going on? Where are your robes and your hat? I've never seen you this wa—"

"Please, just be quiet for a moment and allow me to enjoy my victory."

I am puzzled by his words, I assumed I will deliver her to him, and he will perform an exorcism, perhaps lock her in a cage and deliver her back to London to be dealt with.

I round the corner to Charity and pull her to me, kissing her hair.

"Did you know about this?" she whispers.

I don't move; I just keep my eyes on Domenico, the man I clearly didn't know at all.

Dragging Freyja to the other side of the room, I watch as he passes a large mirror above the mantle, and he is not there. I only see Freyja struggling to get free.

"*What?*" I whisper, blinking my eyes, refusing to believe what I am seeing.

Domenico shoves Freyja down into a chair next to a large four-poster bed, where a young blonde with ringlets sleeps. He fastens the other end of the collar to a metal bar screwed in the floor.

My mind races, and I force myself to stand still, even though I want to go to her, stroke her hair, and comfort her.

Her pain is all my fault...all my doing.

"What are you going to do with her?" I ask loudly, Charity gripping my shirt tightly in her hands.

"My son, she is but the missing puzzle piece, and you have delivered her to me...to my Melody." His voice is calm and even, something that used to put me at ease, but now it just sounds menacing.

"Was she even responsible for the deaths? Or did you lie about more than just my purpose in Bethlehem?" I hold Charity tighter, my chest heavy at the thought of leading her into every danger she's encountered along this journey. All for what? God's will?

Monsters aren't real. I am having a nightmare, and I'll wake up soon.

"You see...I've been around for quite some time. Oddly enough, those *most* respected, *most feared*, seem to be the men of the clergy...so that is what I became." He spreads his hands wide, smiling, but his fangs are gone now.

He moves about the room, picking up objects as if he is preparing to leave.

"Then why do you want her? She's a witch. Isn't she one of your kind?" I force my voice to sound strong, something Domenico has taught me.

He laughs, low and incredulous. "You can say that...I do *need* her. If I ever want my little girl to awaken again... she's the only one that can lift the curse. So, thank you! Charles! I am forever indebted to you."

"Fine, then you have what you wanted...now Charity and I can go home." I turn Charity toward the doorway, her sobs muffled inside her hands. I know she doesn't want to leave Freyja here.

All I can think about is getting away from him, and getting Charity away from him. We can make it back home, and we can have our own life together, even if we have to do it somewhere else. After all we have endured, surely, we can find a new town to take us in.

"No, no, no...come back, come back. You can't leave yet."

I turn back to him, and he is no longer standing beside Freyja, cowering in the corner; he is right in front of us, his fangs bared again. "When she wakes—which she will once this succubus enters her dreams—she will need to feed. From her..." he shifts his pale eyes to my sweet Charity, and she darts behind me.

I reach around behind me, shielding her, proving my protectiveness with that one small gesture.

This is because of me. My guilt causes my doubt, and even though my heart wants them both, my brain won't allow it. If I have only been strong enough to silence that voice—that guilt—perhaps the three of us will have been able to live in blissful harmony all together. We have all we can ever want, so why do I have to fuck it all up?

I have already fucked up Charity's perfect dream come to life.

I try to wrap my mind around his words, *curse.... enter her dreams*...but my mind still hovers by the fireplace where the three of us made love. I will give anything to return there again, blissful, comatose, dripping together in love and lust.

I do the only thing I can think of to save Charity, try and salvage the real mess I have made.

Bringing Charity along with me, straight from the stove and into the fire.

My eyes are drawn to a single rose in a vase next to the bed; it looks out of place in the dust of the old house —blossomed into a vibrant red, the color of fresh blood.

Two men in black coats descend onto Freyja while she hisses and shouts curses. She gives them a rather good fight as Charity and I both look on in shock.

"Come, brown eyes, it is time to go." Domenico reaches out a pale hand to Charity, and I can see something in him has changed, softened.

"Who is she?" I ask, my arm still protectively wrapped around Charity's waist.

Domenico locks eyes with mine, and I can remember his kind words to me as a boy when I was full of questions and concerns—*you only need to trust in God.*

"Someone *very* special to me. Just trust me, Charles, my boy. Return to the little town, collect your things, and I will send a carriage soon. So *unfortunate* for Thomas...a pity really," he sneers in a way that makes me feel uneasy.

I won't let him take Charity. I can't.

"I don't need anything there; I will accompany you *now.*"

Domenico draws his hands back, tucking them both behind him, and gently nods. "Well enough."

One of the taller two men who has dragged Freyja from the house approaches Charity and I. "No, I will take her. I can keep an eye on her for Dom."

The man looks at Dom, and after a small exchange, he nods.

"Where are we going?" Charity whispers behind me, and I lead her out of the dark house and into the dawning light outside.

"London, I assume."

A small part of me is elated to return there. I can show Charity all the things I have wanted too so badly. She will be under my care with no pressure of being taken from me by another.

I just need to figure out who this sleeping girl is and why she is so important to Dom.

There are two carriages already waiting outside, and I shiver as I watch four of the men in black coats load a dark, cherry wood coffin into the back of one.

A wheeled pallet is hitched to the one we are led to, and a large cage sits atop it with a thrashing Freyja inside.

Charity gasps, clutching at my arm, and I pull her head to look into my eyes. "It's time to act exactly the way you did before you met her. God-fearing and humble...despondent. Do you understand?"

Tears threaten to break at the corner of her eyes, but she nods twice, casting her eyes to the ground.

My heart sinks as I watch her become the scared and quiet maiden once again, desperately trying to act like the woman she loves wasn't in a cage like an animal.

I squeeze her hand but look at Freyja one last time before we step inside the carriage.

She looks different in the morning light, her black hair in wild snarls around her face. Her eyes are green no more but black, a startling contrast to her fair skin. Her fangs are bared, and she shakes the cage, reciting chants in a language I do not understand. She looks wild—feral.

Just as I adjust myself into my seat, the tall man reappears, tying Charity's hands behind her back while she looks up at me in the carriage with fear in her eyes.

I swallow hard, but the man stuffs her inside beside me, and I pull her close.

She is crying again, and I kiss her hair, shushing her with gentle strokes along her back.

"All will be well, my little light. I will always keep you safe."

THE SECRET OF THE WOODS

Lilith bows to no one

Lilith is an ancient Goddess, and Domenico is one of the most revered vampires in France.

When these two forces combine, love and bloodshed soon follow.

But after a betrayal of the heart, a curse claims a life for a life, leaving Domenico searching for answers through an ancient lineage.

Domenico believes Freyja is the key to unlocking the curse, but he should have known better than to force a witch to do his bidding.

Charles and Charity want to escape the shadows, but little do they know, they're just pawns in a grand scheme.

Corruption, lust, and power linger inside the corridors and hidden rooms of Castle DeLesepps, but just who will reveal their truth?

PROLOGUE

The Dark Mother was what Hel called me after I was banished to The Underworld.

I refused to lay beneath my husband and remain in the garden...so here I was, forced into darkness and fire, plummeting through realms and sinking down into the depth of the sea...only I did not once feel fear.

I felt freedom, unrestraint...clarity.

The soft, curvy human body I once inhabited; felt lighter yet stronger...

Cold, black floor pressed against my cheek, and once I had enough strength to open my eyes, it was not pain and despair I was met with.

"Another fallen angel." Hel gave a heavy sigh. "One would think I would be used to this by now. Stand up and drink, fair one."

Pushing myself off the cold floor, I turned toward the voice and sat up, curling and uncurling my fingers and toes. I blinked a few times as the figure before me became clearer, towering over me like the apple trees in the garden I once called home. Two black and white snakes curled into coils beside me, and I smiled, stroking one's scales and feeling great comfort.

"Am I dead?" I asked the shadowed figure.

She laughed, chilling and sweet. "No, but you will feed on lust, and if you do not have it, you will wither away."

I nodded, looking down at my hands, and they seemed to blur, like fog. I waved them around and watched in awe as I floated in and out of solid form, red light glowing through my skin.

"You must rest now, gather your strength. You are nothing short of a Goddess, Dark Mother, and stories will be told of your contempt and resistance. Women will praise the Dark Mother. Just remember, even if they fear you, you will still thrive."

Contempt? Resistance?

I was strength embodied; I did not bow to anyone. Why was it called resistance and not curiosity to see outside of the Garden?

I would rest, and I would gain strength.

I was a Goddess now, her words permeating inside my soul.

I needed to find a way to be worshipped...there must be someone who could fill that role.

It was then that I bargained with Hel, for another chance somewhere else.

I couldn't deny the empty feeling inside my chest, the crushing feeling of rejection and ridicule. I ached to be loved and needed, but I refused to submit to another. It was the price I paid for choosing such insolence.

My only choice was given to me by her and her alone:

The mortal world, the Welsh lands that held magic.

It was only there that I would be able to retain a new beginning.

And so, she birthed me through the green moss and tall trees, not quite a demon but also not a God. I would start over in a time that was not kind to women; but I would show them exactly what it meant to be divinely feminine.

CHARLES

1730 FRANCE

The long, arduous carriage ride from Wales to London made my body ache and my mind race.

Charity had fallen asleep in my lap, and I stroked her hair, promising myself I would never let her out of my sight for even just a moment.

I'd never felt so possessive over anyone or anything in all my life.

"Well done, my boy. You did just as I asked...you found the one I needed. As a reward, you can keep your plaything... although we may need her later."

Domenico had been like a father to me, and while I was relieved I'd once again reside inside the walls of the musty, yet wealthy Castle Delesepps, I was worried that the world I once knew had changed forever.

Werewolves...vampires...things talked of only in stories, or fables, walked amongst us. Not many people the wiser.

Except now I knew, and I didn't know how I felt about keeping that secret for Domenico—though I would do just about anything to keep Charity safe.

Would I have to act as if the guise of priesthood was true? After all, it was everything he'd built his life around, the people he interacted with daily...the church he called his home.

What did this mean for Charity and Freyja? What was it Domenico wanted with Freyja, anyhow?

Deep down, I knew I would find out, not much was kept from me, even as a young boy.

I shivered as I remembered the sleeping girl, who looked more dead than asleep, and the way that Freyja had thrashed in that God-awful cage.

Like a wild animal.

"What do you think he'll do with her? With Freyja?"

Charity's soft voice broke my thoughts, and her soft tone brought a smile to my lips, as I looked down at her closed eyes and lashes that fanned her high cheeks.

"There's no telling, little light. I am here though, and we will figure this out together."

I had untied her wrists promptly, but I feared that she'd be held prisoner just as much as Freyja. I made a silent prayer to God that Domenico would not harm Charity—my Charity, the girl that was once my stepsister, but now my lover.

"My mother will be so worried...and Thomas is dead..."

Charity's words trail as a tear slid down her pink, freckled face.

"Your sister is there, and you know Clarise will take care of your mother. Strong willed as she is."

A forced, small pull at the corner of her mouth became visible at my words about her sister, but she quickly returned to her somber mood as the carriage came to a stop.

We'd finally arrived at Castle Delesepps.

And all I wanted to do was lay Charity inside my bed, with only skin, wine, and bread between us for at least one full week.

I wondered if Charity would be able to let Freyja go... let go enough to enjoy only me. Yes, it was a selfish statement to make, but I didn't want to share. I had done what I'd needed to do, and at the time, it was having them both, emotions be damned.

We would find a way to free Freyja; we would all get out of here alive, together. I had to find a way. This was the least I could do, if not to prove to Charity that I really did care for her. Betrayal aside, I had only wanted to please Domenico and do as I was tasked when I came to that small town of Bethlehem.

Surely Charity would want to stay in line with the traditional values of her family and put the immature urges of having us both behind her. She must want a life with me, how could I be wrong about that?

For now, I hoped that my love would be enough to keep Charity safe and happy inside the dark castle walls.

The only woman I had ever loved.

~

Just as I knew he would, Domenico made a big show of what he had to offer us almost immediately.

We were quickly summoned to dinner by one of the many young men who resided here during any given season. We were not being guarded, but we were watched. Closely, I was certain.

I eyed the space around us, searching for the familiar cracks and crevices that withheld so many secrets. So many dark parts of myself were hidden inside of those walls. At least they were safely secured, with only Domenico knowing the truth of our complicated relationship.

Charity held my hand in a death grip, and each time Domenico would smile, she would shudder beside me.

I was a savage boy for thinking carnal thoughts about making her thighs do that little shuddering thing, but I did my best to reign in those thoughts as I tucked her inside my arm, fitting there so perfectly. I was finally getting used to my taller height and bigger body—the body of a man and not a boy. I felt pride in protecting her fragile heart.

Domenico smiled down over us both, the regal and polite man that he was. His smile seemed more menacing now that I knew what he was, an undead bloodsucker, but I tried hard not to think about that right now. I needed to focus on making Charity feel at home, I needed her to trust me—vampires or not.

I doubted Domenico would kill me, especially not after all those chances he had when I was much younger and weaker.

I blushed slightly at the memory of those nights alone with Father Domenico.

"Sit, please. Fear not, girl. I would never hurt anyone as perfect and *youthful* as yourself...with so much life still left ahead of you."

Charity's movements were mechanical at best, and I

watched her sit awkwardly in the chair furthest from where Domenico dined. I took a seat beside her.

Her eyes remained downcast, and Domenico cut away at his steak with an eagerness that made me nervous. I had to say something to break the ice that had formed in the small-time we were apart.

"What did I miss while I was gone? Is everyone... well?" I cleared my throat as I awkwardly said the last part, realizing that vampires probably didn't get sick or ill considering they weren't exactly living beings.

I watched as Charity's eyes grew wider and wider as she watched Domenico chew the bloody meat chunks, a drop of blood escaping in a small rivulet down the corner of his mouth. He gingerly wiped it away and smiled at Charity but returned his gaze to me.

"We've missed you deeply," he said, his smile creased at the corners of his eyes, and I suddenly remembered how beautiful a deep, silvery blue they were.

I swallowed hard, a small pang of guilt shimmering through my vision but dissipating just a quickly. I did what he'd asked of me; there had to be something in it for me.

"I see you've found more than just the woman we sought. Are you in love?"

I nodded stupidly; a grin plastered across my face as I looked over at Charity who remained looking down at the wooden table with a stony expression.

"We are, I'm going to marry her."

I took her hand into mine, and her face was nothing short of shock as she looked at me with her jaw hanging.

Her shocked expression sent a pang of hurt through my chest, and I resisted questioning her right there of her desires. I couldn't do that yet, I needed to wait for a better time.

"Well, that's wonderful. Happy to hear that, Charles." His tone was that of a fondness I couldn't quite name. He was a father figure, but he was more than that—he was home and warmth all wrapped into one.

The large door to the dining room opened loudly, and Domenico stood in greeting. "Brother, welcome. Sit, please."

I recognized the tall, darker man as Darius, the eldest brother. He barely spoke and had a nasty scar on his left eye that made him quite intimidating. I stayed away from the DeLesseps brothers when I lived here, Domenico making it clear that he was the one in charge.

I knew they were from old, royal money, and I heard that you never fucked with old money.

"Please, may I be excused? I would like to go back to the room...I'm not feeling well." Charity's voice was barely above a whisper, and she slid out the chair while she clutched her belly.

"Please, let me know if you need anything at all, darling. Charles, I prefer if you stayed behind. We should probably catch up properly."

I nodded, unmoving.

I should have known this wouldn't be as easy as a good night dinner.

CHAPTER 2
FREYJA

I could smell the blood through the walls of this overzealous castle. It was everywhere, on every surface, but most of it had been cleaned up, the naked eye unaware.

Domenico.

I already knew his name, although I'd never seen this man in my life. I'd crossed many, many men along my path but never one that smelled the way he did.

I gagged at the metal stench, pulling a small piece of ginger from my dress pocket and popping it into my mouth. I smiled at the bitter taste, instantly easing the tug at the top of my belly.

I surveyed the room he'd put me in, and it looked like a guest bedroom fit for a gothic-princess. I rolled my eyes at the thought of his kindness toward me; he could have thrown me into a dungeon that harbored rotting bodies long forgotten, only he didn't. He needed something from me, and I knew that was the reason. I'd explored the depth of castles many times before. I had travelled to France once, but the men there were insatiable, and even a demi-god like me did not have the time to fuck all day, every day.

I walked to the window fogged over from the humidity, and I couldn't see anything except for the green of the trees outside.

Garm would've been searching for me already, following my scent as far as he needed to go. He was either already outside, waiting and planning, or he would soon enough.

Would he storm the castle in his wolf form? Rip out Domenico's throat? I smiled at the thought but had a sinking feeling it would take much time for him to find me.

We'd driven by carriage for nearly two moons and one sun. The cage I had been transported in was a jest, a pitiful way for a man to show the power he held by using an inescapable box on a witch. The only thing holding me in place were the silver bars, searing my skin each time they were touched.

I could astral travel, get help, but I would always return to my body now trapped inside a Castle hundreds of times the size of my cabin.

I needed to find Charity but knew full well that she was by Charles' side. Anger returned a tightness to my chest as I thought of what he had done. How he had fooled me into thinking he could be trusted. I needed to get Charity away from him, soon, before he convinced her this was where she belonged.

He was smooth with his words, one of the only reasons I followed him. He must be stopped, and I needed my pet returned to where she belonged—by *my* side.

The taste of her tangy, sweet cunt was still on my lips. I licked at them, smiling to myself at the way she made me feel—no longer alone, fighting on my own. Her kind, serving demeanor left me with weak knees, and I wanted nothing more than to lie with her again. I thought about stroking the silky walls of her insides with my fingers as I whispered of her rare beauty into her ears. I was not done rewarding her, and I hoped I would get another chance to show her just how much I'd grown to need her.

Run, my child. Get to the outside...and run. Find Garm, and you will be free.

Run? I did not run from *anyone*. I did not fear anyone, men feared *me*.

My pride got the best of me for only a moment before I realized I had no choice but to flee. I didn't want to wait and find out what plans Domenico had for me.

Would he try and harness my magic? Take it from me entirely?

Maybe he'd planned to use me as a personal feeding troth until he eventually drained me of blood entirely.

Better go.

I argued with the internal voice inside my head that never left.

The Dark Mother.

This is not your debt to pay, flee now, my child.

I clenched my fist at my sides, knowing now would not be the time to argue; her voice never steered my wrong.

I pulled on the heavy wooden door, but it would not open—locked from the outside. I peered through the small keyhole, noting the empty hallway on the other side.

Who would knock and disappear? Perhaps someone had let me know the coast was clear?

I let this thought roll over in my mind while I paced.

The only possession left on my body was a hair pin I'd whittled from a piece of bone. I took it from the tangled mess on the top of my head, kneeling back down to the keyhole.

A few minutes had already passed, maybe I'd missed my window.

Fuck it, I must try.

Using my keen eyesight and small fingers, I was able to pick the lock with a click, stepping back as the door opened toward me.

I walked to the door and poked my head around it, just to be sure, and tiptoed to the un-obstructed entrance, waiting, listening. I blinked a few times, feeling the hairs on my body raise.

I was barefoot, and my dress was torn from the bent metal of the cage, but I was well enough to walk. I pulled the door back gently, looking both ways down the long hallway. Not a soul in sight—it was late dusk, and I would guess most of the inhabitants were safely inside their quarters.

I pressed my back against the shadowed wall, careful to watch my breathing in case the blood-sucking creature could hear me or smell me from miles away—surely it was both.

Just as the thought sent a shiver down my spine, my head was slammed back against the wall and a large, pale hand was around my neck, squeezing.

"Sweet, sweet Freyja. Do not run, my darling. Where would you go? We're in the middle of France now...you will not last a moment out there in these unkempt woods."

The smell was back, but now I could barely breathe as he cut off my ability to swallow. I began to see spots, and my eyes were rolling back into my head. Bursts of fire bled behind my eyelids, and the image of a naked woman beside a tree filled my vision. A behemoth of a snake crawled between the branches of the tree she stood beside.

Dark Mother?

"Just close your eyes, Mon cher, we have so much to discuss. *You* are going to bring me back my Melody with your *inherited* magic."

Everything turned black, and the stink of meat floated through my nose, permeating my vision with images of dead animals littered at my feet.

DOMENICO

She had fainted, which didn't give me much confidence in her magical abilities. Freyja's wards had been strong enough to keep my men from her cabin, and the ones who did manage to sneak through had told stories of sexual dreams feeling as if they were real. Bite marks trailed their necks when they returned, and each time I ran my fingers over the cuts, Lilith's scent of honey and fire permeated the air until they left me, bewildered and dazed.

I stared down at the deep purple stone I held inside my lined palm. The night air was cool enough to sting my lungs as I walked the gardens, but the fresh promise of fall lifted my listless mood.

This was the last remnant I had of my Lilith, but she would be returned to me, soon enough. If Freyja obeyed.

I wasn't sure what to expect of Freyja; if she would respect my orders or simply turn this all into a game for her freedom.

What powers did she hold? Was she a danger to me and to Charles?

I had trusted my youngest and most faithful brother, Dante, with the task of keeping watch over Lilith's lineage. And while he reported to me often, his men seemed to have plans of their own.

Was it a mistake for me to ask him to take watch over the woman I loved? The woman that I knew he coveted but hated himself for it?

I had too many churches to over-see, thousands of flocks to pass the word of the Lord onto. If I wanted our true identities kept hidden, this secret must stay nestled deep inside the cover of religion.

"It is done, she has been casted into this stone with a binding spell. Her lineage will never know of the power they hold. We will not have to fear her wrath any longer." I took the stone, turning it over in my hand, feeling a prick of sadness ebb at the corners of my eyes. My one true love, the only woman who saw the monster I was and loved me for it regard-less. We were both monsters, and the euphoria we shared would stay etched in my mind forever.

"But what of Melody? She sleeps forever with no way of undoing it. She is my blood-bound child...I must bring her back."

Dante shifted on his feet, looking back over his shoulder toward his apothecary room filled with potions and dark magic. He never allowed anyone passage into that room, not even me.

"I will find a way—without her."

Only, he hadn't done it yet, and I decided to take matters into my own hands. I didn't want to wait any longer, and if Lilith was the key to waking my sweet girl, then so be it. Deep down, for my own selfish reasons, I wanted—no, *craved* for her return. Would we reunite in love? Would she hate me, blaming me for everything that had happened? I knew bringing her back was reckless. I didn't care, I would pay the price with my own life if I must.

My body felt old, maybe even weaker. I needed something to put back a spark into this endless life—what she did for me that day in the courtyard. I wanted it back, no matter the consequences.

I squeezed the amulet in my palm until it burned, and I hissed her name into the night, into the endless black sky that stretched beyond the forest border, and beyond this dreadful linear timeline called *the present*.

If only I could transport back to that fateful day, the day we met in 1544. Would I have changed it? I knew the answer already. I wouldn't change it, because now, I just wanted to relive it.

CHAPTER 4

CHARLES

After Charity excused herself from the dinner table, I made a move to follow her, but Domenico quickly stopped me, grabbing my arm.

"So, we have some catching up to do, do we not?" He smiled, a knowing smile, the small secret between us living inside my head rose to the surface, and I pushed it down.

"I really didn't want you to know the truth about what I was, because, well, I didn't want to *frighten* you. Though, I do think a lot will make more sense to you now...about your...*unique* upbringing. It was not a traditional one, I know we can agree on that." Standing, he walked to my side of the table and leaned on it, his hand very close to my arm.

He was handsome and fit. He smelled of pepper and musk, creating a perfectly heady cocktail of confidence and sex.

If I had to admit it, I was most definitely attracted to him in every way I wasn't supposed to be. But he was right, our relationship was not one that was traditional in any way.

I'm sure it hurt a little at my announcement, but he wanted what was best for me after all, and he would want me to have the most traditional relationship for a boy raised by a priest.

"I'm not frightened." I wasn't certain why my brain picked that one part of the sentence to focus on, but it struck me somewhere deep, and I needed to make that clear to Domenico.

I was not afraid.

"Good, good. You are safe here...I swear by the Grace of God."

Ironic how he kept mentioning God, but I didn't know if God had allowed a spawn of Satan to walk among his crosses and statues. I'm sure God wasn't pleased with this situation.

I moved away from the table, pushing back away from Domenico and his sweet, spicy smell.

My thoughts hovered over Charity and if she was all right. I needed to be there for her if she was sick or needed comfort. I wanted to be her rock.

"And what will you do with Freyja?" I asked, feeling the need to further prove my point that I was not scared of him.

"We will know soon enough," he said, returning to his seat at the head of the sprawling table full of wine and food.

I had forgotten about the sleeping girl and resisted bringing her up, since I knew that was the real reason behind this. Domenico thought I was foolish, I knew that much. At this point, I would continue to let him think that way of me. It would only make it easier for me to find out more.

However, I wasn't brave enough to push the issue. Not quite yet anyway. I excused myself abruptly and hurried down the long, narrow hallways to our sleeping quarters, only to find Charity was gone.

I mean, really, I should've known better.

Of course, she searched for Freyja. It was her idea to venture into the woods that morning beside me, refusing to turn back. Of course, she would go in search of someone she cared for so deeply.

A pit began to form at the bottom of my stomach, and I fought back the urge to sob.

Did she still want me *and* Freyja? Or was I just a way for her to get inside these walls and rescue her beloved? A sharp dagger of jealousy pinched my heart, and I decided that I would not let Freyja interfere with my plans. Even if it was the last thing I did, I would marry Charity and she would be mine. I didn't *need to* share.

Doubt flooded my mind, even as I said it to myself. A nagging at the back of my mind wouldn't let me entertain the idea that she only had eyes for me. I knew that she didn't; I knew how she felt about Freyja. Was I selfishly trying to help Freyja, just so I could get her out of the way? Or did I truly want to see Charity safe and happy? I didn't have the answers to that yet, but I told myself it would all work out in the end. God would see to it, and I knew now that he would favor me over these *monsters*.

CHAPTER 5
LILITH
THE PAST

The mortal world was a boring one. I was stoned if I was naked in front of humans, cat called and ostracized. There was no endless supply of food or water; I must find those things on my own, and often, that meant someone must die in the process. I didn't fit in sixteenth century France either. I'd noticed a theme around that. I craved acceptance and needed mercy, but how does one receive mercy and acceptance when they were destined for adoration and devotion? Mercy was given to the poor, the inept. I wasn't kind to men, and women seemed to fear me at the very least. It was no bother, I didn't care for the opinions of others—I was a Goddess, and I would walk to the ends of the earth until I was rightfully worshipped.

The clothes of this century were uncomfortable to say the least, the corset hugging my waist and hips made me feel as though I'd suffocate. What was living if it wasn't steeped in the small pleasures of life? Why would I ever want to squeeze my insides so that I may have a small waist? I would rather jiggle my hips and my arse all the way down the dirt and stone pathways, without one care in the world. Let them stare, let them say what they may —it didn't affect the way I felt about myself. It was them who were bothered by it, not me. Perhaps I should remain deep inside the woods and stay in my naked, natural form beside the animals. It would be much like Eden, which was exactly what I didn't want. I came here looking for more, and more was what I would have.

I sat at the edge of a fountain in the middle of someone's courtyard. I'd fallen asleep against a tree this morning, after an   invigorating kill—a deer and her fawns. They were delicious, the meat gently warmed by a fire. I had also taken some cheese from old lady Marie, who had a habit of leaving her doors unlocked at night after her husband died suddenly.

The courtyard was not modest by any means, but there were no horses with carts, only crosses and heavy iron gates. The full moon hung above me, and I looked up at it longingly, reaching out a hand as the white light bathed my body.

I was naked again, but my wavy hair reached my thighs and covered my breasts. I crossed my legs, eating an apple and surveying the tall steeples and windows that surrounded me.

Someone must have brought me here, I was powerful, but not powerful enough to travel by thought, not yet. I was working on that. My strength was unmatched, and I'd killed bears bigger than I. I was unsure of my immortality, but I was most fearful of being caged again.

A man, taller than I, emerged from the shadows below the eaves of the windows. His hair was black as night, with grey dusted at his temples. His body was tall and lean, and his smile was nothing less of the Devil's—

sinister and full of mischief. He was clothed in a tight fitting, grey tunic with a high collar. He looked regal, royal almost. Yet his dark eyes held something inside of them that I couldn't quite put my finger on. I squeezed my thighs together as he walked towards me, sparks tittered up my lower abdomen and flourished around my hips and around to my lower back. I took a sharp breath in as he reached me far quicker than I anticipated, his hands folded behind his back.

"Breathtaking, *and* bold. Not very often I meet a woman like that anymore. You are seated naked, without shame, in front of a priest. Do you feel ashamed?"

His voice was deep, and the bass of it hit my nipples. I grinned at this question.

Feel ashamed? I was a damned woman, I didn't know how to feel ashamed.

I had never met a man like this before, commanding my attention with just his smile and honey-dripped words.

"Ashamed? Would you like it if I felt ashamed?"

His smile was shadowed by the steeples, and I couldn't tell if he was pleased with me. Something told me he was.

"Darling, my *job* is to make people recognize shame, and why. Atonement is the end goal. Do you atone for your sins?"

I straightened up at this, pushing my shoulders back and canting my head. "If by atonement, you mean *payment*, then yes, I have atoned for my *sins.*"

I didn't need to answer him, he had no right to judge me. No man did. Did he feel he had the right simply because he had dedicated himself to an unseen deity? That sounded like ignorance to me.

He let his gaze slide down my body, down my legs. His eyes looked hungry, as he fixed his stare on my face.

"Sins are tricky things...after all, one man's sin could be another man's guilty pleasure. It all depends on whose eyes it is seen through."

I blinked slowly a few times, letting his words sink in.

My sins were not claimed as my own, they were claimed sins by another.

"Is insolence a sin, father?"

His eyes flicked down to the ground, as if deep in thought at this question.

Good.

"To some...yes. But not to all, that is my point."

I bit my lip at his answer, and a wave of electricity whips through me like the wind. I like this man.

My pupils expand, the feral Goddess inside of me begging to be worshipped, knowing this was the precipice of what I desperately desired. Perhaps, this could be the one, the man who would fall so deeply in love with me that he would speak my name more times than his own, a holy sermon to me, hour after hour. My name, a commandment on his lips.

"Not often I meet a man that can make my cunt a slippery mess just by his mere presence." I smiled, uncrossing my legs and opening them a little, eager to see his response.

I couldn't count the number of times I'd seduced a man this way before, but never had I found the one who would remain beside me eternally.

I wondered momentarily if my crass words would offend him or intrigue him, but he only reached for the blanket he held under his arm, extending it to me. I took it, wrapping it around me, remembering how offended these humans were of the naked form.

Pathetic mortals.

"I am Domenico, the Deacon here at Castle DeLeseeps. I see you are not fearful of strangers, but aside from your wet middle...are you well?"

I scoffed at his jest, taking his hand, and following him to a large wooden door to the left of the tall, front entrance.

"I am well...but perhaps I could stay with you for a while?"

He turned to me, that devilish grin plastered on his face once again. "You may stay here as long as you need, this is mine and my brother's congregation. All who are lost are welcomed."

"Lost? I am never lost."

CHAPTER 6
DOMENICO
THE PAST

I lusted again. Boredom wracking my mind until I felt I had sunken into complete madness, my body too keen on a pliable, soft body that desperately needed plundering. She was divinity embodied—rich curves of womanly hips and thighs, an ethereal aura of power and strength. She was naked, appearing enchanting, even intimidating in her pure form.

She was brought here last night by a distraught Dante, my youngest brother, who just wanted to make sure she was not dead. After careful inspection, the church's physician deemed her abnormally healthy and could not explain the blood that smeared her body.

She must have tried to escape but failed, the heavy gates locked each night. Now she sat at the fountain in the middle of my courtyard, looking like a fallen angel.

My fangs and my cock tingle in unison, like a beating heart, something I no longer had. I was already hard for her, steel straining against cloth, and I absentmindedly stroked it, just before I revealed myself from the shadows.

It didn't take much to convince her to stay, as if she

had already decided it once she saw me, eyes wide and pupils as large as saucers.

There wasn't one soul who knew what I really was, what my brothers were. Hiding behind the guise of Holy men, and not one person ever dared to challenge that.

We did our part in leading the surrounding communities to the word of God, and there was no harm in that, only good.

I ushered her inside, and as we walked down the winding corridors, I looked back at her, watching as she dragged her hand along the stone walls.

"This place is beautiful...and large. How many people live here?"

She was curious, and I tried to talk myself out of the desire to fuck her, to pierce her with my fangs and find out what she tasted like. From the way that she smelled —flowers sprinkled with cinnamon—I'd wager she tasted sweet. I could feed until I was drunk on blood and adrenaline, after satiating myself inside every warm crevice within her. I swallowed hard, fighting with myself to keep the promise I'd made. Purity over desire, it was best this way.

"Ah, here we are. You do not need to worry, no one beyond our clergy men and sometimes students of the church reside within these walls. Please, make yourself at home and stay as long as you need."

I unlocked the old door of the familiar castle that my family had for centuries, opening it wide for her and stepping back against the wall.

Her breath came heavy and fast, but she did not move to the inside of the room. Rather, she stood in front of me with her gaze locked on me, so sweet, so right that it could bring any holy man to his knees. Her face straight from a painting of the Heavens.

She was on me in an instant before I could collect anymore responsible thoughts. Sometimes our bodies knew better what we needed than even our minds.

Her eyes were filled with black, leaving no irises to be seen. I steeled myself against the opposite wall, observing the vibrations that emanated from her glowing body.

"I am Lilith, The Dark Mother."

Her tongue stroked my lower lip the way a serpent would—slow, rhythmic, zig zags. I'd done well at controlling the inner monster that threatened to show itself daily. It was easy to fight these urges when I was alone day in and day out, with nothing to occupy me but books and papers.

This was an entirely uncharted terrain. But a mistake, and something I chastised myself over, ever since.

I didn't even try to resist her; I knew exactly what I was...who I was. I was Domenico DeLesepps, one among the three second generation of vampires to ever walk the earth.

I grabbed her by the waist, crushing her body into mine and moving my hands down to her ass as she wrapped her arms around my shoulders.

The feel of her body pressed against mine was a blessing, her sweat an anointing drip of Holy water to cool the fires of sin. A false sense of warmth and greed flooded my body, while I kissed her as if this was my last day in this castle.

"And I'm an ancient being who thirsts for the very blood that is smeared on your skin."

I hoisted her legs up around my waist with ease and

we kissed, as I quickly led her through the doorway and into the chamber.

The powerful vibration that coursed through her body made me feel alive, the beating heart that I lacked, pumped from her to me.

A vision of Melody, her soft skin and blonde hair bouncing around her, gave me a small sting of guilt. The youngling vampire was new to this life, and it was my responsibility to teach her our way of survival—just how delicate human life was. I didn't need another distraction from tending to her, responsibility nagging at the edges of my mind.

I never missed being alive until I was fucking, and that was when the nostalgia of having real feelings and emotions would call to me.

And here I was, in the throes of passion with a stranger—no, a Goddess.

This was the only way, to ensure the discretion of others when it comes to our family name. We are Princes, and we must make sure it stays that way. No one can know our secret, or we will be forced out...as monsters. We must never disgrace the family name.

"Kiss me, *holy man.*"

I smiled down over her, knowing a man of Christ would never commit such acts, but I did. I craved it, loved it. Sex, power, the rush I would get of committing such a blasphemous act, even after all these years. While my other brothers followed closely to the line of guise in holiness, I did not.

I loved doing all the things I was not supposed to do.

I needed it to be able to continue.

And isn't that only natural for a vampire? A being born out of darkness.

I was warned to keep a close eye on my kills and indiscretions, and I did. I was never sloppy.

The how wasn't as important as the why, but I couldn't think about that now. Not while this walking Goddess sucked on my neck the way I wanted to do to hers.

She was not the type of woman to shy away from desires, a rare find, and exactly what I'd looked for to curb the hunger of my raw, primal need.

This is wrong, and you should fight this.

The voice in my head wasn't my own, but my brother, Dante.

He was nothing like me, sometimes going years without feeding until he was so weak, we had to force him into the woods for sustenance. I had no problem taking exactly what I needed.

I moved us both to the canopied bed with a quickness, and my stole was discarded without care to the floor. Fire burned through me while we devoured each other with teeth, nails and tongues. It was glorious, a feeling I hadn't experienced since my youth.

Her ass was plump, round, and so pliable. I roughly squeezed it, a low groan escaping her lips, urging me on.

"Please, yes..." Her breathy words against my ears drove the carnal urges inside me into a frenzy, and I reached between her thighs eager to find the warmth and wetness that awaited my cold fingertips. I brushed her seam, and she let out a low hiss.

Was this her first time? She did not speak as though this was her first time.

I paused, wondering if I would be willing to take a virgin. The thought of her blood spilling over my cock almost sending me over the edge.

"What are you waiting for? Fuck me the way I *deserve* to be fucked. *Let me atone with you.*"

Three small, shiny snakes unfurled from beneath the bed, and instead of screaming at the abrupt invasion, she smiled.

Her words resonated deeply inside of me. She appeared as a mortal woman, but something surrounded her like a cloud of light.

I wouldn't be shocked by another immortal, I was what I was, after all. Darkness embodied, a fable built on fears and rumor.

I knew such things existed beyond our family, and these creatures also existed in secret.

I couldn't take the teasing any longer, the years of withholding this act from myself. My fangs tingled, and I parted my lips ever so slightly so she could see exactly what I was.

Monster, blood sucker, *the devil.*

Skating my hand down to her breast, then her hips, I eagerly plunged one finger inside her, then two, and her body writhed as I curled my fingers against her warm wall.

It was everything I imagined and more.

My mouth hung agape, watching her writhe against my hand, a vision of beauty and strength, and all I could think about was burying myself inside of her—fangs and cock—while she screamed, blood running down her neck.

Her head flung back as she was seated half on the bed, held still by my hand in between her legs. One leg was hitched up on the bed, and I worked her with one hand, my palm against her clit while I stroked the firm spot inside her. Her cheeks were a rosy pink, and her glassy eyes opened, falling onto my mouth.

The blood in her veins sang to me, called to me.

Her brows furrowed as she reached out to touch a fang with her clawed fingertip. She pressed on it, until I could hear the pop of skin and a single drop of blood dripped down the digit. Her eyes were wide and still a pool of black, as she pulled her fingertip to her own mouth while I continued to pump into her wet cunt.

She sucked her finger, eyes closing at the taste. She gained pleasure from the very thing that gave me sustainability. I grabbed her finger, pulling it into my mouth and sucking, hard. She gasped, and I removed my hand from her warmth, wrapping my arm around her waist in a flash and bringing her up to the head of the bed. We were chest to chest now, and I grabbed her throat in sudden fury. Something flashed inside her eyes that made me want to live in this moment forever, chase this excitement with her for as long as I could. I reached down, fisting my cock, smiling to myself at the ample size. I found her slick entrance again and lined myself up, letting the crown ease in, slowly.

Bringing my head down to her neck, she arched her back, giving it to me as if her life depended on it.

I thrust home, to the hilt, and my fangs sunk in synchronically.

Her hands on my ass, pulling me deeper into her, and I feel her scratches draw blood on my clenched cheeks.

Blood filled my mouth, and she cried out. "Yesss... please...more."

As I swallowed, fireworks flashed behind my eyelids, and the taste of sweet berries and honey flooded my senses. I floated, my soul separated from my body, and I watched from above as I fucked her and suckled at her scarlet neck. When the swallows were over, I blinked, and I was back inside my own body once again, feeling brand new.

All my energy restored, a tingle of hope and happiness left lingering on my lips. I looked down over her, and she was rubbing the blood that ran down her neck from the bites, out and around it, down her chest. She wrapped my thick hand around her throat, and it was then I realized I needed to stop the bleeding before she was too drained to recover. She quickly grew pale, but the sight of her blood and the low moans that escaped her lips made me pump harder, chasing an orgasm that promised to be nothing less than holy.

The pressure builds as I watch her body roll against me. The band that began at the bottom of my sack and stretched to the sensitive tip of my cock stretched, threatening to break at any moment. One last, deep thrust up, and it snapped; my lifeless seed spilling inside of her. Her pussy clenched around me as she met me there with luster, and we were both panting and smiling at one another when it was finished.

I bit my wrist, bringing it to her red stained mouth, and without a word or direction, she drank.

She laid there, eyes closed, but chest falling gently up and down. She looked sated, as the blood began to dry on her skin in shiny crimson streaks.

"I thought I'd lost you…just as I realized I wanted to worship you," I whispered, motioning over her body.

I felt a flutter in my chest where my heart used to be, causing me to squeeze her hand as I laid beside her. A smile played on her lips, and as she opened her eyes, I could see they were no longer entranced and now a unique color of lavender. She was simply breathtaking, and I wanted her to be my secret for all of eternity if she would let me.

"You will never lose me as long as you worship me."

CHAPTER 7
FREYJA
1733 FRANCE

When I woke again, I was in a cold, dark place. At first, it felt like I may be outside, but when I felt the jagged edges of rock and cement beneath my fingertips, I opened my eyes to realize I was underground in a very inhospitable cellar.

I must still be in the dreadful castle because the stench of blood is still all around me. Panic rose in my chest when I felt the weighted chain around my ankle. I screamed, I raged with all my might until I was a pile of sobbing flesh and bone on the floor. I should have known better than to try and fight my way out of these chains, I am helpless against metal. I'd done nothing but weakened myself in a childish fit of rage.

I needed to sleep, to rest, and gather all the strength I had to use my magic and astral project. It was my only hope of getting out of here.

My eyelids were heavy, and that matronly voice inside telling me to rest and not be foolish in the presence of The Red King.

The Red King?

Is that who this man was, a king? Perhaps I could leverage this.

Do not provoke him, you must flee as soon as you can.

Flee? I dif not flee.

I needed to find Charity first.

There had to be a way out of here, there always was. It may not be obvious to me right now, but I could figure it out. From what I had seen, I was not being guarded. I could not sense a single heartbeat within a mile and if someone lurked, my hairs would be standing on end.

Surely blood-bag would bet on me being weak, although he seemed to think that I would be able to wake up his progeny from a curse.

I remember now, after the fog inside of my head cleared, mention of The Red King.

I had passed many years in those Welsh woods, and I had seen dozens of men in black coats. Killed nearly all of them...except for a select few.

One of them called himself Dante, and the control I held over the others was not easily held over him. Dante liked me—enjoyed me, and I half wondered if he never tried to kill me simply because he enjoyed the sexual deviance of my powers.

Or he was afraid.

He never spoke much, but he did speak of The Red King.

I clawed at the silver cuff around my ankle, cursing at it until my leg was red and raw. I laid back, one small but scratchy blanket balled up below my head. Closing my eyes, I envisioned Charity and her freckled cheeks, the soft curves of her body that I reveled in touching. I felt my body begin to tingle, then warm as I smiled to myself. The memory of the hot springs forever played on a loop inside my head. S day filled with heartfelt exchanges and a true vulnerability I'd only ever seen in Charity's eyes. My sweet, soft pet.

I rose, beginning to separate my soul from my body, and as I levitated, I began to see the beauty of the castle I was being held prisoner in.

The structure itself was sturdy, stone and mortar surrounded the stained-glass windows that were taller than a man. Paintings hung on the walls beside the massive tapestries that covered most of the halls and windows.

The quiet of the castle was deafening, and when I heard crying, I knew exactly who was responsible.

Charity.

The smell of blood is back inside my senses, and I balked, wiggling my fingers back at my body. I was returned, and not by choice...it was as if the trance was broken completely. I gasped, sitting up as I returned to my full five senses.

He was nearby.

I was not afraid, but I did not yet have a plan. If I ever wanted to get out of here; alongside Charity, I would have to plan. Thoughts of Charity brought my thoughts to Charles and what he did.

I would not forget.

Did Charity feel as betrayed as I did? Or was she simply blind to the fact that Charles hand fed me to a monster because she was now inside of his protection? Was she crying because she was sorrowful of my being taken prisoner or was she upset because she was betrayed by a person she thought she loved?

Charles.

I couldn't be sure of either until I found her. Just as I

began to think about the last moment I had her on my lips, my chin was snatched, and I was looking into the vampire's silver eyes.

I moved back, but I hit a wall.

"Screaming will get you nowhere. I didn't want to put you down here, but you have fought so hard that I had no choice."

He unhitched the chain from my ankle, and his grip was like steel against my arm.

As if I was weightless, the trap door above me was flung open and in a blur, we were up into the castle's main floor, rings of candles above my head, lighting the dark walls.

It felt like we were hovering, moving so fast that my feet never touched the floor.

And then we are in a bedchamber, the sleeping blonde girl motionless under feathered duvets.

"She was placed under a curse, and I believe you are full of enough magic to wake her."

His voice was filled with warning, not direction. It was as if he wasn't even sure *I* could do anything. The tone warned me that if I didn't, I would go back to the hole which I came from.

"If I succeed...you will release me?"

He nodded, closing his eyes at the word *succeed*.

I did the only thing I was naturally drawn to...I climbed into the bed beside her and closed my eyes. I cradled her from the side, pushing into her dreams using my will.

Once I felt a small connection, I pushed into it, and felt like I was falling. The place inside her mind was cold, with a small sliver of light cast on a white patch of snow.

She sat in the middle, holding a wilted flower, blood smeared on her hands.

"Who are you?"

I knelt beside her, taking her bloodied hand and bringing it to my lips. Her face was stained with tears, and when I pulled one finger into my mouth, her eyes closed and her face relaxed.

"Kiss me."

Her loneliness sliced through me like a sharp knife and in that moment, I knew she needed love. It was the remedy.

Her mouth found mine, and the saltiness of the blood, mixed with her rose scent filled my core with fire. Our tongues tangled, and she moaned into my mouth, tangling her hand in my hair.

Breaking our kiss she whispered, "wake me."

For the first time ever, it felt wrong being so intimate with someone besides Charity. With one sharp intake of breath, I blinked twice, and I was back inside my own head, jolting upright in the bed.

"I can't...*she* must return to lift the spell."

I was yanked back by my hair, and torn from the bed, Domenico seething mad.

"If you cannot, then you will remain in that hole like the useless creature that you are!"

And with my failure, I was discarded like a scrap of food, back into the hole.

CHAPTER 8
DOMENICO

I rubbed my forehead as I walked the long, drafty halls of the castle—*my* castle.

Why did tonight feel so different?

I looked at each statue, each painting and I only saw *her*. I saw our handprints on every surface of this place. Perhaps, it was why I had stayed for so long.

Or, perhaps, my loyalty to this family held onto me stronger than I'd like to admit. A generation of a family who'd held place amongst royals, monsters hidden behind religious statues.

It felt nice to have Charles home again safely, even though I knew the reason I'd sent him away that day was because he'd be the only one able to make it past Freyja's wards. It needed to be him, and he delivered to me just as I knew he would.

Lilith's kin.

I slid my hand over the walls, catching the edge of one of the tapestries and darting behind it and inside the hidden tunnels that wound around the castle in its entirety.

The curiosity of a young boy was the only thing I could blame for how I knew of these secret walkways. If I hadn't followed my older brother, I would've been none the wiser.

It is pitch black, but my senses guided me to the spot I would certainly be spending the most time observing. I passed by small holes and streams of light but didn't stop until I reached a small alcove with a bench pressed up against a large slit in the wall.

A view into Charles' quarters.

It wasn't that I didn't trust him, I trusted him enough to take my cock into his mouth when he needed to be punished. I trusted him with the truth of what I really was. But this girl, Charity, was a mouse at best and not what Charles should hold as a prize in this lifetime. She was nothing, miniscule, and possibly not very intelligent. After all, she was from a town so small that most men undoubtedly equally preferred the pigs to the women.

I sneered to myself at the dark jest, but I knew how common it was for a man to fuck livestock. The truth was the truth.

He would grow bored of her soon enough, and once the curse was broken, my Melody would return to me as normal. She would provide a *perfect* distraction from the boring, mousy girl. That was my plan all along.

I needed to return to the oubliette and check on our guest soon, but for now, I wanted the comfort of watching without being seen.

The witch put up such a fight that I had to tuck her far away from the church, I didn't need her scaring off the clergy and the patrons.

I kneeled at the bench, pressing one eye into the lit crack. A ripple of pleasure rolled through me, as I focused my eyes on Charles' golden hair and tall frame. He comforted the girl, and her face was red and puffy from crying so much.

The scene before me reminded me of the night I found Melody, crouching in a corner of the great room, shaking and feeble.

"What is it, child? Why do you cry?" she sniffled, looking up at me in terror...

"I...I know what you are. My parents have told me, and they paid with their lives. Those men...men in the black coats and top hats...I watched them be-head them both...just before they reached the tree line," she let out another jagged sob, burying her head in between her drawn up knees.

If anyone found the truth, it was instant death, no compromise ever. She couldn't have been older than seventeen, and I had never killed a child before.

I knelt beside her, stroking her blonde hair back from her wet face. "Well, then this will be our little secret. What is your name, fair one?"

"Melody."

"You are my family now, Melody. Come with me...I will keep you safe."

Reluctantly, she rose, following me to the hidden passages behind the walls. Her eyes were wide with curiosity, and pride bubbled up, as I readied myself for The Change. I had once been afraid of being blood-bound to another, responsible for their life. But this was the only way, her immortality was the only guarantee she would have to live on.

I'd never turned anyone before—once someone was blood-bound, they could never leave your side. It was a commitment, a sacred oath between two vampires. I would care for her for years to come, as my own, protecting her from the men who had killed her parents. She was mine, and I was hers.

Charles' bed was at the opposite end of the room, and I watched as he gently sat the girl down, his toned arm wrapping protectively around her shoulders.

I was shocked when he placed a gentle kiss on her neck, and she swallowed heavily, turning to him with a look of curiosity in her eyes. I knew that look, and my cock hardened against my thigh beneath my grey slacks. I brushed over it carefully with the backs of my fingers, the urge to fist it, overwhelming. I may not resist the urge altogether, but I did fight it down as much as I could until the feeling broke me. It was then that I allowed my devil out to play.

When I focused again, they kissed ferociously, and the mousy-girl gripped his hand and held it to her neck as they lay back.

I watched as Charles fumbled with the buttons on her dress, but I could see his hard length pressed against his pants in fury. He wanted a release so badly that he forgot he was there with a virile woman, a woman who clearly needed direction. I laughed to myself, but the joy I felt was that of my fondness for Charles and all that he was. Naïve, inexperienced...tender.

I let my hand wander to the stiffness that rested against my thigh, my arousal a heavy burden, constantly needing to find ways to hide it.

I freed myself from the constraints of my breeches, my cock popping out like a beast, as I wrapped my fingers around it in relief. I admired it for a moment, thick and veined even now. Stroking it painfully slow, I continued to watch the couple grind and moan on the bed. I gave two, hard, long strokes down my cock and allowed myself a small groan in sync with theirs, imagining I was there with them, showing Charles exactly what he needed to do to make sure she came.

I bit my lip and cursed, I couldn't do this, not now. I had a church service to lead tonight, and then there was also the matter of Freyja in the Oubliette.

Damn you Lilith, Damn you for taking my love and smashing it to pieces.

I furrowed my brow and wished for a moment that I had never let her go, that I never let her leave.

CHAPTER 9
CHARLES

It wasn't long before Charity returned to the room, mostly out of fear. And I finally got my wish and gave her a thorough fucking after I'd dried her tears. Although, I know I'd not satisfied her in the way Freyja did—she didn't squirt with me.

I'd fucked her with me on top and one leg up. Then, I'd turned her over and fucked her the way I did back in Freyja's cabin. She'd cried out a little, but not the way she'd cried out with Freyja.

I'd come too quickly, pulling out and jacking myself off on her ass, then collapsing. I'd noted her silence but was too glazed by my own euphoria to say anything about it.

Was this something she could always do each time she came? Was it only something she could do with another woman? In a certain position? I thought about it long enough for the fire to go out and for Charity's soft snores to interrupt my questions.

I folded my body around her smaller frame, and I felt thankful for everything I had, for the first time ever.

Should I be afraid that I was amongst vampires? Should I forget about Freyja and her fate and just get Charity away from here?

I didn't feel threatened by Domenico, and I sure as hell was happy to be away from the wolf-man back in Wales. The size of that beast was enough to make any man tremble, and I certainly did not want to stick around and find out if they liked the taste of men. I was most certain they did.

I would keep a close eye on Charity, and slowly introduce her to all the wonderful things this castle had to offer.

She'd miss her family for a little while, but I was sure she would forget about them once we found Freyja and made sure she was safe. I knew she had developed a bond with her, but was it authentic? Or was it only magic? I believed the latter, and I knew Freyja would not be happy with me. After all, I'd led her straight to Domenico, and now who knows where she was kept after that hideous cage. I made a silent prayer to God that Freyja was safe and unharmed, for Charity's sake. Surely if I asked Domenico where she was and if we could see her, he would allow us to.

I held onto that hope while I felt Charity's back rise and fall into my chest. I smiled to myself, sated and sleepy.

Tomorrow, I'd take her to the kitchens and feed her fresh baked muffins with strawberries. That would cheer her up.

I woke up in the middle of the night in a cold sweat.

Dante's words stung the insides of my ears, and I couldn't forget them, no matter how much I tried.

"When you find her, you mustn't fuck her. That is how she will control you...she will own you."

How could Dante have possibly known that? Why didn't he just hand her over to Domenico himself?

I had to fight every urge seated so deeply inside of me, and I had failed. I had given in to my urges, had them both, and still managed to bring her to Domenico. I'd done it, so why did his words fill my head until I couldn't sleep at night?

I stood from the bed, careful not to wake Charity. I would find him, and I'd question him myself.

I knew exactly where he would be, and my feet carried me through the familiar halls until I was downstairs, facing the tall door of the apothecary.

I knocked twice, gently, and then once loudly. He would know it was me.

The door opened with a creak, and Dante's beady eyes found mine, "Charles, come in. Hurry."

"Were you expecting me?" I asked, confused at his eagerness to see me inside.

"I was not, but I had a feeling you would come asking me questions soon enough. Come, I want to show you something."

The moon was high in the sky, and the light filtering in through the tall, oval shaped window to the left of the potion room. I 'd never been allowed inside before, but

Dante ushered me to the sill, lined with deep red tinctures of blood all standing up.

"Behold...the blood of Lilith."

Lilith? Was I to know this name?

His grin was crooked, goofy even. I tried not to laugh, but instead crooked an eyebrow in his direction. "Ok, and?"

"I have collected and studied it for a hundred years. I've compared it to others' blood, I've mixed it with herbs...blended it...shaken it. It's the *most* powerful blood I've tasted to date."

I can see his small fangs now, and for a moment, I wonder if he's brought me in here to take my blood. I swallowed.

"I'm not sure I follow."

He took a vile, uncorking it and tossing it back like a shot of brandy. I grimaced, trying not to imagine how terrible it tasted.

He wiped his mouth with the back of his clawed hand. "The day I fed from her—the first time—I was sick, questioning my life and the never-ending duty of being immortal."

I took a vile of the syrupy tincture, turning it on its side and noticing it shimmer, like small particles of sunshine shimmering off a lake.

I pondered for a moment on what it would be like to be immortal. The fear of ever having to worry about death sounded pretty great to me.

"I dragged myself into the courtyard, ready to meet my death at the sun's arrival—only I didn't burst into flames! I walked right into the sunlight unharmed!"

I blinked a few times, registering what he said. It could only mean that the façade of being human could be proven with this new information. No one would ever be able to accuse them of being undead—not when they could walk in the sunlight just like the rest of us.

My eyes widened in realization, and I watched Dante dance around the room, his black cloak floating behind him like a ball gown.

"And why are you telling me?"

He grabbed the vile from my hand, placing it back in its holder on the windowsill.

"Because you brought me *more* of this blood. The blood of Freyja. Well done, boy."

"Why Freyja?" I asked, stepping back out of the way as he continued his independent celebration.

"She is Lilith's kin, my boy! I was never able to capture her, not like you! You deserve thanks, but you cannot share with Domenico what I have shared with you."

A faded memory of one night in the great room, Domenico seated on the floor with his head in his hands, comes to me. The tapestry that hung before him was that of a naked woman, with long hair, standing beside a large tree. I immediately noticed the snake near her ear, and with a frightened urgency, asked him what story the tapestry told. Lilith, was the only word he spoke, never raising his head to meet my eyes.

"Who is Lilith?"

Dante sat, seemingly out of breath, but how could he be when he too was an immortal.

"It is said that she is a demi-Goddess, sent here from the Underworld. Her and Domenico were in love once."

The sentence shot me through my chest, and I found myself looking around for a seat.

Domenico had been in love? Was Melody their child?

This would explain Domenico's stoic, quiet demeanor. Why he only wanted to do those naughty things with me in private. I had always assumed it was because we were both males, but if he had loved another, perhaps he felt shame in his feelings for me.

Was this jealousy I felt? Would she return someday and reclaim him as her own?

"Did you love her?"

Silence, but then he nodded slowly.

"I should go...it's late."

CHAPTER 10

LILITH

THE PAST

"Why would you worship God when you can just worship me, my love?"

I stroked Domenico's bare chest with my index finger and looked up at him with the most angelic look I could muster in the sunlight.

He smiled. "I do worship you, Dark Mother."

His fingertip skittered up and down my back, sending tingles down my thighs to the tips of my toes. Electricity, something I'd never felt before. I craved it, and I looked forward to the times he would worship my body with more.

"I worshipped every inch of your body last night, and I ate your pussy like it was divine desert."

I shivered at the memory. "Do it again."

He was handsome when he smiled, one small dimple on his left cheek. His stubble was black and gray, and I loved the feeling of it on my thighs as he licked and nibbled me.

Domenico disappeared below the covers, kissing down my body until my back bowed, and I sighed. "You better make it quick, I don't know how long the side effects from my blood will last."

I squealed as he spread me wide, one rough hand on my thigh, the other on my lips. Nudging one finger inside me, then two, until I'm hissing his name and bucking my hips. He steadied me with the hand that was on my thigh, now gripping my hip. The flat of his tongue glides over my clit, and I am molten lava again, lighting up my core. The pressure building behind my needy cunt, as he sucked me off, working my insides at the same time, bumping that tight spot that ached to be stroked.

"Like heaven. You taste like fucking heaven."

The pulse behind my clit spread deep into my hips, and the bubble growing inside me burst, and I came in waves over his fingers. I didn't ever want this feeling to stop, I wanted to fuck all day, every day. Wrapped in a cocoon of pleasure and euphoria created by our two bodies.

A loud knock on the door jolted me from my sexual haze. Domenico lifted his head from the blanket. "I'm getting ready. I'll be there soon."

"It's me. I need to speak to you," Dante said from the other side of the door.

I wrapped the sheet around myself, moving to the edge of the bed to grab my robes. Domenico's hand blocked me, and he smiled as he pushed me back down to sit. A thrill ran through me, maybe he would invite his brother into bed with us and allow me to fuck them together. Or maybe he just wanted to watch me fuck his brother...the possibilities were endless. I raised an eyebrow at him.

"Stay, just like that. Let the sheet fall below your breasts. They are so beautiful; I want him to see."

I did as I'm told, the wetness still between my thighs, a mixture of Domenico's spit and my arousal. My nipples tightened at the thought.

Domenico opened the door, and Dante stood in the doorframe, frozen, as I was revealed to him behind the swing of the door.

"I...um...I have news for you, Dom."

I could see the pleasure Dom received from this all over his face. The smugness never left, and he looked back toward me as if he wanted me to do something.

If he wanted a show...I would give him a show.

I rose from the sheets, completely nude and on display for Dante to see. His jaw nearly hits the floor, his cheeks flushed under his dark beard. The robes he wore were black, so I couldn't tell if I had an arousing effect on him. I reached down to my breast, pushing my long hair back over my shoulder, so he could see the rosy peak as I pinched it.

Breast still in hand, I moved to the edge of the bed, straightening my leg and stepping onto the floor. One step, two steps and by three, I am nearly toe to toe with him.

He swallowed hard, his chest rising and falling quickly, and that's when I saw his pulse beating. He was aroused, or maybe he was just scared. Those emotions invoked the same feeling. I stood on my tip toes, reaching his ear. "Have you ever tasted a woman's pussy?"

I leaned back, and he was silent, still, but shook his head slowly. Reaching down between my legs, I gathered the wetness on my fingertips and brought it to his mouth. He opened, tongue wagging. I giggled, wiping the wetness on his tongue, and his eyes rolled back.

He hit the ground rather softly. Domenico was not the least concerned, only amused.

"You made the poor bastard faint!" He laughed, kicking at his brother's unmoving foot.

I covered my mouth demurely with the same hand I assaulted Dante's mouth with. Domenico pulled me into his chest, squeezing me tightly and sucking the fingers I'd feigned remorse with. I groaned as he bit me, the warmth trickling down to my collarbone as he licked at each drop, sending my body into shivers. He was inside me in an instant, and I rode him with fury as I watched his brother pretend to be asleep on the floor beside us.

My body was no longer my own; we were one. My orgasms belonged to Domenico now, and the bloodlust we shared only solidified our bond. I smiled to myself, becoming lost under his fevered kisses, until I heard someone whisper, "*Whore, witch.*"

Pierre, Dante's right-hand man, watched us move together but not before sweeping a heavy glare over the length of my body.

Domenico's head snapped toward the insult, hissing at the man in the shadowed doorway. His black, hooded cloak floating behind him as he disappeared.

"How *dare* he? I want him dead, Domenico," I whispered.

"And you shall have it, my love."

~

I awoke in the middle of the night, starved and sated by sex. Domenico and I had spent days in bed, and he'd missed two church services, much to his brethren's irritation.

To say I was unwelcome was an understatement. Servant's watched me from the corner of their eyes, and the men of the church watched me closely as I passed by.

I didn't care; they were jealous, *miserable* pests.

With a sheet wrapped around me, I descended the stairs to the kitchens, shadows casted by the still flickering candles above me. I felt oddly at ease here, but it was because of the damp loneliness...the morose setting. My hallowed heart was put at ease by the stone and moss that climbed the outside walls.

Soft voices stopped me in my movement across the floor, and I gripped the doorframe, listening.

"Do you love her?"

It was a gentle female voice, lilting and youthful.

"Love? Love is saved for children and mothers. I don't know if I am able to love in that way. At times, yes, I think I might be."

That was Domenico's hard voice, and a bolt of jealousy hit the back of my neck, edging me closer. I was able to see the pair's profiles by angling my back against the opposite side of the doorway.

The girl was blonde, ringlets of hair brushing her shoulders. She was far too young to be his lover, I thought. But what did I know about vampires? Nothing really, nothing apart from what Domenico had shown me.

"You look tired, father."

They sat closely together at a small table, knees

touching. When she ran the back of her hand down his face, he grabbed it, kissing it softly.

I pulled back from the scene I watched, biting my lip and closing my eyes. My chest felt heavy, like a stone was placed at the center.

Father? As in priest? Or was this another secret?

Anger bubbled inside me, and for the first time, I felt hot tears sting my cheeks.

Do I show myself? Do I make a scene and demand the truth?

Or, should I slink away in defeat, acting as if I never saw a thing?

Even as I thought it, I knew that was not the answer.

I stepped into the moonlight cast across the floor from the large window behind them. It highlighted their silhouette's, and as I stood before them, both of their heads swiveled to me in shock.

I did not speak at first, I just moved to the stove, lighting the burner with a long match that sat beside it.

"My love, you're awake."

I continued to act as if I didn't care about their presence, but the gnawing need to know the truth swallowed me whole.

"Who is *she*?"

Domenico looked behind me, to the girl, and as she stood, I could see her parted mouth, her pointed fangs.

"This is Melody."

At first, he hesitated, and I held her gaze, my shoulders back. I wasn't afraid, and I wanted that to be perfectly clear to her.

"Melody, a pleasure."

I held out my hand to her, and she rushed over, taking it and placing a kiss on the back of it.

Clearly, she meant no disrespect, but if she was a child of Domenico then I had every right to know.

It felt uncomfortable, the three of us standing in the middle of a silent kitchen where only servants and chefs were allowed.

It was a comical picture.

"I've heard so much about you, you are beautiful."

I smiled at this, and a small cloud of sympathy floated through my mind. I was being ridiculous, but I wanted to push further, find out what her intentions were. What was her place here?

"Thank you, oddly, I haven't heard a word of you."

I looked at Domenico, and he smiled, that smile that made my knees weaken. Hot lava pooling at my center, and every nerve ending screamed to be touched. I reached out my hand and mimicked her action from earlier. I stroked his face, and he pulled me to him, roughly.

"I was going to tell you, but when was there a right time?"

He kissed me then, lapping away any doubts I had, and as our tongues collided, and the love within me began to bloom again, I realized this was the first time I'd felt this strange feeling of love and fear at the same time.

Jealousy.

CHAPTER 11
DOMENICO
THE PAST

"The king will be here shortly, and I would love for you to meet His Highness. After all, he oversees all the churches, and respect must be paid."

Lilith looked bored, as she lounged on the chaise in front of the largest fireplace in the castle. She wore a belted black dress, made from a rare, salmon colored snakeskin that was found in the gardens. She snacked on grapes and cheese, her cheeks flushed pink.

"He sounds like a snooze. Why don't you just come fuck me instead? You can come on my neck, decorate my collar with a pretty pearl necklace?" She laughed, filling the high ceilings with an echo that dominated the room.

"Love, we have all night to do that. I have a special surprise for you later, if you're good."

"Good? Do you know me at all?"

I worried my lip, wondering if it would be a bad idea to introduce her to the King. He had been none the wiser of what we were—he praised my dedication and discipline each time he visited, and I didn't want Lilith's candor to prevent that. I knew she would bow to no one unless she was on her knees with a cock in her mouth.

I walked to her side, holding out my hand. She took it, but not before rolling her eyes. The tight belt made her waist look small, but the flair of her hips made my cock twitch, and before I could talk myself out of it, I found the slit of her dress with my hand and let my fingers slide inside. Pushing her up against the window, I found her slit bare, wet with desire for me already. "Dom...you beast."

I smiled, pushing inside of her eagerly with two fingers, then three. She gasped, biting her lip and locking eyes with mine. I wanted to pound into her, fast and hard, until my release was filling her up. I pulled my cock free, hard as stone, moisture on the tip, leaking just for her. She spread her legs wide, curling her tongue out of her mouth. I withdrew my fingers, and they were covered in her blood, I shuddered and swallowed hard. It was no wonder I couldn't resist her; arousal and blood mixed sent me into a heightened state of lust. I couldn't hold back any longer, grabbing her ass cheeks in two hands and lining myself up with her entrance—hot and waiting for me to stretch her, calming the ache inside.

"Please," she whispered, kissing my neck in fevered nips and licks.

I sink inside, just the swollen head at first, but I'm panting now, her cunt squeezing me with need, pulling me in on its own. I thrust up with one pivot of my hips, and I am sheathed; an embrace that only her warm cunt could give me.

Our sex is hard and fast, pumping into her with a ferocity that had both of our bodies arched toward one another, her head bouncing against the painstakingly stained glass.

"You want that pearl necklace, my Goddess?"

She nodded; mouth parted in pleasure.

I pulled out so fast that it was a blur, and she was on her knees in an instant, waiting to take it.

"I need it..."

I jerked my cock fast and hard, the cum spurting in white droplets all over her chest, decorating it so perfectly.

"My dirty little snake. You love the way my cum feels on your skin, don't you?"

I finished icing her chest, hand braced above her head, looking down over her on her knees. I nearly fell to my own knees, to lick it off, but I decided to leave it there, for the King to see.

"Ahem...sir."

I still, tucking myself back into my slacks, helping Lilith up from the floor.

"What? Can it not wait?"

"He has arrived...he waits."

I cursed under my breath, but decided it's what's right.

"I'm not done with you yet...later..."

She pouted her bottom lip but stroked my arm gently.

I licked my fingers clean of her blood and cum, smiling down over her as I turned to the entryway.

Taking her hand, I led her to the doors of the receiving room, silently praying she would not make a mockery of the most important man in the country.

Lilith

I was disappointed that I didn't get my release.

The throb between my legs was palpable, and I resisted the urge to demand Domenico to fuck me until I was satisfied.

His seed still decorated my delicate collarbone, and I decided I would let the droplets remain, even as I felt them slowly making their descent down my chest. The wet feeling made my nipples pebble under my custom dress, and I smiled.

I stood beside Domenico, waiting for the King's entrance, sliding my gaze over each religious statue that made me nauseous at the sight.

Oh well, I could live with them knowing I'd been spoiled by the money of the church that supported the very God that cast me aside.

Ironic.

"Domenico, good man! How are you?"

The king was older than dirt, with a pot belly and grey hair in ringlets beneath his crown.

I crossed both my arms over my chest, my chin raised slightly.

The king was my height, and I feigned a small smile as his eyes slid up and down my frame. "Well, well. Have you taken a mistress and not told me? You sly dog…"

I cringed under his words, slanting my eyes toward Domenico as he cleared his throat. He knew I would not tolerate backhanded insults *or* compliments.

"Not I, your highness. This is Lilith, a traveler on a journey to Greece. She is only staying for a brief rest."

A brief rest?

It takes all but every effort inside my powerful body not to storm from the room at that moment. Instead, I tilted my head slightly, eyeing Domenico. "Oh, but that's not what you said *last night*."

There was venom in my words, and Domenico shifted on his feet nervously.

I love making him nervous, he would pay for that comment later.

"Well, what are you waiting for m'dear? Bow to your king."

My king?

I almost laughed out loud. He did not ask from where I came, or who I belonged to. He only cared if I had lay below his Deacon.

"Bow? To you? I bow to no one."

His face turned a bright shade of red, and Domenico stepped in between us with one broad step. "You must excuse her, she is weary and tired. Why don't you get back to your quarters, Lilith."

I was a Goddess; I wouldn't be spoken to by a *man* this way. I wouldn't let him take a royal piss anywhere near me.

In one swift motion, I used my power to snatch him by the meaty throat, my teeth bared. "Would you rather eat my pussy? Would that be enough?"

Slamming him to the ground as if he was nothing more than a sack of potatoes, I placed my naked foot over his throat, looking down over his now stunned face. I sneered, locking eyes with his.

The red faded, his pupils dilating into huge discs of black, as his mouth went slack. He nodded, in a daze.

Domenico remained behind me, but I could feel his senses on edge, waiting to defend me in a moment if needed.

Good vampy.

"That's what I thought," I purred, lifting my dress up, just enough to draw his gaze to my well of power.

"*Lilith.*"

Domenico's clipped voice took me out of my own tantric spell, and I looked over my shoulder, growling.

I stepped back, ignoring every urge I had to kill him right here.

Perhaps I should be thankful that Domenico intervened—the king had every right to request my head at such an insult.

And as a Goddess, I had every right to do the same.

CHAPTER 12

DOMENICO

THE PAST

Later that night, I held the insolent man who'd called Lilith a whore by his throat. A gift for my Goddess.

He hung limply from my hand, my fist wrapped tightly as his eyes bulged, pushed up against the wall of our bedroom. Lilith purred behind me, pleased with our captive toy for the night.

"You...traitor...bastard...all for a *woman*."

"Shh, shh. No need to make this any harder than it already is. You have *insulted* her beyond repair. Be a man and face your fate with bravery. God would want it that way," I sneered, baring my fangs.

Lilith clapped her hands behind me with excitement. "You thought you could get away with calling me a *whore?* How foolish of you."

She circled behind me until she stood by my side, watching his terrified face fixed on my mouth.

In a blur, I lifted him off the ground, bounding wall-to-wall until he was slung over the large, crystal chandelier in the middle of the room. Face down, he gripped the chains of the suspended light in terror, as he stared down over a now naked Lilith.

"Are you ready to play with our toy, my Goddess?"

Her nude body set me aflame, the warm feeling I hadn't experienced since I was mortal. She was the lifeblood I craved, and there was nothing that could come between what we shared.

She nodded, moving beside me and stroking my chest. She looked up at me from under her lashes, and grinned. "Kill him."

At her command, lightning fast, I grabbed the sharp, silver dagger from our bedside, slashing his belly down the middle.

I rejoined her below him, and as a shower of red, sticky blood and intestines fell around us, I kissed her deeply. The blood coated our bodies in a dark red sheen as our tongues tangled and she shivered. We collapsed together to the floor, laughing, touching, and nipping. I kissed down her neck to her pebbled nipple, bringing it into my mouth, sucking gently as she gasped. It was magnificent, the glimmer in her eyes as we slipped over each other's skin, grinding with urgency for contact.

I licked the blood from her skin, a heady mixture of fear and lust intertwined. "Take me...take me now..."

My cock had never been harder, steel against her thigh, as I found her center. She straddled my hips, and I dug my fingers into hers, piercing her on my length. I pushed home until I was fully sheathed, Lilith shouting my name, completely at my mercy. I wanted more, I wanted forever, I wanted to be greedy with her body night after night. I made a silent vow to keep her, no matter what it took.

"Ride me, my love. Make me come so hard that I forget where we are."

She rolled her hips slowly at first, but the need inside her outweighed any calculation in her movements. She bucked fast, pulling at my hair, forcing my head back. My mouth opened, eyes wide so I could watch her take what she needed. Her hair was matted, sticky with red, drops of blood raining down over us in small trickles now. She licked at the corner of her mouth, running her finger over one of my fangs.

"My love."

"For eternity."

She had been distant with me since the night of the bloody chandelier. I knew she was curious and restless, but I did keep trying to win her heart each day.

I gifted her the best wines and innocent blood when she was feeling overly cynical and dark. I allowed her to drink my blood, which only seemed to make her colder. Locked deep inside her own mind of travesties. I would always question why.

The service I was to lead tonight focused on faith. Faith that the Father would lead us all to redemption, safety, and security. He always provided, and it was up to us to give him our blind faith in that.

I myself began to lose faith that Lilith would remain here, because nothing lasted forever. One fact remained, I needed to stay here in this until it no longer stood or served no larger purpose.

I walked with my hands tucked behind my back, nodding to the men that passed by me, down the winding corridor to the church doors.

Most of my followers were men, and it was best that way. Women needn't worry about God, faith, and politics. Those things were better left to the levelheaded patriarchs that attended my services. At the same time, women tended to be a distraction, and I needed my flock to focus only on the Father.

I stepped up to the pulpit, admiring the empty pews that would soon be filled with my followers.

I may be filled with darkness and sin, but at the very least, I kept my grandfather's legacy alive.

I held my hands out as I spoke, dozens of eyes focused on my words, my teachings. It was just before sunrise, I held mass very early, so I may sleep after. No vampire would dare be caught in sunlight; the irreversible damage of death.

I kept my homily short today; Lilith was returning from her trip to Greece. She had quickly made her way through my library, reading myths and legends that she couldn't get enough of. I spared no expense to get her to the coast, she deserved the world and I intended to give that to her. Some legacies afforded a lavish life and constant donations flooded my walls. Money was never a problem in the DeLesepps family.

I shook hands with a few of the men who regularly visited me for confessions, and as the last few men trickled out, the door remained open, with a timid Lilith peeking around at me through the frame.

She slithered her way inside before the door closed. "The sun will be up soon, we should get back to our room, my love."

I knew something was amiss, but I couldn't quite read her. She laced her fingers through mine, and I pulled her violently to my chest, cradling the back of her head with my hand. I gently tugged on her hair, yanking her head back to look up at me.

"What is it?"

She pushed herself away, hips swaying as she walked to one of the pews and sat. I followed her, feeling a rage begin to rise in my chest.

There were times I was unable to control the animalistic urges that lived inside of me. I hoped this wouldn't serve as one of those instances.

She looked down over her abdomen, ever so slightly rounded, then back to me.

"A baby?" I asked, surprised by the softness in my own voice.

She nodded, not looking at me, but at the old wood floors.

"I didn't think this could be...after what happened. But I'm no mother, Dom...I cannot..." She rubbed her belly absentmindedly, and I could see the torment on her face. She was conflicted, but I knew all of her dark desires and no matter how hard I tried, I could not picture her mothering anyone, it was not her journey. This was, *I* was.

I wanted to tell her that I would worship her in a way that no one else ever could. That I would write hymns and homilies of her beauty and light. If she left me, I would be devastated, unable to unlearn the things she made me feel, the way we made each other come.

"I will help...I will hire others to help..."

"Please Dom, just ask me what you really want to ask. Whose is it? Right?"

I looked at my hands, large and calloused, years upkeeping a thousand year old castle and its worshippers.

When she looked at me this time there were tears in her eyes, I ached to hold her, but I knew she was a force to be reckoned with and would only push my comfort away.

"Well, I was not intimate with anyone but you. So, you tell me."

I narrowed my eyes at her.

Impossible.

"I knew you wouldn't believe me. Therefore, I need to take care of this my way."

"And what does that mean? You will not hurt yourself?"

She stood, gathering her hair in a low braid, and then turning toward the doors.

"I should go."

If she left me, I would not speak of the divine beauty that lay between her legs, no, I would only spread the word of her darkness, her egomania...her deceit. She was lying to me now.

"Do not leave me, please."

She did not stop, did not even turn to see the bloodied tears on my face.

I had larger tasks to think of for now—the entire congregation for one. I had to honor the flock that followed me with full faith.

I couldn't face the possibility that the Goddess I was in love with had been with another.

Not my Lilith...

CHAPTER 13

DANTE

THE PAST

Domenico always got what he wanted.

Even as children, before we were immortal monsters (because that's exactly what we are—monsters) our parents fawned over him and his accomplishments. Darius and I were the second comers, the followers. We were encouraged to be like him, act like him...*Domenico makes us proud, be like Dom.*

My resentment towards him only strengthened even after The Turn. You see, it was a birthright of the Delesepps; once we turned thirty, we were given immortality. If we survived that long.

The canopy of the church was the only thing that insured we would never be discovered, a man of faith was the most powerful man to exist, and not one person would dare to say otherwise.

The day I found Lilith, she was nude, asleep and *oh so remarkable.*

I chose to follow our faith to the line; there was no pretending by me, no, not like Domenico pretended. The only difference was he was *so good* at pretending. It made me sick; it made me *envious*. I simply could not live a life of lies, and when Lilith floated her way into our castle, I was in awe of every curve and peak of her body. Her lips puffed and pouty, her hair like that of a mermaid washed in from the sea. She emanated power, and I knew there was something strange about this woman. I had touched her while she slept, grazing over the soft mounds of her breasts, letting my breath gently hover on her cheeks as I smelled her deeply...like vanilla and sea air. I grew so hard in my trousers that I had to tug on the throb just to get it to stop.

I should've taken her. I should've had my way with her, thrown my vows to the wind and *finally* claimed something as my own. I had eternity to spend here, so why should I not enjoy the carnal pleasures that my body was still able to?

I prayed in the small garden just outside of the castle, rows of flowers and olive trees, accompanied by cracked statues of The Virgin Mary and Arch Angel Michael. It was my favorite spot to pray, and the sunrise shone perfectly just before morning, beyond the grassy field to the left of our sprawling estate.

But tonight, Lilith fled, and I knew something was wrong, just by the way she clutched herself, her steps coming quicker as she reached the front gates.

I closed my eyes, giving a chaste *Amen* as I finished my prayers.

I quietly sidled up to the first gate post, making sure I was out of sight. I watched as she fled down the dirt driveaway, barefoot, with a long, white sheath swirling around her. Her hair trailed behind, a vision of ethereal beauty. I knew exactly what I needed to do. I would follow her, and make sure she never returned, could never make me or anyone else feel those vile delights of the flesh again, she was omnipotent and should be stopped.

I wanted her blood more than life, the vampire hidden inside me ever present, and I needed to figure out a way to keep her under my thumb.

I had heard of trapping demons with sigils, or a talisman, but I still needed to figure out how. The desire to keep her as my own overpowered my loud, logical side.

I wanted revenge, and I wanted blood spilled, but not the precious blood that she held in her veins. I would trap her, somehow, giving myself an endless supply of her magical blood. I would be the only vampire with access to walking in the sun.

~

It didn't take long for a caravan of wanderers to pick Lilith up off the side of the road. I'd followed her for at least a mile, and a few times I'd thought about turning back, but my curiosity got the best of me, I *needed* to know where she was going, what she was up to. It was most certainly nothing *good*, she had upturned our entire castle in the matter of a few years, and now she was fleeing to do the same to someone else.

She must be stopped.

The voice inside my head sounded much like the voice of God, the voice I followed, the voice I gained all wisdom from. It nagged at me, and did not allow me to close my eyes for a second.

I'd hopped on the last carriage of the long line of travelers, abandoning my cassock before I asked for passage.

I was no stranger to being on the road for long periods of time, I was always the one tasked to find new parishioners or seminarians. We would only be able to continue this charade if we had followers, and new followers were my responsibility.

I snacked on apples and honey as we travelled, and I asked vague questions, until I got the answer I looked for.

We were headed to England, to a place that promised growth and opportunity. These people gladly picked up passengers who also sought new beginnings—and my guess was that was exactly Lilith's intention, starting over.

The hate and jealousy I had for her only grew as the weeks passed by. I watched her make friends, flirt with men, get drunk and sleep wherever she pleased. She slept beside men and women alike, sometimes multiple people at once. I gripped my cock as I watched her trysts, and I cursed myself for never being able to feel her snug, wet insides clench around me. I thought about taking her in her sleep, selfishly and unapologetically. Only I never did, I spilled my seed into my hand and whispered her name as pleasure tipped me over and left me empty. I was disgusted, these vile thoughts permeating my mind like a virus I couldn't shake. This was her fault, her doing, she was evil and I would have to repent day after day...sinful thought after sinful regret.

I watched her as her belly grew.

I watched her as she gave birth to a screeching baby girl, and I watched her tuck the new babe inside of her dress with cloth, as she escaped into the night once again.

She did not seek passage inside of a carriage this time, no, she walked...she *floated* to the next town over, looking over her shoulders every few steps.

Domenico couldn't have known this was why...there was no way his controlling behavior would allow that.

I wanted nothing more than to go back, I no longer desired the revenge I thought I would have. She had a child now, I could never commit such an act to a mother.

But Lilith would never be a real mother, I knew that, and as I watched her place the new baby in a basket, leaving on the front steps of a large house just on the outskirts of town—I knew.

I knew she would return, perhaps not today, but she would someday. I needed to return to the castle so I could tell Domenico exactly what she was, what she had done.

I wanted to strike the match that would light the fire of hate for her through Domenico's eyes. I wanted to watch his rage consume him, an ongoing vendetta to eradicate the woman who rejected him, never even cared for him.

Perhaps I would not be able to exact revenge myself, but I knew my brother, and I knew he would do better than I ever could.

CHAPTER 14

FREYJA
1730 FRANCE

It appeared the only way out or in of this pit was through the trap door in the ceiling. I was filthy and hungry, and my body weakened with each night I spent rotting in here.

I had slept for two nights, today would make day three and no one had even checked on me. I was left with a piss pot and a small, ceramic decanter of water. I needed food badly, and my heart ached for the creatures of my forest back at home.

I should have known better than to trust him. I was a fool to believe I could love two people, or that two people would love me. Garm was right, I only got myself into this mess by thinking with my cunt. I hated that he was right. I had failed to use judgement and intuition, only complicating things for me further.

I felt a sob begin to claw the back of my throat, but I swallowed it down, refusing to let this bloodsucker break me down.

I need you...if I ever needed you, it's now.

One tear managed to escape, running down my cheek.

If The Dark Mother was a demon, or an entity, I could conjure her with a sigil and a sacrifice. It wouldn't be easy to do down here, but if I could find a way out of this pit and into the guests' quarters again...I could do it.

I wondered if Charity was treated the same as me, or if she was protected under Charles' wing. He knew this Red King, and he brought me straight to him. Fire burned my insides again, and instead of exhausting myself in a fit, I harnessed that anger inside until it unfurled around me, lifting from the ground, my eyes rolling back inside my head. The cuff around my ankle shook, but did not break, and I cursed at myself. I was not powerful enough to break these chains. My coercion would have to be the tool I used to get me out of here. I stood below the trap door, small cracks of lights beaming through and onto the dirt floor. I squinted my eyes, smiling to myself as I saw a pair of feet guarding the door.

"Please, excuse me? I am desperately parched, could you please fetch me more water? I would be ever so grateful."

The pacing feet stopped, and the door was pulled open slowly, the kneeling guard poking his head inside. "The pitcher."

"Of course," I said, as sweetly as I could, conveying every ounce of innocence I could muster.

I bent down to the pitcher, picking it up and sliding my thumb through the handle, leaving my four fingers free. As the guard reached for the same handle, I grabbed his gloved hand, pulling him down sharply and into the hole with me.

Stupid man, you should have known better than to kneel for me.

A smile stretched across my face as he tumbled on top of me...almost. I stepped back and out of the way at the last minute, the guard now flat on his back on the dirty floor. Dust rises around him, and before he could regain his balance, my foot crushed his neck in one swift motion. Both hands jerk to my ankle, but I am stronger than most men, and this one was small. It was laughable that the Red King would underestimate me, considering he knew exactly what I was; what I was capable of.

I quickly moved my other foot to his shoulder, stomping on his face until his neck snapped.

Too easy.

With the trap door wide open, it wouldn't take much for me to climb out, I just needed to find something steady to stand on.

Dragging the guard's body out of the way, I found a crate full of wine, pulling it just below the edge of the sun-shaped circle. I stood, carefully assessing the room I would climb into. There was only one guard, dead now, and I needed to be as quiet as I could on the creaking wood floor of what looked like a wine cellar.

Any other time, I would have fawned over the trea-sures, but I didn't have time. My escape—and my life, depended on it.

I would not leave without Charity, but I also needed to figure out a way to lose Charles. He could stay with his King, he need not accompany Charity and I any further. She was mine, and it was so clear to me, and I would make that perfectly clear to him.

Otherwise, I would have to kill him, and nobody wanted that. I doubted Charity would.

I slid against the dark walls until I found a door, a very heavy door. I pulled on it, but it didn't open.

My chest rose and fell rapidly now, and although I rarely became scared or even worried, right now my body wanted nothing more than to escape. To see the sunlight, to feel the dirt beneath my toes.

My pets.

I missed the ravens, I missed Lilitu, but somehow the ache deep inside my chest was hallowed only for Charity. I had finally found someone who filled the emptiness inside of me, only to have them ripped from my heart. Again.

It made me think of my parents, of my little sister, Frigg. She was once that person, who made me feel like home, who made me feel like maybe I was exactly where I was supposed to be.

The days that I'd wished I had gone with them to the Americas were rare, but while I was a prisoner inside these unknown walls, I thought maybe it would have been better.

No Charles and Charity, no vendetta against the men in black coats. It would've been easier, simple.

Only I didn't choose that, I chose to rebel. I chose to be my own hero.

As I walked the quieted hallways, I realized it was late at night, but the castle was fully alive.

Servants bustled around with food, and candles were lit in rings above and on the floor below. I remained unseen in the shadows, my instincts far more powerful than any human's. I managed to dodge most of them, until I came upon a set of young women who seemed to be gossiping about what was happening. The castle was abuzz with rumors of the woman Domenico held hostage.

"...she is here to revive the girl! Domenico is sure that she has the remedy..."

"But wouldn't he want to keep her locked in the apothecary? That makes the most sense to me. She will need materials, will she not?"

I smiled to myself, glad that my hearing was as sharp as a foxes.

With this information, I decide I will find the apothecary room and summon Lilith.

I would be beyond these walls by sunrise, the hard part would be taking Charity with me.

CHAPTER 15
CHARLES

Charity paced the room now, our sexual curiosities no longer able to distract her. I was too passive, too submissive, and I knew it. I felt inferior to the lover that Freyja had been...to her...to us both. It was almost as if she completed us, but *all together*. She was the heavy hand, and we were the two pliable participants. Together, we made the perfect balance of soft and rough love. The three of us together were the recipe for a delicious meal that teased all the senses. Part of me longed for that again, and the jealous part of me wanted Charity all to myself. I didn't want to share her, but I also wasn't sure that I would be able to keep her satisfied on my own.

"I can't be stuck in this room any longer! I am beginning to go mad! We have seen the art, the books, we have eaten food that I have only ever heard about—but Charles, where is Freyja? What has he done with her?"

She sounded hysterical, and part of me wanted to make sure she was quiet so that Domenico didn't worry she was a threat to his secrets.

"I will talk to him, little light. I promise you, I will find out where she is. Please do not worry yourself. Freyja is a witch—a strong witch."

Charity's cheeks were flushed, and her snubbed nose looked so cute when she cried, swollen just like her lips. I resisted kissing her face, and instead, I took her hands into mine and squeezed.

"What is he to you anyways? Your master? I see how you look at him...."

My cheeks burned, as if she had struck me. I'm unsure of what to say, but I settled for a simple explanation.

"He was like a father to me."

She squinted at me, as if she wasn't happy with the answer. I couldn't deal with this right now, an explanation of my relationship with Domenico could wait.

The library was the only place I had seen her crack even a small smile. I would bring her there and then I would go to Dom, and I would do whatever it took to find out just what he wanted with Charity's witch.

~

"Here, stay as long as you like, and I will have Fiona bring you some sweet bread and tea."

Charity ran her fingers over the spines that lined the walls to the ceiling. Dusty tomes, and three ladders that slide left and right, a loft just like Freyjas was tucked into the top, and I watched as Charity climbed inside. She would be safe here, and I knew where to find Domenico, the man who was always shadowed in a corner somewhere. But I knew these corridors just as well as he did, him showing them to me all those years ago when I was just a boy.

I winced a little at the memories of late night and wine inside of his office. I saw many things I shouldn't have at the ripe age of twelve. And Domenico continued to exploit those things, using them to manipulate my actions. Guilt was engraved on these walls, not just my own guilt, but the guilt of all the followers of The Delesepps. It was a keen tool to use, the people bowing to it, relinquishing any and all control.

I looked up and down the hallways, and when I was sure Charity would be left well enough alone, I strode to Domenico's large quarters, ready to give him whatever he asked of me, so I could give my Charity all the answers she sought.

It was no mistake why we were all here, I knew what my task had been, and I had completed it. Even at the end, when the larger-than-life Wolf-man nearly gobbled me whole. I still pressed on, delivering what Domenico had asked me to just one year ago.

I knocked on the heavy wooden door, laden with iron bolts and hinges. I knocked twice, then three times, then three more. My secret code, to let him know it was me.

"Come in."

His voice was stern, low. It sent chills down my lower spine, waking something so deep inside of me that could only be described as *primal.* My body reacted to him each time he was near, but that was our secret, something only the two of us shared.

"Domenico, thank you for seeing me."

I felt silly saying this, especially since I had done everything he asked of me without question, submissive as I was. I continued with that notion, my gratitude letting him know I was *still* submissive to him.

Domenico sat behind his desk, looking as handsome and regal as ever. His hair was closely shaven, and small specks of salt a pepper lazily crept up his temples. His skin looked pale to me now, whereas before I thought perhaps, he just never favored the sun. Clearly, that was why he loved to dwell inside of a dark castle.

His jaw was squared and firm, and the rough texture of his lips brought back memories of them on my neck, my thighs...

"You look downright terrified, Charles. What is it?"

He almost laughed, but I could hear the concern in his voice as well.

I rubbed my hands together in nervousness, but I stepped up closer to the desk that looked older than I was. A plush chaise lounge was set up beside it, and as I looked over the deeply red velvet, memories of those nights with Domenico flooded my mind. I shook them away, remembering why I was here.

"It's Charity...she is frightened...morose. She wants to know what happened to Freyja."

I felt as though the last part was blurted out, but he looked thoughtfully at me as he leaned in closer to me on his elbows.

Taking a moment to think about what I've said, finally he leaned back with a big sigh.

"I would have liked to have told you why I asked you to bring Freyja to me...but at the time, it didn't make sense. Now, however, you are home, and we can discuss this—*me*—at length."

I was slightly confused as to why he said '*me*' and not Freyja. What did Freyja have to do with him?

"I was in love once. As silly as that may sound, and the details *really* don't matter. The woman that I loved left me, and I guess I never truly got over that..."

I moved to sit on *the* chaise, and I squirmed a little as I sat.

Domenico's words echoing in my head.

Don't be afraid, you can trust me.

"And is that woman Freyja?" I asked, eager to hear his answers so I could escape this sexual tension that slowly formed at the bottom of my belly.

He laughed at this. "Hardly, but Freyja does *know* her."

Ah, okay, she had information he needed, it made sense. Now I just needed to know where exactly he kept her, that way I could reassure Charity she was safe and in good health.

Domenico stood from the desk, and his musky smell wafted around me, like a comforting blanket. He leaned against the headrest; his large hands very close to me. I shivered, feeling a pull of possessiveness and protection rolling off of him.

I craved being handled, wanted those instructions of exactly what to do and how to do it. I had become reliant on it, and it became a comfort to me at my lowest times.

"Do you remember the night that I caught you...in the bath...?"

My cheeks reddened at the remark, and I felt my cock move as I recounted the night when I was only seventeen, and I couldn't keep my hand off myself anymore. My cock had become a separate entity, something foreign, angry. A need for release that I wasn't even familiar with yet.

Fiona had been changing in the boys' quarters after a flood had ruined all her things. I remembered her crying, and curious as I was, ran to see who needed comfort. I stopped short, her naked body displayed to me. She had shrieked, and shooed me away, but not before I had a full picture of her round tits and pink tips. Wisps of blonde hair curled just above her swollen pubis, and I had licked my lips like an animal.

I told myself it would only be a few absent-minded strokes—just to take the throb away, but the feeling of my own hand heavy on my cock...stroking myself into a pleasure-laced fog...

"I remember..."

He squeezed my knee, then gently worked his way up my thigh.

I looked down at his hand, then to his face, soft and smiling.

"I was so patient and forgiving with you, and I would like you to give me that same patience and forgiveness with me now."

I nodded, biting my lip, and I felt my cock grow hard beneath his hand.

"Good boy."

CHAPTER 16
DANTE
THE PAST: WALES

"I know. I already *know* of the babe."

He was seething mad, but not with Lilith, with me.

"Then how did you just *let her* go?"

"And what was I to do, Dante? Tie her up? Cage her? I loved her."

I stopped pacing in his dark office, and when I faced him, his face had fallen and he looked tired, ancient. Good looks were something that kept our true identities safely hidden, and today he looked every bit his age.

"She wanted freedom, she wanted *worship*. And that's exactly what I gave her...and it still wasn't good enough."

I scrubbed my face, and now I felt anger at him, anger for letting a walking Goddess leave us all.

"I know you fancied her, you half-wit. You were never good enough for her, don't you understand?"

I growled, then I pushed him, knocking him into the tapestry that he had commissioned of Lilith, standing beside a large tree with an even larger snake wrapped around it, lingering beside her ear.

Domenico's fangs sprung free, and he growled back, only he didn't charge me. I knew he wouldn't. When it came down to fighting or fucking, he would always choose fucking. I knew that much of my brother.

"I have never tasted blood as sweet."

"And you think I have? Why do you think I fought so hard for her? It wasn't just her cunt, her lips. It was *everything*."

I sat on the only chair in the room, head in my hands. I wish I didn't feel this way, I wish I had never found her and taken a small taste that night. She had been drunk and laughing, and one thing led to another...

Lilith knew what we were, and she loved it. She loved the blood, the secrets, the *worship*. She *was* a Godsend, she was everything we needed and wanted. It was a damn shame that she fell for Domenico in the first place.

"What else is there to do, Dante? Tell me."

I don't have the answers, I never did—that wasn't my place.

"Aren't you angry? Do you not feel *rejected? Betrayed?*"

This garnered a laugh from him, as if he couldn't be bothered with any of those feelings. After all, we had been dead for centuries, you would think emotions would fail, but they did not—they remained.

"Of course, I feel rejected! Betrayed! I gave her years of my life. Risking being found out. We did every sinful act known to man, I would have been cast aside just as fast as Mary Magdalene."

"Then we just forget her? A Goddess dropped down to us from Heaven, who's blood tastes like life itself?"

Domenico stood, shoving his hands in his trouser pockets, thinking, as he gazed out of the tall stained-glass window. "I guess you're right. I thought perhaps I could just forget, but not without tarnishing her name. I will make a monster out of her, I will tell her story of evil, sexual prowess. The child killer."

I squeezed my fists together, remembering the way it made me feel when I drank from her. I felt alive again, powerful. If there was ever any way of feeling hope in a vampire's world, her blood was it. I felt strong enough to walk into the light, strong enough to reveal my true self to anyone who would listen.

"What about the babe? Would it taste just as sweet, do you think?"

Domenico turned to me this time, grey eyes sharp and pointed. "It is possible...but we would have to wait. Wait and watch."

I nodded, knowing exactly what he meant.

"I will watch, then."

Little did he know, I had plans of my own for Lilith. She *would* be mine. Perhaps not of the flesh, but her blood would be mine.

CHAPTER 17
LILITH
THE PAST

I named her Annabel, and then I left her on the doorstep of a doctor and his wife. He was the only doctor within miles, and I thought perhaps that would be the safest place for my only child.

When I had seen the couple out together at markets, the husband doted on the woman, he spoke soft words to her, he was gentle with her. He looked at her like she was a prize.

Annabel's hair was red, her lips were shaped like a heart. I kissed them gently as I placed her in a basket and on the doorsteps that day. I didn't deserve to be a mother; I was not made for that job.

I was The Dark Mother, the one who refused to submit to a man, who demanded the same treatment as a king. I was not a tender, nurturing matron, but a blood-thirsty and selfish creature.

And now, I was free again, walking away from a baby that I would only be able to love from a distance.

I promise I will always be near, always watching over you.

I suddenly felt weak, and I craved rest.

My snakes had disappeared, and sadness lanced my chest. I didn't cry, I wouldn't allow that.

My magic, my immortality, would always surround her; I could stretch it for miles. I had no doubt in my mind I would always have an eye on her.

Would she inherit my magic? Would my gifts be passed down to her?

All I knew right now was that I would never be a good mother.

~

England 1678

Each time I came to visit Annabel, she looked more and more morose—devoid of any purpose. I knew the man she was with was not the right one, another man who followed the church, another man who would only disappoint her with all his requirements. He did not love my child—he only loved God.

I visited her more and more, leaving her gifts of enhanced crystals, feathers and skulls of small woodland animals. She became stronger, until one day, she had a baby of her own. Another spritely little red head named Lux.

I couldn't have been prouder, as I watched her hone her craft—creating magical wards and spells that could never be undone.

Until one day, the men. They came for her.

I watched, from a cluster of faraway trees, their shadows keeping me hidden. The little girl shouted at her father, begging him not to take her, but it was already done.

I knew exactly who was behind this, and I could do nothing to stop it. I never claimed her as my own, so how would I keep her from harm if she didn't know who I was?

I thought about rushing to Domenico, to Dante, but I knew it would be futile to plead with the men I left behind thirty years ago. This was their revenge, and I should have known Domenico would keep an eye on the baby that I fled from.

He was a man, he craved power, his only gains behind a faceless God that everyone feared.

If you didn't believe—punished. If you sinned— punished again. And the sting had returned at the reminder of the day I was cast out of Eden as a demon, forgotten and discarded.

Women were disposable to men, and the more we were oppressed, the higher up on the food chain they became.

I wept, naked and with my hair curled around my body, caked in dirt and tears. When I pictured Annabel's heart shaped face, and large green eyes, I was transported to the stake.

Flames licked her feet, and she begged for a chance to explain herself.

I'd sunk to my knees, finally giving in to the need to cry, to release my anger and sadness that I held inside of me for too long.

I looked at the sky, the endless rows of clouds and grey. And for the first time since the day I fell through the sky, I spoke to God, full of indignation and hopelessness.

Why have you failed me? Forsaken me? I do not deserve this punishment. You were supposed to love me unconditionally!

I wrapped my arms around myself, letting the tears fall. I rocked myself back and forth, remembering that I was the only one who I'd ever been able to rely on. I crack open, I break, and I allow myself to feel every bitter sting of whips I'd been given. I allowed myself to feel the burn and break of bone that threatened to tear me up from the inside out, but I never let it.

Tears stained my hair, my hands, and my face. I watched as her body became nothing but ash and cinders. I cursed God, and I cursed the men. I was weak, and her death was all because I was not brave enough to be a mother. If I was there, if I had kept her, this would have never happened.

I briefly thought of taking my own life, slicing my wrists and bleeding out at the edge of the forest as I watched her turn into smoke.

Instead, I asked for pity, I asked her for forgiveness.

My sweet child, if only you realized this was just your natural way, you have done nothing wrong except acknowledge the power within you. I'm sorry...I'm so sorry...and I hope that you can forgive me.

Her screams burned inside my ears, and only fed my rage that had once laid dormant inside of me while I was in the arms of Domenico.

I would be lying if I said my heart didn't yearn for him, but I was Lilith and I did not need any man. I was created to walk alone on a path of redemption, a path that led me straight to this very place where I stood, as I watched my child burned alive for her *sins*.

And who was to say that her sins were not theirs? Perhaps her sins were an effect of men's sins? She would never had to protect herself with wards if the man she loved caressed her skin instead of striking it. She would not need love spells on others if her heart was content with the man she called a husband.

I gained invisible wings the day she died, and I flew from place to place without memory or direction. I floated above the clouds, until I had no energy left and had to rest. I had no choice, and I would need food inside of my half-human, half-God body.

I cursed under my breath, finding a small clearing in the Welsh woods from where I'd come.

I thought about returning to the Underworld, only it was a damp and dark place where not much light graced its floors. I had become attached to the sunlight, often bathing in it on days where the loneliness consumed me.

Where would I go from here? Should I go back for the young girl they called Lux?

After expertly trapping two rabbits, I spit them over a small fire. I sat, chewing and plotting.

It was then that I decided I would go to Lux, and I would do whatever I could to keep her safe. I would intervene any way I could, and that included taking her away from whoever I must.

CHAPTER 18

DOMENICO

THE PAST

"She was *burned?* Who ordered such a thing?"

My voice was cross, and as I stood in front of my younger brother, I began to tremble. This was not what I intended; I did not want these men to take matters into their own hands. They were supposed to report back to me immediately after they found her.

Dante looked different; he was sad, guilty.

"Who did it?"

He hung his head and remained silent, and I knew he was guilty, I knew of his jealousy. He was in charge over the small villages and their men, only this time he had gone too far.

I roared, gripping the sides of my desk, my knuckles burning, as I lifted it over my head and threw it across the room.

Dante cowered, he knew what I could do, he didn't want to be on this end of my rage.

He was a coward, and a sorry excuse for the last name Delesepps.

I stalked from the room, intent on walking the hidden

corridors, so I would not see anyone while I was filled with such anger. I could not let my guard down; the mask must remain.

I needed to find Melody, her face was the only thing that could soothe me, bring me back down again.

"Dom, what is it?"

Her blonde ringlets bobbed in front of her pale, freckled face. She kissed me on the cheek gently and I smiled.

It was long ago that she was simply a fledgling in my school for children, a young, supple fifteen. But then her family committed the utmost betrayal—killing a vampire. The violence that followed left Melody bloody and mangled, missing fingers and toes. I had no choice but to turn her, and now she was mine forever.

"Just foolish men who do not know how to wield their power. Come with me."

She followed behind me, down the hidden corridors and to the spot we loved that looked out over the gardens. A large bed overflowing with pillows and blankets piled on top of it. She plopped down on her back, always the bright star in my dark sky.

"You must hide, because there will certainly be repercussions from this act."

She looked at me, confused, but she nodded her head slowly.

"And just what can hurt *me?*"

There it was; the cockiness of a newly turned vampire. I had warned her of this cockiness that would be her demise. We may be immortal, but stakes and sunshine were two very real threats to our kind. There were people who rumored other devices that would kill, but most of them were false.

"You must fear Lilith, The Dark Mother, always. She is the killer of children, and you are no exception."

Her eyes went wide, and I stroked the hair back from her face, gaining a smile from her.

"Is she a vampire as well?"

I sat back, removing the holy collar that I wore around my neck. I was exhausted and planned to take some time away with Melody anyway. I would show her the cliffs of Greece, and the dark hills where we came from.

All would be well, I just needed to make sure we would not be where Lilith last left me.

Would she come back? What would I do if she did? The love of my life who left me when I did not want any such thing.

Memories of our time together washed over me, she was the perfect fit for me, the mate I bonded with in blood. We lived together in the dark, committing sins together, between our naked bodies and her heated breath.

Something gnawed at me, the saying 'an eye for an eye.'

I knew Lilith, and I knew the kind of vengeance she would seek over someone who wronged her. She would want to even the score, she wouldn't rest until her revenge was exacted. Which only meant that Melody would never be safe until I extinguished the monster that was Lilith.

CHAPTER 19

LILITH

THE PAST

I would curse them all.

Domenico and Dante...the entire Delesepps family would feel my wrath in one way or another.

I would not let them swear themselves to me, only to betray me the moment my back was turned. There was no strength in that, there was no loyalty either.

They played God and took Annabel's fate into their own hands. It was not right, it was not 'Godlike.'

But then what did I know about God? I only knew I would never be repressed and controlled by someone who demanded my submission. Submission was not in my vocabulary; it was not something that naturally came to me.

Why did we need to prove our fealty by succumbing to someone else's rules?

Believe in me, or else.

I have whispered into the girl's ear, each night. I'm still unsure if she believes that I was her inner voice or not, but I cannot show myself to her unless I was summoned.

515

Whatever the answer may be, I would only speak my truth, and that I would do through the line I had created. If I was not careful, then she too would be burned, and I would never let that mistake be repeated.

I would burn them all to the ground before I ever watched another day filled with flames of my blood and bone. Never again.

I watched the girl grow from lanky arms and legs to a beautiful, curvaceous young woman who could weaken any man or woman's knees.

I knew exactly what lingered in these Welsh woods, and I knew that there were more monsters among us than only vampires. There was a collection of beasts that would defy any human man that dared try. And When I finally fell upon a Viking who was cast aside; I knew then, he would be her savior.

I could whisper into the ear of anyone I desired, control was one thing, and free will was another. It didn't take much to rouse his lonely heart into a fever. A fever that would burn until he saw her.

It began with dreams, but then I turned into a desire that brought him straight to her.

Once I knew their fates were sealed, I was able to move on to the largest dragon that would need slaying.

The men in the black coats did this to her, and there was only one powerful man who could have been behind it.

Domenico.

I would not rest until I had his blood-bound, Melody, the one he always told me never to fret over. I would have her, by spell, by curses that would entwine her in a sleep that would keep her from him forever.

This would be simple, especially after all I had been

through. I was stronger now, and I would face him with weapons of rage.

I just needed to find him first, which would be an easy feat.

He would be inside the walls of Castle Delessepps.

***

When I saw him again, it was much like a bolt of lightning through my chest. I do not believe it is love, no, it was more like *bloodlust*. Memories soak me, and I was nostalgic for the depravity we committed together. The blood, the sex, the *power*.

I wanted to ravage him and kill him, all at the same time.

Perhaps I will fuck him before I curse him.

I toy with this inside my mind, but I cannot think past setting my plan into motion as soon as possible.

An eye for an eye.

"How *could* you?"

He was silent, and I stalked towards him, night sky be damned. He was sitting in the same place as the day that we first met. Concealed in the shadows of the age-old castle. It seemed to be where he felt like he needed to be, a place familiar and close.

It was where he first laid eyes on me.

"Lilith..."

His voice was scared, and it brought me great pleasure to think that The Red King could be frightened of me. I liked that, quite a lot.

He was no more aged than when I left him last, which also sent a sharp pain through my chest.

"Where is *she?*"

"Please, Lilith, this was not supposed to be this way—"

"Where is SHE?!"

I tore past him, with him barely able to keep up with me. I craved blood, I could smell it. I knew that she would never bleed for me, so instead, I would put her to sleep.

I found her, after three turns in the dark corridors, exactly where I knew he would be hiding her.

Her face was lovely, youthful, the mask of vampirism forever keeping an imprint of her youth. I was not jealous; I was filled with fury.

"You will sleep now, little dove, you will sleep until a submissive man kisses you."

I placed a fingertip between her eyes, aggressively so that she fell backwards, eyes rolling back into her head.

"Damn you, Lilith. It wasn't enough that you betrayed me, left me? Now you take another that I cared for? Will you stop at nothing to feed your bloodlust?"

I laughed, he was one to speak of blood lust—his stronger than my own, I knew.

"Shall we fuck one last time, Dom? Taste my blood one last time?" I ground out the words, holding back a sob that stabbed the back of my throat. No, he wouldn't have my sobs.

It was done, and I laughed to myself, wishing that I had taken Domenico unwillingly before I had done so. It was too late now, and I could hear him hissing behind me. Only I am stronger, and I jump up and away from his grasp and into the sky.

My body trembled in victory, and as I viewed the castle below me, I imagined nothing but pain and loneliness for all that inhabit those vapid, restless walls within.

CHAPTER 20

CHARLES

1730 FRANCE

The question of the evening was simple: Was I willing to do *anything* it took to ensure that Charity got what she wanted? Or was that just too much of a high price to pay after all this time?

I loved her, yes, but my loyalty was undeniably linked to Domenico. I wanted him, my body already deceiving me as I headed back to the room that I shared with Charity.

No, I would not let Domenico worm his way into my mind the way he always did. I would simply manipulate him.

Even as I thought it, I doubted myself.

She still slept, although it was early in the evening now, well after dinner time but not quite time to turn in.

Uncertainty floated through my mind, wondering if I would ever really be enough for her. I had brought sweet cakes and fruit back with me, her favorite, hoping it would lift her mood.

The bed was unmade, and Charity's hair was matted, her eyes puffy from all the lost sleep.

520

"How can you just relax and eat and sleep like we don't know there's a *monster* within these walls, posing as a *priest!?*"

I sat down the tray of food and drink beside her on the bed and closed my eyes as I took in a deep breath. My patience was growing thin with her, but I was trying to understand how she felt. Did I already know, on some level, that he *was* a monster? I knew that a Deacon took oaths, giving their lives to God and only God. However, the things we did in the dark, the acts we had committed were ultimately a sin. And I continued to sin while I was away with Freyja and Charity.

Was it easier to just deny it was happening at all, while still living a life of purity on the surface? Or would a *truly* holy man simply deny himself of his desires for the sake of God's rewards?

I knew the answer, but I wasn't ready to face it yet. Not until I knew how to make my Charity happy.

"It isn't that simple, love. We all do things that we regret, I would say you did things with Freyja that were sinful—are you a monster?"

She looked at me, incredulous and with judgement. "How *dare* you call *me* a monster!"

She began to sob again, and I was beginning to think it would just be easier to put her in a carriage in the middle of the night and send her home. It could be done, I had just as much power over the servants as Domenico did.

I shook the thought from my mind, although that little voice was slowly getting louder as my cock was effectively neglected each day that passed.

I sat beside her and pulled her into my arms, something that I seemed to be doing more than a few times a day lately.

I stroked her hair back. "You should have a bath, would that make you feel better?"

She sniffled, unable to push away the one and only person she trusted here.

I bounced down the hidden stairway behind our bedroom, straight to the servant's quarters and kitchens. It came in handy knowing my way around here, I knew every secret corner and hidden room. I was a curious and easily bored teen back then, probably why I had been in countless *bad* situations.

Self-sabotage at its finest.

After I was able to summon steamed water and soap from a young and timid girl named Tara, I jogged back to our room with a fresh towel that smelled of lavender. This would please her as well, I knew it would.

I pulled Charity over to the clawed foot tub that sat in front of the fireplace that stood taller than I did.

Her cheeks were stained with tears, her bottom lip in a pout.

I grinned, wanting desperately to kiss her, from the tips of her breasts to the velvet seam between her thighs.

My cock was already throbbing, and I adjusted myself before I began to undress her.

She closed her eyes as I unlaced her corset, dropping it to the floor, and just as I slipped the light chiffon over her shoulders, Tara entered with the buckets of steaming water.

She curtsied to me, eyes downcast, filling the basin before exiting the room.

She knew exactly what was about to happen, and that

sent an excited shiver down my spine and straight to my sack.

Charity's long legs stretched over the side of the tub, and I watched her round buttocks descend beneath the simmering mirror. Her eyes were closed, and I knelt beside her, placing a gentle kiss on her temple. I ran a hand down her arm, and she shivered, the tips of her breasts peeking out from the surface of the water, into tight furls of pink beads.

I bit my lips, leaning in to kiss her collarbone, and then taking one of those furls into my mouth. She moaned, arching her back, but she didn't open her eyes.

"Is this okay?" I asked, sinking my hand beneath the water. She nodded ever so slightly, and I trailed my fingers down her belly and stroked the apex of her thighs.

I kissed the bottom of her lip, but she didn't take the opportunity to return, but allowed her leg's to part ever so slightly.

I found the sensitive bud behind her folds, and she hissed as I ran the tip of my finger over it.

"And this, is this, okay?"

She was silent, and an uneasy feeling gnawed at the bottom of my stomach, like something wasn't quite right.

It felt as though I was being judged, watched. Not the way it felt when Charity, Freyja and I were together. Something uninvited.

He was watching us.

I pivoted around to look at the painting to our left. I knew every vantage point he had here, and part of me wished I didn't.

He was watching.

My blood ran cold, and I lost all the courage I had to seduce her.

A sliver of light flashes behind the eyes of the late Marco Delessepps. He had seen me look...

I decided to keep going, he had been caught watching, and now he had fled—I was sure of it.

Feebly, I continued.

DOMENICO

I watched him fumble with his hands, asking for permission from the bratty girl he brought here.

The lust that burned so deliciously inside of me had returned once again. A re-ignition of the flames Lilith spread through my body each time I saw her. It was her who began this lusting, it had all started with her, and I blamed every vile thought I had on her.

I stroked myself under my robes as I watched; my fangs released and hungry. I wanted to show them both what it was like to be in control—full control of another.

The girl did not want to be asked, she wanted to be told. She wanted to be told just how unreasonable she was, how ungrateful...all while punishing her body with pleasures. She wanted it...she craved it. How could he not see?

The answer came easy to me as I gripped the head of myself and thumbed just below the crown.

Charles wanted the same thing.

He wanted to hear how insufferable he was, how *bad* and *wrong* and *dirty*. The punishment was palpable on both their skin—I saw it behind their glassed eyes, I smelled it seeping from their pores.

For a moment, Charles looked back at the painting I stood behind, watching them with languor.

I froze, but he knew exactly what happened behind those oiled eyes; spurred me on.

I would show them.

My steps were steady, and before I breached the door, my thoughts were clouded by possession... ownership.

This was *my* home, my holy sanctuary of worship. By the end of this, they would both respect me.

The girl gasped, covering her chest, and Charles fell back on his hands, away from the tubs edge.

"Shit, Dom, what happened to privacy?"

Unable to control what I felt for Charles, the lingering memories of our countless trysts.

"On your knees."

I commanded the room, my shoulders squared, my robes brushing the tips of his feet. The girl was silent, still clutching her chest, greedily watching the events unfold in front of her like the dirty slut she was.

Charles didn't hesitate to obey, and I grinned as I watched Charity take note of his actions.

A submissive never failed to drop to their knees when commanded, not a good sub anyway.

"Good boy," I said curtly, and his head lowered, his chest bared and his cock hard beneath his breeches.

I hooked my finger below his chin, raising his face to look at mine.

His lashes were long and fanned out below his arched brows. I traced the fullness of his bottom lip, opening it just a little. "Suck."

He did just as he was told, garnering a twitch of my cock, the tightness in my breeches becoming unbearable.

His mouth was the perfect combination of warm and wet, and he sucked with enthusiasm to please me, like always.

I closed my eyes, letting myself fall back into my old patterns, my deviant, dirty, desires.

Waves crashed over me, an arrow pulled back and the tension threatening to break the bow. It was released the moment his tongue brushed over the pad of my thumb. I leaked for him already, but when I flicked my eyes to the girl, she watched intently.

"Do you like watching him suck me, sweet girl?"

She swallowed, darting her eyes to mine, but she did not move.

"Take it out," I commanded, looking over his crown of perfectly messy blonde hair.

He reached up inside my robes, gripping my thighs as he went, cupping my balls tucked tightly inside my breeches. Buttons popped, and I heard him groan quietly as he found my shaft and could scarcely wrap his fist around it.

I lift the robes over my head, discarding them onto the floor and giving Charity the full view of my stony abs and remarkable cock.

I knew of its beauty because there was never a day that passed when Lilith didn't praise its girth, begged for it even.

Charles hand looked small in comparison, and Charity's eyes were wide, her jaw slacken at the sight.

"Now, part her legs, and do *not* ask permission. If she does not do as you please, you will slap those perfect tips gently until she follows your orders."

Reluctantly, he removed his hand from the steel against my belly and stood. Sinking down beside the tub again, he reached between her legs. Not gently, not carefully, but directly.

I was rewarded by a guttural groan from the girl as he entered her.

"Use two fingers, and don't pump them…curl them."

Resting his forehead on the side, he worked her beneath the water as she cries out, her eyes screwed shut.

"Such a good boy…fuck her with your fingers until she comes around them."

He was rewarded with a long, close eyed moan from her. "Ah, you see? She likes that."

He lifted his head to watch her face fall in pleasure, her mouth open.

I watched as his confidence swiftly returned, but he still looked at me over his shoulder, waiting for more instructions.

I laughed to myself, not out loud, it sent a thrill through me, watching his eyes search me for approval. Those innocent eyes…

"Talk her through it, let her know she can let go…but only for you."

Charles surprised me, taking his free hand and stroking the wild hairs away from her face, and speaking low into her ear.

I watched as he stops, moving softly beneath the water now.

"Tell me what you're doing to her now."

He swallowed, looking at me from under long lashes. "I'm stroking the tight bud at the top of her folds. It makes…oh…it makes her shudder."

I closed my eyes, biting my lip, my arousal taking

over. I craved touch just as much as him, it was a weakness we shared.

Slowly, I walk to him, rubbing his shoulder and sliding my thumb along his collarbone. He sighed, every so quietly, and looked up at me. I was lost to his blue eyes and soft lips, and I gave in. Leaning down and kissing him deeply as he continued to flick Charity's clit under the water. It was almost too much, as his tongue tangled with mine, his lips eagerly working over me. He gave me a small moan, and my primal urges threw my logical sense out the window. I grabbed him by the throat, a little to violently, and he gasped. He stood, leaving the girl's mouth agape as she watches us attack one another with hands and teeth. I continued to kiss him; my hand wrapped around his neck. His hands were wrapped around my wrist that held him captive, and I tossed him onto the bed with a guttural growl. He landed on his back, hands splayed at his side, and his eyes never left mine. He knew what I wanted; he knew how I was when I was hungry for him.

I remembered we weren't alone, and the door was still open. Did I want her to escape? Was she just a nuisance that stood in between Charles and I? Or was I hungry enough to allow her to join in carnal pleasure.

I chose the latter.

I stalked to the tub, scooping her into my arms as if she was weightless, she squealed, amping up my adrenaline that was already bursting from my cock.

I threw her onto the bed beside him, and she screamed as she landed. I thought I saw a smile escape from Charles, but he was instantly hushing her, stroking her face. Jealousy rose within me, as I stepped out of my breeches. I climbed on top of Charles with the calculated measure of a cat, and he was my submissive once again, laying back and allowing me to straddle his face.

"Suck my cock like you will never suck a cock again. Just the way you did that night before you left me."

I pushed the dusky head down, and his mouth was already opened and waiting, wet. He licked the tip mischievously, and I tug his hair with my free hand, a warning.

His mouth covered the head, but he can't quite swallow me down from this angle, and the tease is enough to put me over the edge.

"I can't...I can't take you deep this way...please..."

I roar, frustrated with Charity's presence, and angry that he could still make me weak for orgasm. No one could do that...no one except...

Lilith.

Her name was like a curse, and I leaped from the bed, scrubbing my eyes, fangs extended fully.

"Get on top of her, pin her hands above her head."

Charles nodded, roughly pulling her up on the bed and placing himself in between her thighs. He nudged them apart roughly, and I praised him, "That's it...take her, don't ask her."

When he pinned her arms above her head, he held them both with one hand and she moaned. Her nipples were hard, pointing to the ceiling, begging to be sucked.

"Suck her tits, roughly."

He does as he's told, and his lips closed around one, causing her to buck her hips up against his torso.

I dropped my hand to my cock, stroking it in slow, long pulls. The tip dripped, and I swirled my thumb along it. I watched as Charles tried to keep himself from entering her...no easy feat with her hips begging for his entrance.

"She is being impatient; you can force her to stop that bucking..." I stutter, as I stroked myself harder now. I was feral, at the brink of howling.

Charle's took his mouth off her breast, and tugged on her arms, another moan escaping her. "Stay still," he commands, and she stills.

His stern voice sent a ripple down my back, and I can't take it any longer. I wanted him, and I would have my first release since her...damn her...

I get on top of him, pushing his body down onto hers. "Get inside her," I groaned.

He shifts, and I was rewarded with his moan, her squeal. I lay my head against his, trying so hard not to take his ass right here. I can't; it isn't time yet.

My shaft ground against his tight crack, and I rubbed myself between his cheeks until I felt my orgasm building, my balls pulling tight.

"Oh, please, Dom. Fuck my ass...I want it..."

His words send me over, and I already feel the wetness of my seed spill from me.

My breathing was labored, and I kissed his shoulder. "Not again..."

I stood from the bed, picking up my clothes, and pulling them on as Charle's fucked his fleeting obsession into the mattress.

I didn't look back, I could only close and lock the door behind me with shame.

CHAPTER 22
FREYJA

It did not take me long to find the large room that contained every medicinal herb and tincture available to a wealthy family. I had my suspicions, but with a vampire hidden beneath the guise of a holy man—I wasn't sure if that kind of magic was allowed.

The room would normally be located near the food stores, on the ground floor for easy access, so I immediately fled the winding staircase behind the servants' quarters.

Sure enough, a large set of double doors, directly next to the entrance of the cathedral, held everything that I needed.

Jars of herbs lined the walls inside tall bookcases, and empty tincture bottles lined the countertop at the back of the room.

Larger jars of animal skulls and carcasses were tucked away in cupboards beneath them, and I smiled to myself.

The hypocrites were practicing the exact same rituals and spells that they were damning women to hell for. My skin crawled at the thought, but I pushed it away, remembering I was held captive here and needed Lilith now.

I knew that Garm would have followed my scent for miles, but I was not sure if he would be able to sneak inside the castle walls. If I could summon Lilith, Charity and I could escape...but just how far we would make it without Garm's help I wasn't sure. Most of this plan heavily depended on him waiting for us within the woods.

I found the fire still filled with ash, and gathered it into my hands, wiping the sigil of Lilith on my forehead. I closed my eyes, speaking to her with intent and alarm, hoping she would hear my pleas. My clothes were ripped, and my fingernails caked with dirt, and I fantasize of my hot springs and the feeling of Charity heavy breasts beside me.

Making a circle with the ash in the middle of the room, I then gathered the materials I would need: black candles, salt, bay leaves, and wine. I grabbed a pointed knife to cut my own skin with, and lastly, the carcass of a freshly killed snake.

I pinned the bay leaves to the snakes' eyes, placing it in the middle of the circle. I sliced both of my palms, getting on my knees and sprinkling salt around me. The knife clanked to the ground, and I cursed at the noise. The cup of red wine was set beside the snake, and I closed my eyes as I recited my prayer to her:

Oh, Dark Mother, it is you I seek, I call upon you and your powers.
Lilith, queen of snakes, and bringer of curses,
I need you now.

Weak men cower in your presence, and I kneel before you now.
I call upon thee, your power times three,
It beckons you, inside these ancient walls of thee.

I hummed after, keeping my eyes closed, and that's when her voice returned to me.

I am here.

The jolt of her words knocked the breath from me, and my eyes sprung open as I was knocked back.

The candles were all extinguished at once, and my breathing picked up as I surveyed the darkened room.

At first, it was only movement, but the movement comes from the floor—the snake was alive and slithering towards the door.

I needed to find Charity fast.

~

Before I found them…I heard them. Charity's soft moans and cries of pleasure. The door was ajar, and I stood in the frame, watching the three in shock.

It was as if our short time together was reflected back to me, but in a nightmarish way.

Domenico instructed Charles how to fuck Charity

properly, and as I stepped into the room, I see two small snakes slither from under the bed.

Charles sees me first, bent over Charity's behind, and when he stopped, she looked up.

We locked eyes, and hers light up. I couldn't help but smile, relievief and happiness washing over me all at once. It was hard not to run to her, to gather her into my arms and whisper into her hair how I would never let another touch her again.

Domenico was on me in a second, his movements sharp and calculated. His hand was around my throat, and I clawed at it, a gurgling sound coming from my lips.

He bared his teeth, his fangs longer than I remembered, and for a moment I thought I would black out. Charity ran to him, jumping onto his back and pummeling him with all her naked might.

I loved how fierce my little pet could be when she needed to, I would reward her for that later.

"Stop it! Let her go!"

Charles grabbed her from behind, containing her flailing arms as she protested.

"Let her go, please. It's bothering Charity..."

Dom's blackened eyes receded back to gray, and his grip on me loosened.

As if he had been woken from a trance, he set me down, but I remained in his hold. "Of course, I'm so sorry...I don't know what came over me. Charles, close the door and lock it so our guest will not flee."

Charles did as he says, but not before I spat into Domenico's face and hiss.

Like the well-mannered Deacon he claimed to me, he wiped his face gracefully and stepped back.

"Give me the girl and let us go."

Charity scrambled to replace her dress over her naked body and ran to me, flinging her arms around my shoulders. Her honey scent filled my nose, and I hugged her back, inhaling her deeply.

"I've missed you."

"I've missed you, too."

We kissed, and sunshine spread through my body, birds chirped, and I felt light again; only it was the middle of the night and there was no way any of that was real.

Domenico chuckled and took a seat near the fireplace as Charles buttoned up his pants.

"We have been over this, *Freyja,*" he sneered, my name rolling of his tongue in a French accent. He was so cocky and confident that I desperately wanted to backhand him, but I resisted.

I remained with my sweet Charity, feeling her rapid heartbeat and great anxiety about this monster—as she should.

"I *need* you. You will tell me what spell, what tincture will bring back my Melody. And do you know *why?*"

I didn't want to entertain his games, but I played along and shook my head no.

"Because *you* are Lilith's descendant, and Lilith did this to her."

Descendant?

Was this why I could hear her and sometimes see her? New revelations filled my head and pride blossomed inside my chest, knowing just how powerful I had become over the years.

Domenico stood, holding an amethyst crystal in his palm.

"She was captured, inside this stone, and you will

release her. You will bring her back and tell her to undo this.”

“And if I don’t?”

His laugh was low and condescending. “You die…she dies…let’s not travel that path though,” he said as he placed the crystal in my hand as he moved to the door. “Take as long as you like, but now, you three will *all* be my prisoners…until you do.”

With that, the door was closed behind him and locked with a click.

CHAPTER 23

DOMENICO

I didn't want to do this to Charles. I had moments of mistrust after seeing his infatuation with the bratty girl. She was plain and boring in my opinion. I still didn't know what he saw within her. Nothing was as invoking as watching someone submit, and my little submissive was so perfect when he was on his knees.

As a boy, he was eager to please. The blue in his eyes would shine as he would say, *"Yes, Deacon."*

Once he reached fifteen, his insatiable desire showed itself to me. I watched him stroke himself every moment he had alone, he was much like I was when I had been young and naive.

After much time, and many late nights, I had Charles just where I wanted him—a malleable and willing student, taking orders like such a *good boy*. He deserved to be rewarded.

Before he left on his errand in Bethlehem, the rewards were orgasms, beautiful, painful orgasms. I'd edged him until he couldn't take it any longer and had begged me for a release. I missed those moments from our sordid relationship—the begging, the pleading. His rosebud lips, panting and parted. I wanted to hear him beg for me again.

Once I had his trust, I knew he would be the key to breeching the witches' wards.

I walked the courtyard, under the full moon that shown so brightly tonight, that I could see for miles across the fields behind the castle. The rose bushes and moonflowers were a welcomed distraction, I walked each night just to see them. It felt as though this one flower was made just for me—its beautiful white petals opening beneath the moon's influence.

Lilith reminded me of that flower, and I was the moon. Pain lanced my insides, and I cursed myself for allowing someone to ever cause me pain. I was immortal, I was as ancient as this castle. Pain was for the weak, the mortal.

Just as I turned down the cobblestone path, back to the castle, a black snake slithered over my foot. I leaped forward, catching it just behind its head. Bringing it close to my face, it's tongue sliding in and out in a flickering beat. I hadn't seen a snake inside these gardens since Lilith. I surveyed the land, and a thick fog rolled in from the woods that bordered the property, and a foreboding feeling tickled the back of my neck as the snake struggled inside my fist.

I spoke into the sky, "I welcome you back, Dark Mother. It's been a very long time."

CHAPTER 24

DOMENICO

THE PAST: 1725 FRANCE

When Dante brought word of Lilith's two great-granddaughters, I was pleased. So many years waiting, so many years to decide what action needed to be taken.

I had planned on stealing Annabel's child and simply keeping her until Lilith noticed she was missing. If I used the child, it would be easy to bring Lilith to me—she watched over her I was sure, and I knew this because my men could never get close enough. She had wards and protection spells around the girl, and the girl even began to practice witchcraft herself.

It wasn't until I received word that the girl ran away that I began to send the men after her, to no avail. She was enamored with a wolf-man who tore apart men as if they were pieces of paper.

"The couple has two daughters, and one is refusing to leave. She will remain behind alone. I think the time is now."

I steepled my hands as I sat behind the old oak desk

that was once my grandfather's, watching Dante's scarred face. He weakened every day, and it wasn't uncommon that a vampire who no longer had a will to live would crumble into ash the day the last shred of hope in him dies.

"There are wards, I am sure. They have not come this far without them. No, we need to take her in a way that isn't quite so...primal."

Dante nodded, but I was the brains behind it all, he was merely the errand boy, he knew his place. This was exactly what we needed—an errand boy who looked like a handsome prince, someone innocent and pure.

Instantly, my thought was drawn to Charles, his blue eyes and floppy hair, the way his grin slanted, and his skin shined.

"Fetch me Charles, I think I have an idea."

There were plenty of followers whom I could puppeteer easily, and one would be happy to relocate for the Grace of God. Thomas, Annabel's husband.

It was an easy task, getting Charles and Thomas to the small town of Bethlehem near the witch's cabin. I was certain that Charles would be able to breech the wards, but Thomas was also a loose cannon and slightly insane. Perhaps he could teach Charles about the importance of skepticism and a man's iron fist. They really could go a long way if applied, and I wanted Charles to be the one to bring the witch to me.

It wouldn't be an easy sell. The boy had become slightly...attached to me.

I would just have to be as vague as possible and remind him of the rewards he loved so much.

I wanted to tell him that I promised Melody that he

would be hers someday. She was a healthy vampire with a hefty appetite for blood and intimacy. Lust and blood went hand in hand for a vampire, and Charles was the perfect one to meet her desires.

A boy raised in a brothel, what better student could she have? It would happen, even if I had to force it a little.

~

"How long will I be gone?"

"As long as it takes, the first step is to gain the family's trust. Thomas must marry, insert himself into the community, by the way of God, of course."

Charles ran a hand through his messy hair, sighing and looking at the stone floor.

"But *this* is home. I belong here...with you."

We were seated at the dining table in the middle of the common room at the center of the castle. This was where I saw most of my visitors, followers.

I cut into a blood red steak surrounded by grilled carrots and sprouts; I had become accustomed to eating over the years. It brought me great comfort; besides, humans needed to eat.

"If you insist..." He pushed the food around on his plate, looking somber and so irresistible.

"I need you to do this for me...only do no harm to her, she is special. Understand?"

We locked eyes and he nodded. I softened my face as much as possible, and smiled, satisfied with his response.

He nodded again, a smile creeping up one side of his dimpled cheek.

"Perfect. You will leave first thing in the morning. I will tell Thomas, and I will reward you *tonight*."

Charle's eyes shined.

~

When I came to his quarters, he was waiting for me naked atop his sheets with a grin stretched on his face.

"Did you bathe?" I asked softly, shutting the door behind me.

He propped himself up on his hand, elbow bent, nodding.

He looked like a child on the morning of Christmas. Awaiting the one gift he had always wanted—begged for even.

Me.

I never took him the way he begged me too; I couldn't bare it if I hurt him, and I had never been inside a man before. The ultimate sin. If I did this, I accepted my unholiness, my disbelief in everything I ever preached. I would be committing an act so dirty that I would remove any link I ever had to the holy word.

Good. Perhaps it was time.

I held a flask of anointing oil, often used in baptism, the only lubricant aside from the oil used for baking bread.

And that just wouldn't do.

"On your knees."

He does as he's told, standing from the bed, his long, lean body enviable. The tight muscles of his abs make my cock twitch, and I imagine them bunching before he took his release.

He knelt, his head just past my own abdomen, and I tangled my hands in his hair, pulling his head back as I said, "Such a good submissive. I will miss this..."

He didn't say a word, he just looked up at me from under those full lashes, so feminine and soft. I wanted to stroke his cheek, but I didn't want to give him sweetness tonight. I would give him the safety of my rules, my directions.

I brought his cheek to my cock instead, pushing against my dolman, rubbing it until his face was as red as a rose.

He was nearly breathless, and my cock was hard and angry, and I reach under to release it.

My pants fell to the floor, and Charle's lips were already wet.

"I'm going to give you a safe word, I don't want to hurt you, but I will push you."

He nodded, eagerness in his bright eyes.

"What do you think, my soft boy..."

He thought for a moment, and with heat, he replied, "Rapture."

I closed my eyes at this, he was pushing the limits already.

"Yes."

I walked around him, to his back, gathering his wrists into one hand, pulling him to stand.

I pulled him to me and kissed his neck gently, tasting

the salt on his skin. I felt him shiver, and I reached around the front, finding his cock like steel against his belly, dripping from the tip. I lazily gave him one stroke and cupped his balls. He gasped, and I led him backward to the bed.

I laid on top of him, our muscular bodies pressed together. Looking down, I make sure our shafts were lined up perfectly. Charles looked down as well, the heads kissing like two lost lovers. Their crowns shiny and red.

I slowly moved my hips against his, his cock against mine.

"Tell me what it is you want..."

He was gasping now, his eyes locked on my face. Licking his lips, he tried to speak but was overcome, closing his eyes again.

"More...I want more..."

"So greedy for a boy so lost."

I reached for the Chrism that was in a small glass vile in the pile of clothes at the foot of the bed.

Kneeling between his muscular thighs, I poured the holy oil on my fingers and ran them up and down my cock. "I shall bless you with my cock, and I know you will make me proud once you return."

His eyes watched me intently as I lifted his legs onto my shoulders. I dribbled oil on his taught sack, and down his crevice to his tight hole. He hissed, and I began with a gentle tug on his balls, expertly swirling my index and middle finger into his puckered entrance.

With my other hand, I jerked him off slowly, as I press inside.

"Yes...please..."

His groans sounded like a holy hymn to my ears, and my own arousal mounted as I work him with two hands.

I had been with men and women alike, but always promised myself that I would never give myself to another after Lilith.

But I wanted this, I wanted him, and I wanted to claim him as mine just as much as I did with her. Charles was so compliant, and so submissive, I struggled against taking him daily. He was nothing like her... always asking softly, pleading with me, and I wanted to give him just that, changing his life forever. It was a guarantee that he would do what I had asked of him, he wouldn't be able resist me after this.

I leaned down, moving my hands to my own throbbing shaft, and lined myself up with the tight starburst. He squeezed the head, so deliciously tight, and I steadied myself before pushing myself inside.

His cock twitched against his belly, every inch I slid inside forcing a whimper from his lips.

"Fuck," I cursed, forcing myself to slow so I didn't immediately come undone.

Charles eyes were completely closed down, his mouth working into an O, and I was thankful for a moment that he could not see my face.

Keeping my eyes focused on his pleasure, I rolled my hips into him rhythmically, his heavy legs weighing down on my shoulders.

His needy cock throbbed with each thrust, and I reached for it, stroking it gently.

I hit that soft spot deeply inside of him, and I could tell he was close by the way his eyebrows lifted. He grabbed his legs, letting me in deeper.

"This asshole is mine, and mine only..." I grunted, "do you understand?"

He nodded his head frantically and he climaxed,

white ropes of semen spilling from his cock and onto his stomach. The sight shot me over the edge as well, and I unloaded inside of him.

I howled, buried inside of him.

When our breath had slowed, and he opened his eyes again, he smiled up at me. His blue eyes sparkled, and I allowed myself to touch his face, take in his soft beauty.

I stood on shaky legs, and Charles relaxed his body, the euphoria settled on his skin.

Walking to the basin of water near the fireplace, I cleaned myself up, grabbing another towel for him. He smiled as he took it, but he didn't meet my eyes. He was acting shy, and part of me relished in his timidness.

I knew this may be the only time we would be together, especially if I planned on giving him to my Melody.

"Come back to me, okay?"

He replied quietly, "Always."

~

Ever since the wolf-man mangled his hand, Thomas had been reclusive and locked in his room. I took him in without argument, and he only requested that he be left in peace and allowed to attend church. *Of course*, I had said, and now I would call on him to return the favor after all these years. He would agree, I was sure of it. The only thing I needed to do was tell him it was God's Will. Just one small sentence and it would be that easy. It was the very reason my grandfather chose this line of work—persuasion was all too easy.

Charles did not take to his orders lightly, I knew he would make me proud. We had shared pillow talk, life lessons, and seed. But it was time to release my Melody of the sleeping curse, so we could be together again.

I stood from my chair, a young servant girl quickly clearing the plates as I stood. I walked to the far wall where the tapestry of Lilith hung, pulling it back and looking over my shoulder before disappearing behind it.

Her room was the last, after many turns inside the pitch-black corridors. I felt along the walls as I went, but part of my abilities was perfect sight in the darkness.

Moonlight washed over the bed where she slept, a single rose bud in the vase beside of her. The flower never bloomed, and I feared that the prophecy wasn't true. Once the flower bloomed—she would awaken. For years, I had faith that it would, and she would awaken, only it never did. The day she fell into the slumber, the day that Lilith left, I vowed to do whatever it took to bring her back. I often bit my own wrist and trickled the blood into her mouth, hoping it would be enough to sustain her. I held on to faith, and day after day, I was not given anything more than that.

The Witch of the Woods was the key. She had to be; she was Lilith's kin. Magic be damned, I would make sure Melody was brought back to me.

I stroked her soft cheek, which was sharp, and her blonde ringlets still shined with youth, locked in that state forever once she was turned.

If her foolish parents didn't do what they did, she never would have needed to be turned. It was the only choice I had, and once she was orphaned, she became mine.

"We will be together again, angel."

CHAPTER 25

DANTE

THE PAST: 1725 FRANCE

Every woman who ever rejected me would see flames before they died. It brought me great satisfaction to know their death came at my hands, if I could not have them, no one would.

I stood in the apothecary room, surrounded by my tinctures and herbs. This was the only place that I felt like I belonged. Even the small animals I'd sacrificed, they were happy to give their lives to me, they wanted to die for me. I held power here, and when I healed someone of their sickness, or stopped the bleeding from a terminal wound, I was revered, thanked profusely. I was the healer, I was the mad scientist, and no *woman* would ever take that away from me. I crushed belladonna with my mortar and pestle as an old man lay in the make-shift bed to my left. He was dying of a disease that ate his flesh, and the only thing to do now was keep him quarantined and his pain eased. It wouldn't be long before he was gone.

I needed to feed soon, I hadn't drunk a drop of blood in weeks, and I would soon become weak and tired.

My thoughts were catapulted back to the night Lilith let me feed from her.

I awoke to the soft snores of Lilith, Domenico absent from the bed now that it was sunrise. The window drapes were a heavy black to keep the sunlight out, but Domenico preferred his dark corridors to any other place.

I watched them fuck, unable to move from lack of sustenance. I hated who I was, and for that, I rarely fed.

I wiggled my cold fingers, but they only moved a tiny bit. My eyes moved to the edge of the bed to see Lilith peering over the edge with a devilish smile plastered on her face. "Are you hungry?"

I nodded, ever so gently. She crawled from the bed to the floor beside me. She bit her own wrist, bringing it to my mouth. Laying her head on her other arm, she watched me drink deeply from her. We locked eyes as I fed, and I felt small charges of electricity ping through my body. I had never felt healthier, never felt so sure of what I was. I was greedy with her blood, taking long pulls until she's stroking my long hair while droplets fell on my face.

"There, there. All better."

I sat up, reacclimatizing myself to the room but stood quickly, exiting before any of these feelings unfurled any further.

I craved the taste of her blood now, but no one had seen her since she left. I had to lie to Domenico, tell him I was able to trap her within a stone, but now he had made his life revolve around her return. The stone only contained a small amount of her powers, the day I had tried to contain her only to fail miserably.

I had severely underestimated her powers.

Was it because he loved her? Was he determined for

them to be together after all that had happened? Or was it simply the curse that made him cling to her resurrection. I knew the crystal held nothing; it was nothing but a fake talisman. I could never tell him, but if the witch got a hold of it, she would certainly know.

I wondered if her blood tasted the same as Lilith's, like sunshine and flowers, with the same effect. I had to keep her from bringing Lilith back, and the only way I knew how to do that was to take her life myself.

I quietly shut the door behind me, looking down the cold hallways on both sides. Charles' room was the second largest to Domenico's, the spoiled boy who was treated like family but didn't deserve it. Domenico had weak spots, and one of them was the boy—the other was Melody. If she wasn't turned, I would have killed her long ago. Hell, she should've been killed right alongside her parents for betraying us. Humans had a hard time with the information that Vampires and monsters existed.

I had never dared to travel the hidden halls that Domenico thought I knew nothing of.

I mustered up the courage, taking a deep breath and delving into the hidden, shadowed hallways.

I found Charles room, locked from the outside, and stood there for a moment, puzzled.

Why would Domenico lock him up? Unless he felt that he couldn't trust him suddenly, and for what reason would that be?

I had seen how attached he was to the girl he brought with him, which was never a part of the plan. He was ordered to find the witch and bring her here, but he ended up bringing a girl as well, an unforeseen twist for Domenico. That must be why—the girl.

I pushed my nose to the crack of the doorway, and I

can *smell* her. The witch was inside. Her scent strong like patchouli, but soft notes of vanilla laced through it. I began to salivate and decide that I must come up with a plan to lure her out. But how? I had no power here, not without Domenico.

I knew of his plans to bring her to Melody, so that would have to be when.

I would wait, and I would trap her the way I had tried, and failed, to trap Lilith. It took many years of practice, trying to learn the magic of a witch. But with Freyja taken from her cabin, I was able to take the grimoire of spells, and I would use her own spell to trap her forever.

My very own untapped blood bag, full of sunshine and promise.

FREYJA

1730 FRANCE

"Fuck!" I cursed, as Domenico locked us inside the room. I had managed to escape, only to be caught again. How could I be so stupid?

"*Freyja.*"

It's then that I saw my sweet Charity's soft eyes, and she wrapped her arms around my neck, pulling me to her and burying her face in my hair.

"Sweet pet..." I felt warm tears prick my eyes, and I embraced her again, running my hands down her back to cup her ass.

I travelled my hands back up toward her shoulders, cupping her face in my hands and kissing her pouty lips. The kiss was electric, soft and lazy, as if she wanted to savor the moment forever. Our mouths entwined, we kissed until we are both pink cheeked and breathing heavily.

I felt Charles grab for my hand, and I jerked it away as I wrapped my other arm around Charity's waist, pulling her away from him, "*You.*"

At first he seemed confused, but clarity washed over his face as he registered my anger.

This was all Charle's fault. We were here because of him, and Charity was none the wiser.

I felt my fangs extend, and every bone in my body wanted to shred him to pieces right there.

"Please, let me explain."

"There is *nothing* to explain. You lied to us both." I looked down over Charity and her eyes are down casted to the floor. I used my index finger placed under her chin to pull her face to mine. "You see? He is guilty."

Her eyelashes fanned against her cheeks, and a single tear slid down her face. I cannot imagine what she was feeling—witches, vampires and wolf-men, a prisoner trapped inside a castle. I doubted she had ever made it past her humble home in Bethlehem, and with all this new information, she could only be terrified.

I pulled her to me, kissing her cheeks and stroking her hair. I wanted to make her feel safe again so badly, and the only way I knew how involved a lot less clothing and the use of my hands and my tongue.

"Kneel, pet."

She did as she's told but sat back on her heels and leaning her head against my bare thigh.

I stroked her hair gently, admonishing her with a few, *'good girl, it will all be ok.'*

Charles took a seat on the bed, but his eyes remained on us both.

"You may watch, but not participate. Don't even think about touching yourself."

Nodding, he placed his hands on his knees, waiting.

"Would you like to eat my pussy? Would that make you feel better?"

Charity nodded, looking up at me now, like the perfect pet she was.

I pulled my tattered dress to the side, pressing myself to her eager, ready mouth. I placed one hand behind her head, pushing her mouth against my slick folds. Her tongue snaked up the slit, parting my lips and finding my swollen bud. My head fell back, while she made agonizingly slow circles around it.

"Such a good girl, does that taste good? Does that make you wet?"

She sucked my cunt like she needed it to live. The wet sounds of her mouth against me caused me to grind into her face while I tightly fisted her hair.

"Enough, I want to feel your soaked cunt."

She halted her licks and looked up at me with a pouty, so sexy look of disappointment.

My body was wound tight, my climax on the precipice of breaking free, but that could wait. I desperately wanted to feel her cunt squeeze around my fingers first.

"Turn around and get on all fours."

She turned, but before she assumed the position I've asked for, she rucked up her dress around her hips so I had the perfect view of her exposed, wet sex.

I nearly came undone at the sight, and I dropped to my knees, placing a kiss on each of her ass cheeks.

I let my tongue wiggle down her crack until I reached her tight asshole. I probed it but looked up at Charles as I did. He swallowed hard, his hands now braced behind him, and I can see his cock was hard and pushing against his breeches.

I smiled, satisfied with the torture I gave him,

without touching him at all. I hoped it hurt, the throb inside his pants.

Charity released a low moan that had my insides tightening, and I couldn't tease her anymore because I need to feel inside her.

I pulled back, sliding my hand over her velvet seam. She was wet, her clit hard and swollen. I circled it with my middle finger a few times, which had her back bowing. I took the same middle finger and joined it with my ring finger, sinking it inside her tight cunt. "Oh fuck," she squealed, and I gave her three curls as she tightened around me.

I smacked her ass a few times in succession with my fingers, and she bucked against my hand and begged me for more. I watched Charles close his eyes, licking his lips. I enjoyed tipping him over the edge like this, it turned me on even more, him watching us like this.

A few more strokes and curls, and she squirted over my hand, her cum dripping down my arm as I continued to spank her ass with the other.

"Just like that...look at my good girl, coming all over my hand."

Once her spasms stopped, I withdrew my fingers and licked them clean.

As much as I wanted to come, I wanted something inside of me more, and this wasn't home where I had handfuls of glass blown phalluses.

I guess I would just have to put Charles to use after all.

CHAPTER 27

CHARLES

As I watched the two of them together, I was in sheer *agony*.

I had always known I had a strong appetite for sex; man or woman, it didn't matter to me.

But seeing these two together was like a gift...like seeing God. I licked my lips over and over, until I was rubbing my palms against my thighs, desperate to release my erection. Freyja said not to, and I obeyed—it felt *so good* to obey.

When Charity comes, in splashed in rivulets down Freya's arms, I almost come right there. Instead, I closed my eyes and thought of a sad memory of my first days in the castle when I felt so cold and alone.

When I opened my eyes again, she stood in front of me, naked. Her breasts were larger than Charity's, and I reached out to cup one, but she smacked my hand away.

"Take out your cock."

I almost cried out in relief, but I wasn't sure what she had in mind, and my heart thudded inside my chest.

I freed my cock from its cloth prison and it was a dark, dusky red, wetness on the tip.

"Lay on the bed and cover your eyes."

I lay back, but I don't close my eyes just yet. I watched as she turned around, straddling my hips and lining me up with her entrance.

Once she lowered herself, I slung my arm over my face, wincing.

She was so fucking tight, and I curled my fingers and toes as she eased herself down on me. She slowed, balancing herself on the balls of her heels. I snuck glimpses every few thrusts, but I laid there and let her use me like a personal fuck toy. It was wildly erotic, but it took every sad thought in my brain to keep myself from blowing my load right there.

"Come here, pet. Eat me while I sit on his cock."

I watched as Charity moved between her legs, but could only see her head bobbing slowing while Freyja continued to assault my cock.

My balls pulled up tightly to my body and pleasure spun itself around my lower abdomen until I saw stars. I would come right now if she didn't slow down.

"Do you like watching me use him? Yeah? Just a cock for us to use..."

Her words send me flying over the edge, coming and coming, feeling like it would never come to an end. I spend myself inside of her, and she cried out as well, screaming Charity's name, not mine.

I don't know what I expected to happen after, but there was no tenderness with her like there was before. She simply stood, leaving me bereft of her warmth.

I removed my shirt, wiping away what I could of our spend. The pair moved to the washing basin, taking a towel and wiping each other clean, kissing each body part after they've scrubbed.

My heart broke, in that very moment, and I knew Charity would never be mine. She belonged to someone else, and I knew I wouldn't be able to fulfill her the way that Freyja did. I would never give her a feeling of safety, not when I needed to feel the same safety from another.

~

I woke up on the floor beside the bed where the two women slept.

Freyja made it very clear that she would not take my life because I was the reason Charity was not harmed.

I stretched, my back sore from the harsh, cold floors. The fire was burned to ash, and I shivered, moving out of my self-made nest, to the front of the fire.

I had to teach myself many things when I was a boy and starting a fire was one of the most important. Even though I knew there was no making it up to them, I still wanted to please them. It didn't take long before the fire roared again, and both yawned and woke.

"Should I get you breakfast?"

Charity's sleepy eyes tugged at my heart, thinking back to every morning I woke beside her. I would miss her soft sighs, her wandering hands.

Freyja looked exhausted, but she shook her head before hopping down and retrieving the water pitcher.

A heavy knock at the door had me rising to my feet to answer it. I already knew who it was.

"Everyone got some rest?" Domenico crowded the doorway, and for the first time since I came to live here, I felt truly like a captive. I swallowed, daring myself to speak up, "We would like food, please."

He pushed passed me, ignoring my request.

"Are you ready, Freyja? I will bring you to Melody now."

Freyja pulled her tattered dress over her head, and her expression was hard. I wasn't used to seeing her without her tribal makeup drawn in ash. She looked younger, more innocent and not as menacing as she did when we first found her.

"Not like I have a choice."

Domenico led the way, Freyja following closely behind him, but he stopped, turning to face us all. "Don't even think of trying to escape, I am faster and stronger than the three of you combined. You would be dead before you made it out the doors."

With that, Charity and I are left behind as Domenico led Freyja to Melody, the secret Domenico hid from everyone until now.

I wondered how many other skeletons hid inside this castle.

CHAPTER 28

LILITH

Returning to this castle felt *wrong*.

I was never able to return before, the curse wavering upon my arrival. I had wanted Domenico to *suffer*, just as I suffered that day that I watched flames lick up Annabel's roped body.

I had decided I didn't care about clothes anymore after I returned to The Underworld. Things were far different there, but not in the way you would think. There were no eternal fires, no suffering, but rather a quiet and cold place where you were forced to be at peace with your thoughts, alone. The worst part of it was the ebbing loneliness that lingered there, that had the power to swallow you whole if you were not careful. I had everything I could ever want there, besides the company of friends—and love.

I thought perhaps I missed being in love the most. I craved the adornment of another. I dreamed of it night after night.

My hair tickled the backs of my thighs as I slowly

walked up the back staircase, the shadow of night protecting me from being seen. The snakes had followed me of course, but there was nothing I could do about that. Besides, it would be the only clue Domenico would have of my presence. I wanted him to know, I wanted him to be scared.

Could vampires feel fear? I wasn't sure, but I did know that I was a monster too. But could monsters frighten other monsters?

I ran my fingertips over the stones, reminding myself of the reason I was here.

Revenge.

I must protect myself from his charms, which was exactly what got me here in the first place. Was this ever really my home? Or was it all just another way for a man to control me? Was it all a façade that I inhaled like the air inside my lungs? I didn't need him, I was a force all my own, and I would show him as much.

I would find my kin, and we reunite with a vengeance.

I heard footsteps from the top of the stairs and hopped gracefully to the cathedral window above, landing on the sill and crouching down until they had passed.

And there he was, after all these years, and he looked the same. Devilishly handsome, regal, and sexy. I had to bite my lip to bring myself back to the reality that was now, and I watched as the woman behind him followed —*Freyja.*

Her head jerked up in my direction, and I ducked down further, she could hear me, and I knew this because we had communicated since she was a child.

The first one to ever hear me, I was brought back to

my power because of her. She looked just like me—like my Annabel. I covered my mouth as I held in a jagged sob.

I am here my child, and together, we will take back what's ours.

CHAPTER 29
FREYJA

She was here, she had come.

I knew Domenico lied when he gave me the crystal; I knew as soon as I held it. The power and vibration small. *I* brought her back; *I* summoned her here. I had that power, and I knew now just what had to happen.

He led me to the back of the castle where three large tapestries commanded the back wall. The draft of the dark, cold floors sent a shiver through me, and I hugged myself tightly.

She told me what she did, showed me images of the tiny, swaddled baby, the doorstep, the emptiness. I saw the fire that consumed her, whoever she was. I felt a familiarity inside the vision, a resonating that I couldn't explain. She had been a part of my family, part of Lilith's family. *We* were family.

I would follow you to the heavens, or search through the depths of hell. Blood is thicker than water, and my soul will always be tethered to yours.

A tear fell from my eye, a rare feeling of sadness

washing over me. She had felt loss, loneliness, just like me. But she was here now.

"Where are you taking me?"

Pulling back the middle tapestry, the one with the giant tree, his skin looked so pale it glowed.

Be not afraid.

I followed in blind faith, but not for him, for The Dark Mother.

The stone hallway was nearly black, save for the candles that lined the floor. Out of the corner of my eye, I saw movement, and I nearly jumped as a white and black snake wiggled past my feet.

Bumps rose on my arms, and my hair stood on the back of my neck. I straightened my back, remembering exactly who I was—strong, fearless, and *powerful*. I walked the hallway as if I was walking toward my death. I was protected, and I would face whatever it was ahead of me without fear.

The hall gave way to a cluster of small rooms, one large one on the right and a smaller one to the left. Domenico led me into the larger room, and I recognized the sleeping girl from the house back in Wales. A small pang of sympathy hit my chest, but her pale skin and blue lips made me think she was already dead.

Instinctually, I walked over to her still body, taking her hand into mine. I was able to bring dead flowers back to life, breath life back into weeds even saving one half-dead raven after it was mauled by Lilitu. I was a healer, but I was also a killer. Two things that cohesively brought me the power I wielded so carefully.

And now there was Charity, the first person I had ever loved.

I would need to be careful, with her heart, with her love. I needed that just as much as she did.

"She sleeps, a curse placed on her because of me," Domenico appeared beside of me in an instant, startling me. He moved quickly, quietly. It was unnerving.

"Why should I help you? What do I get in return? Only my freedom?"

He was silent for a moment, looking over the beautiful sleeping girl. There was some connection here, but I couldn't quite put my finger on it...

"You and Charity will have your freedom. And I will have my Melody back. A happy ending all around," he smiled, his features soft. He was good at fooling people, he almost had me fooled.

"And what about the women? Will you continue to burn any powerful and unapologetic woman at your will?"

He moved to the chair next to the bed, it was dark, black wood with a faded velvet seat. A bible sat next to the bed.

"Perhaps you think wrong of me. I am still a man of God, undead or not. My reach is far, I have many powerful men of the church inside my pockets. But those *cruel acts* were not done at my hands."

I laughed, unable to contain it as he says *man of God*. "Please, everything you are goes against what God asks. How can you say that?" I asked, backing up close to the bed.

"Forgiveness."

A simple answer, and yet, it left a sour taste in my mouth. It was true, Christianity only required that you believed, it didn't matter what sins were yours—as long as you asked to be forgiven by Him.

Proceed with caution, little Dove.

"Then who was responsible?" I already knew the answer, it was the men in black coats, but who did these men answer to if not Domenico?

He sighed, looking irritated with my questions, but also knowing that he needed to play nice with me if he was going to get what he wanted.

"I have two brothers, who I needed to keep happy... keep inside the family business..."

So, there was more like him; he was not working alone.

Ask for a name.

"What is his name?" I didn't hesitate to do as she told me now, we were united on this mission.

"Dante."

I felt my hackles raise again, and my fingers tingled with this new information. He was who she wanted, not Domenico.

Her rage was palpable, and rain drops began to pound down on the windows. A crack of lightening lit Domenico's face and his pupils were black, his fangs extended.

Three snakes make rapid 's' curves along the floor from beneath the bed, and Domenico jumped from the chair.

He was afraid, and I heard a faraway laughter inside my head.

The flower beside the bed bloomed, red and ripe, the petals unfurling at a breakneck speed.

She returns.

"Tell me! What must be done, girl?"

He was no longer choosing patience in this exchange, I could smell his desperation, feel his fear.

"A kiss...from a submissive man."

~

"Dante! Fetch me Charles, NOW."

I watched as a man moved from the outside of the shadowed doorway, fleeing down the hallway.

Dante.

Just ask quickly as the shadowed, hooded vampire flees—so do I.

I may not have the speed and strength of an immortal, but I had *powers.*

My own, smaller fangs are bared, and I am almost on his heels now, looking back over my shoulder. Domenico remained beside Melody's bed, and it was then I realized that he loved her. He stayed to protect her.

I ducked behind a winding staircase, just as he ascended it. I watched him run to the floor where Charity and Charles were being kept and waited. I heard the door click open, and I quietly waited as he returned with Charle's in tow. I made a silent prayer to Lilith, hoping that he left the door unlocked at the very least.

With both men far enough away, I run on tip toes up the stairway to find Charity. To my shock, the door was ajar, a snake slipping past me. The rain outside crashed down now, and with each crack of thunder, a flash of lightening followed close behind, creating an eerie highlight of the old stone walls and tall windows. Charity was balled up into a heap in front of the fire, and I went to her, wrapping my arms around her, my dress falling across her arms.

"Freyja!"

She was sobbing now, scared as a cat, and as she shivered, I whispered words of comfort into her hair.

"You have to get up, my pet. We need to flea this place before Lilith's wrath comes down upon these men."

Her tear-stained face is puffy, innocent, breathtaking. My heart was full, and all I wanted was to collect her and return home with her. Our home.

She nodded slightly, standing and then taking my hand into hers. She had been through so much since the day we first met, and I wanted to show her what unconditional love and care felt like. I wanted to take care of her forever.

As we fled to the bottom of the stairs, I could see that the large front entrance doors were open, the rain slashing through the night sky like angry stabs.

Run.

I hesitate, pulling Charity behind me, heading straight for the doors. I didn't look behind me, I could only look ahead of us and pray that Garm waited somewhere in the distance.

I knew whatever fate awaited the men that resided inside these castle walls, was deserved. I did not entertain any sympathy, I only pressed on, eager to get to the life on the other side of this nightmare with my sweet pet. We would have our happily ever after. All hail The Dark Mother.

CHAPTER 30
CHARLES

"What is it? Has she awakened?"

Dante doesn't reply, and he looks oddly menacing this way, in his long black coat and his hood raised, shadowing his face.

Once we were inside Melody's room, his icy finger traced my ear, down my neck.

"My sweet boy, it seems that once again you are the answer to all my burning needs..."

Domenico's eyes were a stark black against his pale skin, and for the first time, the sight of his fangs made me shiver.

I thought back to those nights with him, wondering how I could have missed something like fangs. Did he have to resist biting me during those trysts? *Did* he bite me on those nights that I had drunk too much and woke up the next day with a throbbing head? I could remember him telling me that people only believed what they wanted, and I had no reason to think that monsters walked among us. Especially inside a church, a place of peace and sanctuary. The words of God.

"Me? What could I possibly do to wake her?"

"Kiss her. Now."

He pulled me toward the bed, and the blonde-haired beauty looked angelic, but also dead. The lingering sting of Charity's rejection still lay heavily on my heart, but I wanted to help Domenico, I wanted to please him.

"Why me? It cannot be so simple."

I watched as his eyes flicked to the bloomed rose beside the bed, with a nervous drumming of his thumbs against each other.

"What is it?"

It was then that a bolt of lightning stabbed through the sky, the small window above Melody's bed shattering into a million pieces and all over the beauty's face and hair. I fall back, crashing into Domenico. His face is one of terror, and out of the corner of my eye I see Dante flee, as if running for his life.

"Do it, now!"

Blindly, almost mechanically, I turned to her, leaning down and placing a gentle kiss to her cold lips.

Nothing happened at first, and as I pulled back, I almost said *told you so*, but I'm interrupted by her ragged coughing.

My eyes were wide, and Domenico gripped my arms tightly.

I watched in awe as her lavender eyes opened and she gave me a wide, fang filled smile.

She was hopelessly, sinfully, gorgeous. A porcelain doll, with the soft features of a girl, but the demand of a vampire queen.

My knees were weak, and I was thrusted from my haze of lust by my hair, Domenico wrenching my head back.

He bit me, two sharp pangs of pain followed by warm pleasure. I was immobilized, at the mercy of his bite. Blood smeared my neck, and I lazily tried to wipe it away. Domenico lifted his head, pushing me onto Melody, her mouth eagerly wrapping around the wound. It felt like hours, and I think I may have nodded off at one point.

"Enough, Melody. You will drain him if you do not stop."

I was tucked into Melody's four poster bed, and I drifted into a deep, sated sleep.

CHAPTER 31
LILITH

Dante.

All these years, I thought the death of my daughter was at the hands of Domenico.

He had every motive to hurt me, I betrayed him for my freedom, becoming pregnant with a child because of it. His reach was too far to tell, and his sermons were talked about from France, all the way to England. He was everything a powerful man should be, and for that, I should have known he would never waste his time on an orphaned child from his beloved.

It was Dante all along. His jealousy of Domenico shadowing any loyalty he had to his bloodline. His need to be desired married to the fact that rejection was a daily occurrence. I had rejected him on countless occasion, and once felt such pity for him that I let him feed from me. Was that single act a mistake? Did I take my pity for him too far? Leading him to believe that he would ever be able to attain someone like me?

The castle was full of my snakes now, and rain poured

down so fierce, so hard that every window was broken, and water seeped inside through the cracks and crevices.

Water was below my bare feet with each step, and my hair was plastered to my forehead from exertion. I had never taken my powers this far, and it was utterly glorious. The very wind around me was under my control, each crash of thunder, each bolt of lightning.

I took my time walking to the apothecary room, I knew just where he would be cowering, and I knew exactly how to kill him. I was prepared to take a vampires life tonight, but I hadn't thought my spear was angled for Dante.

The door busted open, no need for me to touch the handle. He was there, with vials of red blood in his shaking hands.

"Here...take it back...you can have it back."

I smiled, unsure of what he meant. He kept my blood. What a fool, thinking that this was my reason for my seeking him out.

"So foolish, yet so vindictive."

My hand was around his throat, his strength no match for mine. He should have fed, but he was too ashamed of what he was to do that, and I knew it weakened him.

The sharpened spear in my right hand pulsed with energy, and as I raised it above my head, angled for his chest, a bloody tear slipped down his cheek.

"An eye for an eye..." I said as I thrust, hitting the target with ease. His eyes rolled back, and his body burst into flames as the vials crashed to the floor.

Blood at my feet and flames licking the ceiling, I closed my eyes. The wind picked up and the flames began to spread, catching every dusty surface and cloth that hung from the windows and doors.

I moved with ease through the heat and realized in that moment how badly I wanted to see him again. The one true love of my life, the man that shared my blood lust and passion. The man that I tossed aside like ashes, after he gave me everything I had ever asked for.

CHAPTER 32
DOMENICO

I had gathered most of my followers inside the great hall, assuring them that this storm would pass soon, and we would repair the damages in the morning. Fear not, I would take care of it all.

"We will remain here until the storm passes, all will be well, my brethren."

The men murmured amongst themselves, exchanging worried looks.

My mind was not occupied with what would come of the castle, I was simply filled with joy that the curse was lifted and my blood-bound was awake again.

She needed blood to sustain herself, and Charles was my gift to her. I instructed her to take her feedings in small, separated increments, so as not to drain the boy. He needed sleep and food if she wanted a live host. She agreed sleepily, but not before telling me that she wanted to keep him.

I had no problem giving her that gift as long as she was willing to share.

"Smoke! There's smoke coming from the entryway!"

Panic surged the room full of men, and I raced to the great hall doors and pressed my hands to them.

Scalding heat.

"Lilith."

The doors flung open, and I watched in horror as the tapestry I had made of Lilith was engulfed in flame. It was too late, the castle was aflame; the rain stopped.

I dropped to my knees in front of the flaming flag of our lost love.

It wasn't until after I realized then men had shut the heavy doors behind me, that her naked body came into my view.

"Please, do not take this castle, the legacy my family worked for centuries to keep. Please, Lilith."

"I like to see you on your knees like this, it fills me with lustful memories, Dom."

She was close enough to me now that I could smell her, roses and musk, and I licked my lips, my fangs extending in hunger for both her blood and her body.

She tangled her fingers in my hair, yanking my face to her cunt, wet and ready for my tongue.

I don't even try to resist her, the mixture of fear and love mixing together into a painful tincture of need.

My tongue slid down her parted slit, the bud of her clit beckoning for my mouth. I closed my mouth around it, suckling hungrily.

She sighed with pleasure, as heat fanned us, wooden rafters falling to the ground in small explosions all around us.

"I wished so much this was not how it ended...we were so...oh, Dom..."

I stopped my suckling, looking up at the orange halo of fire around her head, pleading at her with my eyes. "I did not betray you, my love, I did not want her dead. I loved you. It was not at my hands…"

She looked down over me, lovingly, but didn't respond, only stroked my cheek gently.

For a moment, I thought she would relent, give into all our selfish needs no matter what had happened between us. I hold her shining, lavender eyes with mine, and I see one tear slide down her grinning face. "Lie to me, tell me we are like sunset," she whispered.

"We are, my love. Sunsets come with the feeling of accomplishment and freedom from the days end.

But then sunrise always comes—and the sunrise is a reminder that it is a new day, a day full of unknown possibilities. And it's then that we must answer the unasked questions from the evening before, together."

There was a deafening pause, even as the castle burned around us.

"I wish that we could play forever inside the sunset and the sunrise, but we are not creatures of the morning, but eternally of the night."

In one moment, I caressed her with my tongue, my hands gripping her plump cheeks, and in the next she was gone, a nest of snakes now at my feet.

At that moment, I could only make a vow to myself to find her again and again. Making a promise to myself that I would search the ends of the earth for her, until I found a way to prove my love and loyalty. Until we could watch every sun setting.

She was love incarnate—my only love, and every element that graced the earth. The softness and strength of water, the unpredictable chill of the winds, the permanence of the earth below my feet; and the fire that burned through my veins while simultaneously destroying every-thing in its path.

And I would lose her.

I backed away on all fours and watched in horror as Melody appeared in a blur with Charles slumped against her.

"Go!"

We were outside in an instant, and I could hear the cries of the men inside, burning alive.

We ran as fast as we could to the edge of the woods, as far away as we could get from the castle, now just a burning orange glow on the horizon.

I looked down over Charle's lifeless body, laying still on the sodden green grass.

"What did you do?" I asked, searching Melody's eyes for answers. She looked young, fragile. I hated feeling responsible for vampire youngling—it was a heavy burden to bear.

"Dom...I think he's dead."

EPILOGUE

Domenico

The kind neighbor that invited us inside his house gave us all hot tea, and I doubted he realized just who I was after I discarded my robe and swore that I would never again preach the word of God to a soul.

Did I really think that this was punishment for my own sins? Did I want to continue living this lie when deep down, I fought against a blood lust that called to me day in and out?

I wanted to give in to my needs, and now I had two vampire younglings on my hands, two blood-bounds attached to me forever. We needed to start over, there needed to be a fresh new beginning, one where I could put everything behind me, all the men who died because they followed my word.

"You are welcome to stay the night, until you regain your strength. I do not have much food though; I don't think I can offer much past that."

"We appreciate your kindness." I smiled, the steam of

the tea caressing my face like a lost lover. The pain of seeing Lilith again slicing through my stomach, and I held back a gag.

Would I ever truly recover from her absence? Could I move past our unrequited love and find a new reason to exist past her?

I watched Charles' chest rise and fall on the cot by the fireplace. He was pale, and I knew he would have to feed excessively before we would be able to move on in our travels. The woman would have to die, a small sacrifice for my newest blood-bound youngling. His lips were heart shaped, and a small tug of admiration hits me, realizing I had no other choice but to start over. For them both.

Melody stroked his hair, looking lovingly at him. It was the three of us now, a new trio of power that I was determined to make a name for...somewhere.

I turned the purple stone over in my hands, Freyja must have dropped it during their escape, and I squeezed it as I whispered Lilith's name into the fire.

"Where will we go now?" Melody's small voice cuts through my silent prayer.

I didn't want to stay here; I wanted to disappear somewhere far away. A place where I am unknown; a place where I could easily take back my power.

I knew Dante was dead, and I knew this because he was behind the death of her daughter. Lilith was the last to know, but somehow, I knew that she had sealed his fate, as he had for her.

All those years that he watched her family, every detail he relayed was etched into my mind.

There was another girl, another descendant of Lilith,

one who had no thoughts of the monster that lurked inside these woods.

"America. We will sail once Charles is strong enough."

~

Freyja

Charity placed her fingers through mine, and in the firelight, she looked like a dream. I stroked her curved belly with my fingertips, as if to make sure she was really here, really mine.

Garm had waited for us, just past the tree line that circled the castle. Dante had been up to his own dark magic, warding the castle so no one could get in—or out. My grimoire was gone, but I knew many of the spells by heart, and I would simply recreate the book that took me so many years to compile.

His ward was not strong enough to keep us trapped within.

Fool.

"Are we safe? From him, from *them?*"

I laughed low, knowing that they could never have reached me without Charles. My wards were far too strong.

"We are safe, even if they survived the fire. Oh, my pet, my love," I whispered in her ear, stroking down her naked belly, finding the warm apex between her thighs.

It seemed like only yesterday that we laid beside this very fireplace, only Charles was also there.

"Do you miss him?"

I was a little scared that she would not answer me honestly, but if she truly loved him, she wouldn't have left with me.

"I missed *you*. The entire time I was inside that castle, you were all I could think about. His touch became intolerable, and I dreamed of you almost every night," she said as she kissed my fingertips, and I smiled, relieved.

"And now we have this...my pet," she turned an amethyst stone that glittered in the crook of her palm.

"What do you think it is?"

Her eyes twinkled, "Lilith...and all her power. I called her back to me, let me show you just how happy this makes me."

Charity stopped, taking my hand. "I'm sorry...if me being with him hurt you. I think I was just scared, and he felt...safe."

I stroked her hand with my thumb and smiled. "No need for apologies, you are safe within my wards, safe here forever."

I kissed down her belly, and she sighed, eye fluttering shut as she laid down on her back.

Her skin smelled of fresh lavender and soap from our bath. I sat back on my heels, grabbing a small basket from next to the hearth. I had carefully prepared for this moment yesterday after we had returned, caked with dirt and sweat.

Garm was out on a hunt, our meat stores very low from our time away. I had been right, he didn't stop searching for us until he picked up the scent again, tirelessly searching the woods with his clan. He had returned to them, seeking help, and they happily agreed. I think he may have even found a new mate after all these years.

I pulled out a silk sash from the basket and motioned for her to sit. She did as I asked, like always, and my chest felt full of love for my little slice of heaven.

I wrapped the silk around her eyes, tying it just tight enough so that she could not see. Gods, she looked so compliant, beautiful, with the red sash covering her eyes, the ends flowing down the middle of her naked back. First, I grabbed a strawberry, bringing it to her lips, gently, she received the sweet fruit and chewed. Dipping my fingertips into a glass jar filled with honey, I scoop it up with middle and index finger, bringing them to her mouth, "Open, and suck."

Her pink lips parted, her tongue eagerly wrapping around my fingertips as she sucked. "So sweet."

As I watched my fingers disappear into her mouth over and over, I felt a tight pull at the base of my belly, my clit throbbing with each pull. I wanted to claim her, drive orgasms from her over and over again until she was a quivering mess on my floor.

"Such a good girl, licking my fingers clean…mmm."

Lastly, I reached between her legs, pleased with how wet she was. Her crease parted slightly, and I parted her carefully, finding the hard bean in between. "So ready for me, aren't we?"

She nodded, mouth slightly parted, eyes covered. Her nipples pebbled, and I greedily sucked one into my mouth as I made lazy circles around her swollen bud.

"Do you feel an empty ache inside? An ache that needs to be filled?"

Licking her lips, she nodded again, more aggressively this time, and butterflies swirled inside my belly as I reached for the glass-blown phallus inside the basket. Pushing her back down to the floor, she parted her thighs, waiting for me. I knew Charles was the only cock she'd ever had, and sometimes fingers just weren't enough. I wanted to show her just how full I could make her feel with my magic wand.

I brought the dark blue shaft to her apex, running it down her wet seam. I press gently, her cunt opening to me like a flower. She lets out a hiss as I find her entrance, using my other hand to brush light strokes over her clit. Her neck arched, and I eased the fake cock inside of her. Arching her back and spreading her legs wider, she let me inside, swirling it in and out. My thumb worked her clit, while I push all the way inside, keeping it there as she rocked her hips. "Oh fuck, Freyja. It's so big...please don't stop."

I glide deeper, angling it slightly so I would hit the soft spot inside her. "I knew you would love my cock, you love it, don't you?"

Her groans grew louder, soft sighs in between powerful moans, "Yes...yes! I love your cock."

"Is this my pussy? Tell me this pretty pink cunt is all mine."

"It's yours...oh! It's yours."

Using the hand I stroked her clit with, I pressed down gently on her abdomen, just above her pubis bone, and she cried out. Shuddering around the phallus, she comes, and I pressed my face to her thigh, withdrawing my hand and watching her hole spasm with release.

"So prefect," I cooed, stroking her inner thighs and smiling up at her.

Once her body had stopped tremoring, I crawled up her, kneeling above her, straddling her face with my thighs. The blindfold was still in place, and I sink down, lining my soaked crease with her lips. "Lick, pet."

Without question, she licked my cunt with her tongue, flattening it. Her hands found my thighs, wrapping around them, drawing me closer. I gasped as she flicked my clit, and I began to rock my hips, fucking her face. My wetness covered her nose, cheeks, and I pinched my nipples with both hands, closing my eyes so I would not topple over the edge yet.

When I felt her tongue wiggle inside of me, I stopped, stilling as she fucked me with it. Pleasure curled inside my belly, and my asshole throbbed in time with her tongue. I was aching now, needed to be filled and stretched.

I stood, gazing down over her pink cheeks and wet face. I picked up the magic wand, and returned to her, pulling her to a seated position. I straddled her legs, laying back. "Take off the blindfold."

She did as she was ordered, and when her eyes fell on my spread, naked body, she grinned. "Do I get to use it on you now, mistress?"

I shook my head no, running it up and down my folds as she watched. I was so ready that I didn't want to wait any longer, plunging it inside, stretching me.

I watched her face as I fucked myself, my little pet, so eager and needy. "Sit on my face while I fuck myself, pet. Then I want your mouth on my clit until I come."

Awkwardly, she moved to my head, straddling my face the same way I had done to her, except she was facing my hand working the cock in and out.

Her pussy was in my mouth, still so wet for me, and she moaned as I made contact with her swollen bud.

I raised my hips, fucking myself while she rode my

face. "Suck my clit, pet...I'm so close...I need you to help me come."

She lowered her face to my folds and ran the back of her tongue over the throbbing bud. It only took five small circles until I was shuddering, clamping down around the glass cock and crying out around her cunt.

She giggled, and I gave her ass a loud swat for it, but I smiled, feeling warm and replete.

Charity sat beside of me, my eyes still closed, my mind dancing inside of euphoria still.

"I want to do this every day with you."

I opened my eyes, sleepily. "And me too...I love you."

She leaned down to kiss me, my scent on her lips, kissing me deeply. Our tongues fight one another, and the wet sound made me want to throw her on her back and take her again.

For now, we simply snuggled beside the warm fire, feeding each other sweet cakes that I learned how to make just for her. They were her favorite, and I wanted to give her all her favorites for the rest of her life, even if her favorite thing was orgasms.

Acknowledgments

ABOUT THE AUTHOR

Savvy Rose is a self-published author of Romance, Erotic Romance, Fantasy and Paranormal Romance.

Her writing began in middle school and continued through Highschool, fueled by her love of Poetry by the likes of Poe, Bukowski and Shakespeare.

She enjoys writing about magical and complicated people, with steamy romance and thrilling adventures. Her writing pals refer to her as the 'smut fairy' & Scorpion woman.

When she isn't writing, she enjoys spending time with her family in Upstate Ny.

Her many hobbies include: Art, Astrology, Music, Spiritual study and most of all, reading.

Most nights you can find her drinking wine and ugly crying over foreign films, cleansing her house and dancing naked under the full moon.

Check out her Forbidden Fables series, Book one: The Wolf of the Woods

and her Paranormal Romance Series, Coven of Crystals, beginning with Chasing Celeste

Sign up for updates and sneak-peaks on her website: www.savvyroseauthor.com

or follow her on Instagram and Tik Tok: savvyrosewrites

Also by Savvy Rose

Tangled Garden

Twice as Twisted

Coven of Crystals:

Chasing Celeste

Ruins of Ruby- release date TBD

Forbidden Fables:

The Wolf of the Woods

The Wicked Witch of the Woods

The Secret of the Woods

Anthologies:

Getting Witchy with it Volume 4: One Red Candle

Bad for Me: Cheer for Me

Short Stories:

Pegged

Ours

Spring